Readers love *Lickety Split*

"Intensely erotic, *Lickety Split* is a rough-n-tumble cowboy romance as fierce as it is tender. Hot, hip DJ Patch Hastle has taken a rocky road since he ran away from Texas at sixteen, but he could never shake his yearning for Tucker Biggs, the cocky scoundrel he was never supposed to want... This blissful gem of a novel will crack your heart wide open and show you, page after searing page, that maybe, just *maybe*, you can go home again."

—Emily Jordan for Salon.com

"Damon Suede's *Lickety Split* will leave you longing for a dip in a cool pond, the glow of fireflies, and forbidden nights with the lusty older cowboy of your dreams. Equal parts gritty, elegant and beautifully real, this emotional coming-home story is filled with breathtaking imagery, enticingly flawed characters and a generous helping of earthy, edgy kink. The unlikely romance kept me off balance in such a brilliant way that I didn't want the book to end. This author is always worth waiting for!"

—R.G. Alexander,
author of the bestselling *Finn Factor* series

"Damon Suede writes explosively hot, hypnotically well-written gay romance. In *Lickety Split*, he once again takes an archetypal gay erotic fantasy and uses his formidable talents to cast it with two utterly real, unforgettable and deeply sympathetic heroes. Simply put, Damon Suede is one of the most talented and versatile writers of gay romance at work today, if not the most."

—Christopher Rice,
New York Times Bestselling Author of *A Density of Souls*

Readers love
DAMON SUEDE

Pent Up

"Everyone! Damon Suede's new book *Pent Up* is unplug the phone and don't leave the house amazing!"

—Christopher Rice
NYTimes/USA Today bestselling author

"Breathtakingly sexy... A superbly-written, profound and profoundly beautiful novel... One of the deepest and most satisfying books I've read in a long time."

—Sinfully Book Reviews

Bad Idea

"Once you start this ride, you won't want to stop, and as soon as you finish, you'll want nothing more than to go back and read it again. I suggest you strap yourself in right now."

—The Amazon Iowan

"Swoon-worthy romance... heartbreaking, gut wrenching!"

—Boys in Our Books

Horn Gate

"I don't have enough words to tell you how much I enjoyed this..."

—Prism Book Alliance

"Five chocolate dipped strawberries! Horn Gate is the thinking person's sexy story... Damon Suede earned his spot on my auto-buy list!"

—Guilty Indulgence

By DAMON SUEDE

Bad Idea
Horn Gate
Hot Head
Lickety Split
Pent Up

Published by DREAMSPINNER PRESS
www.dreamspinnerpress.com

DAMON SUEDE
LICKETY SPLIT

Published by

DREAMSPINNER PRESS

5032 Capital Circle SW, Suite 2, PMB# 279, Tallahassee, FL 32305-7886 USA
www.dreamspinnerpress.com

Lickety Split
© 2017 Damon Suede.

Cover Art
© 2017 Reese Dante.
http://www.reesedante.com
Cover content is for illustrative purposes only and any person depicted on the cover is a model.

ISBN: 978-1-63533-572-9
Digital ISBN: 978-1-63533-573-6
Library of Congress Control Number: 2017900359
Published March 2017
v. 1.0

Printed in the United States of America
∞
This paper meets the requirements of
ANSI/NISO Z39.48-1992 (Permanence of Paper).

For anyone who's ever heard "Slow down. Where's the fire?" and thought "Right here. *I'm* the fire."

CHAPTER ONE

THE PLANE dropped without warning, a brick through the clouds.

Patch grabbed his laptop in midair and pulled down, clamping it against the meal tray as they plunged. Just as suddenly, the plane crested and steadied, rocking the cabin.

His stomach turned over and clammy sweat congealed on his face. They'd either hit an air pocket or Texas was trying to kill him again.

The groaning girl in the window seat, all of sixteen and gray-green from the turbulence, clamped her hand over her mouth. She'd chatted shyly with him on the tarmac, taking music recs and then a selfie once she'd recognized him, downed a Monster Energy Lo-Carb, and promptly dozed off. Usually he avoided chatting on planes, but she'd seemed so lost. Now she looked on the verge of ralphing for real.

Fall was hurricane bait, but he'd caught this flight so he could make his parents' funeral. They'd probably hit a freak storm outside Houston. The cabin shivered and bounced, then leveled out again.

Patch gripped the seat arms in white-knuckle nausea and glared at the ceiling. *Don't you fucking dare.* He pretended he was talking to God, but more likely he was talking to his dead parents or his fairy godfather, daring the universe.

He refused to die en route and give Tucker Biggs the satisfaction.

The speakers cracked to life overhead. "Sorry 'bout all this rough air, folks." The pilot sounded casual and awful un-sorry.

The girl next to him in 23F twisted and whimpered, eyes narrow. While he had the chance, he tucked his laptop back in his bag and scraped his curly hair back into a short ponytail.

Time's wasting.

Last week his parents raced a train and lost. A cruel joke. Pa had always ducked through the crossing gate near their farm at the last minute, but the passenger side had taken the hit. His mama had died on impact; his father had died on the Life Flight from Hixville to Beaumont. Only person left out there was Pa's best bud, and Tucker probably wished the train on Patch instead.

The plane pitched and rolled. Patch closed his eyes and counted to infinity.

The flight out of JFK was two-thirds empty, and the weary business travelers around him griped and whimpered.

He heard a sour, choking sound as the 23F girl almost puked but fought it down. He smiled in pained sympathy. *My feelings exactly.*

Last night, a lawyer had called one last time about the funeral. To be fair, she'd been trying to get ahold of him for a week, but he'd been DJing in Ibiza and couldn't afford international cell coverage. He'd landed in the States, already wrestling post-partying depression, and caught the messages soon as he turned his phone on. He spoke with the lawyer before he deplaned, and then he carried his duffel of wadded club clothes right to the United counter to beg for an emergency ticket he couldn't afford so he could lay his parents to rest.

They'd discarded him, but Patch was still their son. Someone besides Tucker should be there to pay their respects.

His pulse slammed in his ears. He gripped the seat and held his breath, trying not to count the seconds. He'd just made the 11:04 a.m. flight in time to die.

Around him now, the agitated crew tried to calm folks down and made another apologetic announcement Patch ignored.

Next to him, Miss 23F heaved again.

He fished the little folded sick sack out of the seat pocket. Just as he passed it to her, she curled forward and vomited Monster Energy over his sleeve, her lap, and the side of the airsick bag.

The poor girl whimpered. "Oh God, I'm so—!" Her wet hands shook and dripped. "I can't—"

The passengers around them gawked in that horrified, titillated silence reserved for public humiliation.

"Naw. Shh." He let his accent creep in to seem less scary and shook his head. "Don't you worry. You're okay, hon. I swear." His sleeve and hand were soaked, but he'd certainly done way worse for sillier reasons.

She used her travel blanket to daub at the sweet mess. The plane juddered again. He flashed his best smile to seal the deal. "Cross my heart."

His folks were dead; nothing could make this day any worse.

The only hot flight attendant made his way up the shaking aisle with a clenched jaw and a fistful of cocktail napkins. Patch gave a tight nod so the dude wouldn't stick around to witness the aftermath. She didn't need to feel shamed on top of it.

"Jeez." She coughed and blinked solemnly. "I could *die*."

"Don't sweat it." He shook his head with a dry wheeze of laughter. "Seriously. It coulda been me. F'realz." *Poor kid.* He passed her the napkins and tried to dry his arm.

The plane steadied.

She mopped herself up, glancing at him with mortified, apologetic eyes. "I can't believe I just threw up on a model."

"I done way worse. Promise. My first runway show, I yacked on the designer backstage." His grimace made her grin, at least. "Dehydration." True enough.

"Ugh." She frowned sympathetically.

He raised his eyebrows. "Swimwear, even. Andrew Christian."

At that she giggled. At least she wasn't wigging anymore.

The cabin shimmied again but continued its descent through the soupy clouds outside.

"We're almost there," he said to the girl, like a judge pronouncing a harsh sentence.

As the lights brightened for landing, the hot attendant came by again to "check" on him and apologize for the mess. Swarthy and hung, he was, and whether he recognized Patch from the swimwear ads or had met him at some Circuit party, his timing sucked.

Maybe next time, hombre. Instead he kept his gaze turned out the window past his sick seatmate.

"Ladies and gentlemen, we've begun our descent"—*No shit*—"into Houston."

And finally the plane rocked wheel to wheel as it touched onto the tarmac under wet, gray skies. Houston, flat and muggy and bleak as ever.

His stomach unknotted slowly as the adrenaline subsided. *Time's wasting.* His impatience reared and spun under him like bronco. After the past thirty minutes, he expected a missile strike or a lunatic to open fire.

No such luck. At this hour, they reached the gate before 2:00 p.m. and started deplaning at the usual glacial pace.

Soon as the seat belt light blinked off, he leapt to his feet and pulled down his duffel, then the girl's. He'd change shirts in the bathroom before he picked up the car.

While they stood waiting for folks to shuffle off, Miss 23F thanked him and apologized again and assured him he was the *coolest* and the *cutest*, which was hard to fathom standing in the north of Houston covered in Lo-Carb vomit going home to bury the parents who'd all but banished him, vanished him for being a damn queer.

Cool. Cute.

The faster he wrapped this, the sooner he'd be back in New York where he belonged.

Off the plane, Patch strode at speed past business traveler zombies staggering through the echoing terminal. Thank Christ he hadn't checked baggage. He paused in the bathroom for a cat bath in the sink and a fresher shirt from his bag. The vomit pullover went into the trash.

At the rental counter, Patch checked his phone: No update from the lawyer. No calls at all. An e-mail from a Vegas nightclub with a party offer he ignored; if they found another DJ before he resurfaced, he'd live.

The flirty rental agent handed him the contract to sign and then keys. Parking lot.

There.

A red Impala. His father hated bright cars. Fagmobiles, he called them. Then again, his father didn't have much say anymore. If Patch could have rented a chariot pulled by greased cowboys in tighty-whities, he would've.

Patch tossed his duffel and laptop case into the front seat. He considered pausing for coffee but didn't want to waste the time. At this hour, in the rain, the drive to Hixville should take two hours. With luck and no troopers, half that.

By 2:34, he was on 69 headed up to 105, driving back into the storm that had tried to kill him. Stymied by the car's stereo, he scanned the radio for anything besides church, pop, and country, and gave himself up to hissing highway silence as he fought to stay awake. A couple more hours, he'd be able to stop running. Cold comfort.

Somewhere outside of Kingwood, his phone jangled in the cup holder—scared the pluperfect shit out of him but woke him right up. *Scotty.* His ex was a fellow DJ born in South Carolina—ripped, dark, and sweet as molasses.

God bless Sprint.

Patch poked the speaker phone and grinned in real pleasure. "Scotty! You get my message?" They were opening a club in the spring if he could find backers. *Velocity.*

"'Sup, Hastle? I maybe heard half that mess, but I'm wrecked."
Scotty worked big hip-hop parties these days, which was how he'd
found their amazing space during an after-hours video shoot at a former
factory... practically begging for velvet ropes outside.

"I wish I could say the same." Patch glanced in the rearview and
changed to the slow lane. Car calls sucked, and he didn't want any more
surprises. "I need a favor, my man. Spinning."

"Are you fixin' to ask me to go to Jersey, yo?"

"No. City. Can you cover for me at Beige?" Beige did a Sunday
after-hours disco he spun at on the regular. "Next couple Sundays. Eight
hundred cash per. Three hours each set." He laughed. "You'll dig it.
Pretty fellas. Bread-n-butter mix. Pays easy. And your smoke's fine long
as you keep cool."

Key bait to dangle. They'd dated for about ten minutes last spring,
but with his weed, Scotty was strictly wake and bake and too laid-back
to fake it. In any case, Patch could trust him to shine and not swipe the
job after.

Scotty whuffed with pleasure. "Oh, I see how it is! You're dipping
wick in hot Spanish wax while I'm stuck here, slumming in Queens and
slaving over a hot real estate agent to land us a lease that won't cost me
a kidney." He grunted. "What? Did you miss your flight ?"

"No. I'm stateside, but I never made it out of the airport." He
glanced at the duffel in the passenger seat. At some point he'd need real
clothes, too. Hopefully his parents hadn't thrown all his stuff from high
school out.

"C'mon, man. Where you now? Double-booking it." A warm,
sleepy chuckle.

"Sorta-not-really. I'm down in—" He peeked at the GPS. "Huffman,
Texas. Population: who gives a shit. On my way to way worse. Yee-haw."

Scotty took a swallow of something. "Mmph. Some kinda hanky-
panky?"

"I wish. Family." He didn't want to talk about his folks or the
accident. "Emergency."

"Sorry. You going's the right thing. With your folks."

No. They're gone. But Patch nodded in gratitude, feeling better for
talking to a real person who knew him, liked him. "Mmh. There ain't
nobody 'round here wants to see me."

"They musta dosed your Dr Pepper, boo. You already coming down with a case of the shitkickers."

Patch chuckled. "Fuck, I hope not." Outside the storm picked up speed, pelting the windshield. "Listen, I gotta jet. But you're cool for Beige, right? I'll text the contact and details soon as I stop driving. I really appreciate it, man."

"*So* no problem. Prayers, huh? Stay chill down there."

"Thanks. Owe you."

Scotty laughed and ended the call. Patch sighed in relief and slid back into the passing lane.

At least he had someone to protect his regular jobs until he made it back to the real world. Once Velocity opened, he wouldn't need that money, but for now…. The thought ricocheted inside his head.

Come to think of it, an inheritance might change the game. The farm had to be worth something to someone.

What if he and Scotty didn't *need* other partners? That money might buy him a shortcut. Maybe he could sell the farm, pay for half, and take the city by storm. After-hours impresario at twenty-two, and *suck it, Hixville.*

Evicting Tucker for old times' sake would be a bonus: sweet revenge.

Now rain lashed the car while he battled his exhaustion, shifting his weight and drumming the dash. He hadn't slept last night or on the plane, so now he'd been up for two days straight just in time to get dragged back into his childhood sand trap. A half an hour later, he entered the East Texas terrain of feed stores and future farmers.

Anyone sane would've pointed out there was no future in farming.

Gusts of wind made it harder to hold his lane. A few times he caught himself drifting into the passing lane, but cars stayed too sparse to worry him. Once he veered west on 105, the storm sank lower, slashing the asphalt and blurring the road into a smeary silver tunnel through the kudzu.

He kept his speed steady at ten miles over the limit until a loud honk snapped him fully awake to face an eighteen-wheeler barreling right at him. He jerked the wheel to get back into his lane in time. As Patch swerved clear, the wind of the truck's passage sucked him closer. He swallowed bitter spit and gripped the wheel tightly as he coasted, not daring to slam the unfamiliar brakes on the slick road until the truck had fully passed.

He skidded onto the shoulder of the wet two-lane, glancing at the honking semi in his rearview. Cold sweat. His breath and pulse sounded loud inside the rental car cocoon.

The engine ticked with heat and his hands shook until he squeezed the wheel again. He put the car in Park, turned the engine off, and slowly lifted his foot from the brake. The rain on the rental's window dissolved his view like a sitcom flashback on repeat in all directions. He wanted to be anywhere else, but the choice wasn't his.

Slow down. His mama's soft plea in his head. "Yes, ma'am," he answered, and then did.

Both of them gone and headed into the dirt. No time left. His mother had finally slowed down so much she'd stopped. The only choice was to come say good-bye, even if they couldn't or wouldn't hear.

He knew he should take a nap and call ahead... only there was no one to call. No one except—

Tucker.

He frowned at the thought and started the engine again. He'd sooner jump in front of another eighteen-wheeler than knock on that bastard's door.

After pulling back onto the freeway, he kept his speed at fifty, determined not to give the locals any chance to smash him into homo roadkill.

And so Patch Hastle made it back to Hixville in one piece, ready to burn all his bridges and bury the hatchet in someone's head.

HIXVILLE, TEXAS, was a dusty pimple north of Sour Lake, just shy of the oil fields around Beaumont. *Population 1,537 minus me.*

Patch grew up saddled with his mother's patrician features: aquiline nose, sharp chin, long neck. His face was camera bait in New York and Milan, but out on the saltwater flats of East Texas, it made him an easy target. As a kid, all he'd wanted was to grow into a cowboy; instead he'd grown up a sissified dork with ants in his pants. A skinny, grade-grubbing pretty boy who couldn't throw a ball and didn't like to fight. In Texas? Football was religion and any queer who didn't bow down was fair game.

Didn't matter, ultimately. If Patch had been crushed or twisted by Hixville, he'd grown around and beyond the reach of these dipping dimwits, the way a tree splits rocks to push skyward. No time to waste and no fucks to give.

Hixville proper survived at the edge of the Big Thicket, where the flat coastal plains favored pine trees and stubborn sumbucks. Main Street was a bend in 421, and along its bleached knot of prefab buildings, you could buy gas, burgers, seed, and Jesus... in that order. Texaco, Whataburger, Feed & Seed, Piney Baptist.

He missed his parents every day but knew better than to hope.

East of town, the office of Melinda Landry, Esq. occupied a detached garage behind her house on Bear Creek Drive.

At least the downpour had relented, mellowing to a sluggish drizzle.

As Patch climbed out of the Impala, he pretended to smile and straightened.

"Mr. Hastle?" Ms. Landry stood in the drive in a faded blue cotton dress. She had the raw-boned prettiness of a farm wife, crisped by the sun and faded to brittle poise. She wiped her hands on a tea towel. "I'm so sorry for—" The rain? The towel? *My parents?*

"Not at all, ma'am." He cut her off with a consciously boyish nod. He was twenty-two but knew he looked younger when he wanted. "Thank you."

"Someone musta yanked out the stopper." With a pleased twinkle, she gestured him into the little sheet metal building. The interior had been carpeted (brown), and a window unit (old) worked hard against the muggy swelter outside.

She rubbed her thin hands together. "I been trying to call you these five days. Messages and all." Her accent wasn't local. Louisiana, maybe, this close to the state line.

"I was working in Spain," he said, as if he'd gone to Mars. Same difference.

"Busy man. Off in the big city." She made it a compliment.

"You know how it is," he said, because he knew that she didn't. "Never stops."

Except when you've been smashed by a train.

She eyed his expensive, rumpled clothes. "I know your parents were proud of you." A shameless lie, but maybe she was just being polite to grease the proceedings.

"They raised me to get a move on." He let his eyes glow, using every bit of his looks to get what he wanted from her and get out. Not for nothing had he been modeling since he'd split at sixteen. "My daddy wasn't exactly patient."

"Not what I'd call 'exactly.'" She blushed and paddled the papers in front of her. *The will?* "No."

He smiled at her but didn't fill the silence, telepathically urging her to get moving already.

She didn't. "Have you thought about your plans?"

"That's almost all I think about, ma'am. I'm fixing to open a club in New York." He and Scotty had been busting their asses. Launching it was like holding a slippery bottle. Once they could afford to lease and build out the space as a nightclub…. "Velocity, it's called."

A wrinkle between her eyebrows. "I meant with the farm."

He frowned but quickly hid it. "Sell. Obviously." If he sold the farm, he and Scotty wouldn't need partners to open his club. He'd own the other half free and clear.

Her smile faltered. "Oh." In a town this small, a farm changing hands had seismic consequences.

Wrong tack. "I'm in the process of building out a space in the city. New York, I mean." Almost the truth. Scotty had put up half the cash, but if they didn't need other investors for the reno, Velocity could start *now*. Having his own club was like finally staking a claim on the fast lane. Patch would bring the crowd, and they'd make a fucking mint. He'd give himself two weeks max to give Tucker the boot, find a buyer for the farm, and then hightail it back to New York.

She fidgeted. "Ranching doesn't appeal?"

"It's a hay farm, ma'am. My folks kept a few animals, but the property's always been a baling operation." The past ten years, Texas weather had turned nasty, and many small outfits had sold to escape foreclosure. "I've been gone a long time. The heat kills me."

"Ah." She flipped open the file, glancing at a list of numbers.

Patch shook his head ruefully. "I'd never have time to take care of the property properly."

She gave a sad smile and nod. "Most youngsters do just that. Take off an' all. Not an easy life, farming."

"And time is a problem." He didn't look at the documents on the desk.

"So you'd be looking to—"

"Move quickly. Yes." He turned the full blaze of his charm on her and saw her warm to it. *Good girl.* With luck he could split back to New York in a week.

She softened. "Well, a couple companies were buying up acreage. Farming rice, mostly, 'cause of the water table, but the drought's made rice iffy." Southeast Texas had gone dry back in 2010 for a stretch of years.

Patch shook his head. Big agricompanies would stall and dicker. Eight hundred acres didn't mean much to combines. What he needed was some dipshit from Houston who wanted to play rancher. Or a crazy developer looking to build a suburb in the middle of nowhere. Or maybe a Walmart desperate to ruin this particular county. *Justice.* "What about oil outfits?"

She regarded him with baffled bake-sale eyes. Folks liked the idea of making money on oil, but the byproducts were toxic and nobody wanted the runoff screwing up their land.

Raised eyebrows. Ms. Landry took a moment to respond. Clearly Patch had taken a left turn on this one. "I didn't think you'd be interested—" She sounded shocked.

"I'm not. But their money's good. Texaco's been trying to buy it from my folks for years." For four decades, locals had fended off the intrusion of oil companies. "Or even one of the pipeline companies."

The law would protect him on that front. Texas had never been superconcerned about chemical pollution. What did he care what happened to this hateful place?

"Oh! 'Fore I forget…. Funeral home's asking. We didn't know… your situation, but now you're here, we can set up the service for… a week? Next Monday, say? I can make the necessary arrangements."

"That would be…." Patch swallowed. "That's—Thank you." A long awkward pause while she shuffled papers. "Ma'am? You were saying?" He gave her the smile again to move this along. What was she waiting for? "I'm happy to sign anything you need to get started."

"I should wait." She blinked and looked at her watch. "We'll begin as soon as we're all here."

"We?"

"The other party named in the documents. We're waiting for a Mr."—He thought the name a quarter second before she said it. *Biggs.*—"Biggs."

"As in…." Patch laughed without smiling. "Tucker Dray Biggs?" He snorted and his accent crept loose. "That's a joke. Isn't he in prison yet?"

"Is he a relation?"

"Uh. No." *More my worst nightmare.* "My dad's best friend. Local scoundrel." Patch's hands shook. How did she not know Tucker? Everyone knew him. "Crooked as a bucket of snakes."

"Bit a foofaraw locating him. We've left four messages." The lawyer sniffed. "Phone trouble, I 'spect."

"Football season, probably. He coaches at the high school. Or used to, part-time. Trains horses sometimes. Odd jobs around town." Actually, he had no idea what Tucker Biggs did for a living these days.

"No. Apparently, he's been caretaker for your folks a few years now. He said he wouldn't be long."

Patch squinted in confusion. "Is that necessary?"

"He's the executor. For their estate."

The room rocked, as if about to crash. *Again.* For a moment he was back on the damn plane.

"He—" Patch sat down in the closest chair and blinked slowly. "He what?"

She finally looked up at him. "Executor. You're the beneficiary, but your father left him in charge of the dispensation of your parents' assets. There's a life estate." Spots of hard blush rose on her cheeks.

Patch laughed right out loud, a sharp ugly bark. Pa had resented him so much, and Mama had let him do it. At least he knew. To have hard proof felt like water in the desert, harsh relief.

"Fuck a duck." He shouldn't curse, but he couldn't stop himself. He'd walked into a trap. "Look… if I need to go find him, I will. If he's even home." Tucker's rodeo days were a ways back, but seven years might have changed that. Maybe he was back on the road or, better, dead and dust. "You ever been out to his place?"

She opened and closed her mouth, not liking his tone, not softened by his looks anymore. "Uh, no. No, sir."

"Well, that'll cut to the chase, at least." Shame and terror and lust flooded him. *Just don't make me face him.* Tucker had witnessed everything he wanted hidden: all the insults, bruises, and one-sided scraps. Every time Patch had snuck off looking for trouble, Tucker had hung around, scowling, to dish out guilt and guff.

Flustered now, she drifted to the door to glance out, then to her desk. "I'll give him a jingle just now. See what's keeping him."

Patch scrabbled through his options. All he'd wanted was to pay his respects and scram. Now he had to come up with a way to get around a stupid SOB who'd spent his whole life as a speed bump. "What the hell am I gonna do?" After getting caught and whupped and running like hell, his nemesis had laid in wait like quicksand.

Tucker Biggs. Serves you right.

He knew Tucker dreaded him, and the feeling was mutual.

The awful part: Patch had worshiped the man, dwelled on him the way every awkward boy meditates on a perfect specimen of the male animal… as a scourge, as a god, as a goal. His whole life, Patch had been fascinated by Tucker's giant hands and hard ass, the rodeo drawl and the Skoal ring worn into his Carhartts, and the uneven wad massed under his zipper. Patch knew and feared every thick inch of him.

But Jesus was he sexy.

At eleven years old, Patch figured out his hankerings and why girls didn't keep him awake at night. Hand lotion and the Internet kept him from rushing into anything too dangerous, too fast. *Mostly.* Sophomore year, he'd even found a couple scruffy roughnecks willing to "practice," which was their word for "fuck the skinny kid from chemistry class till they learned to lift skirts." Long as Patch didn't rock any boats and swallowed when they squirted, they left him in peace. He learned how to scrap, joined the football team, rodeoed when he could to get away, and the worst mouthbreathers let him be.

But not Tucker.

Patch's dad, Royce, had been a saggy, sorry sight, but Tucker looked like a cartoon of what a Texan male oughtta be, and his Neanderthal habits only stretched the gulf between them.

Looking back, Tucker had probably seen him as the linchpin to the shotgun wedding that pulled Patch's dad off the rodeo circuit and back home to cut grass for a living. Tucker's family was less than nothing. He'd grown up bouncing around foster care: fistfights and hot-wired trucks. Patch's grandparents had finally taken him in hand and knocked sense into him. Well, as much sense as would fit inside his thick skull.

When Royce stopped bulldogging with him, Tucker had nobody to whore around with. He'd given in to a real job, coaching football at the high school and seeding surly bastards in a fifty-mile radius. At homecoming Patch's junior year, Tucker had at least three sons scattered across both football teams: dumb as hammers, mean as snakes, and sexy to a man. Yet none of his mongrels were as good-looking as their sire.

Tucker had moseyed through life gruff and buff, unattainable in the worst way and vicious to the bone. Before high school, Tucker had avoided Patch altogether, but once they'd collided away from the farm, he'd made Patch's misery a personal mission.

A flash of football junior year. Coach Biggs shaking him by his helmet on the sidelines and calling him a "damn faggot" in front of both teams, while Patch practically pissed his compression shorts. Then himself dawdling in the locker room to watch the brash bastard saunter to the showers wrapped in a towel. Whacking off in the barn after. *Gross*.

Every time he'd screwed up, Tucker had been there to kick his ass.

Patch had wanted him anyway, the way you do when you're too stubborn to be happy and too attached to steer clear. Hell, a twang and a pair of Luccheses and he couldn't be held responsible, so he had run like hell.

Even now, Patch only dated small-town escapees like him, pretty boys his age with clean hands and lean bodies, because he hated that out-of-control hunger he remembered too well. Instead, he skirted insanity… went to bed with sweet farm boys who let him take charge while dreaming about one rugged redneck that wished him dead.

He blinked and turned back to Ms. Landry, schooling his face into hopeful stillness, a little-boy glimmer in his eyes.

She frowned. "Mr. Biggs had no idea you were en route today. I believe he planned to meet you home." *His* home, she meant, because Tucker lived on the farm and Patch did not. What did she know? *Everything*. Hell, she'd written the will. She opened her mouth to say something, but Patch laughed again.

"Tucker Biggs can't pay his water bill. He's a…." *Bigot. Fraud. Sleaze. Loser. Prick. Bully.* He didn't bother to shield his distaste. *And they put him in charge*. "Mess. Hell, he lives in a trailer he stole from an ex-girlfriend in Lake Charles. On *our* land."

She blinked, no longer charmed. "Unfortunately, we're not authorized to take any kind of action without the executor. Do you know if he's willing to sell?"

Shrug. His mind raced. "What can you tell me?"

She sounded distraught. "I assumed you knew."

Head shake. "My parents and I had a falling-out."

"There's insurance, but your daddy might be deemed at fault because of the signals. I can file the paperwork, if you...." She turned toward the door. "...want."

Boots on gravel, a tread he knew better than he'd ever admit out loud. He hated his heart for beating faster, his skin for prickling. A dull roar in his ears as the door flapped open and all the oxygen escaped.

"Patch?" A low rumbling drawl he remembered too well.

Patch braced himself before he looked up.

Sure enough, Tucker filled the doorway in a chambray shirt and a straw work hat that he took off as he stepped inside, likely because the lawyer was a lady.

There he stood, larger than life, with the same square sandpaper chin and twinkle in his wink that got him a free piece of pie anywhere he ordered iced tea. "Well, hell, son! Look at you all growed up." He wiped at his chiseled mouth.

Just the same.

Patch frowned. He couldn't believe Tucker looked so good, even now. He had to be midforties but his body looked— "Hey, Mr. Biggs." He straightened but didn't trust himself to stand.

Tucker hesitated just inside the threshold, letting the last of the cool air escape before bringing the heat inside with him. He blinked, squinted, and turned slightly as he entered, as if his shoulders were too broad to fit through. "Tucker, huh? Boy, it's good to have ya home."

It is?

He rolled the brim of his hat and rocked on his worn boots. *Tough.* "I ain't seen you since... man, look atcha! I wouldn'ta known you." The greeting seemed almost real. Tucker grinned as if he were glad to see Patch. "Lord, I ain't seen you in five years."

The calluses scraped his smooth palm. "Seven." He shook the rough hand, squeezing it hard to make the point.

Tucker didn't react. "Whenever you took off. Right thing, you did there." Without letting go, he pulled Patch to his feet for a thumping hug that pressed their bodies together. "You're a big un, huh?" He smelled like sawdust, machine oil, and sunburned skin.

Patch stepped away and took his seat again. "I'm almost twenty-three." *And now you're old, mofo.* Put out to pasture, only he didn't look so worn out.

"Smart kid." He sat down and squeezed Patch's leg. "Lord, it's good to see you."

Baffled and overwhelmed, Patch nodded in reply, his entire attention focused on the firm pressure. A wet swallow.

Before today, Tucker had been friendly to him exactly twice, both times drunk. Patch's sophomore year, the big cowboy had shaken his hand when he made the football team. The next year, he'd smiled and thumped Patch on the back at the Orange County rodeo. Ten total seconds of humanity in twenty-two-plus years. "Uh, same."

Were they supposed to pretend that they'd been buddies? His dad's best friend had been frank about his dislike from the time Patch was four and spent twelve years treating him like something you scrape off your boots.

Tucker rubbed his chin with his ridiculously thick fingers, dropping his gaze. "Son, I'm sorry for your folks. They *sure* loved you." Except, on his lips the word became *shore* and the bullshit sounded plausible. His charm greased the lie.

Patch grunted acknowledgment but kept his mouth shut. Today was not a day for truth about how narrow and spiteful his parents had been.

Now he'd never get to make peace, no matter how much he'd wrestled with his devils these seven years. Tucker and the lawyer probably took his silence for grief, not regret. *Ballad of the Small-Town Queer.*

By junior year, Patch had become an unwelcome boarder in his parents' house, paying his rent with chores and humiliation. He could talk to his dad a little, but his mama was a sad ghost who prayed for nothing and knitted booties for other people's grandkids.

For ten sorry seconds his freshman year, he'd tried to make friends, play sports, anything to keep him away from the farm.

Coach Biggs killed that hope in the cradle.

Even before high school, Tucker had avoided Patch.

Freshman year, Tucker alternated between ignoring and insulting him, harassing him in front of the team and teachers, smacking him around to toughen him up. No one had blinked. *Friend of the family.* Later, when they'd been nothing more to each other than benchwarmer and bigot, they hadn't exchanged two polite words.

Ms. Landry took a seat behind her desk, facing the two of them, mistaking the silence for affection and proximity for a reunion.

"Well...." Tucker broke the tense silence. Obviously he planned to pretend the past hadn't happened. "Good you're home. We'll take care of ya."

Patch sighed and looked at the linoleum. *Long fucking day.* He looked at his watch. "Ms. Landry?"

The lawyer opened a file and riffled through the pages. "Mr. Biggs?"

"Yes, ma'am. I'm sorry for the hour. I got the messages. Phone works fine, I just gotta be there to answer. We had a situation with a well." The word came out *sitch-ation* and Tucker capped it with that crooked smile that turned panties into pussy willows.

She looked back, pink and fidgety. *Great.* Now she, like everyone else in this shithole county, thought Tucker was wonderful.

Executor. Patch arranged his face into blank distress. "You were saying."

"Yep! Yes, Mr. Hastle. Of course." Her eyes stayed on Tucker. *Panty butter.* Any chance she'd prove an ally in the fight to come had gone adios. "We were discussing...." She'd forgotten. "The farm."

"Oh, it's fine, ma'am." Tucker nodded. "I been taking care."

Patch frowned. He knew how to raise hay, but mostly he'd done what his pa told him. "You did a late cutting?"

Short nod, and cautious, and Tucker walked his hands around the brim of the straw work hat like Patch was his boss. "Every twenty-eight days. We switched from Bahia to Jiggs." Grass, he meant. "Long as the rain holds, that Jiggs grows *fast*. Bale prices have fallen off, but I switched to two-strings, and Janet takes whatever we got, up the Feed & Seed." Again the deferential employee nod.

"Good thing." Patch almost spat on the floor. "Yours anyway. They gave it all to you."

"Hold on, hold on. That ain't—"

"He's only the executor." The lawyer held up a hand. "That's not accurate, Mr.—"

"Good job." Patch turned to the older man, his impatience and disappointment curdling inside him.

Tucker frowned as if flummoxed. "No, son."

"Mr. Biggs has a life estate with the property with all assets held in trust for you." Ms. Landry leaned forward. "If we can all take a breath and go over the—"

"And good riddance, I guess. Pa disapproved of me that much." Patch exhaled, a short puff of rancid air. His folks had put this lazy loser in charge of his future, on purpose, knowing what they knew. They even trusted *Tucker-fucking-Biggs* more than they trusted him.

Outside, his rented fagmobile gleamed red and wet as raw meat, a getaway car with nowhere to go.

"I'm just a caretaker, son." Tucker leaned in, coaxing and gentle.

"Taking care." Patch snorted. "'Cause I don't. Perfect."

"Mr. Hastle, I believe you misunderstand."

The glare from outside made the room bright and blurry as overexposed film. "You drove me off once, and you finally get to cash in—"

"You got no call to say that. Your daddy never—" Tucker kept acting reasonable and looking so ashamed.

Good.

"Mr. Hastle, your parents only wanted to protect your inheritance until you came home."

"Course." Tucker put a steadying hand on Patch's shoulder. "Now, you know your—"

Patch jerked away. "Tell me what I know. Huh? Go ahead, you smug motherfucker." Ms. Landry made a noise. "You and Royce figured it all out."

Tucker squeezed the brim of his work hat hard, glancing at the lawyer with a hangdog expression. "I'm sorry, ma'am. He's upset, is all."

"Upset? The fuck I am," he said just to see Tucker flinch.

Flushed and flustered, the lawyer riffled through the file. "If Mr. Biggs waives his rights and agrees to a sale of the property, there's no reason—"

"Course I agree. It ain't mine. None of it."

Patch raised his voice then. "His rights. To live there till *doomsday*."

"To protect it for later, is all, your folks said. Because you was gone so long." Tucker shook his head, brow knitted. "Royce and your ma was only—"

"Glad I was gone." Patch scowled and swatted him away. "Executor. Estate. I got nothing to do with it. Pa killed her, finally. And himself, rushing around going nowhere. Only right you should squat out here and pick over their goddamn bones." And without realizing he would, he stood and slammed past Tucker and out the door. Knowing he should stop, unable to turn.

"Patch!" Tucker lumbered out into the light right behind him. "Now hang on. Hold up." He gripped Patch's arm.

"Leggo." Patch whipped around, shook him off, indignant and yet in his horrible secret soft center excited Tucker had come after him so fast, that he'd been forced to follow. "Get off me."

Tucker raised his palms and stepped back, his mouth a confused *O*. "You just got here." He shook his head slowly. "You ain't been here five minutes. Why you so mad?"

"Why? You are some joker." But Tucker didn't laugh and the gray eyes looked grateful and sorry and anxious and whatever else normal people felt when they were ruining someone's life. Another damn con, that look had to be. When had Tucker ever had an honest emotion in his bullshit life?

"Patch?" He even managed to sound hurt.

Fuck that. Patch kept his mouth set in cold disdain to minimize confusion on all sides. Maybe everyone else in Hardin County bought this aw-shucks BS, but he knew better. Once Tucker got the upper hand, he had no qualms.

Ms. Landry stood framed behind the screen, watching with eyes blind as two pebbles. Definitely on Tucker's side too. She'd probably bake him a pie next, blow him after, make tea with her panties. She had no idea.

"C'mon now." Tucker crept forward low and steady as a hostage negotiator. "I know how hard this has to be. Folks gone. We're gone make it right, huh? I wanna make things right, like the lady said."

"Jesus, you're good. Fucking pro." Patch sneered, letting each word land like a spear in Tucker's broad, steady frame. How many years had he waited to tell this bastard the truth to his face? He almost wanted Tucker to make another grab so he could shake him off again, just for spite and feeling free. "You fixed me good, old man. Final word on my whole life."

"No, sir. I didn't do nothing but help your dad. I'm so sorry." Tucker frowned, almost in slow motion, as if gravity was bending his face. "Your folks, they loved you something awful."

"Awful is right. Fuck-awful." Patch wanted to punish Tucker more just to see him hurt more but needed to split before he did something foolish or softhearted.

Tucker blinked again. His tan hands squeezed the hat hard, and he swayed gently like a supplicant.

Damn it all to hell. "You did this and my folks let you."

"Naw. Now hand to God, pup. I'm saying." He inched forward as if calming a rabid dog, his arms hovering before him. "You don't worry about the farm, Patch. You wanna sell, we sell and I take off. Honest, now. Please."

That smile and the open arms made him want to give up or give in or something *worse*, so he scowled instead and held his ground. "Farm's awful too. You're welcome to it, jackass."

Ms. Landry opened the screen door to wade in. If Tucker talked much longer, Patch would cave and crawl back after him like a starved dog because he couldn't stop himself. He rocked back on his heels before that strong hand touched him and lurched for his bright red getaway. *Fagmobile.*

"Patch." That humble rumble over his shoulder, but he knew better than to turn.

He yanked the car door open and got in, wanting the last word and a last look to savor Tucker's hurt expression before he pulled onto the road in a skidding curve that scattered gravel, not giving two shits. His hands shook on the wheel and his guts were a cold knot. He felt twelve.

"Just great." He glanced in the rearview, not seeing anything but his own sweaty face, tangled hair. He should've punched Tucker, hugged him, played it cool, spat, anything but that. "Good job, Hastle." It took everything in his body not to drive back and make nice.

While driving out to the farm, the fight leached out of him and his pissy anger crept back into whatever shameful hole it called home. Though he hated to admit it, he'd behaved badly and done himself no favors with that lawyer.

Junior year all over again. Few days after the arrest, he'd split to spare his folks more humiliation, and they'd gone ahead and done the job for him in his absence, sure and slow as stitching a wound.

Getting picked up by the sheriff in the rodeo stalls for indecency at sixteen had nailed the coffin shut, Tucker picking him up at the station then driving him home in awkward silence had buried him. His pa suspecting, but not *knowing* for certain his son was a faggot. They'd already rejected him and finally he'd stopped fighting to change their minds. *Bigger fish to fry.*

Obviously his parents had blamed him as much as he expected... or at least his father had. Still, Patch couldn't imagine his mama handing their land over to a shifty good ol' boy who couldn't keep his fly buttoned. They'd left him the worst of both worlds: the place was his, but he was stuck with it for the foreseeable future. Tucker had all the power now.

He was a man now, and he knew better. Being impetuous and irrational only gave the dipshit locals ammo. Deep breath. Tucker had won this round without taking a swing. Tough shit.

He'd spend the night here and drive over to the bank in the morning to finagle some kind of reverse mortgage. Or maybe against all odds, Tucker really would give him the go-ahead to sell. But he wouldn't hold his breath.

His problem was time.

Contesting the will would cost months he didn't have to waste. If he wanted to be a full partner, he still had options. The land was paid off ten years ago. Tucker would die at some point, and he'd be free. Maybe he could borrow against the equity or sell it with Tucker still squatting on it. Texaco could just drill around him. Maybe he could still rustle up enough cash to pay for his share of Velocity.

As he pulled up the drive, the house looked smaller and dustier, but the yard was mowed and his mama's flowers weeded. Someone had straightened up for his arrival.

Fuck him.

Tucker had looked too sexy, too strong, too glad to see him. Those sad eyes and huge hands on him. *Nothing's fair and it never was,* his pa had always said. Patch snorted. *Fuck them both.*

Frowning, Patch parked the rental car in the drive. He climbed out and headed to the front door before he realized he didn't have keys to his parents' house. As he came around the side, a small part of him expected his mama's face to bob past the kitchen windows before she called him in to supper. Friendly ghost.

He wondered about the spare key he'd hidden junior year so he could get back inside after sneaking out. *No chance.* He'd break in if he had to, maybe smash a window on the back door. He skinned out of his shirt and wrapped it around his fist so he didn't mangle his hand punching through glass. The late sun dried some of the ripe sweat on him. He probably stank.

He peered through the dark window. No ghostly faces, but he knew every inch inside. He'd forgotten how much he feared this place, even missed this place. He tightened the shirt and had raised his hand to pop the pane when he saw his little toad house by the back door.

By some strange magic, it hadn't moved, and the key inside was gritty but sound. It turned easily, but the crack of the door opening sounded like he'd broken something anyway.

The house felt airless and hot, so he went room to room and opened windows to let the breeze in through the screens. Outside the sun had fallen almost to the horizon.

He returned to the car to grab his bags and, without turning on the lights, deposited it in his childhood room—blue walls and carpet because blue is for boys.

How much time had he spent in this little cell? How many loads had he blown on his chest in the dark? How many secrets, how many escape plans?

Seven years later it had shrunk to a flimsy prison. They'd just shut the door and left it. A wave of missing his folks, even wishing they'd come punish or pray, leaked through him. Once he turned on the lights, they'd be gone for good.

He retreated to the kitchen, but the fridge was dark and empty. So the power was off, and he'd need to go find food. Worse, when he went to the breaker in the mudroom, he found the ancient circuit box in pieces higgledy-piggledy on the floor and a boxed replacement panel on the linoleum. *Fucking Tucker*. No doubt he'd started rewiring because he planned to move into this house soon as he could. Patch scowled. He hadn't even bothered to finish. *Lazy asshole*.

Besides, a teardown doesn't need improvements; he could live without lights till he got things sorted. He'd have to charge his phone in the barn or the car. At least Tucker'd left the water pump running.

At the thought of that voice, his dick thickened in his shorts. He pulled on his shirt and decided to check Tucker's trailer, just to spy, like he had as a teenager. Hating himself, ashamed and horny, he snuck over in the dusk only to find it dark and locked tight. Tucker had plans somewhere else, apparently.

The storm had scattered the clouds, leaving the sky full of crimson fish.

He told himself that he'd have apologized, but no one was home. It might've been true. On Tucker's porch he dug out his phone to call someone, anyone in New York who could remind him that he was an adult with options.

No signal. Perfect.

Even so, he texted Scotty the details about the gig at Beige, wondering what all those club kids would say if they could see him locked outside this little grubby box. *Real glamorous.* The message would get delivered once he drove into civilization where his phone had coverage, because obviously Sprint and Hixville didn't get along.

Feeling irrationally jealous and foiled and annoyed, Patch trudged back across the fields, resenting his boner and vowing to deal with this place before two weeks had passed. No eviction, but faster he was packed, faster he'd be gone, faster his nightclub would come to life. *Velocity.*

He made it back to his parents' house by sunset, shedding his sweaty shirt again halfway there. He'd deal with that bastard tomorrow.

Standing on the porch, conscious of his bare torso, he stretched and cracked his back.

He'd always suspected the sky looked so much bigger in Texas because of the earth's bulge. *Welcome to the fucking buckle.* The horizon glowed like a bruised peach, fuzzy violet and orange. Patch knew that crazy air pollution made for all those spectacular sunrises and sunsets, but Christ, they were gorgeous.

His energy died with the light. He'd been up almost thirty-one hours. He'd wait till the morning to duke it out with Tucker. *New day, new play.*

Rather than his room, he opted for the couch, asleep before he stopped thinking about Tucker's hand on his leg and dreaming things that pinked his cheeks in the dark.

CHAPTER TWO

PATCH WOKE up about nine, practically midday on a farm. Not that he had any intention of farming ever again.

Sounded like someone was mowing outside with the small tractor.

His morning stiff stretched uncomfortably inside his briefs. In New York he slept bare, but he couldn't shake the feeling that any second his father would bang on the wall and yell at him to *feed the damn dogs*. His dogs had all been dead a long time.

"I hate this fucking place." His whisper echoed in the room's stale air. The "fucking place" said nothing back.

His stomach rumbled. He'd been in such a hurry he hadn't planned for things like food and memories.

The kitchen was dark even with the sun up. The pear tree in the yard had grown so wide that no sun could reach the kitchen. It yielded piles of cooking pears: hard, round, and tart. When he was seven, Patch once had ridden to a rodeo in the back of a horse trailer in the rain, eating them until he got a stomachache.

The cabinets were still full of cans and jars, but the cupboard was definitely bare. His parents had died so quickly that there were still messages in his mother's loopy handwriting on the fridge and a box of his pa's Thin Mints stash thawed in the freezer.

Someone had cleaned out the perishables. Tucker, probably. *Interfering asshole.*

Standing in his underwear, Patch ate a bowl of dry cornflakes that tasted like straw.

What am I waiting for?

Outside the tractor passed, Tucker steering with one hand as he mowed. More handsome than he'd been seven years ago, if anything. The Marlboro Man with a shit attitude. Why couldn't he have been fat, foul, and fucked-up? How did he manage to grow hotter out here in the sticks? That perfect squint, the lazy power of his body jouncing on the tractor. Nothing to do and nowhere to go but get sexier so he could drive the queer kid out of his mind.

Patch shook his head and looked away, scowling at his own weakness. At least he'd calmed down.

Better to face Tucker first thing and sort the land out now, but he couldn't make himself do it without coffee or food or serious drugs. He needed a clear head and a full belly to face his old adversary.

He knew how it'd go. He'd eat crow and offer a share of the proceeds. Tucker, lazy and greedy as he was, would bluff and bluster, and they'd come to some scummy agreement. The life insurance money would clear his path till the farm sold, and Patch would get his nightclub. *Velocity ahead.*

Patch rinsed. Just to piss the locals off, he pulled on a slouchy White Party T-shirt featuring a rooster and a lollipop, and a pair of jeans too expensive and tight for any kind of actual work. *City slicker.*

He hopped in the muddy rental car and headed into town.

Hardin County had only the one school. Till eighth grade, local kids bussed it an hour over to Lumberton. High school was closer to home. Up at Gumsapp Road, some state senator had seen fit to dump a low flat building and fill it with God-fearing folk who could give a little shitkicker the basics. Back in the '50s, Texaco had dumped money into Hixville High in the hopes they could keep a couple of ambitious good ol' boys around to work the plant. Nowadays, they didn't bother. The locals ran and Texaco just dragged in cheap labor from out-state. Since the recession, work was hard to come by, and the oil companies paid real dollars.

Almost no one stayed anymore. Farmers and ranchers barely made enough to starve slowly. Teenagers hightailed it to Beaumont or Houston any way they could. The whole town smelled like the oil refineries sucking the stink out of the soil.

Patch drove through Hixville without seeing any changes: a gas station, a boarded-up Baptist church, a Whataburger, and the Feed & Seed. These days, folks bought groceries in Sour Lake or at the Walmart in Lumberton. Most other shopping was mail order.

The Hixville Feed & Seed survived by selling hardware, tools, and a range of basic supplies from flour to aspirin to the dwindling local population. It filled a wide single-story barn crammed with fifty yards of metal shelves and all the oddments big box stores didn't stock. Owned and operated by the Rodman family, the Feed & Seed had lasted close to thirty years and acted as hive, hub, and hotspot for the community.

Kids bought comics there and tailgated in the parking lot. Moms shopped for fabric and presents. Hell, Patch's family had sold 80 percent of their bales to local ranchers from the pallets right out front. Before he had his license, he'd driven the tractor over at sunup when the highway was dead and unloaded the hay himself. And after, the Rodmans always thanked him with a popsicle or a Big Red.

Already the sun baked the parking lot gravel. Under the roof's overhang, a wire rack of faded seed packets stood next to a leaking ice machine and a row of potted sunflowers. The bell tinkled as Patch stepped inside. Ceiling fans stirred the air under the tarpaper, keeping it slightly cooler... but only slightly.

"One sec!"

A hoarse female bray he knew and had missed.

"Janet, it's me. Patch." His accent crept out a bit. If anyone would know Tucker's deal, she would. "Janet?"

"Hastle? Bullshit! What in tarnation?" Huffing and puffing from the other side of the store, a big woman with a long auburn ponytail stepped into the central aisle. "Patrick! Fuck, you're skinny."

"I'm home." He held out his arms as if to demonstrate his Patch-ness.

"Aww, kid. That's terrible."

Patch rolled his eyes. "Tell me."

"Didn't I just?" She hugged him hard and fast, as if she thought he'd bolt, but let him go when he stepped back. Most folks clung but she knew better. "The hell y'doing back in this shit pit?" Then she nodded with a tight frown. "Funeral."

"Mmh." He held her stare and that said plenty.

"Damn shame, all of it. Waste and worse." Janet stomped behind the register, her large, square bosom like the prow of a ship. She had to be in her midfifties, but she looked exactly as she had when he was a wimpy seventh grader: a woman of fierce will and absolute purpose. She narrowed her eyes at him. "Lemme get a look."

The booming voice came honestly. She had been a junior high teacher for about twenty years.

"Fuck a duck! Skinny as a lizard, but you're prettier than my daughter now."

"I don't know about that. But your tits got bigger." He grabbed a handbasket.

She eyed his rooster/lollipop T-shirt. "I get it. A cock and a sucker." She looked proud. "Oh, you're terrible." The word sounded like *turble*.

"Your fault, Miz Rodman." Patch winked and started up and down the aisles gathering the essentials: bread, canned chili, peanut butter, soup, a plastic half gallon of vodka. Survival rations. "I'm staying at the house for a week or so."

Janet wiped the counter with a rag without looking at it. "Kiddo, I'm real sorry about your folks." She made a glum sound and didn't elaborate, as if waiting to see if he was in a whitewashing mood. She knew about the fights and had kept him on track during high school in hopes he'd graduate. She'd hid him here more than once. She had a niece who was a "lesbo" and wouldn't take guff from anyone.

"Janet. Everyone told him. Hell, my mama told him. Stubborn, stupid. Fuckin' coward." His anger sounded ugly even to him, but Janet would understand.

"Dead." She knew his pa and how they'd died, but she was old-school enough to make the right noises. A sniff of pity.

"Suicide is what. Only they won't call it that." Patch unloaded his basket on the counter.

"Still a fuckin' shame. Ten years younger than me, and I'm a veal cutlet. Your dad's always in a goddamn hurry. And now what? Death and dumb." She sighed and stopped barking like a teacher. "You okay? All things considered?"

Patch forced his fists open. "Sure."

She ignored the lie.

"Yesterday I was in Spain, now I'm insane." He went to refill his basket, talking over his shoulder as he eyed the refrigerated wall: fresh eggs, skim milk, sliced baloney, hamburger that he couldn't store with no fridge. Instead he topped up the basket with SpaghettiOs and Pop-Tarts. He only needed enough to survive until he sold the place.

"How you? Big city. You doing all them pornos still?" One of her favorite jokes since she'd seen him wearing a Speedo in a perfume ad he'd e-mailed to her his first year in New York. He sent postcards and clippings every once in a while.

"Jesus. No. I'm too old now. I wish." *Bullshit.* Modeling bored the hell out of him, but the money could be very convincing when he was strapped. "I model a little still, when there's time, but I'm a DJ mostly. A disk jockey."

"I know what a DJ— Fuckin' wiseass. What, like radio or y'know... weddings?" She grimaced.

"I can't stand weddings. No. Big, fancy clubs. Music's paying my bills."

"Good for you. Give 'em hell." She probably had no idea what a disco even looked like outside of *Love Boat* reruns. She held up the vodka bottle he'd set on the counter. "You're not old enough for this shit."

He laughed. "C'mon. I'm twenty-two now."

"Which makes me one hundred and fifty-seven, at least. Still getting plenty too." She leered and lifted an eyebrow at him.

"Dave good?"

"He won at the rodeo again last year. Large livestock." She winked and weighed imaginary bull balls in the air. Janet loved to boast about her husband, a shy salt-of-the-earth guy who would've died of shame if he knew. "Kinky bastard." An affectionate smile.

"'S good to see you."

"Same." She arranged his groceries on the counter in neat rows and nodded at the fridge wall. "You need breakfast stuff? Them eggs come from Tucker's."

He gave her a weird look to match the weird tightening in his belly. He went looking for paper towels, twine, boxes, and trash bags.

"He brings 'em in three times a week. Sells them at his trailer too. Little extra money on the side."

"Wait, Tucker keeps chickens at his trailer?"

"Kiddo, he's just trying to make his bills. Good eggs too." She slapped the counter. "Been a long damn time. You seen anyone yet?"

"Uhh, no." Did she mean school? Church? Between the closet cases he'd sucked off in high school and the homophobes he'd scrapped with, not too many locals were likely to cut him slack. Plenty of people in Hixville outright shunned him. "Just for the funeral, the will, and all. I gotta deal with the house."

Janet regarded him with gentle pity. "You're gone sell." No lilt of a question because she knew better.

A shrug. "You know I gotta. Only, my pa did a real number on me." He shook the twine at her.

"What now?"

"Janet, he made Tucker Biggs the fucking executor."

"Oh." Janet smiled until she registered his scowl. "That's a bad thing?"

"That man doesn't like me much. Only reason Pa did it was to hassle me one last time."

"I don't know. Tucker's pretty reasonable these days. Mellow. More than you think. He'll do right. And he sure is easy on the eyes. Coming and going. *Girth*!" Saucy raised eyebrows again, daring him to disagree.

Standing next to the trash bags, Patch grunted. He resented the interest his body took in Tucker, hated that he was one in the herd of unwilling admirers. "Like he should have any say in my life."

"He giving you trouble?" Janet pressed.

He shook his head. "Not yet, but he will. He claims he'll give me whatever I want."

"See? Then what's the problem?" She handed him an icy can of Big Red, because she remembered his life better than he did.

He beetled his brow and pretended to look at a pack of cherry bubblegum, weighing it. "I don't believe anything that hick dickhead tells me. Reasonable. *Pfft*."

"Kiddo, that's what they call a gift horse." Janet laughed. "Maybe Tucker's gone help you get clear so all your daddy's shit don't touch you. Maybe he's so lazy or busy he won't bother to get in the way. You don't know."

"Maybe." The thought still rankled.

"Then, what?"

"Nothing. I dunno." Patch put the gum back. "I don't wanna trust that dumbass. For anything. Even if he does right, I don't wanna owe him."

Janet goggled. "Then you're a dumbass too. Take the deal and clear out, why dontcha? I bet he gives you your money. You'll go back to the city and do your disco thing. Who's gone know Tucker had anything to do with it?"

"*I'll* know. But I guess I'll get over it. Right?" He returned to the counter with the packing supplies. "I think this is everything. I'm only here a week or two. Funeral's Monday "

A pause, and he realized she was watching him gently.

"You gone be okay out there?"

"Yeah. Of course." Patch spun the rack of greeting cards.

Three months into his junior year, Patch had left a thank-you card from this rack on the kitchen counter and hitched a ride to Beaumont without warning his parents. *Who's the dumbass?*

Janet rang him up. They exchanged cell numbers before she hugged him to her bosom.

"Too fucking skinny you are." She jabbed a finger at his ribs.

"Maybe you can fatten me up while I'm here." He hoped he'd be gone long before that happened.

She peered at him. "You'll come to dinner one night. Dave would love to see ya."

"Yes, ma'am."

"Don't you 'ma'am' me. You're gone take off, and before you set foot in this dump again, I'll be ashes in an urn on my daughter-in-law's piano."

"You could come to New York. Get Dave to come model some swimsuits."

They smiled at the thought. Dave weighed about two-sixty, even if Janet raved about his endowment.

"Great idea, kiddo." Janet slapped the counter. "I swear that man has a negative ass. I wish I could push on his stomach and give him an ass."

Outside, Patch loaded the car and drove back past the same church, Whataburger, and hardscrabble ranches he'd hitchhiked past seven years ago looking for trouble in tight jeans.

At Hob Warren Road, an old woman selling unshucked corn on the corner raised her hand and smiled. He did the same but felt like a liar. He didn't belong here; Hixville had spat him out like gristle at sixteen.

Nothing changes in this place. He hadn't seen Janet in all this time and it felt like yesterday he'd ditched his folks for someplace faster.

In Beaumont, Patch had kept his nose down, running deliveries to save money for the bus ticket to Houston, then spent March and April bussing drinks and dodging hands in Montrose until he could afford the plane to New York. No job, no plan, no chance, but he'd managed to make a place for himself by flashing his smile and his abs. Pretty boy makes good.

He waited tables and got his GED and worked his tail off. *Eyes on prize.* He flirted when he needed to and stuck to one-night stands. Last thing he wanted to do was put down roots. He just kept hauling ass and didn't look to either side.

In all that time, he'd never set foot in Hixville again. Until now.

Well, not in person.

At night sometimes, when leaving a club, he'd wander back in his head, to June bugs and MoonPies, rugged yokels with barbwire scars and cocks that leaked honey. The city was cooler, but some part of his heart must've stayed in the sticks. *Fenced off.*

He'd run all the way to New York City and then spent too many years trying to find a country boy to call his own. *Sick.* Every dude he dated came from West Bumfuck: Nebraska, Kentucky, Arkansas, South Dakota, and about sixteen goddamn Texans. Lanky boys who'd made their own escapes. Even Scotty had grown up raising soybeans. Apparently, Patch gave off some sick signal that brought the rednecks running.

Gathering all his hayseeds made him feel like those self-hating suckers who advertised for straight guys looking to cheat on their wives and girlfriends. Stolen moments with thieving bastards. Fantasies were bullshit; he wanted a life.

Patch deserved someone who deserved him back, someone who could keep up... but in the dead of night when he was listening to the traffic sounds on Ninth Avenue, he dreamed about well-filled Wranglers with a Skoal ring and the smell of fresh hay. He replayed the two times Tucker Biggs had forgotten they loathed each other and treated him like a person: at his first football practice and at that rodeo. Both memories he kept buried deep and only visited by himself in the dark.

Every full moon he saw took him back to varsity tryouts, Tucker sitting with the other two coaches to share a flask. Patch in hand-me-down pads and loose shorts that should've been looser.

Or worse.... the fairground bleachers junior year, a couple days after the arrest, with Tucker breathing beer in his ear, squeezing the back of his neck. "Hold your horses." That low drawl and wink. "Havin' fun, son?" The teasing growl so quiet Patch had to run whack it in the porta-john, right into his hand, and lick it clean. That hard, sweet grip and quick hug had almost torn a terrible public confession out of him. The next day Patch had run for his life and left all that, all *this* behind.

Two times, Tucker had noticed him, and both had stopped him in his tracks.

There would never be a third.

Climbing out back at the house, Patch spat at the dust.

Hold your horses.

As he unloaded the car, he made a deal with himself. He'd walk over to Tucker's right now and get things sorted. In, out, and no shouting.

If everything went right, they'd never have to see each other again.

THE SUN was high when Patch walked up the road past the little pond on the back twenty to an uneven dogleg acre never used for hay. Back here, Tucker's double-wide trailer sat at the end of a little circular drive

on a fake rise over a fake pond a couple hundred yards away that he and
Royce had dug with a backhoe and stocked with catfish.

The trailer had faded. Red and purple flowers filled a little patch
below both front windows. A crawling blob of kudzu smothered the trees
behind it. Fat chickens roamed the yard between the little porch and
Terrapin Road, pecking through a graveyard of old plumbing and rusted
metal: rescued toilets, tubs, and tractor parts bleached by the sun in neat
rows. A garden of garbage.

Under the vine-strangled trees round back, a sedate quarter horse
nosed the grass and raised her head toward him. Nugget, her name was,
and she'd arrived with Tucker when Patch was twelve.

The trailer wasn't even Tucker's. With Royce's help, they'd stolen it
from Tucker's ex-girlfriend and covered the holes in the floor with plywood
so he'd have a place to whore around. They'd put it back here on the farm's
dogleg so he didn't have neighbors to piss off and so Royce could sneak off
for a beer most nights. Their old wooden picnic table still sat in the front
yard, two chickens dozing up on the benches, surrounded by plumber's junk.

This early in the day, Tucker shouldn't have started discing, but he
was nowhere to be seen. His old blue pickup was, and a rusted Suzuki
jeep with holes worn through the roof.

Buh-gawk! A couple chickens squawked and squabbled out back.

Patch heard loud barking as soon as he climbed out and closed the door
of the Impala. Tucker usually kept a work dog. The barking came closer.

A grayish-goldish blur rounded the corner of the trailer and came
straight at him. A pit bull, champagne-colored, with floppy ears and a
cropped tail wagging furiously. She sniffed at him happily, nosing at his
knees and balls, and then bounded up onto the picnic table, then back
down, circling him.

Patch smiled in spite of himself. He missed having a dog in the
city. He bent to pet her ghosty coat and let her slobber on him. "Hey, girl.
Hey. Hi." He scratched her square head roughly and stroked her soft ears
as she wiggled with pleasure. "You're beautiful. Uh-huh! You are."

She climbed onto the picnic table again to lick his face and let him
rub her roughly. Down her back, a cluster of old knotty scars ran right
along her spine, rubbery and pink. She'd been stitched up after some
ugly altercation, but she didn't seem sensitive about him touching them.
She slobbered him again and wriggled before bouncing away and down
to the ground on the other side of the table.

"Hey there. Yeah. Hi."

She jumped up to put her paws on him, showing a white tuxedo splash down her chest and belly.

"Botchy, get off." A gruff growl from inside the trailer, but not Tucker's voice. "She bothering you? Botchy!" Heavy tread. "Sorry 'bout that. I was on the john."

The dog dropped and trotted up the little steps to the front porch of the trailer as the screen door opened with a *splat-smack*, and Patch had to swallow a mouthful of spit.

Out stepped a thick, bearded blond with a trucker's face holding a bottle of Bud. Midforties and stocky, swaggering like an ex-con under a stained gimme cap. He stood about Patch's height but probably had forty pounds on him. Hot in a roughneck way, but obviously bad news.

Patch stiffened. *Rough trade.* For realz. He could imagine the punches.

The man moseyed down the three steps, eying Patch with the hungry boredom of an overfed crocodile. "You the kid?" One hand rested on Botchy's head idly while she panted in Patch's direction. He dug at his gums with a finger and spat on the grass. A real genius. "Pat?"

"Patch." He didn't want to get any closer. Where the hell was Tucker? Who the fuck was this ugly, sexy numbskull? "Hastle."

"Wayne Bixby, but most everyone calls me Bix." He offered a tattooed hand to shake but came no closer, then let it drop. He smelled like diesel. "Buddy of Tucker's. I knew your folks some. But, uh, they didn't like me much, y'know."

"Bix." Patch knew the signals from growing up queer in a small town: the lazy eyes, the low voice, the intense, lingering focus. The man stood a little too close, too chummy and aggressive for a stranger, his fingertips grazing his packed crotch like a flashing BBQ sign: ALL U CAN EAT. Out here cocksuckers learned how to flag each other so they could bust a nut without getting beat to death.

Bix wet his lips and stroked his beard while he gave Patch a head-to-toe once-over like a plate of hot ribs that only needed sauce. Hot and creepy both. This was the type of bastard who fucked runaways at rest stops and slapped them around after. Good-old-boy dominance shone from him, sly and sleazy.

Queer… meet bait.

The gross part? Patch started to get turned on by the idea of blowing one of Tucker's inbred buddies on his rented couch just to make the point. The grimy danger revved his motor. *Sick, sick, sick.* A trickle of sweat crept out of his scalp and trailed down his neck.

Just to make his offer completely clear, Bix palmed his crotch, adjusting the contents. *Jesus.* His meat plumped up until the cockhead's ridge showed plain under his sunburned fingers. *Hypermale.* Why didn't men in the city know how to flirt like this? Why did Patch miss this when he hated home so much?

Bix sniffed at him, as if he found the sexual tension vaguely disappointing. "Hot day, huh? Y'hungry?"

Gulp. Patch eyed the beefy arms and oil-stained jeans and prison ink. Was he about to blow some grizzled bubba at 11:40 a.m. on the porch of Tucker's double-wide? The idea terrified and teased him. Part of him wanted to make trouble, to mark territory, to milk the cream out of this thick hick so he could smear it on Tucker's wall as a fuck-you. To prove he wasn't powerless, didn't care, wouldn't apologize for what he wanted.

Except he was, did, and would. In high school he would've blown this guy at a truck stop and come back later to do it again, but now he knew better. *Right?*

Patch closed his mouth and tried to focus on the pit bull circling their legs. He kept his voice level. "He at school?" Tucker, he meant. Coaching, he meant.

"For football?" Big wet chuckle and Bix smiled slow. "Naw, man. Them folks fired his ass years back. Got caught porking the principal's wife during a game." Head shake and that dirty chuckle again.

Patch nodded like he knew. He could imagine, in color.

"Long-dickin' her under the bleachers. Some such. Big scene. Hauled off. He cain't even go to them games no more." He licked his lip and grunted. "Dumbfuck."

Botchy panted beside the big man's thigh, regarding Patch with blond eyes and a slobbery Joker smile.

"Aww. He don't care... all his bastards growed up and gone off 'cept the one, an' he's up the prison in Conroe." Slowly, Bix's muscular arm brought the beer to his lips, and he made a show of taking a swallow, then wiping his springy brass beard, his bicep a sweaty knot and a glimmer of gold fuzz in his armpit. The wet August air slid between them, and Patch fought his ugliest urges.

Tires on gravel.

Bix raised his eyebrows but didn't look away. Brown eyes on green. Patch turned.

Tucker pulled up and swung to the ground, grinning and gorgeous, as if to remind Patch what Texas sexy *actually* looked like. Just like that, Bix might as well have been invisible. Tucker tapped the brim of his straw hat. "Morning, boys."

Patch swallowed and nodded. Testosterone swamped him. *Overload.*

"Y'all had lunch?" Tucker squinted.

Bix raised his beer, hesitating before he took the sip to say, "Naw. I'm good."

Yeah. Right.

Tucker thumped the blond on a meaty shoulder. Bix looked up and wiped his loose mouth, obviously interested in more than breakfast.

Patch watched them. Did Tucker know his friend was a big butch queer? A cold hope snagged him. Had he and Tucker ever fooled—?

"You met my girl, huh?" Tucker nodded at the sturdy dog pacing around them.

Botchy slobbered on his hand and bumped her head under it, petting herself and panting with joyful purpose.

"She's great." Patch smiled down at her and, without meaning to, looked up and caught himself sharing the smile with Tucker.

Because Tucker grinned right back at him. *Blink.* The force of it knocked the wind out Patch. "Good." Tucker's eyes glittered, gunmetal gray flecked with light. He held Patch with them and rasped over his jaw.

Patch swallowed, nervous for no good reason. Why was Tucker being nice to him? Why was Bix here? Down below, Botchy squirmed in a circle, panting and pushing closer to his denim thighs as he squeezed and stroked her pale coat. Solid muscle, like her daddy. The scars didn't seem to bother her a bit.

Bix grunted, maybe at the tense vibe, maybe at the dog, but it broke the moment.

Patch fought the urge to crouch beside her down there, this near to the men's legs. He knew he was already too close to be safe. "So happy."

"She's got it pretty good." Tucker's big hands rubbed her back, and her pale eyes squinted in pleasure. His deep drawl vibrated in Patch's bones. "Food, love, room to run. Pretty much heaven." He squeezed and stroked her floppy ears and tugged at them. "Your mom loved her to bits. Brought her treats. Sewed her a blanket, even."

"Ma did?" Patch couldn't believe it; she hadn't liked anything four-legged. "Well, great dog." He shrugged.

"She's a rescue. Some kids over in Sour Lake beat on her, dogfighting and worse. Her back got infected, and they dumped her to die." The scars.

"Dumped her here?"

"Naw. Janet called from up the Feed & Seed to tell me the vet planned to put her down. I stopped that shit quick. She's my best bitch, huh? You are, you are." Tucker squatted to stroke her, kneeling where Patch wouldn't. His sturdy thighs bulged on either side, and his face hovered all of two feet from Patch's zipper.

Sure enough, Patch felt his cock perk up at the fantasy, if not the reality, of Tucker on his knees grunting in front of him.

Bix stared past Tucker at his zipper with open interest. He swallowed more beer and wiped his loose mouth again. Bix dropped his thumb to his belt; his blunt fingers curled over the bulge in his pants, petting it absently while he eyed Tucker's face and Patch's bulge and did the math.

The fuck was going on?

For one sick second, Patch wondered if Tucker knew, if this was some sicko setup. He thought about Ms. Landry and the building in New York, and frowned at Bix, declining the invitation to be his bitch for a half hour of caveman throat fucking behind the barn.

Oblivious, Tucker reached into one of the low planters on the ground and pulled out an egg, holding it carefully in his dirty hand. "Them chickens get lost sometimes." Botchy panted up at them, tongue lolling. "I'm-a warm up some chili for us if you're hungry, pup."

"I'm good." Patch followed him anyway.

Tucker glanced back and held his gaze. "D'you wanna talk?"

"Oh. Right. Yeah. Sure." Patch felt his face heat.

"Then I better hit the road, ladies. I gotta make Kerrville by morning." Bix jingled his keys in his pocket and scratched. "Rodeo."

Patch nodded. *Another cowboy?* He didn't trust himself to make a sensible sound till this sleazebag split.

Tucker tossed his buddy the egg as Bix nudged past and clomped into the trailer. "In the bowl."

Bix thumped around, away, and then back to the door.

Tucker squinted like a joker. "Wayne's a clown."

"Fuck you, Biggs," Bix said through the screen as he emerged with a tattered Army duffel balanced on one shoulder. "Rodeo clown, he means. Not Bozo. Bullfighter, they call us now. I keep the livestock from killing folks."

Tucker chuckled. "'S why he's so fuck-ugly. Them beefs keep stepping on his head."

"An' why I get so much tail." Bix cupped his balls. "Least that's what your ma said."

Tucker swatted at him and laughed.

Their affectionate macho squabbling gave Patch a funny feeling in the pit of his stomach. The other two didn't seem to realize he didn't belong there between them. He'd felt like this constantly as a kid watching the older boys on the team who knew what to say and how to act around each other. A spy in a secret club.

Bix clomped down the steps and threw his bag in the back of the old Suzuki, rocking it on its bald tires.

Tucker eyed the vehicle. "That piece of shit ain't gonna make it to San Antone."

A dirty wink from Bix. "You know me. I can always find a ride." He gave Tucker a thumping hug and nodded knowingly at Patch, and then he was in his battered jeep and gone.

"Sorry about that." Tucker rubbed the back of his neck. "Bix is crazy." He paused at the screen door to turn fully. "He *bother* you any?" His eyes were shadowed.

Patch blinked. What was he asking? That "bother" had sounded funny to his ears. Did Tucker know that Bix fucked around with guys after all? Was Tucker being protective? "No."

Tucker gave a tight nod and held the door open. Botchy headed straight inside.

Inside, the trailer looked tidy and handsome: a leather love seat, a small color TV, a table in the kitchenette with four chairs. Patch covered his surprise with a nod. "Didn't know we mowed this late in the year. I thought all the tops were down and dried."

Tucker doffed his sweaty hat and gestured with it at the window. "I needed to disc. We seed in the fall with tops and they's a short window." Planting the tops of mature plants offered one of the cheapest ways to seed. "Whatever you do, this way the land's planted for spring."

Patch shifted his weight. Lot of work for someone who'd said he had no claim. "Wish you'd asked, Tucker. Unless we sell to a farmer, no one's gonna care if the fields are seeded."

Tucker scrunched his face. "Who'd buy this place but a farmer?"

Patch tried to imagine living in a world that ended at the blacktop. "I dunno. I just hate you did the work."

Botchy reappeared inside the door, watching them talk.

Tucker's forehead wrinkled. "Sorry, son. Your folks never wanted to—"

Patch nodded tight and walked back out into the junked yard before the rest of that thought emerged. Tucker didn't know shit about his parents. Not really. He'd been Royce's satellite, maybe, but kids and church? No way.

Awkward silence as the screen door slapped open again and Tucker emerged behind him. They didn't know how to talk to each other.

"I can come up to the house if you want." Tucker looked over the odd scatter of toilets and fenders. "To help get you situated." *Sitch-ated.* He dropped the hat on his head, not raising his eyes.

"I got it."

"Yes, sir. You do. I just didn't feel right after what that lawyer said an' all." He stood as still as a barn cat watching a snake. "About me living here." Tucker squinted at him, arms crossed. "That ain't right." His voice was gravel.

Patch didn't pretend to disagree, still spoiling for an ugly fight. "No shit."

Tucker sat down on the porch steps and looked up, his jaw set. "Your daddy shouldn'ta done that." Head shake. "Stubborn."

"You don't know."

"Well, I do, Patch. Who you think he talked to? I told Royce no, and he paid no fucking attention."

Patch gave a weary snort.

"So we fix it. That lawyer said. Didn't you hear her?"

Patch disagreed. "I knew better." His frustration left him jittery and hostile. "I knew he'd take a shit on me if he could."

"Now hold on—"

Patch's face heated. "Everything I done, I did. Fucking stupid to think my family would take a second look."

Tucker's lips clamped, his face darkened.

"See?" Patch laughed raw. "My folks had one last chance to—"

"—make sure you got took care of, Patch. They loved you."

Patch wiped his nose, not breaking, but close. "Faggot. Loser."

"You stop that." Tucker's coach voice slammed down. "Stop now. You ain't none of that."

"Yeah. Good. Right." Patch rocked on his feet. *I'm all of that.*

"They loved you, son."

Patch wanted to break something. "I hate this place." The words slithered out of him like tears.

"So...." Tucker stood up and dusted his hands off on his dirty jeans. He came to Patch and paused, the musty sawdust smell of him warm and dangerous. "Then let's sell it." Breathing. "They's folks would buy if we put it up."

"You're not gonna let me sell."

"You gotta listen sometimes. Royce didn't *give* it to me. I'm the caretaker, is all. Your daddy gave me a life estate because he didn't think you'd come back. I'm just here to take care of it for you."

"Why would you do that?"

"Do right by him. To help you get along?" Tucker gave a weak smile. "Patch, you got all these ideas about me that ain't right."

Patch opened his mouth and closed it. It *had* to be harder to get what he wanted out of Tucker Biggs. "I don't believe you." The fight churned in his belly with nowhere to go.

"It don't belong to me, pup." Tucker frowned. Botchy paced around his legs. "I'm gonna go eat. I'll call that lawyer later. It ain't science."

A cold ball in Patch's stomach. "Don't bullshit me."

"What bullshit? It's your durn land. They said already and that lawyer told you so, but you was in a hurry." His eyes fell. "I ain't funnin' you. Royce gave me a place to stay, is all. I don't own nothing. That's truth."

Was he serious?

"Hell, we could tell Janet, and she'd have this place under contract in a week. Plenty a snap in her garters. But I can call that Landry woman and get it taken care of, legal."

Patch rolled his eyes. "You'd never—"

"You got no idea what I'd ever or never. I'm saying right now what we gonna do."

The thought made Patch's knees gummy. He resented the hot stab of relief that went through him and let all the fight spill right out.

Tucker peered at him. "That's what you want, son?" He didn't mention that it'd make him homeless and jobless.

Patch nodded, which probably looked like permission to call him that. And as much as he hated to admit it, the word "son" made him nervous-relieved-hopeful. Maybe Tucker truly felt guilty enough to give up his claim.

Just like that Tucker moseyed back to his door, handsome and plausible. "Patch, you coming? Lunch."

"Nah." Patch shook his head. Stepping inside the trailer seemed dangerous, loaded somehow, after talking with Bix. What if they *had* fucked, what if he could smell cum and smoke, what if he couldn't help himself and popped a bone? "No." He hooked a thumb over his shoulder. "I got all that packing to do up the house."

"Well, alright, then." Tucker squinted, almost sad, it seemed, and opened the screen door again.

Patch rested his eyes on the sturdy body and gave in to the gratitude flooding through him. "Thanks... Tucker. Thank you." Claws on the deck as the dog ambled out.

"Y'welcome." Botchy licked Tucker's hand. "And I think we're gonna eat now."

They shared an awkward smile.

Before he said or did anything irrevocable, Patch went back to the rental car and climbed in. Behind him the screen door thwacked shut as he turned the key.

He'd get his check, take it back to New York. With nine months for construction, Velocity could open for the club crowd next summer. He could publicize it at his parties all winter. Even beyond New York and Vegas, he was booked for Prague, Rome, and two hours at the White Party in Palm Springs.

Money from the farm would buy him a future he'd earned. Tucker had said as much, and that should've settled his doubts. That cowboy was a shiftless son of a bitch, but he was pretty honest, all things considered.

Why was he willing to help? Where would he live? Patch shook off the questions. Maybe Tucker Biggs was making amends. *Not my problem.* He wagged his head, giddy with relief.

Hell, maybe he'd give Tucker a little bonus as a parting gift. A grand would be more than enough and he'd be grateful.

Still, the inequity nagged at him. If Patch sold this place, Tucker would... be fine. He belonged out here tugging his pud in the ragweed. What did he have to be sad about? Hell, everyone knew him, loved him, looked out for him, so he always landed on his feet with some kinda work, a place to crash, and a bed to get sticky.

Patch frowned. He'd never see Tucker again, and what of it? No better than they both deserved.

At the house he opened a warm can of SpaghettiOs and ate from it standing up in the dim kitchen, embarrassed that he hadn't stayed for chili and private jokes he'd never heard. Pretending to be compadres seemed dangerous and dumb. Besides, he knew himself too well to tempt fate. Last thing he needed was Tucker changing his damn mind.

Instead, Patch packed for the next seven hours, beginning in the living room because it seemed safest. To start, he cleared all the old furniture to one wall. He attacked the closets and cabinets, bagging the obvious garbage. At first, throwing out the past exhilarated him, but it was lonely, sweaty work.

His mother had squirreled away decades of catalogs and clippings. His father had piles of magazines going back thirty years, but occasionally Patch found money and memories tucked in between. Every dollar counted, so sorting it all was slow sweaty work. By two, his initial glee had faltered: rummaging through his childhood seemed poisonous and pointless.

He stopped for PB & J with his mama's kudzu jelly, standing on the porch so his sandwich didn't get dusty. Then back in and boxing till the light failed. About eight, he did make it to Janet's for overcooked roast beef and an awkward chat with Dave, who'd gotten paunchier and friendlier with time. She sent him back to the farm with leftovers and a hard hug.

On the way out of town, he called Scotty again, who picked right up.

"I got the deets. You're all set." His ex was talking very loud with bar voices and house music in the background. "We aces." Wherever he was, he almost had to shout to be heard.

Patch grinned in relief. "Well, that's something, at least."

"I gave 'em a shout, so they don't expect me in them shorts you got." Scotty was built like bricks, but parties didn't hire him for his look. "And hey, looks like we got the lease sewed up. Ten years."

"For real? Aww, man. I'm gonna find us the money."

"All fine, Patch. Get some sleep, huh?"

"That's great, Scotty. I owe you. Serious."

"C'mon, man. We partners. You don't owe nothin'. I gotta go, huh? These crazies are climbing the walls. Later." And he was gone, laughing at something the crowd was doing around him, and Patch was left holding the dead phone in the rented Impala, missing his life in the city.

Back at the house, he went right back to work, trying to focus on New York and Velocity instead of the shit he needed to shovel. As the moon rose, Patch pulled out a camping lantern rather than fight with Tucker's abandoned circuit breaker.

Gradually the small, hot house shrank around him. The stacked boxes made it worse, taking up what space remained in the sticky air stirred by his rushed inventory.

He glanced at the black windows. *Gotta be ten or eleven by now.* Outside the crickets fiddled at each other.

The lantern made the house into a ghostly echo of itself. Too much regret. Twenty-plus years of bullshit since before Patch had come home from the hospital.

He kept expecting his father's shouting, thumps on the table, or his mama muttering passive-aggressive church blab at him to make him sit still, act right, hush up. He had half a mind to burn this place down just to sweep it all away.

Instead he had a glass of warm vodka. *Who needs TV?* His boredom and memories rose up till they felt like terror.

He'd go for a drive. Hell, Beaumont had gay bars, and Grindr worked out here—maybe he could find himself some willing bohunk to rope and ride. One thing about Texas: it offered hot-n-cold running rednecks and cowboys on tap in every flavor, if that was your kink. Patch didn't DJ in towns with this many sweet farmboys, so he might as well take advantage. Like a drunk in a brewery. *Wolf in the fold.*

His cock shifted. He wet his lips. He knew how small towns worked. Even ugly, he could say "New York" and they'd be on their knees stuffing his joint down their throats. "Big city" meant exotic. He wasn't afraid or gangly, not anymore. He was a city slicker now. Moving around had sanded off his awkward edges and lumps. *Yeehaw.* He'd get duded up, and they'd fall easy. They'd seen him on billboards and better.

Small-town boy makes bad.

Strike while the iron is hot, right? Patch peeled down to his briefs and eyed himself in the mirror, a hostage to vanity. Before he hopped in the lukewarm shower, he did push-ups and crunches to put blood in his sore muscles. The water pump outside delivered killer pressure at least. He rinsed off in the dark, not bothering with any product or cologne, 'cause out here that was for sissies. He let his hair dry and curl in loose waves. "Pussy hair," his dad woulda said. *Fuck you, old man.* His agency called it "dark butterscotch" on his comp card, and they should know.

Wasting no time, he dug jeans and a V-neck out of his bag and toed into old sneakers from high school. He ducked outside in happy anticipation. For once he'd show the locals how—

He stalled on the steps. Why would he let just any old small-town queer to know him and blow him? No. He didn't want none of them. Blushing, he stopped dead in the front yard. *Pathetic.*

No. He wanted a cowboy, a greaser, a jock, some rough sumbuck who'd toss him around and make him crazy. He wanted—

"Tucker," he whispered. *So help me.*

The sky churned overhead like a storm with no clouds, no rain.

Patch looked out toward the trailer, hidden across the property behind a small break and a cowshed. He thought of Tucker kneeling in front of his zipper to love on that goofy dog and again wondered what the hell he and the other cowboys and convicts got up to out there when nobody was looking. *Maybe.... Surely....*

A half mile away, Tucker Biggs sat lonely in his shorts. Or not lonely, humping some waitress. Or his own hand. Or some rodeo clown, even. Not like he'd ever had any modesty, but living out here alone? No chance. He probably put on a show every night.

For a full five minutes Patch fought the impulse to just go see for himself. He'd never unsee it, and yet if he didn't, he'd never have the chance again. In a week he'd be back in New York and he'd never see Tucker Biggs again. *Thank fuck.*

Before he could second-guess himself, Patch walked up the drive and turned onto the dark shoulder headed the right direction, even though he knew it was the wrong way.

Out here the county didn't even have lights, leaving it truly pitch dark. His eyes adjusted as he walked the half mile to the pond, the trailer, and Tucker.

Like I'm thirteen.

Back then, Patch had snuck over to spy on this trailer plenty. *Duh.* Hot cowboy next door. He remembered hanging around the locker room for a glimpse of Coach Biggs's perfect bare chest. Going camping and washing in the creek as slow as he dared. Or that one night he'd spotted his dad's best friend under the barn shower, the flash of his perfect pale butt. He'd been too afraid to sneak closer. Too petrified of getting busted, but now, here, he was grown and it was just the two of them.

Us.

The trailer sat bright and still. Tinny voices, from the TV, sounded like, but nothing alive. Someone was home.

He padded along surefooted as a fox. He crossed the ditch and ducked through the split-rail fence like he was still a kid. He circled the yard slowly, coming no closer to the trailer just yet. His gaze strayed to the lit windows, ready to catch Tucker and his local skank or maybe his sleazy buddy doing something raunchy and embarrassing.

The windows spilled amber light onto the patchy front yard and its clutter. Inside, television voices rose and fell, but no overt cock show. *Duh.*

Patch walked on, disappointed and also somehow relieved. At this point, the notion of Tucker as a closet case would've been even more humiliating. Bix had gone to Kerrville. Now he remembered and felt foolish.

He walked on, keeping to the road's unlit shoulder, ready to be inside. Then, just as he passed out of sight, a phone's ring and movement drew his eye back to the trailer.

Tucker walked naked past both open windows. The angle hid most of his body, but the root of his fat slab of cock was visible under the dark pubes that led up a trail to fan out over his chest. *Jesus, his body.* His arms, his back—even with the farmer tan he looked like a statue. Tucker passed from sight, but Patch stood frozen, waiting for another chance.

Television laughter echoed. The rise and fall of Tucker's raw, drawling bass wove through it, wordless and seductive. Why didn't any of the small-town dumbasses in New York sound like that, look like that, feel like that?

Patch's hands squeezed into powerless fists.

He refused to creep closer, but he stepped sideways into a stand of live oak and wiped sweat from his face. Not like he'd ever have the chance again. Minutes ticked by until he started to feel ridiculous squinting at empty windows on a double-wide. And then....

Tucker drifted back. Smiling at something and talking on the phone notched against his shoulder. He paused, and for a crazy moment, stood exposed face to knees, shadowed and splendid, in the rectangle of the window. He rubbed at his armpit, raised the hand to his face and frowned skeptically at the smell. Absently, he tugged at one tiny nipple and dropped his hand.

If possible, Tucker looked even sexier, even stronger than he had seven years ago. He wore that wear and tear like a prize buckle.

Patch crouched lower, wincing at the crack of a stick under his foot. From somewhere inside, Botchy *ruffed* lazily. He saw her nosing at the window screen. *Shit*. She'd come right to him if she got out. His heart galloped.

Tucker leaned to look out over his yard and said something to the dog. As he leaned closer, his chiseled bare body blocked the lamp glow, silhouetting him, but if anything, that made it worse. Alpha male, ready for trouble.

Patch held his breath, aware of his pulse in his ears. His cock rose into an impatient ridge inside his stupid pants. He'd never wanted anyone so much in his life.

I can't stand him. But he knew that for a bluff. Patch refused to move.

Turning, Tucker laughed at something and rubbed the tight abdomen over the lazy thick swing. *Hold your horses.*

Light-headed, Patch swallowed and exhaled. *Fourteen again.* He knew he couldn't be seen in the dark, but no way was he gonna get caught spying.

Tucker cracked his neck and nodded.

That ridiculous impulse to stay and spy warned him how much he needed to leave this place, like *yesterday*, split before he did something stupid or got himself beat. He'd seen what he wanted. He couldn't have it. The end.

In the trailer, Tucker turned away, muscle playing across his back and shoulders, then the tight swell of his haunch before he sat, vanishing from sight.

The end. *Run.*

Ignoring his embarrassing erection, Patch crossed his arms and hurried back to his parents' house like a thief, his mind full of that rugged silhouette and the sound of Tucker's low laughter. Hopefully he could make his escape before his fantasies caught up with him.

CHAPTER THREE

PATCH PROBABLY slept three hours in the hot house, and then only after he'd jerked off twice thinking of Tucker in the trailer window.

When he woke he didn't remember where he was until he saw a rubbery golden drip on the wall. His childhood room was paneled in rough pine that bled sap every summer, even twenty years after his pa had built it. He tossed the sheet back.

A new day made him feel like a solution might be possible. As of this morning, two-thirds of the garbage was bagged for the dump. He could see more clearly, at least.

His parents had left about twenty grand in savings, and that'd get him part of the way. If he couldn't sell the place right away, maybe he could sell off some of the crap to scrape together capital. To get Velocity open, he was about ready to rustle cattle or boost an armored truck.

Around 5:00 a.m. he got himself moving.

He found his old school clothes laundered and folded in the dresser as if Mama had expected him home any second. He'd grown a couple of inches and put on muscle, but the basics were useable: briefs, T-shirts, shorts still fit well enough. Otherwise, his only clothes were from his beach gig in Ibiza last weekend, so he didn't have many practical options. Without A/C or bothering to shower, he opted for a pair of baggy khaki shorts and sneakers. By sundown he'd stink, but who'd care?

He tied his hair back in a ponytail and queued an old mix on his laptop, four hours of tech house that shook the windows and kept him moving. If anyone pulled up the drive, they'd hear thumping synths that said, *In a hurry, fuck off.* He'd recharge it in the barn later.

Looking at the place as an asset helped keep him steady and unemotional. This wasn't a home, it was a fire sale.

First he did a catalog of appliances. He could probably get two grand for them, and way more for the tack. In the mudroom he'd found a bunch of show saddles, worth six or seven grand. He moved through his childhood home like an adding machine. *TV, one-fifty. Air conditioners, eight hundred.*

No way could he raise a quarter-million dollars to match Scotty and buy the full partnership. But he might be able to scrape together fifty or sixty grand and convince a bank to make him a loan against the farm's value if he couldn't dump it.

In Ms. Landry's driveway, Tucker had offered to help, but Patch didn't want any distractions. The sooner this house was cleared, the sooner he could catch a plane back to his real life out in the world. He didn't live here anymore and didn't want to remember when he had.

Patch decided to ignore the breakers and tough out the week without power. One less thing to hassle with and an expense he didn't need.

It took him all the rest of that second full day to clear the closets, his pa's den, and the back porch.

Nostalgia didn't interest him, and he'd emptied most of the hiding places yesterday. Last thing he wanted was to pick through his memories. Most of them were crappy anyway. He'd cried plenty in this house, and he had no intention of spending more tears on it. He didn't have room in New York for a bunch of souvenirs of his shitty childhood.

Instead of pausing and musing, he emptied drawers and hangers into trash bags and tagged furniture for hauling. Aside from photographs, most of the knickknacks would go to charity. Poverty out here was real. Surely someone needed this flotsam and jetsam more than him.

The past only interrupted him when he slowed down long enough to notice details: Trophies on the mantel. The iron scorch on the carpet from seventh grade. The broken teapot he'd mended with epoxy.

In one drawer in his pa's desk, he found a folder labeled PATRICK in his father's stern block capitals. Inside was the schoolwork he'd left behind and a sheaf of school photos and report cards in no order. "Patch can't seem to get along" and "combative and creative." All the small-town code words for *angry fag* turned up plenty. Proof he'd survived. The old man had scraped together all the evidence a kid existed in his house and stuffed it here, out of sight and mind.

A few sweet memories hid in there too: tickets to a long-ago corn maze in Honey Island, a card for his junior high graduation with "Love, Mama" in her careful cursive, a painted handprint turkey with giant feet that forced a smile out of him. The most recent thing was a magazine page with an old Macy's ad featuring Patch in a seersucker suit with his long hair a curly mess and a redhead in a sundress hanging on his flexed arm. Someone must've passed it along. Seeing it here on his pa's desk made him queasy, lit a funny flicker in his gut, like damp wood catching fire.

His parents *had* known about him modeling, then. Living in Manhattan. He could imagine his father's reaction. At least they'd known he was alive and cared enough to keep it.

Patch set the folder aside to sort later. Now he had evidence he'd grown up somewhere. He didn't have time to waste now, but maybe one day he would.

As he was emptying papers out of his father's sideboard of junk, he heard the front door crack open.

"The hell?" That was Tucker.

"Back here." Patch straightened and dropped a stack of yellowed newspapers for recycling. "One sec." He wiped his face and realized he'd only smeared the dust. He went to the bathroom to splash water on himself and dried his face with a towel in the dim room. He really did stink.

When he reached the front hall, Tucker was flipping a switch and staring at the ceiling. He wore a faded chambray shirt and seam-ripped Wranglers. Some cowboys sliced the bottom seams at the ankle of jeans so they fit boots better and the hem couldn't catch and drag them if they got thrown.

"Oh Lord: them lights is still off. I'm sorry, pup." Tucker's brow creased. "You want me to go fix the breaker?"

"No. 'S fine. I don't need lights." Patch crossed his arms over his soaked T-shirt, self-conscious of his sweaty skin.

"Only reason I even pulled out the electrical is 'cause it needed doin'. Didn't want to pay nobody. I told Royce forever that panel were dangerous. An' I figgered you'd want the house right when you came...." Tucker's voice trailed off and his face softened. "Home."

"Nope. It's fine. I'm only working during the day, and it's one less expense."

"Patch, you shouldn't be working in the heat like this," complained the man who worked outdoors in August.

"I ain't spun glass." As soon as Patch said it, he froze. It was one of his pa's stock answers. He'd even said it with the same cadence.

Tucker didn't react, didn't seem to remember. "You say so, son."

"You okay?"

"I was gonna ask you the same." That good-ol'-boy grin and drawl. He looked at Patch's torso, no doubt baffled at him doing any work at all. "I didn't know if you wanted me."

No comment.

Patch didn't look him in the eye.

Somewhere back in his gorilla brain, he associated the smell of sweat, chaw, and beer with being a real man... which meant in that same part of his brain, he wasn't anything of the kind.

Grass, greener.

Patch closed his eyes and pressed the heels of his hands into the sockets hard. Soon as he could afford it, he needed to get his ass into therapy.

He'd spent his whole life lusting after hot bastards with a wad of tobacco wedged against their gums. *Dippers.* Hell on teeth, but safer than smoking when you worked a ranch.

Tucker turned back to him. "You done a lot. Organized and all."

"I'm not, though. But thanks."

"Fool me."

"Well, I've learned to fake it, then." Patch shrugged, scooped up the next taped box, edged past Tucker, and lugged it out to the car.

His pa used to say that pretending to be confident or patient or neat was the same thing as *being* brave or patient or neat because the virtue was in the doing. Acting brave was bravery. Pretend that you're patient and you just were. Fake tidiness and you lived tidy. *Same thing*, he'd say. *Just pretend.*

Patch had to move all the way to Manhattan to make sense of that, but damned if it didn't turn out to be true now that he couldn't admit it to his family.

He dropped the box in the backseat and didn't hurry back. What the hell was Tucker doing hanging around?

When he made it back to the front door, Tucker was there, one hand on the knob.

"Guess you got things covered. Sorry 'bout them wires." Tight smile. "I'm gone go run eggs and bales to the Feed & Seed."

Patch nodded but didn't offer to help. He knew full well what Tucker's muscles looked like pitching bales.

Tucker stepped outside and Patch followed him. "Thanks, Tucker." The words slipped out, but he found he'd meant them.

Tucker swung into the cab of his truck before he turned, a strange look on his face. "Y'welcome." He touched his hat and turned down the drive, then drove past the pond toward his trailer as Patch stepped back inside the dark house.

Around noon, the living room phone rang and rang and rang, but he ignored it. Who had a landline anymore? Last thing he needed was grief from his parents' church or the Shriners in Lumberton, but it just kept ringing. By two, he gave in and picked up. "Patch Hastle."

A woman's husky contralto. "Well, hello there, stranger! I been calling and calling."

He didn't recognize the voice. "Beg pardon, ma'am. Who is this?"

"Look at me screwing up twice." She chortled. "This's *Vicky*. Vicky Jean Thibault." Her voice hung in space as if he was supposed to squeal in recognition. "From up the high school."

"Oh, hi. Yeah, Vicky." He still had no idea. "Great."

"I just wan' say how sorry I am. Your daddy, rest him, was a caution, but he was good people. And your mama helped out Sunday school when I had my twins senior year. How you?"

His eyes bugged. *Who are you, crazy lady?* He almost said the words aloud, but then he remembered: a lean girl who'd helped him with... *math.* "Vicky! Hey. Hi. You and Fred get married after graduation?" She was a bona fide treasure.

Again that little hoarse chuckle that made her sound twice her age. "And them babies come about four months after. You been up in that city so long you didn't know. They's at school now, and their sister almost three."

She'd been a year behind him and nursed a crush on him till Coach Biggs started calling him a faggot during practice in front of her boyfriend. Back then Fred had been a lanky ding-dong with lowhangers and a used BMX. *Probably dumber and danglier now, with no time for dirt bikes.*

"Well, I'm working part-time up the funeral home in Kountze."

"Oh." *Right.* "For my folks. The service."

"Clothes is the truth. Sounds weird, but they want whatever you think your folks should wear for the burying. Lord, that sounds something. I'm so sorry, Patch."

"What kinda clothes?"

"Suit and dress, I 'spect. But whatever you think best. You know what they want."

Actually he didn't. "I dunno."

"I could swing by y'all's place, maybe. Look in the closet. For something."

Was that a subtle hint? She had to know he dug dudes, right? To her credit, she'd driven him home a couple of times when the team had whaled on him, sparing him the worst of the bus. Fred at least hadn't picked on him, probably on her say-so. She meant well. "You know, I'm coming out that way later. How 'bout I swing by with a couple options and you can pick?" he replied.

And that's what he did, stopping at Foulain's Mortuary with two handfuls of coat hangers. She met him up front in reception with a careful hug after he slung the piles onto the desk and dropped the bag of shoes he'd cobbled together. She was a little chubby now, her black hair shorter and streaked. She looked pretty and pleased and happy to be squeezed.

"Jeez howdy." She sighed and stepped back. "You're even more gorgeous than high school. I seen some of them pictures. It's that city living. Heartbreaker." She poked his chest.

He smiled easily. "Not really. Me, I'm more what you call a heart bumper. Folks bounce right off me." He'd forgotten how sweet she could be, how casually kind.

"You always running around, is all. You so lean. Between kids and sitting here, I kept all my baby ballast." She rubbed her hips and whispered, "Fred likes a little extra to hold inna sack." Again the conspiratorial chortle. Her face softened. "Now what about them clothes?"

"You pick." He nodded. "I trust you."

She flicked through the options and pulled a shirt and a tie to go with the old man's suit, a pale blue dress for his mother. "We, uhhhh. Don't need shoes, actually. I mean—" Her face tightened and her eyes flared. She held up the outfits. "Even these is just for them, really. We cain't do open casket on account of—"

He nodded. "'S okay."

She separated her picks from the rest and set them aside. "You good, hon?"

"I am. Yeah. Thanks, Vick." He scooped up all the remaining hangers. "I'm gonna run these up the Purple Heart center. Seems wrong to waste clothes."

He made it there in under twenty minutes, unloading the entire heap of hangers and bags for a grateful trio of elderly volunteers.

Headed west out of Hixville, Patch tried to find something on the radio other than Bible beating or country griping, and then gave up to drive in silence through the flat green.

Twice more he made the round trip, loading the Impala's backseat with clothing and linens dragged from the closets and driving back to the Purple Heart to donate everything. No way would he donate anything to a church, and the Salvation Army was nasty to gay people on the regular, but he knew military families often scraped by on crumbs and duct tape. He filled out donation paperwork for the first load, but for the second load he took near sundown, he didn't bother. The volunteers helped him pick out a black suit (shapeless) and shoes (stiff) for Monday. One less thing to stress about.

On the way both times, he passed Tucker's trailer. The windows and doors were shut tight like he'd gone into town for something.

Once done, he grabbed a pulled pork sandwich at a sketchy gas station. No way he could eat healthy out in the sticks, and *Christ*, was it delicious. He'd make up for it when he got back to civilization.

He didn't starve himself, but he knew his eight-pack came at a cost. In the city he'd ditched bacon and lard for kale salads. He'd always been skinny, but twenty-two wasn't seventeen. *Biology, yo*. Same reason he'd skipped tattoos. Photographers paid real dollars, and ink was an encumbrance.

Besides, half his success as a DJ came out of his look, and he knew it. Clubs didn't want a real farmboy from Texas; they wanted a drawling fantasy with shaved pubes, gym pecs, and a salon-cut mane. They gave him enough money to live his life, so he couldn't complain.

Walking back to the car with his sandwich, he spotted a couple of bohunks clowning and jumping on each other outside the gas station, lower lips packed and pulled sideways by chaw. Eying them as he passed, he was sincerely glad of his loose jeans and his mirrored aviator shades. Sunglasses are a small-town queer's best friend; nothing better for discreet cruising of clueless jocks so you didn't get beat.

Coming back down 326, Patch spotted Tucker riding the fence on his quarter horse in the low gold light with his happy champagne pit bull trotting beside.

They raised hands at each other, and Nugget slowed to a walk, but Patch didn't even tap the brakes. He hated the warm flush and smile that snuck over his face. *Idiot*. His dick thinking. In two seconds, Tucker made those sunburned no-necks up in Kountze look like cardboard facsimiles. If he'd been ugly, reliving all their history would've been easier.

Just because Tucker had been civil didn't make them friends. Just because he was hot didn't make him friendly. If all his exes and bastards steered clear, they must know better. The man was a bigoted clodhopper living in a rut. The only difference between him and those rowdy jerks in town was *time*. The last half mile to the house, Patch reminded himself of the insults and petty tortures visited upon him by someone who could've protected him.

Still, a picture formed in his mind of Tucker alone in the trailer, along with a ridiculous urge to invite him out to supper.

You don't like him, Patch reminded himself. Who cared that he'd mellowed or knew some truck stop gay bait with a fat pecker and prison tattoos?

At least Bix had fucked off to Kerrville where he could cause less trouble.

When he pulled into the drive, sunset striped the yard bright orange and streaked the sky amber and pink like a tulip. He'd missed all that crazy sky, surely, and the quiet.

A folded note was tucked under the door knocker. He read it as he entered the hot, dim house.

If you get hungry, I got steaks. T.

He smiled, then scowled.

Asshole. Never mind that he'd had the same thought. Never mind he wanted to go. Never mind the warmth in Tucker's eyes this morning.

"Peacemaking after the fact. All it is." *Do-overs don't happen.* Even if he was starving, he'd sooner cut off his leg and eat that. Tucker meant the meal as some kind of overdue apology, and he wasn't about to accept that. *Fuck you.*

Outside, the sprinklers cast over the flowerbeds in lazy circles—water from the well and power off the barn. Why hadn't Tucker torn them up too? *Hsst, hsst, hsst* as they kept his mama's lawn green and smooth on autopilot.

She's dead. Patch hugged himself. *Both of 'em.* Just then, his mother's tuneless kitchen humming came to him through the dimness, as if she were standing on the other side of the door slicing pears for a pie.

He'd never felt so alone. Even in New York that first year, when he'd known no one, the knowledge that his folks were out here gave him a point of reference. A place to sit a spell should he ever get the urge. Maybe that's why he ended up with all those farmboys.

The rooms loomed and his family's foolishness echoed in the quiet. They'd cared enough to fight him, and that had to count for something. Somewhere along the way, he'd forgotten how young sixteen was.

Standing around, treading water, nothing to do, aggravated the bejeezus out of him, but in this hot dark, he had no choice. He shook his hands impatiently. A wild urge to get out, go anywhere, surged into his throat until he thought he'd shout.

Why hadn't he let Tucker turn the power on? *Stupid.* He had zero cell reception and his laptop was on death's door.

He stalled until it was too late for steak. He should've gone, but he didn't think he could take watching Tucker flex and sweat over the grill or laughing and wiping juice off his lips.

Like a hick. Even the thought woke his dick up. *Sick.* Compulsive and juvenile. High school was a long time ago, and he knew better now, didn't he? He'd gotten past this kind of stubborn inferiority. He'd forgotten how much his fetish for good ol' boys drove him growing up, the sense of challenge and the lust for their approval, *real* men. It was the same reason millions of sane gay men fantasized about "straight-acting" jerks. Self-loathing and self-destructive posturing, and he knew it. He'd slept with some of the hottest tail on three continents, *models,* for the love of Pete, but this craziness ran deep in him.

He remembered every insult and every time he'd tried to catch a glimpse of Tucker as a teenager and failed. Shame seeped through him for spending his life trying and failing to measure up to someone he loathed, who loathed him even more.

The dark room didn't help him any and memories of the past twenty-four hours preyed upon him until he felt thirteen and miserable in the depths of his adolescent crush and Tucker's cruelty. He resented his own weakness and lust. Coming back offered an ugly reminder of how far he hadn't come. Confirmation that his intense farmboy kinks were radioactive, with a half-life of forever.

The faded bulge in Tucker's jeans. The scent of iron and sawdust. The cleft chin and twang rumbling from chiseled mouth. The knotted sinew of his arms and giant hands, so big the sight of them made Patch think of words like *spank* and *milk* and *prod.* He rolled the shoulder Tucker had squeezed, and the imprint of those ridiculously thick fingers burned there still.

His tormentor. His worst enemy. His father's best bud.

Patch gripped his hardness and squeezed till it hurt, till even the pain felt satisfying. *Disgusting.* But it didn't disgust him one bit. By moonrise, he'd spent three hours talking himself out of sneaking over to spy on Tucker, only to give up when he knew better.

A sweet flutter of anticipation at the thought of seeing Tucker naked; a boyish rush of adrenaline and anticipation. Pathetic, but he wouldn't have many more chances. Hell, he should go look his fill now. All these years later, he could finally get an eyeful and knock Tucker off that pedestal in his mind. After years of idolatry, maybe it'd get the man out of his system. He would not whack off over Tucker Biggs ever again.

He raised a finger and touched another drip of amber sap on the wall of his room, squeezed out by the heat.

In a week, he'd go back to Manhattan, open his club, and never lay eyes on that prick in his lifetime. Tucker deserved to be forgotten. *Happily Never After.*

Tucker was only a man, after all, and the reality couldn't possibly match his fantasy. Some redneck in a trailer? Already forty-three and living alone. A lonely loser who only looked like a winner out in the middle of nowhere where he had no competition.

Patch swallowed as the idea took root in the silent house. Who'd know and who'd care? Didn't he want to look his fill, to outrun his past and get clear of this? Soon he'd split and he'd lose the chance forever. Tucker never needed to know about his infatuation, and Patch would be free, his whole fabulous life ahead of him at a million miles a minute.

He nodded to no one.

Anger and lust swirled together, propelling Patch out the door into the starry night, moving fast enough to outrun his reservations.

AND SO for the third night in a row, Patch snuck over to Tucker's trailer like a common pervert on parole.

Instead of risking the road, he cut across the field so he wouldn't be spotted. As he made his way, fireflies speckled the dark, winking on and off at each other in a way that always made him smile and hold his breath. He hadn't seen lightning bugs in seven years.

He felt as pathetic and ridiculous as a Peeping Tom, but having caught a glimpse of the man's body already, he'd be damned if he wouldn't take advantage of his last chance to see his high school fantasy in the flesh at close range.

As a kid, Patch had caught fireflies in plenty of jars, even knowing they'd die. The soft winking glow would falter and fail. Why catch them at all? He'd known better but couldn't resist.

What if spying on Tucker was like that? Maybe catching his fantasy once and for all would kill it. Or kill him.

No.

Out back, the quarter horse was dozing at the fence, and Patch could hear a muffled squawk from two horse-haulers on the side of her stall, serving as makeshift henhouses. The rusted Shoops sat on flat tires, and inside were rows of laying boxes and sleepy hens. There's where Tucker got those eggs.

Placing his steps carefully and hugging the blobby silhouettes of the live oaks, he let the shadows hide him as he crept up on the warm light from the windows and the open screen door.

Jackpot.

Tucker sat in the tatty armchair Patch's mama had kept in the sewing room. Her thinking chair, she'd called it. The chenille was dull purple paisley, and the back was ragged from their old tabby Skeet clawing it.

He was buck-ass naked, and fewer than ten feet and Patch's pants separated their erections.

Tucker Biggs had to be the most beautiful man he'd ever seen in twenty-two years, on four continents. The broad, flat chest carved by manual labor… the thick-veined forearms and the wide shoulders… the powerful legs and the bull-rider's ass… the deep cleft at his chin and the cheeky twinkle of his eyes. His hard torso flexed under the layer of extra meat that beer and grease had put on him, flesh that softened the chiseled edges Patch remembered on his coach, or the cowboy he'd been before that.

And his cock. *Jesus.*

Tucker's fat bat was every bit as broad and brutal as Patch had dreamed, a beer can battering ram with a stubby upturned knob.

Tucker took his time and then some, tugging the shaft, scrubbing that juicy snout with calm focus, his eyes half-lidded. How long had he been playing? His shaft looked dark and swollen, his balls pulled up tight. He could have been jerking it at least an hour or more. He was in no kind of hurry. All the time in the world and plenty to play with.

The sight of it paralyzed Patch. Ordinary length, but goddamn was it *wide*, wide as hell. What the farmhands would have called a certified pussy-splitter. A broad root to make you shout at the time and ache for a week after.

He suspected it was uncut but couldn't be certain because it was so stiff in Tucker's fist. Extra skin for stroking, definitely, and a wet crown. The balls beneath sat plump in their fuzzy sac, bouncing as Tucker tugged lazily and closed his eyes, milking himself with painstaking purpose. He rolled his head back to face the ceiling. A distant smile played over his mouth, and his tongue snuck out to taste the corner of his mouth.

Patch inched closer to the lit window. Stealing this private moment from his old nemesis made him anxious and proud and ready to bust. He gloated over the twisted instinct that had steered him to this spot to spy tonight.

He had never taken his time with anything, but for the first time he understood, at least: of all people, Tucker had nothing to rush for.

Patch swallowed as clarity dawned. When you live nowhere by yourself, what the hell else is there to do? *Hold your horses.* How could it be a waste of time when he was so alone?

Inside, Tucker seemed hypnotized by the sight of his own hard-on, testing and tasting its thickness with his blunt fingers. Every third or fourth stroke, his index finger lingered just under the knob, petting the stretched skin so lightly that it gave Patch goose bumps at twenty paces. His sac jounced in a plump, fuzzy knot.

He'd wondered what the fuck someone did out here all day, and now he knew. You developed masturbation as a martial art till you were a hand job ninja. Tucker's girth glistened dark, whether from grease or the slow ooze of juice from its tip. His steel-band arms were slick as well, and his legs quivered with restrained power while he worshiped his own flesh.

Edging.

This was whacking off taken to a whole other level. Self-pleasure as a sport.

Tucker stroked with a patience that seemed to slow the clock and stop the moon until the night slid past his pleasure like the sweet sap oozing out of him. *No rush.*

Without turning, he scooped two fingers of something white out of a jar on the side table, lard or lube. He closed the hand and scrubbed the white

lump into slickness inside his fist before polishing it onto his cock gingerly…
slower still, almost cautious in getting the fresh grease onto himself. He
paused again and held his hands away from his straining erection.

Jesus.

Tucker shivered, a slow ripple that shut his eyes and tightened
his torso for a moment. He clamped his lips shut and breathed through
his nose as if carrying something heavy. He let his throbber bob before
him as he pulled one leg up onto the chair. Even his movements had an
underwater languor, as if he'd put himself in a trance. His slack jaw and
drowsy eyelids seemed drunk.

Patch heard heavy breathing and knew it for his own. He opened
his mouth to stop the sound. His heart knocked slow and sleazy against
his ribs. *Can Patch come out to play?*

As if ordered, Patch dug his own handful of pork out of his briefs,
his tight balls crushed up by the waistband. He leaned over and drooled a
ribbon of saliva for lube, catching it and smearing it onto himself roughly.
Popping with Tucker like this would be a once in a lifetime, better than
anything he could've planned.

Hurry up.

Patch shook his head at his own impatience. He didn't want it over
so fast. He wanted— He shook his head again and stopped jerking himself
for fear he'd go too quick. What was his hurry? *Hold your horses, son.*
He almost said the words aloud.

Inside the trailer Tucker cracked his neck and gave his meat three
short strokes. A grin, and he tasted his sweaty upper lip absently as he
let go of the straining column again. It jerked in midair like a cobra but
didn't squirt.

Tucker held his breath with hands held up as if a cop had given
the order. He stared at his vein-strapped shaft a moment before exhaling
raggedly. His eyes closed as he inhaled again, then hitched his pelvis
forward, exposing the trench of his muscular rump, pale and smooth
with a light scatter of dark hair at the center.

Patch licked his lips involuntarily and let go of his dick, too,
mesmerized with longing.

Tucker flicked his tits with lazy thumbs and then reached down
under his nuts to stroke the tiny pink aperture hidden there.

Patch realized his chest was rising and falling in tandem with
Tucker's. Hell, they were breathing together too. *C'mon.* Maybe he just

had to watch and Tucker would do the work for him, violate himself. Did Tucker play with his own ass? *Do it, man.*

As if he'd heard the request, Tucker tipped his pelvis again and screwed a thick finger into his butt. As it sank, he growled at some magic it worked inside him.

The sight made Patch horny and nervous. He'd never let anyone poke around inside him. Butt stuff seemed complicated and scary. "Too tight," he told 'em, and "My dick feels plenty good on its own." It seemed too scary, too personal, too permanent.

Tucker slid the fat finger out and then in, out and in, slow as spit. His dark dick strained beside his forearm. He definitely knew what to do with his wide hands.

In the sweaty dark outside the trailer, Patch tried to imagine what they could do to him.

Truth was, New York had made him lazy in bed. His looks let him get away with a lot, and these days he was happy to kick back. "Cocky," his exes called him, but after years of groveling and worrying, he'd earned a little worship. Still, seeing that raw who-gives-a-fuck confidence in a guy always knocked him sideways.

A long shaky exhale as Tucker slid his fingers out of his ass and breathed raggedly. His hands hovered in midair, arms knotted with muscle, and he swallowed and blinked, fighting something inside him.

The pulse ticked in Patch's throat, and a trickle of sweat down his spine. He didn't dare touch himself or it'd be over. *Hold your horses.*

Tucker stroked his chest, belly, and downward, everything but his fat rammer, tracing the base and balls and his inner thighs with sleepy intensity. He tasted his lower lip and watched his greasy bone.

No rush. Patch nodded sluggishly. *No worries.* If he lived out here, what else would he do to entertain himself? If he looked like Tucker, he'd tell everyone to fuck off and live in front of a mirror.

Tucker drove the fingers back inside himself gradually. His engorged dick bobbed before his eyes, the crown glossy and firm. Precum dripped to the floor in slow motion. Once. Twice. A spasm shook his sinews and bunched his sturdy legs. Again he held his breath, straining against some internal pressure.

Patch froze. His breath tight, his knees mushy, he could feel his own climax rising, unbidden. *No fucking way.* His balls tightened with Tucker's.

Squinting, Tucker pushed inside himself again, with two fingers this time, and twisted his hand. A head shake, a sharp intake of breath as his toes clenched. His rod jerked and locked rigid. A gasp, a lazy grin, and his eyes widened at whatever it was.

What I wouldn't give.... Patch almost grunted in mute aggression.

While Tucker probed himself, he began to brush the knuckles of his other hand up the top of his shaft, lazy grazes from root to crown. Another drip. His jaw tightened, and his hard quads, and his balls.

He's gonna. We're gonna—

Tucker's grimace locked and stretched, and he roared painfully.

Patch held his breath as Tucker lost control. *BLAM* came the wet fireworks.

"Shiii-iit." As if he was still fighting a losing battle, gummy loops of semen seethed out of him and smacked into his face, chest, navel, pubes. His thighs flexed, hips hunched at the *squeeze-squeeze-squeeze* as the goo erupted onto one cheek, his heaving chest, his treasure trail.

Patch was nearly there himself. He tugged at his stiff joint frantically, pulling his cock hard and fast, racing to get there too while he could stare at his fantasy in the flesh for the last time.

What would it be like to kiss him?

Inside, Tucker gasped and settled with a lazy chuckle, jizz running and branching down his torso while his honker settled a heartbeat at a time to roll onto his knotted thigh. A shiver chased up his torso and his head wobbled.

Cresting pleasure pushed Patch closer, closer to his own cliff. He began jerking fast enough to sting. *Almost there.* The crown of his cock swelled under his curled fingers, and his balls rose too high to bounce. Any second, any second he'd bust—

"Patch, you wanna finish that up in here?"

He froze, hand wrapped around his meat, and looked up, pulse knocking in his throat. *Busted.*

Throat clearing. Glittering eyes on him through the screen.

Patch's stomach turned over and his balls turned to ice cubes. Free of his hand, his spitty pole bobbed in the dark. *Caught.*

"C'mon, c'mere now." Tucker didn't move from the armchair but stared straight at him, cool eyes boring into his through the screen, as he dabbled lazily in the spray of jism coating him to the hollow of his throat. "Either close the fucking door or help me clean all this sauce up."

Obviously Patch wasn't as hidden by the dark as he'd assumed.

"C'mon in outta the crickets, boy." Tucker's blunt fingers played in the puddle of semen sliding down his abs.

Patch shook his head and made an apology face. His erection flagged. He could still bolt and bluff his way out.

"Suit yourself. But, way you been watching me, a Kleenex seems like a fucking waste of all this good nut. And maybe you need to get off proper."

A step. Another. Patch started moving to the steps and door without tucking his dick away before he could stop himself. At the doorway, he paused till he got another nod of permission that brought him inside and across the creaking trailer floor.

"Waste-a time, y'ask me." Tucker's musky iron and sawdust stink was everywhere and his softening dick rolled to a stop across his balls.

Patch crossed the dim living room, right to his ruin.

Tucker raised his wet thumb to his mouth and sucked the cum off it. He swiped at the puddle again, then offered the hand to Patch. "Y'hungry?"

Hypnotized, powerless, Patch dropped to his knees between the spread thighs. The air there seemed briny and thick as chowder.

"I figgered you might be." Tucker's tan fingers glistened with the hot bleachy load. A milky smear ran slowly down his hip like melted tallow.

Patch took a breath, and another, silently begging Tucker to put those fingers in his mouth, to make the choice for both of them.

Tucker did no such thing. His flecked-gray eyes twinkled and his index and middle fingers curled. "Unless you don't wannit." A sleepy grin.

In one motion, Patch shook his head, leaned up, and licked Tucker's fingers into his mouth, sliding his tongue between them and sucking them clean of semen. Filthy exhilaration flooded his body, blood drummed in his ears.

"Good boy. That's a good boy." Tucker pushed the broad fingers deeper, pressing at the back of his throat with a salty, gagging pressure. "Get all that good spew."

Patch grunted, extending his tongue to swipe at Tucker's calloused palm, pulling more fingers inside his mouth and sucking the sweet salt off them too.

"Some mouth you got, pup."

That gravelly, drawling bass unleashed something frantic in him. Lust coursed through Patch, ugly and glorious as a hurricane. *I shouldn't want this, but I do.* The twang, the sweaty reek, the rugged, arrogant indifference. Tucker pressed buttons he'd tried to forget he had. So many kinks without breaking a sweat: straight, cowboy, coach, dickhead, daddy. His cock thickened uncomfortably, bent down over his balls until he dug in to flip it up.

Tucker nodded and smiled at that, letting Patch worship him with spit ribbons. Instead of removing his hand, he pressed all four fingers inside the wet heat and caressed Patch's cheek with a blunt thumb. "Look't you. So fucking dirty, so handsome. Good boy."

Made him curse. Patch blushed and nursed on each finger of that big hand like a calf, and as Tucker lowered his hand back toward his meat Patch followed it right down, gratefully nursing on the thumb. Then, as if he'd been waiting to do it his whole life, he lowered his lips to the stout snout of Tucker's spout, taking the sauce from the source.

"*Unnngghhph.*" He growled as he suckled, and Tucker echoed it above him.

Why didn't the posers in New York know how to steer him right and sound like this? The guilty, grasping pleasure felt sweet as found money, like birthday cake for breakfast.

Tucker slid his fingers free and took hold of Patch's curly hair with a filthy, growling chuckle. "Now go on, pup." He jerked his chin at the semen on his lean belly and hip.

Patch obeyed, pressing his face into the warm ooze and licking it up with wide strokes of his tongue. His breath came hard as he slobbered and bit lightly at Tucker's ridged abdominal muscles. *I'm starving.*

Of all the bastards who would have tripped his switch, didn't it just have to be Tucker Biggs?

"Fucking-A, that mouth." Tucker hunched his pelvis so Patch could snuffle along his balls.

Patch learned Tucker was ticklish on his sides and that he liked his balls licked. The head of Tucker's dick was too sensitive for sucking, maybe because he'd already popped. Patch tasted the underside of the head, licking in small dabs that made the older man jerk and moan above him.

"Jesus! *Jay*-sus H. *Crickets*, pup. Ho!" Tucker twisted and arched under his mouth but let Patch clean him like a Sunday plate. His thighs were pale next to the farmer tan on his arms.

The dark curly hair smelled salty and clean. Even soft, the fat branching vein on the top of his cock stayed spongy under Patch's tongue.

He stroked Tucker's butthole lightly with a finger, not testing it, but keeping it awake. He pressed forward and tasted it, licking the seam right up the ridge to the underside of his fat balls for one perfect moment.

Sharp inhale from overhead. Tucker bared his teeth, and his eyes glittered wild. "Easy... easy there. Holy fuck." Tucker's taint hadn't softened fully, which meant another boner, another load wasn't out of the question.

Patch's meat felt like a hammer. He gnawed and drooled on the underside of the shaft, worrying the tender spot under the head with his lips and teeth. Long, slow licks until Tucker's tool shifted and rolled over and started to firm up again. He inhaled the salty scent from the tufts of dark hair.

"Agh!" Tucker made a strangled grunting sound deep in his throat and pressed down on the armrests till he rose off the chair. His back arched and his hips locked. "Hang on, Patch. Gimme two secs. Y'gone kill me with that fuckin' mouth." He scootched his butt an inch forward. The leg over the chair arm squeezed and released. "I'm gonna pass out."

That's more like it. Patch liked the idea of taking control, of big bad Tucker in his power, squealing and squirming. For once he had the upper hand, even if it was on his knees.

"Easy now. Wait a sec. Hold up. Jeez."

Patch ignored him, licking up his twisting torso to his throat, bringing their faces together. *Finally mine.* Kissing distance.

"Look at me now. I'm too old to go that quick, son. You gotta remember—"

Son.

Patch stopped cold. Eyes wide, he fell back on his ass and wiped his mouth roughly, ashamed and exposed. "The fuck am I doing?" He couldn't stand hearing his accent flare up. Ice in his heart, face burning, he scrabbled back.

Tucker planted both feet on the floor and leaned forward. His cockhead dropped and bumped the seat, leaving a dot of seed there. "Look at me."

"What the fuck are *you* doing?" The room reappeared at the edges of Patch's vision, blurring back into focus. The trailer door still stood open to the night with the crickets scraping all around them. Patch could smell Tucker's crotch and semen all over himself—face, hands, hair.

Marked. He'd crossed a line forever. "Oh my God. What'd you just do to me?"

"What *I* did? Now hang on, Patch." Tucker sounded like a coach again, stern and steady. The voice he used to make rotten kids mind him at school. "It ain't like that, now."

"How is it, then?" His dick drooped. This was every kind of wrong. Heart a mile a minute, Patch rose one knee, two, and backed toward the open front door, pushing his dick back into his jeans. His pa would kill him if he ever—*Pa's dead.* Grief and nausea raced through his veins like cold acid.

"We're both of us here. Stop, boy." The stern coach voice again.

"I'm not your *boy.*" Patch shook. "Jesus. You're my father's best friend." One thing to lust over the local ladies' man, quite another to blow him five days before the funeral. For a horrible moment, he felt the corners of his eyes sting with tears.

Before Tucker could use that coach voice again to nail his feet in place, Patch fled, tumbling down the little stairs, and wished he'd driven. His slimy hands shook.

Tucker's irritated alpha bellow sounded behind him. "Patch, don't be a pussy."

Too late.

"Patrick."

Without lurching toward the lights or looking back at the trailer, Patch stumbled away in a blind scatter of gravel and hightailed it back to his parents' house, trying to ignore the smooth burn of Tucker Biggs in his mouth and down his throat.

Chapter Four

Patch didn't sleep.

Oh, he lay down in his jeans and socks and looked at the ceiling. He paced around the dead house and stared out at the moonlit yard. He took a piss and drank some water and then pissed that out too. But sleep stayed far the fuck away, in Manhattan maybe.

Instead what he had was the grunt of Tucker, the musk of Tucker, the spice of Tucker, the heat of Tucker Biggs over his hands and in his belly and on his skin. As much as he wanted rid of it, he didn't rinse it off for fear he'd miss it once it was gone. He couldn't jerk off for fear that one act of delicious self-defeating treachery would come back to haunt him. Why had Tucker invited him inside? He chided himself for reveling in the memory and cursed the boner under his buckle that refused to surrender. Instead, he stared at the empty dark.

What do you do when your obsession gives you the go-ahead?

Run.

Sometime around dawn, when the horizon started to pale and the dew got heavy enough to leave snail trails on the windows, Patch gave up and got up for good. If he couldn't stay still and stay sane, at least he could escape faster and get his ass back to NYC and the fast lane ASAP.

He packed.

Mama's sewing room seemed safe enough and unsexy in every sense. He lugged a pile of flat boxes in there and began loading them for charity. One of the local schools, or maybe a shelter, would want all her crafting supplies. Out in the middle of nowhere, smart folks needed these mind-numbing hobbies to keep from climbing the walls.

About ten, the sound of wheels on gravel froze him with his arms full of acrylic yarn.

For one horrible, happy moment, he thought it was Tucker. *Nausea. Guilt. Lust. Hope. Panic.* And in that order.

Tugging back the sheers, he saw a faded station wagon he'd never seen and a man he'd seen plenty.

Before the wagon had rocked to a stop, Patch went out right to the driver's side. "Pastor Snell."

The window rolled down and the jowly face gave him a somber smile. "Patrick. Morning." Snell, an overfed blowhard about as sharp as a mashed potato. He made free with the brimstone in his sermons and acted like he *knew* sin, up close and oily, but Patch had never managed to catch him with his pants down.

Not for lack of trying.

"Thanks for coming out." He'd always suspected the pastor ostracized him on principle—town queer and all—but maybe he'd misjudged, maybe the guy was only a grinning Puritan with no other agenda.

Snell squeezed his steering wheel. "That Landry woman arranged things last week, and then she called yesterday, mentioned you was back."

"Prodigal son."

"No, sir! Your mama-rest-her-soul tol' me you done great up north." He blinked sadly, as though Patch were a refugee from a glamorous war zone. "Photography, she said. And music something."

"Uhh. Getting by. Yeah." Patch smiled in spite of himself and wiped his hands on his T-shirt. "Listen, I'd offer you something, but the house—"

Snell pursed his lips. "No need, Patch. I just came up to pay my respects. See if there's anything—"

"No, sir." Imagining if this sanctimonious crank had spied the raunchiness in the trailer last night. Patch tried to make his grin look like gratitude. "Ms. Landry knows what they wanted. With the service."

"Seemed to." An absent nod. Snell looked at the house and the yard. "They's so proud of what you done up there in the big city. Your folks, I mean. You was always a good boy."

Patch blinked at that. "I dunno about that, Pastor." He could still smell Tucker all over himself.

"Well, I do. I won't keep you none. See you Monday." The funeral, he meant.

Patch nodded, dumb, but didn't wave.

Before he could second-guess himself, he hooked a trailer up to the rental car and ran three loads of furniture to the charity shop in Kountze. He'd be sleeping on the floor now, but finally he began to see some progress. *Going, going, gone.*

After he'd dropped off the sofas and the sideboard, the repetitiveness and frustration had scoured away any lingering sexiness. He'd *just* about forgotten the Tucker run-in. Maybe Tucker had too.

Before the day slipped away, he called Ms. Landry. She'd followed up with the Texaco scouts, but better still, she'd put feelers out to a few brokers in Houston and Nacogdoches. A wealthy family named Killinger wanted to have a look-see, along with a couple of ranchers and maybe a dairy outfit if they could get a variance. Anyone'd be an easier sell to the locals than big oil. To speed the sale, he urged her to drop the price and gave her leeway to cut corners. *Sooner done, sooner won.* Great, thanks, bye.

He went back to work with a second wind. Apart from the furniture, he'd stacked the sewing room's contents into twenty-odd boxes against the south wall. He stopped to eat a couple of cold Pop-Tarts and chug three cupfuls of lukewarm water. His Manhattan gang would've been horrified, but *needs must.*

To seal the deal, he finally used the mudroom sink to scrub the rich stink of Tucker Biggs off his hands and face. He went to his room to strip off the ripe jeans and put on clean clothes he hadn't worn since junior year. He scraped his curls back into a blunt ponytail.

He ignored his stiff poker trapped in overshrunk BVDs. Mostly forgotten, then.

He built boxes and tried to fill them without thinking too much, but dismantling his folks' bedroom took even longer. The wall of photos staring from the hall gave him a sick, sad feeling.

Patch as ring bearer, age five. Patch, older and laughing at a home-baked birthday cake. Patch's first rodeo in Sour Lake. Patch sunburned, digging postholes with the Humphrey kids. Patch up to his knees in mud after a hurricane. Patch in football pads. All him, all bullshit. He was in every photo, but the life they described had happened to some other boy.

Objects in mirror are closer than they appear.

How had he forgotten so many big chunks of his life here? Hixville *had* been kind to him every once in a while, only, he'd outgrown it.

The weirdest part was that in every picture the winning smile that got him so much work as a model slowly developed as he'd practiced it: it was a lie from corner to corner, but it'd protected him from the worst.

The wall didn't show the shit kids called him, or him slowly shriveling on the pew in church, or sitting apart as a bullied benchwarmer, or his collection of middle school shiners or the years pining over the sexy rednecks who doled them out, or the endless scraps with his old man. Trying to live, wanting to die.

These photos were of some other life, his mother's idea of home and heaven, with the scuffs buffed off.

Only that practiced, perfect smile, little Patch's one magic trick. If nothing else, home had taught him to tell a lie with his face. *Life skill.* When he'd moved to New York, that smile had put food on the table till he stopped feeling hungry all the time. *Life's kill.*

Patch scooped up a flat stack of boxes and hefted them into the kitchen. Memories tangled his legs and made his grip shaky, but he had no time to lose. If he got this done soon he could haul a load of dishes and knickknacks to Goodwill before the end of the day. After he unfolded and taped a couple of cartons, he started on the cabinets: stacking pans and small appliances on the table before sorting them into containers.

Packing the third box of dishes, he caught the scent of greasy metal and raised his hand to his face to inhale. He couldn't be sure if the musty smell was real or a radioactive memory.

He wished he'd sucked the rest of the load off his fingers and regretted he'd snuck over to spy on Tucker in the first place. The sight and taste were burned into his brain.

"Unnph." Just like that, his stupid pecker popped a salute at the thought of Mr. Biggs. He scowled down at it, annoyed at his self-destructiveness. At twenty-two, he might be a grown-up and know better, but his informed consent didn't tame his animal impulses. *Embarrassing.* All the gross 2D porn that flipped his switch: cowboy coach daddy dick. Fantasy made flesh, flesh made foolish.

Make me, take me, break me.

He frowned. He knew better. Hell, he'd been *taught* better by the man himself for twelve-plus god-awful years.

Staring out at the barn, he flashed on a memory of Tucker driving him home after a rainy game sophomore year: Patch had been soaked through, and Tucker loaned him a stretched undershirt that reeked of pipe tobacco and clean sweat to wear.

Those were the moments when he'd forgotten that Tucker detested him, that the feeling was mutual. Not all bad.

Boned up and silent, Patch had sat skinny in the borrowed shirt next to Tucker thumping along to Reba McEntire on the frayed steering wheel. As they pulled up the drive, Tucker patted his leg, just missing his stiffy. Patch had almost fallen out of the car, mumbling thanks as he jogged through the rain. Tucker tooted a good-bye on the horn.

He'd forgotten until this second.

Trying to hold the memory of the muggy front seat and Tucker's husky rumble, his veiny hand squeezing Patch's jeans *once, twice*, Patch had dashed inside and jerked off as soon as he could get to the barn, spraying his chest twice and leaving both loads to dry on his torso the rest of the night.

What else had he lost track of while he'd been gone? By twenty-two, he'd gotten smarter, right? He had better things to do than waste loads on a lazy roughneck who could talk the pennies off a dead man's eyes.

Patch blinked. Older and wiser wasn't enough, apparently, not at three on a Thursday with Tucker across the field and willing to wait for him to give in.

Sniffing his fingers again, all he detected was Ivory soap, *99.44 percent pure*, even though he still felt 99.44 percent filthy. *Texas crude.*

Hixville was a poisoned trap. He needed to pack up and get back to his real life in New York, far far away from stuff he shouldn't and couldn't want.

He closed the fourth carton of dishes and stacked it against the wall with the boxes of appliances and flatware. He needed some oxygen and light. Maybe he'd rinse off and sit in the sun to dry.

The idea of taking a shower in water the temperature of blood made him shudder. Prissy maybe, but he'd earned a break. He stank and streaks of dust and worse gummed his sweaty skin, shirt, shorts.

He ducked out of the house, climbed the back fence, and cut east toward the clutch of trees that ran alongside part of the neighbors' property. The path, long overgrown, snaked through mulberry trees and pine to where a small creek led into a tight stand of trees his pa had left up as a windbreak. He pushed into the scrubby little stand using the thread of water to lead his feet.

Sure enough, he remembered the path fine. At one point the ground rose to a small clearing dotted with crude headstones over a hundred years old in a small stand of beech trees. That small graveyard had been Patch's thinking place as a kid. Even then, the ragweed and kudzu had choked off most points of access, surrounding it with a dusty green wall.

In there, the air was always cool, still, quiet. Nobody came out here but him.

Sixteen gravestones in pitted stone, the details worn flat. Nine still stood up in the bunched grass. A few of the markers were flat stones set right into the soil and hidden by weeds. But on his favorite, a statue of an angel perched, its wings curled like parentheses around the bent head and clasped hands. Probably for a long-ago kid, his pa had said.

Freshman year, after Tucker brought his trailer and discovered the swimming hole, Patch had come up here to sneak a beer and have a tug. At first he'd felt guilty, but he quickly rationalized that anyone buried out here must've been so bored that they'd appreciate the show. On the whole farm, this was *his* place.

But right now, sitting among the graves to cool off sounded morbid. Patch wanted to get wet and clean up, so instead of stopping, he followed the path down to a half-acre pond shaped like a crazy jug shaded by leaves at its handle.

Nobody would know, and he'd feel so much better for rinsing off properly and getting some air. Patch turned toward the rustling trees. Nothing. He twisted back to face the house and the highway a half mile away. Silence. The overgrown trees and a barbed wire fence kept the large livestock out. Nobody ever remembered this little puddle hidden in their back twenty.

A dull breeze carried the grape candy smell of the kudzu blossoms, which made him think of his ma putting up jelly when he was a kid: rows and rows of hot pink jars every summer.

The plop of a fish turned his head.

Before he could second-guess, Patch shucked out of his ancient sneakers, the grimy gym shorts, and gummy T-shirt. The sunlight baked his bare skin until he waded in and dunked himself before swimming for the other shore sixty feet away.

Tucker's side.

Originally, no one had lived on this eastward stretch of the property. His pa left the trees and kudzu because they provided a windbreak in hurricane season and hid the road. Patch had come swimming out here every day after chores.

This was his other retreat. Obviously Tucker thought the same now, because a muddle of boot prints and bare footprints showed plain around the north end of the pond under a bald cypress. The trailer sat up the rise only about two-hundred-fifty yards away.

Patch scrubbed his skin with his wet hands underwater. *Should have brought soap.* Didn't matter. The coolness was what he wanted, and a break from that house and all those damn pictures. Plus, his favorite place on the farm hid only a short hike into the trees.

Ten years ago, Tucker had still lived in Kountze and stuck to torturing Patch in front of the JV team. The bastard hadn't moved into the trailer till freshman year. And Patch had only come when he knew Tucker and his pa were off somewhere else.

On the big rock near the center, Patch stood again and scraped the water from his wavy hair. He had a memory of his pa balancing him on a horse as a boy. *Steady now.* The sun felt like heaven through his closed eyes. He turned and dove back in.

Even at its deepest, the water only came up to his chest and the carp at the bottom weren't something he'd ever eat. The bottom was broken rock at one end and cool mud at the other.

Patch had learned to jerk off against those flat rocks, snuck beers, and smoked the only two cigarettes of his life too. Sophomore year, he'd fooled around on the rockier shore with teammates because it was private and navigable in the dark. Against that tree, he'd kissed his first girl (*meh*) and blown his first boy (*yeah!*).

"Afternoon."

Patch stiffened and straightened, twisted to face the gravelly drawl with a cold twist in his gut.

Tucker stood on the opposite shore in Carhartt overalls and that straw work hat. His muscular arms looked tan and greasy against his white undershirt. "I guess we had the same idea." He glanced at the sky, the water. "It's hot as a whorehouse on nickel night." He shifted his weight but came no closer.

A flicker of Tucker naked in the armchair, glittering eyes gazing down at him, the taste of his semen pinning them both in place... Patch blinked it away, hyperconscious of his wet, bare skin and the distance between them. He went no closer to the pebbly shore.

They eyed each other. *One Mississippi, two Mississippi, three—*

"So.... Uhh." Tucker took his hat off with one hand and wiped his brow and mouth with the other. "We talking?"

Patch frowned, trapped by his nudity and the water.

"I mean, do we talk about what we done?" Tucker crouched at the water's edge, his boots sinking into the smooth mud. No one had a right to look that good. "Last night. Or are you fixin' to run off again?" He said *run* like a cuss word, painting Patch a coward for having some sense.

Patch started to snap back at him out of habit, but then he thought better of it. "Naw."

"How you today?" Tucker seemed to be actually asking a legitimate question. "Better?"

He shrugged. "I guess. Sure." Exposed and motionless, he let Tucker's gaze rest on him across the water. Whatever had passed between them last night had not vanished in sunlight.

Tucker looked relaxed, and cautious.

Patch swallowed, his shaft fattening underwater. "I shouldn't have done that."

He crossed his arms. "Which part?" Tucker squinted. "Come to visit? Squirted the side of my trailer? Eaten my load?"

"None. All." Knowing it was a mistake, certain he would regret it, he pushed through the cool water toward the one person he had no business wanting. He moved as he would've for a racy photo shoot, fucking the imaginary lens with his presence, demanding a reaction.

Tucker watched him warily from under the trees still, overalls hanging from one strap. "I guess we are." A crooked smile bent the edge of his mouth. "Talking."

The closer Patch got to the shore the more of his torso was revealed: nipples, navel, and gradually the darkened trail down to his pubes. His dick thickened and shifted in the water, swirling around his waist as he advanced. Now his body was clean but his thoughts were everything else.

Tucker stared as if hypnotized. He wiped his lower face, lip to chin, and swallowed. He was sweating now. Was that a boner in his overalls?

Patch strode in slow motion, stirring the calm pond water as if sleepwalking. He shouldn't want this so much but couldn't make himself care. Conscious of the picture he made, he crooked a sinful grin just for effect.

Eyes wider, Tucker stood and took a step back. "Well, okay, now. Okay."

"You afraid of me now?" Patch paused one step before his erection broke the surface. Tucker stood as if rooted to the shore. "Or you gonna come for a swim?"

"I'm good." Tucker swallowed and his tongue slipped out to taste his lips. He couldn't seem to look at Patch's face. "Fine. Y'know." His hands squeezed and released beside his pockets.

So Patch took the step that brought his knob out of the water and his boner dripped between them. Way too much fun watching the big cowboy squirm. He'd come out here looking for trouble; Patch was happy to give it to him.

On the shady shore, Tucker rocked back on his heels and shifted his straw hat to cover the lump under his coveralls.

Patch couldn't look anywhere else. Another step. The cool mud sucked at his toes in the water dripped from his skin with each step he shouldn't take.

How had he gotten here? Naked on the family farm, thigh-deep in stagnant water, walking toward a bear trap. New York City and all its fancy bullshit seemed like the other side of the world. Hot wind pushed through the trees overhead; the cattails hissed and the live oaks whispered above them.

Tucker stood waiting and wary now, a sexy, lazy no-account who'd only ever wanted to scare him straight. They both knew better, but now they stood a yard apart with disaster churning between them.

"Unff." The low grunt in Tucker's throat made him look up into those eyes. He must've come out here on purpose, right? "You're all clean."

Patch nodded, again mesmerized by desire. His cock was iron below, pointed where it shouldn't like a bad compass, but Tucker didn't look down, wouldn't look down. Patch stretched and skimmed water off his hip. "I forgot to bring a towel."

"Sun'll take care of you." Tucker wiped his brow and crossed his arms.

Another breeze heavy with the grape bubblegum haze of the kudzu. The pond stirred behind him. If Patch wanted anything to happen, he'd have to make the move. Another step. Now his boner really was within bumping distance. "Feels good to cool off. Stressed out, you know?"

And at that, Tucker matched his snaky grin and the gray eyes glittered. "I bet. Sometimes you just need a little relief. Where no one's gonna bug you."

Patch wobbled but ventured no closer. He glanced toward the road.

Tucker followed his line of sight and uncrossed his arms. "Don't you worry, pup."

Patch paused and looked down at the dirt.

"Nobody comes out this way."

With a cold fold in his heart, Patch knew Tucker had brought other folks out here to mess around before, maybe even when Patch's parents had still lived up the road. He didn't examine the thought too closely, but the image soured his cowboy coach daddy fantasy. He was only a notch on the post, a scalp collected. *Duh.* Tucker used everyone.

Then again, what'd he care? He'd never get stuck in this place again. He'd never have another opportunity to watch his high school crush abasing himself in the mud. He'd fuck Tucker over before Tucker could do the honors. Only fair.

Still, sucky.

What'd it matter anyway? Two consenting adults with time to kill. Maybe this way they wouldn't end up at each other's throat and he could unload the farm in time to build Velocity.

He reached for his briefs, ignoring Tucker long as he could.

"Naw." Tucker shook his head slowly

"What?"

The next words came out as a sexy threat. "Patch, you pull them shorts on again, and I can't be held responsible."

"Shorts?"

"Unless you want me to get down on my knees and eat the seat out." He reached around and cupped Patch's cheek, carefully, reverently, as if afraid he'd bolt.

Like I'm an unbroke horse.

Patch held his breath, and his entire consciousness tightened to that contact, the perfect socketed fit of the four thick fingers across his damp haunch and the blunt thumb teasing the top of his crack, just so.

Wind rustled in the leaves again and wrinkled the water.

"Anything worth doing is worth doing well." Tucker glanced back up. "Sex's s'posed to take time. Feels good longer. Huh? You don't gotta thrash around breakneck."

Patch blinked, aware of the thudding in his ears, the close air between them. "You mean jacking."

"Hell, I jerk off two, three hours in a night when I can. Tease it out, make it last. Then when I blow…. Whew." Grin in slow motion. "And I always been one to take my time."

"No shit." He looked down.

"Buddies is buddies. Giving a hand. Tight as sliced bread." Tucker's tone was offhand, but with one hand he kneaded the lump at his lap.

Patch swayed closer, unsure.

Tucker rubbed the back of his neck. "Now me? I love edging. Milking the bull. Getting right up to the point of no return over and over till you goon out."

Patch peered down at his knob knocking at Tucker's bulge through the overalls. "That's what you were doing." *When I spied on you,* he meant.

"You ever done that before? Edged yourself?" Tucker tipped his head and squinted. "Let someone milk you. You oughhta."

He nodded, mute. His meat hitched. "Ye-no. Well, not like— No."

Tucker lowered his voice and leaned closer. "Then yeah. You need help."

Patch swallowed and stood his ground.

Tucker studied his face. "I don't mean to yourself. I mean with a buddy. Teasing it long as you can." And just like that, his massive, rough hand took hold of Patch's straining shaft. Not stroking, just learning the length and weight of it.

"No." He swallowed. "I don't think—I don't have any buddies that way."

Tucker closer. "Well, pup...." For a moment he looked ready to kiss Patch, swaying a bit, but instead he just hung there breathing deeply, the warm, sweet air hovering between them. "Now you do."

Patch nodded, paralyzed. This wasn't coach and cocksucker, cowboy and faggot, daddy and dumbass. Tucker was flirting with him like a *man*, like something needed to happen between them while they had the chance.

Tucker turned him to face the water, pressing his own hardness through the canvas against Patch's damp backside.

Patch sagged against the overalls. If they'd been face-to-face, they'd still be in kissing distance, but thank God, they weren't. The wide hand milked him expertly, patiently. He whimpered.

"I gotcha." Tucker sounded smug as hell, but when Patch reached back for the bulge in his pants, he made a disapproving noise. "Not just yet. I gotcha."

"I gotta.... I can't...." His legs trembled and he let his breath escape.

"You're fine. You're good." Then Tucker bent and bit his buttcheek.

"Hey!" Patch turned. "Tucker."

Big grin, and Tucker squinted up at him. "I ain't worried about mud. I gotcha. Let me help out."

Patch choked and nodded permission his cock had already given. *Well, since you asked so nicely.* The coarse fingers milked his full length in an unvarying stroke and squeeze, stroke and squeeze. His mouth fell open and his hands twitched, powerless.

The pond shone, throwing the sky back up at itself. The live oaks shifted overhead, but no sunlight found them now under the hissing branches.

Tucker's hungry eyes glittered but never made it above his waist. Lust, loneliness, and nothing more. His big fist worked, pitiless and powerful, around Patch's shaft.

The hard hand knew its business. Perfect pressure, strong and smooth, as Tucker tugged at him with all the patience in the world.

There was something too about Tucker servicing him without stripping, the careworn cowboy kneeling in the mud to pleasure him leisurely. Tucker reached behind Patch's knee and pulled, trying to bring him down into the mud at the pond's edge. "You come on down here." The stroking hand teased and tugged in an easy rhythm.

"Fucking hell." Patch's jaw trembled. This shouldn't feel this good, being manhandled and milked by someone twice his age who hated his guts. The pleasure paralyzed him.

Why didn't the boys in New York have grips like this? Why didn't they smell like tractor parts and fresh sawdust? How did Tucker know exactly how fast, how far, how firm a stroke would pull the pleasure out of him?

"C'mon down here with me." From his knees, Tucker beckoned with his eyes. "Lemme help ya some."

Patch did just that, kneeling in the soft mud. He leaned and Tucker leaned, and then they were pressed together at a snug angle on their knees. With a groan, Patch pushed his rod through Tucker's gentle fingers deliberately.

"Yeah? Is that it? Somebody oughtta be takin' care of you regular." Tucker's stubbled mouth brushed his ear, and his mutter was low and urgent. "You need to get milked like clockwork by someone who knows how."

Tucker definitely knew how, shucking the skin lazily, which made his horniness feel all the more urgent.

Tucker's other hand came out to Patch's face and the thick thumb pushed between his lips. Without thinking, Patch sucked it a moment before it slipped free and joined the other hand making him crazy. The wet pad of Tucker's thumb slid over his cockknob and made him shiver and yelp.

"Easy…. We got time. Huh?" With that other hand, Tucker cupped his balls and felt their weight. He pushed his fingertips behind to rub the ridge of his taint. "Lemme do it."

Patch swallowed. *Bad. This is bad.* Everything would change, had changed. He should stop all this before Tucker started making him happy.

But Tucker had other ideas. He rocked back to sit square in the soft wet soil, pulling Patch against his chest without ever releasing his meat.

At first Patch was sitting in his lap, on top of the firm mound of Tucker's trapped excitement. Tucker pushed him forward, forcing Patch to sit in the mud.

"Ugh."

"Mud won't hurt you none." Tucker crossed his arms. "Ain't even cows come here to mess things."

Patch's shoulders settled. It did feel good, in a gross way, the cool, wet press of it against his suntan.

On either side of him Tucker's legs, Tucker's arms folded against him and his face against Patch's temple. The pitiless hand went back to work on Patch's erection.

"You don't even know. Nobody ever showed you."

Patch stared down at the swollen, slick flesh in Tucker's grip, a smear of precum on the crown. Each tug teased more sap out of him.

"You a leaker?" Tucker squeezed his joint tight for a moment.

"No. Not really." He'd never dripped like this before, maybe because he'd never given himself a chance to get so worked up. "Please, Tucker."

"Please what? There something you need?" A low chuckle. "We got all the time. I'm just getting started with you." The relentless stroke stayed steady, strong, stubborn.

Patch growled in frustration. He lifted his right hand to move things along and got swatted for his efforts.

"Aww. You're fine. You stay outta my way, now. Lemme do my job." He pressed Patch's hand into the wet shore and hooked his chin over Patch's shoulder. "I'm the caretaker, ain't I? Let me take care of you."

Patch grunted in electric irritation. The cool mud sucked at his wrists and his fingers clawed deeper, but he relented and let Tucker wring the bliss out of his body.

Tucker's fist made a scalding, slippery sleeve for Patch to drill through.

Patch did exactly that. "Oh. Ohh yeah, Tuck-*ker*. Fuck."

"Nice. Aww. So good now." His fingers tapped Patch's nuts. "Loaded. I can feel you bunching up down there." Tucker took hold of the top of the pole, both thumbs rubbing the cap roughly and rhythmically.

Patch shook and hissed, squirming to get free. "Ahh! Ugh-acchhh! Too much. Jesus! Ohhh man!" That last shout lifted birds from the live oaks.

Tucker let go completely, let the rigid flesh stab the air, held him and stroked his torso, ribs, and nipples. "Shhh. Okay now. Let it back down some."

Patch panted, muscles locked defensively. Little by little, his cock stilled and the jittery panic drained out of him. He slowed his breathing, taking deep draughts of the kudzu breeze until his heart slowed.

"Better?"

"Mmh." Patch exhaled through his nose. Bit by bit, his tension gave way and he sagged against Tucker's rough overalls, yet somehow the need to pop had expanded beyond his crotch. His charged skin and his jerking muscles simply stretched to contain the pressure and pleasure. The pond lapped against his muddy ankles. "Goddamn."

"See, most folks make a mistake about getting off. Rush round, get 'er done." Tucker's hand closed on his shaft again. "That's all wrong. If it feels good, why do you wannit over?" Slow and sure, he slid his fist up the full slick length of Patch's throbber. "What's your damn hurry?"

Patch concentrated on the feathery brush of the bristle at his ear. The heavy arms holding him close. The patient fingers teasing sap out of Patch's meat. The iron and sawdust stink of him. "I guess."

"I know. You saw last night, didn't ya?" Another stroke and another. "And the night before that, I expect."

A chill stiffened the hairs on Patch's neck. Tucker had known the whole time. *Fuck.* Icy shame pierced him.

"I seen you spying on me, pup. I don't mind none." The stroke steadied now into a long up-squeeze down-squeeze that felt like a reward. "I don't mind a show." Tucker had messed with him, knowing full well.

"I had to see for once." Patch's sac tightened again, and the veins on his cock stood firm as the urge rose again.

"More'n once. Fair 'nuff." Like he knew, Tucker sped up a little. "Yeah? Look at that good stuff. Good boy."

Patch whimpered, driving his hips up and fucking the fist in earnest. *Almost.... Almost....* He tried to control his breathing so Tucker wouldn't know, so he could make it over the edge and—

Tucker let go. "I ain't that stupid."

"Prick." Patch snarled in impatience. The rushing in his ears made him light-headed. His skin was slick with sweat. His poor, punished dick tingled and bobbed in his lap, only slackening when a few seconds had passed, its corona oozing nectar.

Tucker chuckled. "You got no idea." He held Patch's hands in the mud again, as if his fingers were slimy manacles. "You ever give me a chance, I'll be happy to show you." A strong arm wrapped across his chest like a saddle strap. "I'll show you till you can't see straight."

Fuming and flying, Patch relaxed by degrees. What was Tucker doing to him? How long had they been out here? Why didn't he want to leave?

Perspiration slid down Patch's chest and belly. His heart hammered triple time and his muscles locked and loosed in woozy impatience. "C'mon, Tucker." Tucker liked to edge for hours. Impatience was a foreign concept to him because he never had a reason to hurry. For Tucker, blue balls were the *goal*. "Please let me."

"Not yet. Let me take care of you right. Settle down. Relax back." Tucker scooted closer, squeezing Patch tight against his torso, the overalls buckles pressing into his back, the thick arms making his ribs creak. "Mmmh. That's the way. Gimme all of it." The fat thumb again swiped the crown of his cock.

Patch twitched. The steady ooze from his skin, from his scalp, from his knob, made him crazy. Any second he'd lose it. The only thing holding him together was Tucker. Powerless, he dropped his wet head back against Tucker, the notch of his throat and meaty shoulder. "*Muh-haughhh.*" He squirmed, rocking against the muscle behind him and the mud beneath.

Tucker inhaled at his ear, sliding the skin forward, shucking it back, an unvarying stroke steady as a heartbeat. "Got somethin' good for me?"

"Ah-ahh-uhh." Patch gasped. He'd been holding his breath like a diver, taking swift gulps and then bearing down against the crushing pressure of his pleasure.

"Yeah? That so?"

Every mouthful of air tasted like Tucker. He shuddered. "You're gonna— That's.... Make me—"

"Hold your horses, son. Hang on now." Tucker's fist slowed, slowed, slowed but didn't let go. It settled into a faint casual stroke that gave no relief.

Patch's erection held rock solid for a moment as he fought toward squirting and back from the point of no return at the same time. His sanity did a somersault. "Fuck."

"Take a breath, boy. 'At's it. Shhh. I didn't say you could yet, now did I? You hold that seed for me a while longer now. Make it last." Tucker sounded like he was smiling.

Patch could feel his heartbeat there, held in Tucker's big hand. The firm ridge of his knob stood out, glossy and deep rose. One fat branching vein he'd never noticed before ran firmly up the side, swollen thick for the first time. Tucker was teaching him what was possible.

"Got it now?"

Patch nodded. "I think." Not rushing meant he had to be in his skin, right there while it was happening. He couldn't think or be or go anywhere that Tucker wasn't. The mud sucked at his hands up to the wrist, immobilizing him sure as cuffs. "Yes, sir."

The blunt fingers plucked at the top of Patch's crown over and over. The sensation was so intense that Patch didn't bother to fight it, just rode the twitching insanity. It wouldn't make him cum, but it felt like heaven. He groaned and sagged in submission, giving Tucker his full loose weight, everything boneless except the greasy spike in Tucker's grip.

"Nice. Nice job. That makes me so happy, seeing you like that. Feeling you fight it. Making it last." He gripped the length again and milked it slowly. "Milking a bull right."

Far away, a dog barked. Patch glanced out across the still pond, the hot grass, the blinding sky. *Too much.* The same hypnotizing paralysis he'd felt last night stole over his limbs. He closed his eyes again and dropped his head to the side, turning his face toward Tucker's heart, unable to take it all in.

—*too strong too slow too perfect*—

"Yeah. Good boy. Let loose." His rough hand began to twist at the end of the stroke. A small shift in the rhythm that made Patch brace his legs and press his heels into the mud.

"More. *Al*-most. Please." Patch's hips rocked involuntarily, tipping up to drive his impatient cock into Tucker's punishing grip more directly.

Tucker chuckled in his hair. "Is that so?" But he didn't stop, and his stiff hog ground at Patch's back. "You fixin' to bust?"

Patch whimpered and shook his head, but his load wouldn't wait. Letting this happen was so wrong, and he knew it. He fought the inevitable with everything he had. "Ungh. Uh-hungh. More. *Nuhh.*"

"You got a big load stored up for me? You carrying a lotta squirt in them balls?" His voice rumbled behind Patch's ribs. "I want every fuckin' drop."

The steady dribble of precum had started to smack and slip under Tucker's fingers, letting the skin slither and his swollen knob jam under Tucker's knuckles whenever he swept up to polish it.

Patch moaned and shook uncontrollably. "I'm gonna go now. Tuck! You're gonna make me—Uhh, *augh*! You're gonna make me—" The rising pressure expanded inside him, under him... an inexorable tidal swell he could only ride without reins.

"See? That's the way."

Tucker was right. Patch had never felt anything like this lazy blazing stillness for... not in all his years of messing around. This was the way, this right here, only he'd never been patient enough to find it with anyone.

Patch's legs shook. His heavy balls tightened, tightened again. He wanted to twist and crush their lips together so he could shout into that mouth.

Tucker grunted in his ear and licked the back of his neck. "Uh-*huh.* All of it. Every drop now."

"Wha—? Whoa!" Patch's heels drove down into the clean mud. His hands clamped down on Tucker's knees cradling him. "Guh-*odd.*" Patch's hips stuttered and squeezed.

"Take your time. That's it, man."

And as Tucker's fingers slowly stroked the underside of Patch's erection, the bubble of lightning at Patch's core expanded until it fried his resistance and blew his head wide open. "I'm ab—that's gonna—Tucker!" He convulsed and roared and thundering sunlight poured out of him over Tucker's knuckles.

"Yeah. Yeah. Everything, Patch." The raspy drawl against his neck made Patch shiver. "Every damn drop for me."

No strain. No effort. No hurry. As soon as he crossed the crest his boneless weight gave way, and Tucker took it happily while the thick jism streamed out of Patch in hazy, crazy ribbons.

"Oh, yeahhh...." His hands stroked Patch's arms and chest roughly, smearing him with semen and sweat. Tucker inhaled at his nape, just shy of kissing it, and squeezed his ribs tightly. "I ain't satisfied till I find the quiver in a body."

"Fu-*huck*." Patch's head rolled on his neck and his arms flopped, useless. "I can't move." A low laugh.

"You don't have to."

"That was—"

"Mmmph. Me too." Tucker held him firmly and kept petting his limbs in long steady strokes, as if calming a wild colt. "I knew. I figgered on that."

Patch shivered juddery aftershocks. The brightness almost hurt his eyes so he kept them closed and focused on the sweltering breeze.

With one hand Tucker gripped his slackening balls and with the other he milked Patch's bone hard, almost painfully, forcing a final fat dollop of cream from him.

Patch struggled against the hand and the muscle wrapped around him. "Aaggh! Hfft. Hey."

"You gone fight me?" Tucker sounded evil and hopeful and pleased as pie. "You sure?" He scrubbed his hot, jammy palm over Patch's raw cockhead and sent an electric spasm along his limbs.

Twitching and laughing, Patch pretended to fight back in the squelching mud, but he wasn't going anywhere and wouldn't have if he could. "Naw."

Tucker growled. "You'd best let me do my job."

Patch stilled and settled again. The spew on his skin had begun to cool. "Job?"

"I'm your caretaker. Ranch hand." Tucker milked his softening dick again, and this time Patch didn't struggle. "You need to let me handle what needs to be." Tucker shifted and stood.

"Yes, sir." Even sitting in the mud at Tucker's feet, he meant it. Exhaustion and expectation warred inside his chest. "I think I will." He felt selfish and stupid, biddable and beddable, but he didn't regret anything. He twisted toward Tucker. "Do you want—?" He faced the lump in Tucker's lap and rose to his knees.

Tucker chuckled. "Hope's a fine thing." He cupped his crotch and a soaked spot spreading across his left thigh. "That ship sailed, pup."

"You sure?" Patch squinted.

Tucker squenched one side of his face in disbelief. "I dumped my sauce 'fore you did. Alla you pressed up against me, coming apart. I was a goner."

Something splashed in the pond. A curious catfish, maybe. The dappled shadow of the trees had shifted to cover them and half the water.

"Nobody ever took their time like that. With me, I mean. Edging. Fucking hell." Patch wheezed and frowned at himself or all those other assholes who hadn't known what they were doing. His bone had finally softened and his balls dropped back into their sac. "Like a five-course meal."

"Fuckin' stupid, they were. Milking a bull takes a while. No point in racing past a good time."

"I guess." Patch did feel stupid, but he liked Tucker calling him a bull rather than a boy.

"You need milking steady. 'S why you get so anxious and pissy. All that sap backed up, and no one to tap it. Hell, you need that regular."

Patch nodded, hungry and dumb with desire. He'd agree to anything.

Tucker reached down and hauled Patch to his feet with one sticky mitt. Before Patch could feel weird about standing naked next to a fully-dressed farmhand, Tucker raised a foot and tugged his boots off. He straightened to pop the one closed clip at his shoulder and peeled out of his overalls and undershirt, revealing saggy boxers, the left leg translucent with jizz over his dark pubic hair. "That's my favorite way to blow."

Patch looked up at that and pushed the damp hair off his face.

"No hands, while I crack someone's nut." He peeled off his socks, then boxers, and stretched, a stocky, cocky motherfucker thirty pounds over the limit.

Jesus, he's strong.

Tucker let him browse. All country and no shit: scars and farmer tan over forty years of work muscle. A spray of dark fuzz on his lower chest tightened into a narrow trail pointing toward his thick dick and low balls. The fine hairs on his left thigh were lumped and matted with fresh semen. He smelled delicious. "What?"

Patch shook his head. Too much and nothing to say. He had Tucker's scent on him again, and he didn't want to wash.

Tucker jerked his cleft chin toward the pond. "Rinse?"

"Sure." *Shore.* Patch could hear the accent creep back into his own voice echoing Tucker's, but for once he didn't mind. He grew a big grin as he shoved Tucker and jogged into the water before Tucker laughed and tackled him.

"Sneaky li'l sumbuck. I'll whup you. You 'bout broke my ass." He wrapped Patch in his arms and then fell sideways, pulling them both under the lukewarm water, spluttering and laughing. Not so much with the whupping, actually. He didn't even mind getting clean like this.

Patch closed his eyes underwater and focused on the slick squeeze of Tucker's muscle wrapped around him and the sizzle of their cocks knocking together. Was this even possible? Shouldn't he be running in the other direction? Didn't he know what a mistake felt like?

Still....

Patch would be gone in a little under a week, the farm sold and Tucker planted in some other dead-end setup. Why shouldn't they make the most? Two grown men, too many years of fantasies and fuckups to worry about wasting time that needed killing.

Tucker stood up in the water and bent over him, holding his floating body loosely, their mouths only inches apart. A breath, another, as Patch listened to his heartbeat in his ears.

Tucker let him go abruptly, pushing free. *He doesn't kiss, then.*

Patch twisted to set his feet on the pond's bottom and stood, skimming his hair out of his face and the water out of his eyes. He blinked at the brightness.

Tucker's stillness created a gravitational pull that kept Patch anchored to his lust and laziness. The still air and whirr of insects restored the pressure behind his eyes. He scraped dry as he returned to shore. *Sure.*

A whistle.

Sure enough, Tucker stood on the shaded edge of the pond, scrubbing the droplets from his darkened hair as he eyed Patch openly from under the live oak. "Fuck, pup." He wiped his mouth and shook his head. "Butt like that, folks get ideas. Men, women, both."

Patch crossed his arms.

Tucker looked around at the empty field beyond the pond. They *were* alone out here. "Why you so shy?"

Patch had turned around. "I'm not shy. It's— You surprised me."

"Scoping your tail? You oughtta get out more."

"I guess."

Actually, Patch didn't like his butt. He felt like it was too high and too small. He'd always wanted big haunches, like a wrestler, or square jogger glutes, but his lanky frame made that impossible.

"I fuckin' *love* to eat ass." Tucker made it sound like a casual hobby: macramé or fly-fishing. "*Ungh.* For hours if you'll let me. Push my face up in there and make you scream. I like eating pussy too, but I'm a butt man, no two ways. *Mmph.*" He shook his head. "That's what I want every fucking day. You sit yourself down and let me lick you till you pop." He stuck out his tongue for a sec like a panting dog and then grinned, winked.

"I never had anybody do that." Patch touched his glute experimentally, as if Tucker's appraisal had changed it.

"Then you been fucking idjits all these years. I swear." Tucker's mouth quirked and he squatted. "Y'all get in a fucking hurry. That's what porno does. Everybody trying to get a nut. Like it's a race."

Tucker's face was right at his erection, his breath brushing the balls, but he stared at Patch as he slid the other hand around, squeezing his ass gently, testing it like a nectarine.

Tucker sighed. "Breakfast, lunch, supper right there."

"I guess." He struggled to stand still, exposed and expectant.

Without explanation, Tucker pushed between his legs, crawling right through so Patch's balls dragged over his hair a moment before twisting so his hot breath brushed Patch's backside.

Kneeling behind him now, Tucker ran his two thumbs over the bunched muscle and spread the cheeks. For one endless moment, his tongue pressed right at the hole, not inside but nuzzling and testing the little iris. His sandpaper cheek tickled.

Patch shivered, but didn't fight him, just gave in to the fizzy pleasure of all that delicious attention.

Finally, Tucker rocked back again on his heels to sit on the pebbled shore. "Jesus, that's something. *Yuh'mmmph.*" He licked his lips and spread his legs comfortably.

Patch bent and picked up his briefs.

"I swear. You in them skivvies." He rubbed his flat belly and his fat cock bobbed in answer. "You sat on my face three hours a day, I'd die happy."

Inhale. Milking the moment, Patch let all of it drizzle over him: the sun, the water, the fierce rake of Tucker's regard. *Exhale.* Rather than break the spell, he focused on his scalding skin and the drip-plip of the water falling back to the pond's surface while Tucker took him apart with those stern eyes.

"You sure are something, Patch." *Shore*. Tucker studied him from a couple of yards away. "Way you look. You are a *caution*."

Patch knew the glow of vanity, the secret tendril of power over another that made grooming and training himself worth it. Never in his life had he expected Tucker Biggs to fall victim to it, to come under his sway even for an afternoon. *Beggars, choosers*.

"*Fheww*." Tucker exhaled and whistled at the cloudless blue. The water's agitated surface lapped at his calves. "That's enough of that already."

Of what? Patch hesitated, wanting Tucker to stare at him that way again, nervous about leaving. On the other hand, watching Tucker's meaty rump stride through the water toward his muddy overalls, the flex of his back, the heft of his thick arms, took away any sting of regret. "Same."

"*Pfft*." Tucker screwed up his face and raised his brows. "I ain't no male model."

Patch eyed him openly. "Says you. You ever came to New York, they'd eat you up and suck the bones."

"I guess it's lucky I ain't never been." Tucker turned away and reached for his Carhartts. Apparently playtime was over. *Well, hell.*

Irked and addled, Patch went to fetch the rest of his clothes about ten feet away, not looking in that direction, because one sleaze-out a day was plenty. He could hear Tucker's footsteps behind him.

"I gotta get back to packing."

"A damn shame, that is." Tucker sounded amused over his shoulder. "You fixing to flip out again?"

He didn't turn. "No, sir." He sat on the smooth pebbles to tug on his socks.

"I bet you are. Jittery as a colt." Tucker squatted behind him and wrapped an arm around his chest, not an embrace, but a joke. "Heart like a hammer."

"I'm fine."

"I know." Tucker's coarse chin scraped the back of his damp neck, and his skin puckered with gooseflesh. "You *feel* fine."

"Jesus cats!" Patch choked. Still seated, he yanked his shorts on, not wanting to be naked or near because he couldn't trust his body's reactions at all.

Tucker rolled him forward onto all fours and dropped his weight along Patch's back, his bulge pressed at the seam of his ass, those rough hands on his ribs. Stubble scraped at his cheek and ear and then a hoarse whisper. "Smell like salt still. Cum."

"*Huh*-ungh." Patch groaned under the weight of all that strength holding him down in the pebbles and grass. *Playtime not over?*

"Don't squeal till you get stuck, pup." Tucker's hips stilled and his voice too. "I don't wanna hurt you none. No fucking. I don't wanna put nothing in you but my tongue, not even if you beg nice." Tucker squirmed against his back. "But I'll get all that cream out where it'd do us both some good."

"Mmh."

"Know what?" Tucker hunched against his backside. "You *feel* like you still need milking. It might take a while." His zipper dug into the trench hard enough to sting. "That make you nervous?"

Patch's heart stuttered. The anxious sissy in him still worried about getting roped and groped by a redneck. The stupid, stubborn side trusted Tucker to keep him safe. "Little." He shut his eyes.

"It should. But that's all. Just enough to keep you awake." Tucker's meat felt like a trailer hitch back there.

Patch shook his head. "*Huh-umm.*" Breathing under two hundred twenty pounds of cowboy muscle was tough, and he filled his lungs with effort. His bent cock hurt now, but no matter how much he raised his hips, he couldn't give it enough space to flip forward.

Big hands at his hips and that rough cheek brushing his ear. "You gonna fight me, pup? Good deal. I like fighting fine."

"No, sir." Gradually the wind and the light came back to him, and the sound of the weeds cricking in the heat distracted Patch now.

Tucker chuckled and inhaled. "Yes, you are. You're up in your skull. Trying to go somewhere else. You watch. I know you pretty good by now."

Patch gasped. "Agh. Ow. My dick." His erection hurt for real now, at the weird angle. He twisted and lifted his pelvis.

"Aw, yeah. Yeah." Tucker's hands snaked around his ribs and squeezed the breath out of him. "Maybe I'll just tie you down till I'm done with you." He hunched Patch's hindquarters like a locked dog. "Rope you so's you cain't run off nowhere."

Patch didn't think he could stand, let alone run. "I don't like the sound of that."

"You gone make me? So I can make you and make you."

Patch swallowed before he got the words out. "Yessir. If you want." He opened his dry lips, his face crushed into the cool pebbles.

"Truss you up so I can get in there and milk you right. Lick you out and pull you off." He humped Patch's crack again. "Take our sweet Texas time." He breathed hot on Patch's neck, mouth hovering just above his skin. *So close.* "Whaddaya reckon?"

"Dunno." But he had a pretty solid idea and a stiff in his shorts.

Tucker grunted and hunched again. "I do. I know plenty." His thick bone notched against the crack of Patch's ass through thin cotton. "And I'm gonna teach you if you let me."

Patch closed his eyes but nodded. *Please.*

"Well. So." Tucker's weight vanished.

Patch rolled over to his knee. "What?"

"Nothing." Tucker considered him for a moment. The grin stayed put as he ambled toward his boots on the stone ledge. "Not a damn thing."

Hold your horses. But before Patch could reply or shrug back into his shirt, Tucker tapped his hat brim and left him watching across the water as his cowboy walked back home.

CHAPTER FIVE

HOW PATCH made it back, he never remembered after.

Limbs loose and head muzzy, he must've stumbled across the fresh-disced fields in a stupor. By the time he opened his parents' door, the clock said six. He figured it was p.m. because the sun was still up, but he couldn't have said for certain. Apparently he'd been out letting Tucker work him over for more than two hours. It could've been five minutes or five years.

When was a mistake not a mistake?

Now he was back inside his parents' house and the claustrophobia was real. Without the furniture, the house actually seemed smaller somehow, as if his family had stretched the walls by living in it.

Tucker's confidence at the pond had woken him up, scared the crap out of him, showed him something irrevocable and ferocious that had no place in his future.

He spent the evening clearing out the shelves in the garage, ate chili out of a can, and put himself to bed around ten on the musty blue carpet, wrapping himself in a comforter like an exhaustion burrito.

He didn't regret what they'd done, but it scared the tar out of him.

Whatever niggling doubt remained only confirmed that he'd made the right decision. The farm would go fast. In a couple weeks he'd sign the contracts and Velocity would happen. Tucker would go back to being a guilty hankering in the wee hours. *The role not taken.*

The sun woke him in the morning. Too queasy to eat, he grabbed a big bottle of water and tugged down the folded ceiling ladder next to the laundry room. The house's attic was more of a crawlspace, about five feet high. Because of the constant flooding, East Texas storage was usually overhead, and after the sun hammering down all summer, it still felt stuffy and sweltering at 7:00 a.m.

His folks had squirreled away decades of junk and jetsam: plastic tubs of Christmas decorations dragged out each November, a dusty bassinet and highchair his ma had loaned out to young couples, neat boxes of hand-me-down clothes passed along from church, a pair of oars he'd never seen used, a shelf of his sneakers going back from size eleven to baby. And shelves of toys his pa picked up at auction all year long for donation. Boxes of dolls and bears and board games. The cramped space looked like a fallout shelter for an orphanage.

With no room to work, he opted to pull the toys down and deal with them for the next couple of hours. Emptying the attic took maneuvering, but as the toys made their way downstairs, things went quicker. Creating logical piles, he began sorting everything into labeled stacks of boxes: *games, stuffed, doll, sport, crafts, figures*. Handling all these imaginary friends and projects gave him a lost, creepy feeling. Still, they were only unwanted by their original owners; plenty of local services needed stuff for kids.

His mama had been adopted, so every summer his folks took presents up to Boys and Girls Country, a foster community outside Houston. Every Easter they'd hauled a load of toys up to the pediatric ward in Lumberton, along with little animals his ma crocheted all year.

His pa told him, over and over, "Never forget you're blessed."

Had he? Memory's a fine thing, but most people remembered what they wished was true. He knew how lucky he'd been, compared to some kids. Even at the end, he'd been strong and smart enough to get while the going was good. Hadn't that been a cruel blessing in itself?

Patch left the boxes unfinished and went out to the barn. Tucker had loaded bales for delivery, the trailer hitched to the truck and the keys inside.

Rather than sit and dwell on impossible bullshit, Patch decided to run the load into Hixville proper for the Feed & Seed. If nothing else, it was money and afterward he could duck inside to buy a Big Red and grill Janet for any facts she had about Tucker Biggs.

Way things stood, he wanted to do right, at least. Eviction was no joke, and Tucker deserved better.

He pulled up and stacked the bales on the pallets inside the largest of her sheds. Unloading the trailer was sweaty, thankless work that made him feel fifteen. Soon as he finished, Janet ambled out with an apron over her bosom and, because she never forgot, threw him a can of Big Red.

He caught it. "Hey!"

"Sure is." She nodded at the bales and picked up a small bag of ant poison, cradling it like a baby. "It's hotter'n hell with the blowers on."

"How'd you know?" He chugged the soda so fast his brain hurt.

"Thirsty."

"Fuck's sake, kiddo. You look like a used condom." She held the door so he could step through into the A/C. "We got plenty soda, y'know."

"Sold!" Patch rolled his eyes at her as he passed. He hit the fridge for a second soda so fast they both made it to the counter at the same time. He dug out his wallet to pay.

"Oh my God, you got laid." Her face lit up with gossipy glee.

"Bullshit."

"Kiddo, I been married twenty-six years." She hefted the poison onto the counter and wiped her hands on the apron. "You think I don't know what blue balls look like? Seriously?"

Patch pressed the cold can to his face. "Sure. Yeah. I let the sheriff blow me. Out front." He huffed sarcasm and nodded at the windows. "Standing in the birdbath."

"Good for you. Long arm of the law." She nodded in approval, her mouth a smug arch of approval. "No, who was it?"

"Nobody." He leaned on the counter and exhaled. "I didn't."

"Fine. Lie if you like. Boys are so screwy." She perused his neck, his arms, his zipper, even. "I know! It's that organist over at Piney Baptist. Twenty-five, cute as a button, hung like a *bear*. Right? I thought I detected a hint of mint in the hymns."

"What? No!"

"Gimme a minute, okay now, I'm getting something." She waggled her hands over him like a soothsayer. "Got it, I got it: you poked the new barbecue chef up at Honey Island. *Oof.* Zowie-*wowie*. Everyone's tried to nail that slab. Big sad eyes and an ass like a warm muffin. C'mon, you can tell me. 'S better with butter, huh?"

"Janet, I did not fuck a piney organ or barbecue anything." She'd given him a reason to blush, so now it didn't matter. "With or without butter." He laughed without meaning to.

"Have pity on him. Margarine, at least. It's on sale?" She flashed a wide, wicked grin and pointed at the fridge wall in back.

"No." At least he knew he had no hickeys. Whatever the fuck had happened with Tucker had left no marks visible. *Yet.* "I do not wanna fuck around in my hometown, Janet." Of course, he hadn't said he hadn't or wasn't *going* to fuck around. "This whole town is like boner-bane. Ugh. Are you crazy?"

She arched an eyebrow and leveled a skeptical stare at him.

"Withdraw that. Jesus. We're both crazy."

"I know what I know." She rang up the sodas on her old punch register. "And I suppose that means you're done packing? If you've got plenty of time to pillage the locals."

"Not even." He popped the second Big Red and shrugged. "Halfway? A third? No idea."

"Oh. Good! I could call my cousin Rhonda to come help if you want."

"Listen. Seriously. Janet? I was thinking about something you said the day I came. Gift horses and all."

Janet didn't bite. "She's fast as a rattler and she won't steal anything important. I mean, unless you care about Beanie Babies and that Hallmark figurine shit. Your ma's Hummels would prob'ly vanish. That's truth."

"Listen, Janet." He rapped on the counter. "I am gonna sell the place. Farm."

Janet stilled, frowned, exhaled. "Oh. Yeah? Oh." Sad smile.

"I got to. The hell would I do with a place down here? The money's good."

"Sure." She didn't or wouldn't look at him. "You got an offer, then."

"No, but soon."

"All sorted?"

"Except Tucker. He's gonna have to vacate the property." He tried to sound casual. "So I was hoping he had people left. Around? Y'know." Surely she knew something.

"Nobody who'd pay his bail."

He frowned. "Shit." He needed to tread lightly lest he set off her small-town Geiger counter. "Not even family?"

"Naw." She rocked back and eyed the ceiling. "The Biggses? Least I didn't think so."

Patch frowned. *Well, damn.* So much for easy solutions.

Janet rubbed the counter with a rag. "I think they all died or went to prison. His dad did, and uncle, both. I think. Or maybe just died *in* prison? Whole town singing 'For he's a jolly good felon.' And his mom took off for Alaska long time ago. With some junkie. Before you was born. Long time gone."

"Mmh?" He took a sweet sip of soda to cover his curiosity.

She didn't bite anyway.

"Look, I've got a question—"

"Tucker's not...." Janet crossed her arms and leaned forward with a conspiratorial gleam. "He's not had such a good run the last ten years. Lotta screwing around, dim friends, loaning tools to crooks. Works summers at Texaco, whenever they're short. Lost the job at the school 'cause he knobbed the principal's little wife. None of his women stick around. Plus he's got all them kids all over, but none of 'em officially his, you know. On paper."

"I guess. So he doesn't have a regular girlfriend he stays with."

"Well, he used to see that real estate lady in Lufkin, but her husband bought her a Caddy and she told Tucker to clear out. Good thing too. That woman couldn't arrange a two-car funeral." She rolled her eyes in exaggerated contempt.

"Uh-huh." Again, not a topic Patch wanted to visit just now.

"Tucker Biggs ain't so bad as he seems, kiddo. Or if he is, he might ought to be worse. With what he come from? He's a fucking saint."

He needed to be careful how interested he got. "Then why's he stay?"

Janet shrugged. "Why's anybody do anything? Why did I retire from swimsuit modeling?" She squeezed one breast. "Tits got too small. No, kiddo. They do it 'cause it's *easy*."

"That's not—"

"Even you. You run 'cause you're fast." He looked up at that. "But not everybody's fast. Some people are good at sitting still and being patient, so they spend their lives waiting. 'Cause that's what they're good with."

"Good at." Patch frowned. Something about her stolid certainty bugged him.

"What's he got's so great? Thick stiffy, strong back, dimples in all them cheeks. Nobody, is what. Out here, that's superglue." Janet wiped the counter.

Patch nodded. He'd wanted to know, and now he didn't. What if Janet got curious?

"He's going along with the sale, right? He's not stopping you." Her blue eyes weighed him quietly.

"Janet, I can't keep the farm so he has a place to putz around and jerk off regular." Why had he said that? "My dad did right by him. He's not crippled." *Stop making him a big deal.* "Tucker's not my problem, I mean."

Janet looked at him a moment too long. *Tricky, tricky.* "Nobody said he was." She polished the clean counter again, but her eyes stayed on him, watching him with the patience of a trap spider. She wasn't trying to make trouble, but a born gossip didn't need to try. "I just said he's been straight with you."

Straight.

Patch ignored that one entirely. "Some folks are just lazy."

"Lazy? What lazy? There's different kindsa work, kiddo." She snorted. "Dave likes ribs, so he can stand out there in hundred degree heat and smoke meat in August. Folks visit the church that makes 'em feel holy, or jerk off to the porn that pokes their no-no, or, or nurse the in-laws they stuck with." She wiped the counter again, absently. "None of that's *lazy*."

"Easy, then. At ease." He took a swig of cold sweet soda.

"Sure, yeah. And you're not easy here. So you fucked off to the big Wahoo exactly like you shoulda. You stayed away 'cause it came easy. You model 'cause it's easy. And you fucked some local kid 'cause he was easy."

"Not a kid," slipped out, and then he pinked.

"Ha! I knew it."

"Screw you, Rodman." She was right, though. "It was a fluke. Didn't mean a thing."

"Not much does. Doing shit is *hard*. Most of us drift, kiddo." She poked his chest. "Even you. We hatch our problems. Don't matter how fast we do it, if we just keep on letting it happen. If it ain't chickens, it's feathers."

"Well…" He'd spent so much time dwelling on his problem that saying it out loud felt… cruel. "Tucker's gonna have to move. Away."

She bobbed her head. "Guess so. He'll figure it out. He lived over in Silsbee a while before he came to help Royce and your ma with the cutting. Not quick. That man's slower than a breakfast wagon with biscuit wheels. He just sorta made his way back."

"Drifted."

"Exactly so. See?" She looked him over again, scalp to sneakers. "All he's got's a passel of bastards who hate him and grandkids he won't never meet, scattered from here to Lubbock. You just give him notice so he's got time. He's gone need plenty."

Patch could see her putting something together in her head. *Time to go.* "I should get back. Sorry about the hay."

"*Pffft*, hay?"

"Killing your supply. Leaving you in the lurch so sudden."

"Like I give a shit. Bales, we can find. I want you happy, kiddo. You need help, I'm gone come out there with my lucky chainsaw." She slapped the counter like they'd made a bargain.

"Thanks, Janet."

She hugged him hard and patted his cheek roughly. "Who loves you more than me?"

"I wouldn't know."

He polished off the second Big Red on the walk back to the battered pickup, tossing the can in the skip. He swung into the cab like a real farmer and caught himself pretending to be bowlegged. Turned him on a little, actually, which was worse. Some sick part of him wished a photog would snap shots of him getting dirt under his nails.

The stuffy interior of the car made his skin feel clammy, and the air-conditioning made that worse. His balls throbbed like a sore tooth, but he was determined to make it back to the house before he let himself jerk off inside his shorts.

Reward for a job done right. Again his pa's words came to him, which took the edge off his boner quick. "Don't whack it," he muttered to himself. "Pack." Time to get a move on.

Back on Terrapin Road, he almost ditched the empty trailer in the front drive but instead did the grown-up thing: put it where it belonged in the old clapboard barn where they stored bales. Tucker could pile it high again and run the next order to the Feed & Seed on his next trip into town.

Patch had climbed out to unhitch when he heard paws and dogtags in the knee-high grass.

Sure enough, Botchy *whuff*ed and butted his leg with her blocky head, bounding around him in doggy invitation.

"Hey, girl! Hi. Yeah!" He rubbed her back roughly and stroked her ears. He missed having a dog so much. One downside of being crammed into a studio in the city and traveling all the time. Maybe after the club opened, he could. "Good *girl*. Hey." He rubbed her sides roughly, and she wriggled in a happy circle, then led him through the dark door.

Inside, someone had piled the back barn twenty feet high with fresh hay bales. Patch had never seen it so full. Small two-string bales stacked like bricks to the rafters. Had to be ten or fifteen grand at least. "Jesus."

"Right?" A drawl and chuckle he should've expected.

Patch stiffened and turned.

Tucker wore gloves and a sheen of sweat better than anyone he'd ever seen.

Patch nodded at the steep slope of bales. "Lotta damn work, Tuck. You bucked all them bales solo?" Being out here he started sounding like his pa. *Those bales*. He knew how to talk now.

Tucker let out a heavy sigh. "We finally started getting rain in May, and now I'm baling every twenty-eight days so it don't rot."

Patch walked toward the dry mountain. "This the Jiggs?" He didn't know shit about different grasses, but this was a hell of a lot of hay to be storing. Ten grand easily. Mold would be an issue down near the bottom.

"I guess it's a lot, huh. If you're selling this place, we're gonna have to clear it out pretty fast. I can cut the price and dump it."

Botchy sprang onto a bale and then bounced up the mountain of straw like a marionette goat. *Boing-gaboink-ga-boing*. She panted at the top happily, pink tongue lolling, and then bounded down again when they laughed at her.

Soon as she reached the floor, Botchy rushed up and licked his leg, making him giggle and squirm away.

"Tears and sweat." Tucker rubbed her scarred back firmly, and she braced herself in obvious pleasure. "That dog loves salt." She tipped up her square head to lick his hand and cheek.

"So, you've been wuffling and baling all this by yourself? On that ole shit tractor?" Patch knew he had. Who else could help? He'd never seen so much hay at one time. He was looking at a thousand hours of backbreaking work for no salary, no guarantee. "For how long?"

Botchy nosed around the edges of the barn and then back up onto the bales.

"Last year-two, I got a couple guys from the veterans center came out to lend your folks a hand, but mostly I just chipped away at it." Tucker shrugged. "Pays okay. I wanted to cover the taxes, utilities, an' all. And then after your folks...." He frowned at the ground. "One less thing for you."

Patch nodded. Much as it shamed him to admit it, Tucker had done him a favor.

"I weren't gonna let it rot, Patch. That's your money. Farm's still got bills an' all." He waved a hand at the barn stacked high. "Whatever we cain't sell, I'll just burn." All that work. *Ash*. His expression didn't change.

Up on top of the mountain of straw again, Botchy raised her panting head.

Patch smiled back at her in spite of himself. "Why's she get up there?"

"That crazy dog always goes the highest place, I swear. She'd sleep up on the damn roof if she could. Folks ask about them scars, I tell 'em that's where they cut off her wings."

Up in the rafters, Botchy seemed to know she was under discussion. She hopped back up and bounded up and down across several bales before settling again to lick her own stomach.

Patch turned. "But why?"

"Do I know? Maybe 'cause them kids hurt her. Caution. Boredom. Maybe she likes licking the stars. She's a dog." Tucker smiled up at her and smoothed a hand over his rough jaw. "She needs someplace to run to, huh? Somewhere to get."

Botchy nosed in the straw and then sprang down a bale at a time like a slobbering mountain goat. She bumped his leg with her happy panting skull till he stroked it.

"That's right. We're talking about you. My best bitch."

Patch shifted, eying the hard lines of Tucker's mouth. The cool dimness of the barn made him want to take a nap or get his fuck on. Around them the fields crackled with heat, and the farm's quiet privacy stretched several hundred acres in all directions. The easy option of fooling around any second swirled around them silently.

Out in this old barn, nothing stopping them but habit and daylight, after all. Patch eyed the mountain of bales and Tucker's buckle. He could make it happen in under ten seconds if he wanted, and they'd be on each other like flapjacks on a griddle.

Stop it. For some odd reason he wanted Tucker to make the move. Then he did, but not the way Patch had expected.

"Uhh, Patch. You wanna grab supper?" Tucker pointed between them, as if Patch might imagine he was talking to the dog. "Y'know. Later?"

No should have been the answer. Instead Patch flashed a relieved grin. "Yeah. I guess."

"If not, no salt." Tucker jammed his hands in his pockets. "I just figgered we both gotta eat, some point."

He shrugged and put a hand on Tucker's back, the first time in four days he'd touched him when they weren't naked or fighting. "Sure. Sure, if you think so." For reasons he couldn't sort, his joint thickened in his pants at the idea of a date. *Not a date.*

Tucker grinned. "Fine. They's a couple places up in Kountze you'd like… just two whoops and a holler. Or barbecue up at Honey Island."

"Are we…." Patch opened the truck door, then nudged it closed. He'd walk back. "I dunno, friends now?"

"I'da thought so. Friendly for sure." *Shore.* A grin crept over Tucker's lips. "Ya think?"

He grinned back. "Yeah. Yes. Friendly." He glanced at Tucker's rough knuckles and remembered them covered with his jizz, Tucker's teeth tugging his earlobe while they busted together in the mud.

Tucker blinked and dropped his smoky eyes to the lump in Patch's pants. "You have fun? I had fun. That's about that."

Balls, man. That easy boldness paralyzed him. Most folks who came after him played bullshit games and hung back, intimidated by his bod or his rep or his swagger. Hot guys made everyone uncomfortable. When he'd first moved to New York, he'd had coffee with anyone with the nerve because it was the *nerve* he wanted.

"I got enough time, they's no problem I cain't lick." Tucker smiled wider and winked, lazy and dirty.

Patch asked, "So what does that make us?" He knew better.

For a beat, they eyed each other through the sulky air.

"I dunno. Live close. Working close. We get off together pretty good, huh?" Tucker winked. "Friendly. Playing around. Makes us tug buds, at least."

Tucker just wanted him flat-out and had the guts to say as much. Maybe what he found so damn sexy was Tucker's relentless self-assurance. *All balls.* That was his real kink—not the boots or the drawl or the looks, but the raw male confidence. It made his legs freeze, his dick drip, and his hairs stand on end.

"I guess so. Dinner, then." They needed to talk about the sale options anyway: locals and oil company both. And maybe after, Tucker would be horny enough to play some more.

Tucker took his silence for hesitation. "It's weird for me too, pup. You're a stranger to me most ways. So, I guess it's nice to meet ya."

Patch scoffed. "C'mon. Tucker, you known me my whole life."

"Naw." Tucker plucked straw off his chest. "Never did I ever."

"What do you mean?"

"You was Royce's kid. I didn't *know* you, know you. I mean, you looked fine and all, but mostly you were the reason we couldn't go drinking and whoring. Just there and a headache. He stopped wanting to rodeo 'cause he had a family."

Patch nodded. "And you didn't."

"Well, I did and I didn't. Luanne left when we was kids, and I couldn't see myself getting hitched twice. I coached and rodeoed. I never thought about you as nothing but a skinny pain in the ass." Tucker ran a hand across Patch's shoulders. "You ain't a kid now."

"Not for a long time." The casual affection raised goose bumps on his arms and his scalp tightened like a lug nut.

"No, sir." Tucker gave him a hard thump that felt... right, good, strong, real. "All man now." The bullshit compliment sounded funny coming out of the rugged face, but if Tucker could tell the lie, Patch was willing to hear it.

Patch stretched lazily. "I guess. New York toughened me up."

"Sure did." *Shore.* Like toughness was somewhere you could go.

Patch realized his old coach wasn't making fun. "What's that mean?"

"I could never do what you done. Gone off north to the concrete. Big city. By yourself."

Patch made a goofy face and made himself sound like a local. "Bull. You're the toughest guy I know."

"Patch." Tucker laughed and shook his head, didn't look up. "I lived around these folks my whole life. I ain't never been nowhere. Not outta Texas. Hell, only time I left Hardin County was to rodeo when I was your age. Bulldogging. Hay bucking. Traveling puts good miles on you."

Patch grinned at that.

"So, case in point." Tucker patted his chest with his knuckles and grunted in satisfaction, swaying closer. "Tougher than me. Skinny an' all."

"Am not." He stood his ground.

"Tough as a two-dollar steak." Instead of flirting back, Tucker nudged him and winked. "Go on now." That grin again. "*Git.*"

Patch left him working and walked back to the house.

Tucker's voice over his shoulder. "Pick you up 'round six." Because down here folks ate before sundown. Patch had forgotten that too.

Fuck buddies, then. Tucker could be wary of him and still get off. *Keep it casual.*

Messing around seemed safe, getting off together seemed almost innocent. Except Patch knew that they weren't kids and this wasn't school. They both had adult lives and problems. At this point, whatever he needed to do to survive home-sweet-home sounded sensible.

Any actual intimacy seemed downright dangerous. The way Patch figured, modern dating treated cocksucking and hand jobs as kinda casual anyway, but putting two bodies too close together for long stretches of privacy might confuse the situation.

Patch knew what would change if they ended up sweaty face-to-face for an extended period of time. He knew what he'd start feeling and telling himself. Not even he was that stupid.

No strings, no matter what.

The difference in their ages was bad enough, but Patch knew what would happen if he let the man get close enough to get tangled.

Nobody needed to get attached to anything.

They were just fooling around because they were horny and bored, acting out fantasies for each other: coach and jock, daddy and boy, shitkicker and city slicker.

He needed to get off, and this way he didn't have to drive to Beaumont, which was a damn waste of time. Fooling around with Tucker? Incentive, that's what it was. *Reward for a job done right.* Only this time he heard the words in his own voice and he almost believed them.

The sweat had soaked his clothes by the time he made it back to the dark house and drank two glasses of water from the tap. The impossible task of tackling the photo drawer made him queasy. *Tomorrow, then.* When he felt steadier. These would keep. They could wait.

Without air-conditioning, he opted to strip and change into dry shorts, not bothering with a shirt and scraping his curls into a messy ponytail to keep them off his face. If he had to dig through hell, at least he wanted to be able to see.

As he went back to trying to make sense of the attic toys, Patch checked his cell phone for a signal and called Ms. Landry while he continued sorting stuffed animals.

"Mr. Hastle!" she said. Rustling paper and her voice got clearer. "I meant to call you yesterday."

"With good news, I hope." He found his stuffed animal pile.

"Potentially. I 'spect not the good news you wanted."

"Meaning…."

"Insurance company's paying the life policy." She paused. "Not on the accidental clause because of the police report."

Because of his pa running the signal, she meant. "We knew that. That's not bad news."

"No, but… the dairy passed. No way for them to get the variance. And the Killingers decided to keep closer to Arkansas for now."

Patch scrubbed his forehead with one dusty hand. "Ah. That doesn't sound too hopeful. Where do we stand, then?"

"Them oil guys want to come back for a geological survey. Sample and such."

"Texaco." Patch frowned. Drilling would do all kinds of things to the neighbors, and he knew it. Then again, maybe everyone could sell up and get out. Maybe this would end up a good thing for all concerned. Patch wavered, a plush snail in one hand.

"You still there?" She sounded skeptical.

"How fast could they move?"

"Very." She cleared her throat. "Apparently they've been monitoring the property. This much land so close to the refineries is a rare prospect. Beaumont and Port Arthur keep sprawling and—"

He interrupted, facing a heap of unclaimed baby dolls. "Give them the okay on the geologist. And please do a little digging with the county. Just to clear the decks." Maybe this would all work out.

"You're sure?" Not a warning, but she knew how to cover her ass. "I'm headed down to Sour Lake for dinner at my daughter's later. I can drop the prospectus off in your mailbox." Once news of this got out, locals would have plenty of opinions about the Hastles' faggot son. Texaco already had plenty of enemies, and here he was letting the fox into the henhouse.

None of that mattered. In one stroke he'd slough off his past at a substantial profit and make Velocity happen for himself.

The only problem was Tucker, and he could find no solution that made any sense.

TRUE TO his word, Tucker swung by in his beat-up truck when the sun got low. He climbed down wearing a pressed pink dress shirt with a collar and a stiff, unfaded pair of Wranglers.

"You look sharp." If anything Patch was glad he'd opted for a knit shirt because now they were both wearing collars. "This place we're going fancy?"

"Hardly." Tucker held the front door for him. "Least, there ain't straw on the floor."

Was this a date? "Well, I never." Patch mocked him.

"I just thought you might be getting tired of canned beans and fast food."

"Truth."

"Well, this place is pretty good and pretty close." Tucker shrugged. "You gotta eat."

"Right." So it wasn't a date? "Is it just us?"

"Far's I know." Tucker twisted to eye the porch. "You got somebody else hiding in one-a them boxes?"

"Didn't know if Bix or somebody was meeting us."

Tucker squinted at him like he was nutty. "Uh, no. He's still out working in Kerrville far as I know." He gave a slow shake of his head. "Did you want him to come?"

"What? Naw. Nothing. Sorry. I think I've been inside here too long today." He faked a smile he didn't feel, wishing he hadn't said anything. Now Tucker thought he was psycho or jealous. "I was hoping it'd be us."

That was the right thing to say. Tucker smiled and opened the door for him. "Good deal, then."

Guilty, Patch lifted his hand to squeeze Tucker's shoulder as he passed and thought better of it. They weren't friends, exactly. Barely fuck buddies when you got right down to it. But against all odds, he'd started to give a shit. He knew better, for all that mattered.

Some pair we are.

Tucker's faded blue pickup idled in the drive. They climbed in and the A/C felt like heaven.

Tucker shifted the truck into Reverse and then Drive. "I figured you hadta be roastin' in that house." The cab rode so damn high.

"No shit."

He pulled them around and headed for the road. "I thought maybe you wanted to bring Janet and Dave."

"Why?" Patch asked. "You did?"

"Yup. Well, you ran a load an' all. I went by the Feed & Seed with them other bales 'cause I'd forgot you took 'em. Janet comes out angrier'n a goat in a garter belt." He laughed. "You'd filled her shed already, so she was yelling and screaming, using cursive words."

Patch turned. "Cursive?"

"Profanity. *F* this and *F* all that."

Patch beamed and buckled himself in. Stupid affection bubbled up in him, but he didn't do anything about it. "Me, I love cursive words."

"No shit." Tucker looked annoyed, but happy about it, if that made sense.

It did to Patch.

"Music okay?" Tucker snapped on the radio.

Low music filled the cab—country, of course, but less twangy and doleful than he expected. *Small mercies.* In a funny way, it made him feel like he belonged here beside this guy he barely knew, when push came to pull.

They drove in companionable quiet. Wet farmland sped past, the speeding truck so fast and sturdy its progress unnerved him. He'd never thought much about Tucker's plans, his disappointments, his options. He'd never cared much one way or the other. Until a couple days ago, Tucker had been a dumb fantasy he'd played with behind his locked door. *Cowboy coach daddy.* Real life didn't enter into it. Why should it?

Come to think of it, what did Tucker know about *him* besides the bullshit he'd heard from Royce? At most Patch had been a pain in his ass while he worked at the school, a benchwarmer, the smartass faggot, his best friend's runaway fuckup son.

Patch understood how young he must seem. The twenty years between them felt like a washed-out bridge over rapids. Maybe the fantasy was safer because they could never really touch each other while standing on opposite shores.

Tucker drummed the wheel, a small smile creasing his cheek. *"Givin' me the devil 'cause I wouldn't hoe corn."* He sang along under his breath, and it didn't sound silly. It sounded true.

"Y'know." Patch nodded at Tucker. "You got a nice voice, Biggs."

"Piss off." But Tucker sounded pleased.

"I mean it."

"I just bet." Tucker checked the rearview mirror and changed lanes. "You hungry yet?"

He was. He nodded and quietly made the decision to pick up the check. He knew Tucker couldn't afford to eat in restaurants. Hell, he couldn't even fill up his tank at the station. The only reason Tucker had driven out here was to impress the city boy. "Starving, now you mention."

At that Tucker grinned. "Good thing. We'll get you fixed up. Put some meat on you." His big hand came down on Patch's thigh and squeezed, leaving it there.

Patch flinched and grunted. It shouldn't feel that good, but it did. His cock rose, juicy and fat in his jeans. He glanced down, wishing Tucker would grope him in the truck. He slid his eyes over.

No deal. At least Tucker left the hand hot on his leg, the top of his knuckles nudging Patch's ball sac through the denim. "Not just now, pup."

"What?"

"That load you're carrying." He rubbed Patch's thigh. "Dinner first, cream after."

"Yessir." Patch had been horny before, but now his trapped wood ached inside his jeans.

"Don't you worry none. We got all night to milk you proper." *Melllk*, it sounded like. "You'd best let me drive for now."

Fuck. Now he really was hungry.

On the outskirts of Kountze the farms got closer together and the lights got brighter. They crossed a narrow creek on a two-lane bridge barely wide enough for the pickup. Up ahead a Texaco station and a farm supply setup indicated they were approaching town.

Tucker glanced sideways in the dark cab. "Nearly there." He drummed the steering wheel with his hands.

"I can wait." For once that was true.

"This place is solid. Bix brought me here a while back, and he's real picky about food an' all."

He probably should have been annoyed, but for some reason the idea of Tucker's ex-con rodeo-clown fuck buddy as a connoisseur of fine dining seemed so ridiculous.

"He knew a gal. Well, he banged her. She waits tables when they get crowded." Tucker sounded nervous and formal both.

Out of pure orneriness, Patch asked him straight: "Tucker Biggs, is this a *date*?"

No answer. The hands on the steering wheel stilled, and Tucker let up on the gas. His lips shifted over his teeth.

"You grabbing food with me to be neighborly or is this us socializing because we're fooling around?" Patch put his gaze back front. "Or 'cause my folks died?"

"I didn't.... I just figgered—" As the road shushed past, the signs got brighter. "You could use a nice dinner."

"All due respect, that's what you'd say to a lady." Patch turned to check his reaction.

Tucker made a strange face. "I was being polite." He glanced over. "We been buddies for—"

"All of two days. So I call bullshit, big-time. I avoided you mosta my life. And with good reason."

"C'mon now."

"You remember ratting me out to my folks? Smacking me around at football games? Dragging me home all hours?"

"You was a kid. I was doing the right thing 'cause it was dangerous, what you done. Sneaking around to mess around."

"You got no idea what it was like for me."

Tucker shook his head. "No. I don't. But you was a boy and I didn't wanna see you hurt."

Why did that sound right to him, warm him inside? *Asshole*. Still, Tucker protecting him sounded so good, he could almost forget how scary it had been. "Then you're protecting me again. This dinner and all. Baling all that hay. Sex in the mud and more."

"No. Well… yeah."

"Well, we've messed around. Chucked our muck on each other more'n once." Somehow it didn't sound as funny or casual as he'd intended. "All of a sudden, we're talking regular. Grabbing a bite. And you're wearing an ironed shirt with all its buttons. I wanna know if it's a date."

Tucker tapped the brake and didn't give him an answer. "Hope we can find parking."

A flashing red stoplight at a four-way intersection. Past that, the road curved past a Sonic Burger and the stand of pecan trees.

"Seriously?" Patch couldn't imagine anyplace out here seeing enough traffic to make space a problem.

Slick Dick's, the neon said without shame or any sense of a raunchy interpretation. *Ah, Texas.*

The lights played across Tucker's rugged frown. "Dick's family built this place back during World War I. Mostly his grandkids run it these days, but he's still the cook. Best chicken-fried steak in East Texas. Folks drive out here from Nederland and Port Arthur. I'm telling you. I always wanted to have a place like this."

Sure enough, they made a left onto an unpaved lot where rows of cars, trucks, and everything in between filled a rutted yard higgledy-piggledy in front of a rambling frame house with a wraparound porch. High sodium lamps spilled peach light over the bustle. Kids running around. Middle of Shitkick, Nowhere, and a line out the damn door.

This public? No way was this a date. "Jesus!"

Tucker winked at him. "Don't worry none. They know me good. We'll cut the line and eat out back. Dick's wife'll take care of us." He found a spot and nosed in.

Patch said nothing. Maybe Mrs. Dick was another one of Tucker's sad-sack booty calls. Maybe he was too. Hometown three-way. The thought chafed at him.

"So it is a date."

"Well, hell…." Tucker killed the engine and unbuckled the seat belt. He exhaled and inhaled.

"I guess if you're not saying no, then it's at least partly a date. Partly not too. Or not?" Place looked nice. He didn't see too many folks inside, but this was fancier than Whataburger.

The truck's hood pinged and ticked as it cooled. "I just thought you'd be hungry."

"Bull. Bull—" Patch laughed. "Shit. And you know it. You got dressed. I mean, good boots and everything."

"So did you."

"So what in hell's that mean? Yes, this is a date because now we're officially fooling around?"

"We're buddies."

"With butthole benefits."

"If you like." Tucker sounded confused. "Guess that works. It's only dinner. I ain't brought you a damn corsage."

"Fuck buddies, then. With some freaky history."

Tucker looked nonplussed. "If you want. Taking care of business. Ain't hurting nobody."

"Until this last week, I'd never had a conversation with you that didn't end bad. Till three days ago, you were just my dad's asshole friend who gave me shit for laughs and made school a fucking nightmare."

"Okay. And?"

"We're the same people, Tucker. We didn't—*poof*—turn into two amigos that like to share beers and bitches."

Laughter as Slick Dick's side door opened. A young Mexican couple emerged and wobbled across the gravel to a battered jeep. So couples came here at least.

Tucker squinted at him as if expecting him to rattle and strike. "It's dinner, pup. I thought it'd be nice."

"Right." Patch crossed his arms and turned to face Tucker head-on. "I've eaten your nut, hoss. And you've returned the favor, right out the spigot. A couple times now." But they hadn't kissed.

Tucker raised an eyebrow. "Patch, that don't scare me none."

"I don't believe you." He twisted in the seat to really look at Tucker.

"Then don't believe me. Hell, I've had my face in your crack and licked your jam off my fingers. I'm gonna do it again, I reckon. Maybe tonight. That'sa truth." He grinned. *Jesus.* "I'll eat your tail right here if it'd calm you the hell down."

Patch flashed a tight smile. "I guess I don't understand."

"That so?" Tucker dropped his gaze. "You can't just sneak over nights when you're horny, then act like we're strangers."

I do. "I don't."

"Patch...."

"I don't mean to, then." He took a deep breath and held it like cigarette smoke before letting it out. "I didn't think you gave a shit."

"I told you I did." Tucker's dark brows knitted and his brow clouded. *Stern coach.*

"Sorry."

"Don't never be sorry for thinking. At least you bothered to think." Tucker opened his door, hopped out. "I'm starved. You comin'?"

Patch just nodded, stupid and stunned. He climbed out and slammed the door.

Tucker frowned at him across the truck bed. *Grouchy ranch hand.* "You gotta problem messing around with me, then don't. You wanna be my friend, be one. I'm too old to put up with wishy-washy horseshit."

"Yes, sir." He couldn't believe they were having this argument in a juke-joint parking lot.

"We're two grown men. Act like it." Tucker squinted and crossed his arms. *Disappointed daddy.* "Seriously. Bad enough you call me sir. I feel old enough."

"You call me *son* and *pup* and what all."

"Maybe I do. You're right. It's all too much for me to figure out. But if we gonna mess around, I wish you'd treat me like a person instead of one-a them magazines."

Patch just swallowed. *Busted.* Tucker kept on being smarter than he should've been. His moods kept lurching and spinning and bucking. The conversation was like riding a bull.

"I swear you wear me out." Tucker waved his hand in irritation. "If we're consenting adults, then I wish you'd consent already."

Patch scowled back. "Yeah. You should talk."

"You should listen."

He wavered, knowing he'd been caught and called out.

"Well?" Tucker stood waiting on the steps, one boot on the crowded porch, thumb behind his belt, fingers over the wide buckle. "Make up your mind."

Patch laughed at his lap. *I'm making up everything else, so why not that too?*

Over Tucker's shoulders, a couple diners looked their way. The front door smacked open again, and a gabby family emerged.

Tucker crossed his arms and squinted. "No salt, huh? I can run you back home quick, if you want."

Patch studied him, looking for whatever answers hid there on the surface before he made whichever mistake would be worse. *Making it up as we go.*

"I don't wanna."

"Wanna what?" The sodium lights overhead threw Tucker's face into deep shadow.

Instead of answering, Patch ambled in his direction, closing the distance slowly and feeling better with each step, the weight melting.

"All right, then." Tucker went to open the door for him, which he kinda hated, kinda loved.

A couple of girls in A&M T-shirts trotted through, giving Tucker the twice-over and looking back to check again. The big cowboy didn't give 'em a glance.

Patch sympathized. The way Tucker filled those Wranglers shouldn't have been legal. The fat bulge under his buckle, the cool eyes, and the thick muscle stretching his shirt dared anyone to give him shit.

Fools rush in.

Patch stepped through into the air-conditioning with a sigh of relief, his mind made up. When he turned back to his date, Tucker winked from a few inches away and nudged him forward.

"Hope you're hungry."

As soon as they stepped through the door, the smell of grease and black pepper smacked him in the face like a salty pillow fight. His stomach growled.

They ordered at a counter and then the food would be brought out. They grabbed beers and headed back.

The waitstaff wore matching red polos and black jeans. Tables were covered in red-checked vinyl, with plastic plates and rolls of paper towels on each table. Televisions on each wall blared various sports. Guys watched and gals maneuvered food into the roaming kids whenever they sat still enough to chew.

The Lone Star State of Affairs.

Patch didn't want to sit near the families where they couldn't talk plain, so he was relieved when Tucker steered him out to the back deck, a screened-in dining area like an oversized veranda, where ceiling fans stirred the air. All the other patrons had opted for the A/C.

A big sign on the wall said LIQUOR IN THE FRONT. POKER IN THE REAR. "Perfect, man."

That damn grin. "Yeah?" Tucker pulled out the chair to his right rather than across the table.

"Better without all the little buckaroos."

"Amen. I had enough kids to last me." He had been a coach, after all.

Patch gave a slow nod. "Good thinking."

Tucker plopped down and rubbed his hands together. "Good deal."

"I had a friend who says you can turn tragedy into comedy by sitting down." Patch rocked back.

Tucker chuckled. "Smart friend."

Patch looked at his lap and back. "Ex-boyfriend." *Eek.*

Tucker just nodded. "Then maybe not so smart." He regarded Patch with steady pleasure.

"We're building a club together. So it's all good." Right? Patch blinked the thought loose. "Scotty's a music producer too. Real wheeler-dealer. He lived nine blocks away in New York, but I met him on the Circuit."

"Howzat?" Tucker unrolled his silverware from the paper napkin.

"The Circuit's like a...." Patch sat back.

Tucker's forehead wrinkled in confusion. "A dance place?"

"Yeah. No. More like a traveling circus. A whole buncha parties in different cities all year long. All over the world. But the same folks go."

"Like the rodeo."

"Yeah!" Patch nodded and blinked at his quick insight. "Exactly. I say that all the time. But for guys who party. No animals." He stifled the laugh. "Well, not that kinda animal. No livestock."

"So you was playing the music and this fella was there. But y'all didn't work out, like, together." Tucker sounded like he understood, but there was no way he could.

"Not that way." What the hell was happening? Was he actually talking about his love life with Tucker Biggs? "Business, yeah, but the rest, no. Is that weird?"

Tucker sipped and cocked his head. "What?"

"Guys together. I dunno. Gay stuff."

"Sex ain't so complicated out here as you think. Folks get busy when they wanna. Like Bix and me. They don't talk about it too much, but... well. Yeah." Tucker crooked his lips.

"Well, that isn't what I thought you'd say."

"Why?" Tucker leaned forward, looking into the busy restaurant. "Mosta them guys inside is queer for beer."

Patch fought back a grin. "What's that—?"

"You get a six-pack in 'em, they happy to choke on it till I nut."

Patch coughed his beer in midswallow.

Tucker leaned forward and lowered his voice. "Son, just 'cause I mess with guys sometimes don't mean I'm a sissy."

Patch nodded in sympathy. He knew this song. "It ain't a club, Tucker. Either/or. There's all kindsa gay people. Some them live Catholic and vote Republican."

"I guess."

"I just mean it just changes your perspective, but it isn't everything you are."

Tucker shrugged. "They's thirty-one families in Hixville. A couple hundred people work for them. If I want to get off without driving fifty miles and paying someone to give me crabs or grief, I can't hold out for a centerfold. Man or woman. It's sex."

Patch shrugged. He got it.

"Sometimes jerking off just don't cut it with me, and Houston is too fucking far to drive to get my coals raked. Beaumont, even. A man's got needs. Nothing to be 'shamed of." Maybe he meant it.

"A man after my own heart." Patch had made the same fucking speech to friends on the Circuit. Wicks needed dipping and there was plenty of wax to go round.

"I'm not a queer—I'm practical."

Patch didn't take offense and didn't argue. *Got it.* Long as he stayed in town, they would be friends with benefits. Once the farm sold, shake hands and sayonara. No future, no entanglements, no problems.

Makes sense to me.

If he had any lingering worry, the thrill of conquest, of living out a few fantasies, wiped his concerns away. And it'd make his time in purgatory pass that much faster.

The waitress brought their dinner. Chicken-fried steak, okra, mashed potatoes in cream gravy. He'd live to regret it, but he'd live. They still hadn't talked about the farm. How was he supposed to bring up Texaco?

Tucker tucked in with his knife and fork, then looked up. "I don't know why I told you all that shit. Now I feel silly."

Patch swallowed and frowned. "What's that supposed to mean?"

"I'm just a man, Patch. You gotta see that. I'm stupid and stubborn, headed nowhere fast. Whatever bullshit you imagine about me, I can't never measure up. I'm just some old cracker, used to wrestle steer. Nobody needs to call me sir."

"You're forty-three, Tuck. Not exactly time for the glue factory." Patch took another bite and lowered his voice. "And if it's all the same, I like calling you 'sir.'"

"Yeah." Tucker looked sheepish. He looked down at the ridge in Patch's jeans. "That for me?"

"Yessir. You fuck me right up. You always did."

Tucker reached across and cupped it, stroking it through the denim right there in Slick Dick's where anyone might walk in. "I had no idea, pup. Never did I ever." He sounded incredulous.

Patch saw that first crack and pumped oil into it to keep things moving smoothly. "That's 'cause you were getting hot tail all over Hardin County. Man, I used to watch you."

Tucker made a face. "How?"

"At the rodeo. Up in the barn. Hell, behind the diner in Sour Lake once." Patch bobbed his head. That weird hypnotic slowness stole over him and he didn't fight it. "You'd talk up some girl and wink and whisper. Next thing you'd be porking her against your truck in the parking lot. Or on a bench. Jeans slid down as little as possible so you could hump her hard." He pushed on his throbber below the table.

Tucker saw. "Jesus, boy."

"Fucking hot. Hell, you were my porno. Who else was I gonna watch? My folks? Janet? You were the town stud, so I made sure I got an eyeful. I spied on a lot of humping alfresco."

Tucker laughed right out loud, pleased as punch.

"Man, I knew your backside so good. Every inch. I swear. The way your balls slapped when you swung into women. The exact rhythm you liked, the roll of your hips. The dimples at the small of your back. Your little hole when the cheeks spread. So fucking pink. The sounds you made. And faces. Your mouth on 'em, licking 'em till they broke. You don't fucking know."

"Patch."

"I dumped quarts of spunk all over this county watching you pound 'em with your pants on."

"That true?"

"Used to make me nuts, wanting to see you all the way naked." Now he was seriously boned up. "Stupid. I thought you hated me."

"Naw. How could I hate you? Hell, mostly I didn't see you at all because you was a kid. I cain't stand kids." He shook his head. "No. That's a lie. I worked at the school and I 'spect had more than my share of kids. Last thing I wanted was some little shit who needed me to be the responsible party."

"Fair enough."

"But it weren't good, that's sure. I did plenty that was outta line. I know that and I'm sorry."

Patch swallowed. "Okay."

"Not okay. No kid deserves that kinda hell, but I was hurting and lazy, and you kept getting in my way and always doing dangerous shit. Royce mad all the time. It was easy to blame you, which made it even worse."

Here he was apologizing, and Patch felt like apologizing back. He shook his head, annoyed.

"What?"

Patch shook his head again. "Nothing. I didn't know anything."

"You was a kid. You're not supposed to know nothing."

"Well, I'm not a kid now."

"No shit. You're stronger than me."

Patch excused himself to the bathroom, but in truth he slipped his credit card to their waitress to head off the inevitable check wrestle. He squinted at her name badge. "I get the check, Sally. Deal?"

"Deal. Y'all was talking so I didn't wanna interrupt. You need anything else, just give a holler. I wanted y'all to have your time."

What did that mean? "Sorry. We're just talking." A cold gnawing in his midsection.

"So I see. Well, you go ahead. Nobody else is in that section anyhow." Sally chewed her lip and peeked toward the table.

Prickling at the back of his neck; Tucker was probably watching them. "No hurry with that." He gave her the smile.

"Sure thing." She tucked the card into her little apron.

Once he was back at the table, Tucker gave him a funny look but said nothing. They demolished their dinners. No way could Patch finish, but Tucker cleaned both platters. Where did he put all of it?

Patch watched him with real pleasure in his pleasure. "Good?"

"Better than." Tucker patted his hard, flat belly. "Man. Now I want dessert. So do you."

"Dessert! No way, man."

"Don't you worry." Tucker's lids went lazy, and he tasted a corner of his lip with his tongue. "I'm gonna eat it. You're gonna make it for me."

Oh. He closed his mouth. *Gulp.* South of the buckle, his cock jerked.

"You think you can?" Tucker sucked the pad of his thumb. "That sound good?"

"Yes, sir. Real good." Two sentences and Tucker had his bone fit to bust in his damn shorts. "Jesus."

Tucker brushed his arm with those broad knuckles. "Worth waiting for, huh? The longer the better. Dee-licious."

"In case you hadn't noticed, I'm fuck-awful at delayed gratification."

"Well, now." Tucker scanned Patch's face a moment, his eyes, his mouth. "I can fix that."

Sally came back with the check, rushed and flushed, but exactly the way she'd promised not to, handed it right to Tucker without hesitation. Probably because he looked *in charge*.

"Uh, no." Patch reached for it too late.

"What in hell?" Tucker pulled it away and flipped the receipt over. "This ain't right." He held up Patch's card. "No, ma'am." He gave her a stern look.

Sally's mouth opened into an embarrassed pink *O*. "Oh, I'm so sorry, mister. I didn't think."

"Wait just one minute...."

"Tucker, it's taken care of. Done. Why do you get the check?"

Tucker wouldn't relinquish it, holding it high. Mexican standoff. "Now, hold—"

Rather than playing fair, Patch stood up and plucked it out of his hand. "Nope. Already paid and all. You drove. This is mine. Next time you pay all you want." He tipped, signed, and handed it back. "Please, Tucker." That last seemed to calm the waters.

Sally grimaced at him apologetically and scurried away.

"I swear you're ornery as a steer on skates. That was uncalled for." Tucker stood and pushed in his chair, then slid his wallet into his back pocket. He followed Patch closely all the way out of the restaurant, bumping their shoulders and hips in front of all those families who couldn't have imagined the kink passing by. Or maybe they could. "Boy, that was *some* mean trick."

"I seen meaner."

A naughty chuckle. "You will at that. Don't forget, dessert's on you too."

Patch held the front door. "I don't think you'll let me."

Outside they walked right into the shit: five beefy teenage boys goofing off next to a pickup with a full-sized Confederate flag flying from their gun rack like a cape behind the cab. Somewhere else they'd have been in college, but out here they probably had grandkids. They swayed on their boots, just beered up enough to argue back.

"The hell?" Standing off the porch, Tucker frowned and said clearly, "I don't like that. Stars and bars bullshit." Without a beat, he walked right up to them like he wanted a fistfight and jail after. "Shame on y'all." He addressed the whole fucking parking lot in his coach voice, loud and certain.

What in fuck?

The overfed teenagers shuffled back, wary and pig-ignorant. They didn't glance in Patch's direction, and he didn't know what he'd have done if they did. This was the kinda fight he steered around as a matter of survival.

Not Tucker.

"See, that there's a flag we beat." Tucker's forehead bunched. "Idjits put that shit up and pretend it means something else. If it's for the Civil War, then it's for traitors. But most folks do it to scare blacks." He spat like he was fixing to hit someone. "Bullshit both ways." He crossed his arms and the biceps bulged.

Patch moved toward him. He had no idea what he could do to help, but he wasn't gonna let Tucker go down solo.

"Free speech." The pimply one piped up, face like a purple fist. "It's cuz we're proud." He squinted like he was leaning into a dusty wind.

Tucker crossed his arms. "Prouda what? You're Americans. That side lost their *ass*. If you don't know better it's 'cause you're ignorant, and if you do know better, you should be ashamed. People murdered, raped, and worse under that fuckin' flag." Coach voice again. His face a thundercloud.

The driver held up both hands, keys dangling, his belly large from biscuits and brisket. He scratched his throat and stared over the lot for something, backup maybe. He didn't want trouble either.

The three others shuffled closer to their ride, unsure and unsteady, suddenly fascinated by the concrete under their feet.

"Free speech an' all." Tucker took another step, and the night tightened around them all like a threaded bolt. "Proud." He made the word a deadly insult, and the veins in his neck stood out pencil thick. He looked ready to go to jail right there.

Pimples opened and closed his mouth while the boys squinted at each other. They acted as confused as Patch felt. What was some local yokel barking at them for? Plenty folks around here sported reb tattoos and reb murals and reb bikinis without getting the fifth degree.

"Y'all take that shit down before someone gets hurt." Tucker wasn't budging and the tic in his jaw made it clear how ugly things might get. *Big dog with a bone.*

"Yes, sir." The fat one bobbed his head and—*whuup*—the Confederate flag came down. Pimples eyed Tucker warily and climbed into the cab. None of the kids blinked or mumbled as they piled inside.

Tucker didn't move.

The truck scattered gravel as it pulled out onto the highway.

"Little bugfuckers." He spat. Patch nodded. "Ain't served their country, not old enough to vote, but they can pretend Jim Crow's a good idea. Like they don't know what they saying. Black folks die on foreign dirt to keep them free enough to burn crosses, march around in sheets." He spat again.

Patch could never have done that, even now. He'd spent his whole life keeping his head down around bigots and bullies. Once they'd pulled out onto the road, he asked quietly, "You okay?"

"Mad." Tucker was still watching the retreating taillights.

He'd always imagined how good it would feel to fight back, but Tucker didn't look happy at all. His jaw was set and his hands wiped and rewiped the legs of his jeans as if covered in oil that wouldn't wash off.

"I ain't that backward, Patch."

"That's not—" He meant it. "I'm sorry."

"For what?"

"You're right. More than. And I just stood here pissing my pants."

Tucker ducked his head and his voice softened. "Not hardly. This ain't your town and ain't your mess to clean up. Nobody's born a bigot. Them kids know better, 'cept nobody says nothing." A slow blink. "Well, that ain't a problem I got."

Patch smiled at him, a real one instead of the camera-ready bullshit that paid his bills. "You're a good man, Tucker Biggs."

"Yeah?" Tucker repaid him with a big startled grin. "News to me."

They walked back to the dusty pickup side by side, shoulders and arms bumping easily. Tucker popped the locks and opened Patch's door for him before circling around to the driver seat and climbing inside.

Nothing else for a while. The truck ate the road, the wind whipped his hair, and Patch kept his eyes on the green mush of kudzu crawling over the Big Thicket. "I forgot you fought."

"I didn't for long. Knee." Tucker thumped the offending bone. When he frowned, the faint crow's-feet made his rugged face look tired and sad. "I signed up and humped cars for three years. Still an' all, I know plenty guys't died."

Patch watched his handsome face, surprised at the vulnerability there. "They're just kids. They don't know."

"Jackasses. Only folks fighting wars are the ones need the money. They ain't rich kids went to I-raq and Bosnia and what-the-hell. You learn quick." Tucker shook his head. "I fought next to all kinds, all colors. Not one of 'em rich and most of 'em died… either there or once they got home. And those little pissants tooling around in daddy's truck proud of the wrong flag."

Patch nodded and looked out the window.

Tucker frowned at the asphalt ahead, drumming the wheel with his blunt fingers. "Sorry."

"Don't be. Don't ever be. That was the bravest thing I ever seen in my life." Without thinking, Patch reached back to squeeze his neck.

Tucker's mute sadness lapped between them, like water against a rowboat. Finally he snapped on the radio and soft bluegrass trilled out of the speakers, a woman crooning in a fragile, crystalline soprano that made Patch forget he'd never felt at home here.

End of discussion.

Small-town wingers always said they wanted their country *back,* the way it *was,* as if the United States was a rock band that had changed styles. Way he saw it, politics all sounded like bullshit, but he tended to side with the folks that didn't burn crosses and lynch anyone.

Tucker kept being more thoughtful than he'd expected. Again, he wished Tucker could visit New York. Hell, even Houston, just to climb out of the small-town sauce he'd basted in his whole life.

Patch started to check his phone and realized he'd left it at the house. Hell, he hadn't charged it today. What was wrong with him? Worse, there was no one he wanted to call. Nothing he needed to check. Nowhere he wanted to go but Tucker's bed.

Insane.

Past the Sonic Burger, the highway bent gradually into a long arc to the west, and Patch let himself brush against Tucker.

"Now you know why they call them S.O.B. curves."

Patch turned. "What?"

"Slide over, baby." Tucker dropped a friendly arm around Patch, who didn't move a muscle for fear of breaking whatever spell the curve had cast.

Patch glanced at him then back at the road. "That's pretty good."

"It's okay to get comfortable. After I eat at Dick's, I gotta take my belt off just so's I can breathe." Tucker's big paw slid over his tented meat to pop the top button on Patch's jeans.

Patch dropped his head back against the seat, sliding down into his chicken-fried steak coma. "I'm pretty stuffed."

"Not yet you're not." Tucker's teeth gleamed in the dashboard glow. "'Sides, we got a big dessert back home, huh?"

The tension had drained out of him. Patch spread his legs to give Tucker access whether or not he wanted it.

"First we got chores." Tucker gave him a wicked grin.

"Chores. What chores?"

"Well, I figger you need to shuck down and rinse off. Put them nice clothes away." Tucker reached over and patted Patch's full belly, rubbing it in firm circles before reaching down to cup Patch's balls hard. "And I got serious milking to do. Hour, at least. You think?"

Patch swallowed noisily.

Tucker leaned closer, his voice gravel but his gaze still on the road. "That is, if you say so."

"I'd say so." His right hand twitched on the seat beside him, unused. He felt powerless and powerful both.

Tucker squeezed his thigh, making him jump. "Good deal."

Patch hitched his hips forward. Tucker would ask him in and sit him down and do crazy shit to him until he couldn't speak or think in complete sentences. Patch didn't plan to even sit in the big recliner. He saw himself kneeling and sweaty and roped on the floor like a steer, straining and groaning under Tucker's expert hands. *Just dessert.*

"Fucking juicy." Tucker's fat thumb tapped the wet spot on his shorts where he'd leaked through the cotton. "You thinking again?" He squeezed the shaft gently, scraping its skin through the briefs.

Patch hunched against his hand and grunted. "I guess."

"I like that fine." Tucker slid his hand under to cup Patch's sore balls. "Maybe thought you'd get started early, work up a big nut for me."

"Yeah. Yes, sir."

The rough fingers plucked at his hard-on, brushing it with glancing pressure from several directions. His wet spot got bigger.

Tucker checked the rearview and scanned the two-way ahead, not even needing to look over at his handful of Patch. "Course, your nuts gonna start to hurt sooner, but I reckon you know what you can take. All this buildup, I'm gonna need a real thick spew outta you. Y'hear?"

"Uh-huh." *Loud and clear and wet as hell.* He hunched against the hard palm, boned for real now at the idea of getting a nut in Tucker's truck while they drove past sleepy homesteads in the dark.

"You know why cowboys are so good in the bedroom?" Tucker steered with one hand, with that easy grin. "We got all damn day to dwell. We spend time thinking about what's comin' and makin' a plan so we can enjoy it while we got it."

Patch nodded, dumb with desire and nailed in place. Even his blood thudded sluggish in his ears while he watched Tucker teasing his sap out.

The calloused hands stroked Patch's smooth skin in long steady strokes, skimming the heat off him till he shivered. "We spend all day talking to things can't talk back, calming 'em down, no matter how skittish. Big animals. Listen with our legs and hands to know what they sayin'. And we wanna come home and bury ourselves in something sweet."

"Tuck—" Patch gripped his wrist then, with both hands, to stop the sweet friction before he dumped it. "You're gonna make me."

With a chuckle. Tucker patted his thigh and returned his paw to the wheel, rugged face smug in the dashboard glow.

A few minutes later, they made the left onto 326 and down the dark road in silence, Tucker muttering smut and kneading Patch's meat with detached affection.

But when they got back to the trailer, they didn't go inside, even though he was so ready. No kneeling, no squirming, no rope.

Tucker fetched beers from his little fridge and brought them out on the deck, his silhouette stark against the upturned bowl of stars as he rolled the bottom of the bottle on the wood rail. "Hey up!" he muttered as he bent over an unweeded planter. "Lookee there." He stood back up holding a perfect white egg, making them smile at each other. "Free range." He put it on the sill.

Again Tucker'd knocked him right off-balance, not doing what seemed likely, in favor of something that seemed… what?

Important.

From inside the house, that crisp bluegrass soprano again singing about a simple love. Patch looked across at Nugget in her the lone stall and the two Shoop trailers full of sleepy hens. "Nngh. Jeez."

"Right?" A ragged smile. "Alison Krauss is pretty much heaven." Tucker tossed him the other beer.

Patch caught it and popped the cap. "I'm gonna have to buy all her stuff."

"I guess you couldn't play her none. At your Circuit doohickey."

Patch shook his head and took a long cool swallow. "T'yeah. No. Not for club dancing. She's amazing, though." Another deep swallow that almost drained his beer.

They sipped and watched as more and more fireflies bobbed and blinked their disco sparkle in the dark leaves.

"Nice." Patch sighed and stretched.

Tucker put his bottle down and walked down the steps onto the edge of the hard-packed, moonlit drive where the dirt had been pounded and scorched into a surface like dusty granite. He turned to say, "C'mere."

Heart thumping, Patch did just that, clambering down into the dappled light at the side of the trailer.

"Pup." Tucker took his beer, stole the last mouthful, and put the empty on the steps. "Okay if I show you something?" His face was shadows and glitter. He took Patch's right hand in his left.

Patch said, "Yes, sir."

"You ever two-step?"

Tongue thick and guts tight, Patch shook his head. He'd avoided all that down-home *kicker* business.

"It's easy." Tucker took him in his arms, nudging his thigh against Patch's hard-on and holding his back with one broad palm. "Hell, cowboys do it drunk. How hard can it be?"

Then everything was the huge sky and the musty rust and sawdust of Tucker holding him close enough for their rods to knock.

"It's gonna go… quick-quick, slow, slow." As he said the words, Tucker just rocked at the same tempo against him, shifting their joined weight right-left with that whisper in his hair: "Quick-quick, slow, slow. Quick-quick, *slow, slow.*" And then their feet were scuffing over the smooth driveway at the same pace. "'At's it. Yeah!" Tucker's hand tightened on his back and his breath caught. "Aww, man. You're born to it. Good deal."

They were moving now in a tight circle, and Patch started to get the sense of it in his legs because the music and Tucker's body told him where to go. Hell, even with his eyes closed he knew what Tucker needed him to do. Tucker's erection rode his gently, but for some reason all he could feel was Tucker's hands and his heartbeat in that close frame of their arms.

Patch blinked in surprise. "Quick-quick, slow, slow," he said it back, and Tucker just breathed against his ear, cradling him close as their little circle expanded.

Tucker nodded against his head. "Good. Now push back a little. Gimme some tension. Between us. Make me chase you and hold on both. Fight me just a little." He grinned. "That's it."

Patch did just that, pressing back into Tucker's spread palm and against his hand, creating a kind of springy tension that let them cover more ground as they danced. One thing with two bodies and their faces at kissing distance. "Oh!" It felt like gliding, or floating or skating over the dry, hard dirt smooth as ice. Their joined strength kept them steady. *Quick-quick, slow, slow.*

They weren't pressed together anymore, but the closed loop of their hands and Tucker's hold on his back kept a charged space between them that felt even more intimate, as if he were dreaming with his body under the lopsided moon while Tucker did the same.

"*Yeahhh.* Good boy. You're two-stepping!" Tucker chuckled. "Lookit you now." And he didn't look at anything else.

Patch nodded. This was what dancing was supposed to be, this shared dreaming spiral together, like smoke from a snuffed candle. He hadn't known until this moment.

He smiled at Tucker in the dark while Alison Krauss took them exactly where they needed to go, together.

Both their dicks stiff and he didn't give a good goddamn. His heart jarred his ribs, chugging so hard he worried Tucker would be able to feel it through that hand cupping his shoulder blade.

Hold your horses.

Even after Alison Krauss stopped singing, the wistful picking spiraled to a lingering close for a minute or more. *God bless her.* Because he didn't want to go in or get off or anything other than this-this-this.

All Patch could wish was that he and Tucker could dance out here hidden in the firefly dark until the stars fell and the moon melted, that the bittersweet guitar and piano wouldn't stop for anything.

But it did, winding to a soft double chord that gave him goose bumps. After, the black silence seemed immense and suffocating around them, except for his cowboy.

His. When had that happened? And had it really?

They weren't fooling around now. Whatever ties he felt had nothing to do with rope and rough hands. Patch opened his eyes again but couldn't see much but the fireflies wavering in the warm air, calling quietly to each other in bright code.

Tucker pulled him close for a warm, slow squeeze. "Thanks." His voice seemed more rumble than sound as he bent closer.

"Course." Patch nodded against his chest. "You too." *Too much, too good, too soon.* He stepped back, wanting the sweet certainty to last, not knowing why he should be so sure. If Tucker did kiss him, he'd… something. *Anything, everything.* "I'm—I guess—" His hands were trembling. "I better get back."

In the darkness, Tucker gave him a funny look, shadowy eyes inscrutable, but didn't say anything. "You say so, son." He gave Patch another friendly squeeze. "You gonna let me drive you home?"

"Thanks. Uhh." Patch wavered like he felt drunker than he did. No kiss, then. "I wanna walk, I think." His feet wanted to run, and his heart was already racing.

"Sure." *Shore*.

The silent breeze shifted his hair, and Tucker smiled till Patch smiled back. *Caught*. The dark glinted and hinted at stuff he shouldn't want and someone he couldn't be anymore. He'd forgotten how beautiful the farm could be, how huge the sky seemed and how still the stars. *Everything in its place.*

"I'll get there safe. Promise." He wasn't safe here, and he knew it.

Tucker didn't fight the idea, but he didn't seem happy. "I had a good time, pup. Real good."

"Me too. Thanks, Tucker." Patch could still feel that springy, dreaming tension between them without touching, even across the drive, as if they were still two-stepping. *Quick-quick, slow, slow.*

Tucker climbed the steps to his deck and gave a funny little bow. He didn't try to kiss Patch or shake his hand or anything. Then again, what was he supposed to do?

Thumbs in his belt, Patch rocked back on his heels and went quick without looking back once like a fool. Hopefully Tucker watched him go. Hopefully he didn't.

Shaking, horny, in a big rush to nowhere, Patch strode through a thousand woozy fireflies across a half mile of fresh-mowed fields to the wrong house, the wrong bed, still dancing those two damn steps in his head with the wrong man.

CHAPTER SIX

NEXT MORNING he swung by the trailer to give Tucker the Texaco papers Ms. Landry had left and found him sipping coffee on the porch.

They nodded good morning at each other as Patch climbed out of the Impala, sharing a sigh as he closed the distance.

"Late start?" Tucker's voice sounded scratchy still.

"I bet you been up for hours."

Tucker shrugged. "Couple. I had good dreams." If he smiled, he'd hidden it with a deep sip from his mug.

"I brought you papers to look over. Geologist still has to come and all. Real offer, might be."

"Good deal." Tucker accepted the creased envelope and patted the porch.

"Thanks, naw. I gotta...." He hooked his thumb back toward the house, his insides fizzy with suppressed pleasure. "I should get my ass to packing. I'm running outta time."

"Want some coffee?" Tucker held up the mug.

"Just a sip." Patch stole a mouthful, unexpectedly sweet and thick as cough syrup. "Jeez."

Tucker chuckled. "I shoulda warned you. I got a helluva sweet tooth." His eyes twinkled.

Patch considered him a moment, a pleasant heat blooming in his belly. "Good to know." He hesitated, perusing Tucker's body.

"No, pup. Go on, now. We both got work to do." He swatted at Patch with the envelope. "Dinner later. Bix coming."

Patch stopped midnod, midflirt.

"On his way to Nacogdoches. He cain't even stay the night, just on up to work some fair. Just barbecue and a piss 'fore he takes off." Whatever their plan, Patch was welcome too, apparently. "But only if you want."

"I'm good." He'd make himself scarce.

Tucker squinted at him strangely. "Why you say that?"

"I'd be a third wheel." Patch knew the tingle of trouble. After last night, Bix was bound to pick up on the vibe and come at him or make a play or worse. *Whatever worse might be*. A whole can of worms, and not his to open. "Y'all go on. I've got to get through the rest of the house today." He nodded toward the mess waiting in his parents' house.

Tucker eyed him for a stiff moment. "You sure? You gotta eat. Place is just up the road."

"Yep. Too hot to be up there during the day anyways. You say hi for me." A night wasted with no time together. Next week he'd head back to New York, and he begrudged losing any time with Tucker, but Bix creeped him all the hell out.

"You say so." Tucker shrugged. "I could bring something back, then. If you want."

"Sure. I'd appreciate it." Maybe they'd still be able to spend the night together.

Still, the sight of Tucker sipping his syrupy coffee alone was a cold gut punch. A warning he decided to ignore.

This fuck down memory lane was too perishable to matter, nothing but kinky nostalgia. In a week or two it'd be academic and he'd be back on top of the world.

Back in the dark, hot house, Patch kept reminding himself that he didn't give a damn. Bix and rodeos and what all had nothing to do with his life in the fast lane. *Velocity*. Messing around with Tucker was anything but serious, and they both knew it.

Care about Tucker Biggs? He had fresher fish to fry.

STILL TOO sapped to do much hauling, Patch spent the afternoon in the sewing room with the big drawer of photos and albums and promptly fell into a family tar pit. Boxes and boxes of their unframed personal photos. With all the big packing done, this flotsam and jetsam was the last task left to empty the house.

To his surprise he discovered that in addition to the framed pictures on the walls, his mother had kept careful photo albums, labeled and dated. Their entire family story stacked by year in neat boxes. *I can't toss these*. He had no room for them in his apartment, but they meant too much to simply dump. He'd have them scanned or something.

A car crunched up the drive outside. He couldn't invite anybody inside with the house all pulled apart, so he zipped out onto the porch to eyeball the burgundy Chrysler parked at a sloppy angle across the drive.

Studying his mother's azalea bed were two elderly ladies, as fussy and feathered as molting birds. One of them he remembered pretty well: Doreen Keister, from the little lending library down in Sour Lake. He could only remember her because she smelled like spearmint and the whole school had made fun of her name. She'd unwittingly turned him onto the Hardy Boys, who he'd lusted after, right up to the day he met the surly cowboy who'd rewritten his rules.

The sound of his boots creaking on the porch and coming down the steps turned their fluffy white heads.

Doreen minced toward him, extending a pink, powdered hand. "Patrick, I just had to come say sorry. How *sorry* we are for your loss." The other woman hung back, bashful and pie-eyed, every inch of her some pastel shade.

"Y'all didn't need to do that, Miss Doreen." Manners by reflex. He even drawled a little to put her at her ease. "But thank you, ma'am."

"This my sister Fay. She didn't know your folks none, but your daddy changed her tire once on a Sunday after services."

The sister favored him with a mournful smile and a knobby handshake that felt like bones wrapped in satin. "We so sorry, Patrick. He's a good man, your daddy."

With tires, at least. "Thank you, ma'am."

The two ladies didn't budge, and he didn't know how to step around them.

"Ladies, I'd ask you in for something, but the kitchen's empty."

Doreen pursed her lips, businesslike. "Don't you bother none. Hear? We come to pick music. You know their hymns? Their favorites, I mean to say." She shifted her stocky body left-right like a wrestler. "For Fay's little organ."

"Organ?"

"At the parlor. The funeral and all. Just to make it nice for your people."

Patch goggled. How did you make a funeral nice?

"See, Fay plays organ up the funeral parlor, and I do the family flowers, so we thought it'd—"

"Uh, no. I dunno, Miss Fay." He closed his mouth because he felt stupid standing there like a guppy, not knowing any hymns to name. "'Bringing in the Sheaves,' maybe. And my ma liked 'Come Away from Rush and Hurry.'"

"That's the one," Fay said as if he'd reminded her instead of plucking titles out of the air. She pinked and wiggled in pleasure at his practiced catalog smile.

"And for your casket spray, I thought delphinium. And mums." Doreen leaned in. "I think roses is tacky this late in the summer."

Funeral fashions. *What the actual fuck?*

Fay sniffed and frowned. "Roses my favorite."

"Roses her favorites," Doreen repeated helpfully and nodded. "But they's expensive and everybody piles up roses for closed casket. If that ain't a fact, God's a possum." She patted his forearm, wise and patient as a bingo card. "You look, you'll see. All that money gone down a hole."

"That is not so," said Fay. "I cain't believe you'd say that, working with flowers."

Patch nodded and schooled his face into a reasonable expression as best he could. Were these two actually squabbling over the decor? "I guess. I never thought about it."

What was the point of flowers either way? Better if folks donated money, but then again, what charity? Not like his folks had died of something curable. Train safety? Anger management? LGBT runaway assistance? Maybe flowers just gave everyone sympathetic an easy out. *Jesus.* He didn't know how to put the brakes on.

The sisters looked ready to duke it out in the front yard… with ugly oaths and pinking shears at dawn, so he stepped in with his softest smile.

"Whatever y'all think is best sounds good by me. You know what my folks would want." Which they didn't, but the Keister sisters could squawk over the details back at the funeral parlor. "I haven't been sleeping much… since." *True.* And the weariness in his look wasn't for effect.

Doreen patted his hand again and ladled warm affection over him like she'd never spread gossip about him. "Terrible thing." *Turble.* "They's so prouda you up there. Big city an' all."

"Uh-huh." Patch nodded at the polite lie.

Fay raised her eyebrows. "New *York* City." Full of awed meaning. "Makes me giddy to think on. Giddy."

He wrung his hands so they'd know to go.

"Well." Doreen took the hint and glanced back at her old Chrysler. "You a busy man, and here we stand raising sand and depressing all the spirit outta you."

Patch gave them both his smile again, hoping his impatience didn't show. "Not at all, ma'am. But I'd best get back to work in there. Thank y'all again."

"You are so very welcome. And thank you, young man," Fay said and gave him a slow, humble blink like he'd done them some gigantic favor by coming to the porch and *yes-ma'am*ing them.

"We don't wan' keep you, none." Doreen held up her hand, a little salute as she backed toward the Chrysler. "You need anything t'all, you just holler. You's always such a nice young fella."

Patch waved as they pulled out and swore if anyone else turned up uninvited, he'd hide in the attic. Heading back inside, he lugged all four boxes of photos out to the living room and spent the next nine hours digging through a family history he didn't remember.

Pictures of some long-ago barbecue at a fairground. Tucker and his pa laughing with a bunch of other guys with Brylcreemed hair and stiff jeans. Arms laced lazily over each other's shoulders, retro facial hair and a distinct underwear shortage if the crotches told the truth. Maybe they'd been off fucking each other in the trees ten minutes later. Horniness and dread at that thought.

He didn't want to toss everything, so the easiest thing was to just box it all and stick it in storage until he had enough space and time in New York to go through them. An envelope of yellowing pictures without any names. Who were they? Who could he ask?

Hell, weren't many folks left who could give him any answers worth having.

A sudden sick certainty took hold that for the rest of his life a bunch of strangers from these family albums would always be just that. He'd never know anything again. *All future, no past.*

Used to be, when he didn't recognize a relative or know history, his mama filled in who was who and why. She'd kept all their memories, and now she was dead and he was alone. A sharp pang of missing her, wishing he could apologize-explain-forgive.

Now the only person remembered his family was *him*, and he'd spent a third of his life making sure he forgot. *Well, not exactly.* He had one other reliable source.

Tucker.

The only person who could identify the faces in this picture was a hot loser who'd jerked him off in the mud. But about Patch's grandparents and aunts, actual ancestors who'd died back before he could've known them? No chance. Tucker wouldn't know shit about the Hastles or Grogans. Even with these rodeo folks, Tucker was hardly neutral at this point.

He shook his head, but the thought wouldn't go. What did Tucker want anyway?

Sure enough, Tucker popped up in a couple photos, rude and handsome. But Patch found himself looking at his parents instead. Had they been happy living out here at the ass end of nowhere? The photos said yes. If they'd been miserable, all the smiling made no sense. Even Patch looked more healthy and normal that he'd ever felt.

Even this proof was bullshit. He thought of an old joke about a cheating husband caught by his wife. *"Who are you gonna believe, me or your lying eyes?"* In the albums, their family had been happy, but maybe that was a pleasant fiction Mama had glued together out of paper and Polaroids.

Only, Hixville wasn't like he remembered, so maybe he and his folks weren't either. *I'm so sorry.*

He caught himself crying before he felt the tears come. Wiping his dusty face only smeared the dust and cobwebs. *Dumb.* The harsh edge of missing his parents sliced through him, so cold and slow he gasped out loud.

Tears now were like tossing coins in a ditch. No matter how much he hurt, he'd never see them again, never touch them or laugh or fight with them. They'd never understood him, that he knew of. At least... he'd never understood them and that amounted to the same thing.

Sixteen was way younger than he'd remembered.

He didn't hate anything or anyone. And anyways, hate was the wrong word for something he'd felt at sixteen years old. He'd only *lost* them, and come back too late to find them again.

"You okay?" The low voice scared the ever-loving fuck out of him.

"Jesus crap!" Patch's heart raced. "Tucker."

"Sorry, pup. I knocked, but weren't no answer." He held up a brown paper bag. "Brung you dinner."

Patch nodded. His heart slammed around inside him like a trapped bird. He rubbed his wet face, probably smearing it worse.

Tucker looked sad. "Your folks was good people. And they loved you."

Even knowing it was a lie, Patch nodded, crying again. *Why?*

"No way they coulda understood all them things you was gonna do. Out there." He raised his chin, as if to encompass the entire world beyond the Hardin County line. "But they were so proud." The gravelly croon of his voice pinned Patch in one spot. "Of you."

"I don't remember."

Tucker put the bag down on the table and came closer. "Course not. Kids is supposed to run."

"I guess." Maybe Tucker's memory was as much of a lie as the albums, as all the photos he didn't remember smiling for.

"Well, I know."

Patch wrapped his arms around himself. "I didn't realize how dark it had got."

"We should put the lights on, but we can't." Tucker took another step. "You come on back to mine." His eyes shone.

Patch swallowed, pretending to think, but his whole body wanted to do nothing else but crawl into Tucker's bed and forget the world. He nodded.

And just like that Tucker was holding him, pulling him into the circle of those hard arms, against the smell of sawdust and greasy metal. "It's a lot."

"Yeah." Patch's face fit right into the hollow of his throat. An inch at a time, he relaxed, surrendering his weight and his tension to Tucker. Giving in and standing still.

"Good." Tucker just held him firm and fast. "They missed you, pup. Every day."

Patch squeezed his eyes shut, but the regret leaked out anyway.

"C'mon." Tucker turned and tugged him toward the door, looping one arm over his neck, not like a lover but a teammate headed off the field after a crappy game. "You c'mon over now, and I'll fix you some supper, put you to bed." He picked up the bag of food, and then they were outside ambling through the dark.

Without streetlamps, the warm night churned around their gritty tread. The fields ticked with crickets and the sky loomed overhead, vast and cast with stars. *God's disco.* Patch remembered his terrible sophomore year hitching rides into Beaumont that coulda got him killed, then sneaking back in with the toad-house key or crawling through his window in the back of the house. He could see he'd been lucky.

At the trailer, Botchy dozed on the porch. Her blocky head didn't stir until they climbed the steps past her. She nosed his ankles and huffed in assent.

"Some guard dog." Patch said.

Stepping inside the trailer felt like going below deck on a ship, with the creaky give of the floor and the low ceiling.

Tucker turned on the TV and went back to the kitchenette with the bag. "Two shakes."

Patch stood in Tucker's tidy living area while Animal Planet told him about the aerodynamics of cheetahs. The couch and hand-me-down armchair looked more worn up close, and his face felt grimy and stiff.

Somehow Tucker knew to leave him be. When had the man stopped being an asshole?

Patch ducked into the bathroom and splashed his face with water, then dried it on a towel that smelled like Tucker. He smiled and then immediately fought the smile back into a corner. "That's enough of that," he muttered.

The smell of barbecue pulled him back down the hall.

Tucker wiped his hands on a dishrag and put a plate on the table. Ribs and brisket and potato salad.

Patch sat. "Wow." The saliva factor was real.

"Ain't nothing ails a man that meat can't fix."

Patch dug in and groaned at the flavor. "God that's good." By the time he'd cleaned his plate, he'd swallowed the strange bubble of sadness that had welled up earlier. "Thank you for making me eat." He cupped his junk and pushed back in the chair.

Tucker chuckled. "Bix knows a buncha guys who barbecue on the Circuit. These folks is up at Honey Island. Mostly ribs, but I think brisket travels better."

Patch nodded. "He good?"

"Bixby? He's fine." He eyed Patch a moment. "He's headed up to Arkansas next week. Why?"

Shrug. "Curious. He's your friend." His jealousy didn't need voicing, now or ever. He drifted into the living room.

"I ain't got many friends, Patch, and most of 'em I had a long time." Tucker eyed him for a moment. If he sensed the simmering envy, he didn't react. "I only see him when he's out this way for a rodeo."

"Oh. I figured he was local." In rural Texas, local could mean anywhere in a hundred-mile radius.

"He's got a place down in Clute, but mostly he's always running around." Tucker shrugged.

Nosy as hell, Patch pushed open the door to Tucker's bedroom, which was practically filled with an antique brass bed made up with a homemade quilt.

"Only thing of my family's I managed to save." Tucker had his hand over his belly, still seated. His eyes were lost in unreadable shadow.

"'S beautiful." It was. The whole trailer felt real around it. Solid.

Patch blinked. Just then, he saw several Tuckers sitting across from him in one chair. His father's drunken sidekick. The bigoted coach from high school. The hot rodeo loser with nowhere to go. The daddy fantasy he'd made up in his head. The weather-beaten caretaker sitting in front of him shooting the breeze. And the man, the man, the man.

"What's all that about?" Tucker raised his eyebrows and stuck his square chin out.

"All what?" Patch stood and stretched.

"I can see you." Tucker squinted at him. "Running your skull. Scurrying and worrying." Sip of beer and a chuckle. "Going eight ways at once like you do." He gave Patch what seemed like an affectionate grin.

Rather than give an honest answer, Patch developed a sudden interest in the snapshots and junk scattered around the trailer's living area: a lot of goofing off at rodeos, Tucker with laughing strangers. The only folks who turned up more than once were Bix and Patch's dad. *Buddies.* A few faded pictures of him as a young man, so handsome he looked like a trick. None of Tucker as a boy, and no family that that Patch could see.

"They's a bunch of Royce younger. I can make copies if you want." Tucker spoke from over his shoulder. "Your dad was something else back then."

What else? He nodded, but said, "Nah. That's okay. I just haven't seen these."

"We whored around like anything. Young and foolish." Tucker raised a can of beer in a toast and took a sip. "That is to say: young."

Patch couldn't remember his dad ever looking this relaxed. "Y'all didn't...." *Fool around. Blow each other. Fuck.* Tricky turf.

Tucker's eyebrows almost hit his hairline. "Lord, no!" Head shake. "Your dad flirted with the girls, but he never— He weren't that way."

Patch nodded. "Hadta ask."

Tucker frowned. "All this is wrong. Jesus." His lips scrubbed his teeth. "In answer to your question, no. Royce and I didn't do nothing. Hell, you think I'd...?"

Of course he did. And Tucker knew he did, and that's why he'd asked. They eyed each other uncomfortably.

Tucker cleared his throat and put his thumbs in his waistband. "Well, no. He was a stiff sumbuck. And back then I didn't.... Well, I wasn't as easygoing about that neither. Fellas and all."

Patch lobbed it out there on the table. "But you and Bix screw around." Steady gaze.

"Ah." Tucker sighed. "Well, that ain't your business, pup. But yeah, we mess around some." A dark blush rose under his weathered skin.

"Sorry." Patch leaned forward. What he'd give to be a fly on that pair of jeans. "'S fucking hot."

Tucker looked up. "Why?"

Patch grinned. "You're both fucking sexy, is all. That is something I'd love to see." But half of that was a lie because he didn't want to see Tucker touching anyone else.

"Oh." Tucker's mouth shifted down and his brow furrowed. He nodded. "Okay, then. If you like Bix, I'm pretty sure he'd volunteer for duty."

"Uh, no. Nossir." Patch frowned. He didn't even a little. But Tucker jealous, he liked fine. "On second thought, maybe not."

"Howzat?"

"You and Bix." He cleared his throat and spoke up. "Makes no sense to me. At all. Is all."

Tucker tipped his head and crossed his arms. "That so?"

"Better just us. Easier."

"Patch, ain't nothing easy 'bout us." A rasp of skin as Tucker wiped his stubbled mouth with one wide hand. "I hope that ain't a problem for you."

Patch didn't laugh and their eyes caught. The charge built in his belly and the mound at his fly thickened. His face flushed, and his mouth fell open.

Tucker stepped back and turned his face to the side. "What're you doing?" His raised his hands to hold Patch's ribs gently. The pulse ticked in his throat.

"Asking nicely?" He hadn't felt safe before, and now he didn't feel safe anywhere else.

Tucker turned back to him. "Pup, I don't know if—"

To shut him up and shut down his brain, Patch cupped his balls and pressed his bone into Tucker's leg.

Tucker scanned him. "Lord."

He took a step closer.

"Patch."

Another step, right into Tucker's body heat and the rusted musk of him. "Mmmmh." He leaned in, planning to push his face against Tucker's for some quality beard burn.

"How d'you mess me up so quick?" Tucker breathed deeply and his fingers tightened on Patch's ribs. "I can't."

Patch hefted the soft weight of Tucker's balls. "No?" The stiffness bent above them proved him a liar. "Feel's like you're gonna anyhow."

Tucker winced, stuck his hand inside his jeans, and rocked his hips back to readjust so that the stiff bulge stretched behind his fly. "Fucker." He didn't sound too angry.

"Just messing around, Coach."

Tucker scowled. "Hey."

"C'mon." Patch didn't back down, just spoke right at him, close enough that he could smell the beer on his own breath bouncing back. "We're buddies, right? I'm fixin' to bust." He knocked their cocks together lightly, then slid side to side, bumping them across each other.

"Don't call me that. I'm not your coach."

Anymore. Patch rocked his hips forward, humping their rigid flesh together. *My cowboy.*

"Or anything else."

"Nossir."

Eyes half-lidded now, Tucker gave a husky wheeze of laughter. "You're crazy." He licked his lips. "I don't know what. *Hsss.* Easy." Tucker grunted and ground his blunt pole forward.

"What?" He kept at the slow, gentle hunching. He could feel the urgency in his nuts, how easily he could bust just dry humping Tucker hard enough with their eyes locked. "I could go like this. Right here. You?"

A nod. "Yeah."

Patch knocked his hips side to side again, scraping their baskets across and back with slow sullen electricity. "What do you want, huh?"

"Don't know." Tucker's massive hay-bucker's hands on his ribs pushed around into a near embrace, pulling them tightly together. "Don't much matter."

"Then...." Patch didn't look away, paralyzed by the possibilities. He wanted the full ride. "Tie me up."

Tucker raised his head, his dark eyes inscrutable.

"I mean it." *Like you want.*

Tucker's next words came out scratchy. "What do you mean?"

"At the pond, you took over like you wanted. Handled me." A glance up. Taking charge, negotiating his own surrender, gave him a freaky sizzle of pleasure. "Am I wrong?"

Tucker shook his head. He looked stunned.

"I'm asking nice as I know how." Patch stilled and stared at him. "If you don't, I'm about to make a sticky fucking mess all over both of us any second." He ground his rigid cock against the muscular thigh. "Which seems like a damn waste."

Tucker stood still and let him. "Are you asking for real?"

The tension humming in Tucker's thick muscles made Patch brave.

"I want that, like that." *Shameless.* "Tie me down and make me shoot. Take me apart, man." He was stiff as an axe handle.

Tucker seemed to weigh the notion, jaw clamped and stiff hands gripping him.

Patch raised his fingers to unbutton his shirt. "Right?"

Tucker swatted his hand away, then cupped it gently. "You'd best let me do that." He smoothed the front of the shirt with his palms. "Hear?"

"Yessir."

THE FIRST thing Patch learned was that brass beds were sturdy for a reason.

While Tucker went to get something down the hall, Patch went up and sat on the side of that antique bed. It almost filled the trailer's master bedroom, and the sheets were ironed, crisp and white. With the little lamp on, the room was a dim cave, and the brass swirls and loops threw the amber light back in slices.

Patch fought the urge to fidget or snoop, trying to anticipate and stave off the heart attack that seemed likely.

Anxious after only a couple minutes, he started to toe off his boots.

"Hold on." Tucker stood at the door, bare chested and barefoot, in a loose pair of work jeans buttoned just high enough to hang on his hips. He held a skein of rope in his right hand and his low voice sounded stern. "Where you going?"

"Nowhere." Patch sat back, chest thumping.

"I wanna do it." Tucker tossed the rope on the mattress and knelt to tug Patch's boots loose and set them against the wall. He rose up close and unbuttoned Patch's sweaty jeans with firm, slow fingers: one button, two, three, four. He ran his big hands down Patch's legs and tugged at the hem, shucking the denim free and exposing the red briefs beneath without acknowledging the hard-on under them.

"Tucker."

At his name, Tucker looked up. "No. You stay put now." He stood between Patch's legs and skinned the damp T-shirt off. "Hold up."

Hair tumbled in front of Patch's face until those coarse hands smoothed it back.

"You look real nice like that." Tucker shifted the obscene bulge tenting his jeans but left Patch's in his briefs with the cotton-covered ridge straining between them.

Touch me. But Tucker didn't, until Patch reached for himself.

"Slow down, sport." Tucker held his wrist and pushed his hand to the sheet. "Scoot back."

He crabwalked back, and Tucker knelt on the mattress and crawled forward in lazy pursuit.

Without warning, Patch's back pressed against the freezing brass. "Hss-hfff." His nipples and skin stiffened, and he shivered.

"Cold."

Patch nodded.

"A/C blows on it all damn day." Reaching toward the bottom of the mattress, Tucker snagged the skein of rope and plucked at the knot holding it together. "You'll warm it up quick."

Sure enough, as Patch relaxed against the metal, it ate his heat and braced his muscles.

"So, I'm fixing to tie some knots." Tucker sat back on his heels and regarded Patch. "Won't hurt none." He unspooled a few loops of the rope. "But you won't be able to move much." He slid the rope through his coarse hands. "Or at all."

Panicked heat surged through Patch's abdomen. His heart stuttered and heat washed up his torso into his face.

"At least the idea don't turn you off none." Tucker looked down at Patch's crotch and laced the pale rope between his tanned hands. "You ever been roped up?"

"Naw. No." The headboard didn't feel cold anymore, and his dick was doing something freaky down below. His balls shifted involuntarily. "Claustrophobic."

"I get that." Tucker nodded and smiled at the trailer bedroom around them. "Big open room, big ol' bed. I'm not gonna smother you."

Patch blinked some kind of assent. He stretched his arms out and rested them against the brass.

"But you're gonna stay still a bit. Right here in my bed. Can you do that for me?" Tucker's soft dark eyes stayed steady on his. "Stay with me a while?"

"I think so."

Tucker blinked. "We'll see."

He shifted forward but Tucker's hand held him in place.

"See now? That's what I mean. Rushing around."

Patch shook his head, swallowed, and then nodded.

Tucker's rough knuckles scraped down his chest. "Let me take care of you." A stiff ridge showed to the left of his button fly.

His fingers tightened on the brass. Talking about it made him more anxious. "Okay."

"I ain't making you, Patch. I'm asking."

"Yeah. Naw." Why had he said that? He was always in control of himself. "I want you to." He did. Seeing Tucker so turned on made him feel oddly calm.

"Sure?"

"Yessir. I promise." If anyone in New York saw him like this, they'd laugh.

"Just a few simple ties. Nothing hard or scary. I just want to do this proper."

Patch gave a snuffed exhale of laughter at the idea of being *properly* stiff, stripped, and strapped to Tucker's old brass bed somewhere in East Texas. He flexed his hips and his boner between them. "Yessir."

The *sir* slipped out again, but saying it tightened the knot in his balls.

Tucker grinned. "I like that." He slapped Patch's hard-on. "You like it too."

He moaned. He felt exposed, frozen, weightless, and empty. His body rendered in blown glass, his fear nothing but glitter between them. His mouth fell open.

"You look so handsome like that." Tucker whistled between his teeth. "Like I got no right to see something so handsome."

And somehow he held himself together in the terrible stillness until Tucker touched him again.

The second thing Patch learned was that in the right hands rope didn't hurt one bit. Actually, felt kinda good when you gave in to 'em.

Tucker knelt between his open legs, breathing deeply and grunting with satisfaction as he laced and wrapped and knotted the new nylon rope. "I got a couple buddies get fancy with knots, Japanese tricks an' all, but I'm a country boy."

At first Patch tried to focus on the firm grip of his fingers, the rust and sawdust warmth of his smell, the obvious erection a foot away. He battled the urge to run, to struggle, to push back.

Tucker worked methodically, with maddening patience, the nylon rope heating Patch's skin in dull lines. A loop here, a clove hitch there, the rope snaked around Patch's spread arms until he realized he actually couldn't move at all. His wrists were secured to the headboard with a loop. And another set of loops immobilized his elbows and crossed under his armpits to pin him in place.

He swallowed. Sweat snaked down the right side of his face, and he struggled to control his breathing. *Calm down.* Even in the cool room, the heat was terrific and the urge for panicked flight implacable.

Tucker wrapped another rope around his chest, four strands laid snugly against each other to make a wide strap across his pecs, then another at his waist.

I sure must look stupid right now. Patch's heart began to trot and another droplet of sweat traced his cheek and dripped from his chin. How could he be freezing and sweating at the same time? Light-headed, he closed his eyes hard. Within minutes, soft cord bound his chest, waist, and shoulders to the headboard. The loose loops on his wrists had widened by several coils. Several stacked strands just under his pecs held his muscles in high relief. There would be marks.

Tucker muttered and stroked the ropes and his skin, smoothing and patting and testing. "Easy now." He might have been talking to Nugget and tugging her reins. "Easy there, pup."

He bent his knees on either side of Tucker's body.

Tucker held up another loop of rope, flipping it into a half hitch. He dragged it down Patch's left leg to his foot. "Just so you don't kick around none." He used the rope to stroke the sole of Patch's foot lightly, just this side of tickling. "Look at that."

Patch refused to react or flinch, but he couldn't stop the goose bumps. His pulse throbbed under his skin, and he wriggled in place. He could do this. A chill wave surged over him.

"You're okay," Tucker muttered.

He'd secured Patch to the brass headboard from wrist to ribs. The metal at his back felt oddly comfortable, and the only things he could move properly were his head and his legs.

Except when Tucker reached under his knees and bent them all the way, pushing them toward his chest.

"Wait."

"Nope." And then Tucker pushed his face right into the seat of his briefs, and Patch froze at the impossible electric sensation.

Tucker bit the muscle and licked at the seams of his underwear. His fingers were there too, testing the hole through the cotton and skimming the elastic edges.

The hair on Patch's legs rose, and gooseflesh crawled down his arms. With him immobilized, Tucker might do anything. "I never—" His heart began a rolling canter.

Tucker didn't answer with words, but his spit started to soak through. The scratch of his stubble scraped Patch's skin. He tugged the elastic to one side, trying to get inside them. He grunted and growled down there while Patch tried to keep his legs bent and still.

"Umm." Tucker dragged his sandpaper cheek across Patch's thigh and looked up.

"You feel that? Made for eatin'."

He did. Tucker's thumb pressed at the little knot under the briefs in a way that paralyzed him, that made him want to agree to anything, everything. Patch inhaled sharply, legs shaking, but didn't answer.

"You ain't had nobody taking care of you. Crazy shame." Tucker ducked back down and licked his crack in low slow swipes that soaked the seat of his briefs. Then the thick fingers, yanking again, pulling and biting the briefs until Patch heard the tear.

Tucker didn't hesitate. Feeling for the breach, he ripped the seat of the briefs open over Patch's crack and laved it with his tongue. A moan that teased his taint with its hot exhale. Pushing deeper with his face, he tore the interfering cotton back and away until all Patch could feel was stubble against the soft flesh.

Patch yelped and pleaded. "Tucker! Jeez-us." His legs flopped but Tucker growled and pushed them back, folding him against the headboard in a way that hurt good.

Tucker took his time. Long, slow licks, tasting the skin and testing the hole. "Feel that," he muttered. "I need to— You feel how good it is?"

Gradually Tucker pulled the briefs all to pieces, growling and tearing while he worshiped the muscle with his mouth. The cotton shreds kept getting in his way until he finally ripped them free and rolled his face against Patch's thigh and sighed raggedly. "That's better."

Patch tried to breathe. No one had ever done that to him. He'd never let anyone close enough to pin him down, which made him feel crazy and brave at the same time. A shudder passed over him.

"What's the matter?" Tucker sat back slowly.

Patch shook his head. Vulnerable. Freaked out. Excited. Embarrassed. "Fuck, Tucker. Nothing's wrong." He giggled and pushed his cock forward best he could. "You're making me... I dunno what."

The big hand stroked his crack. "Ain't nobody ever ate your butt proper?"

Besides you? Patch swallowed, embarrassed, and shook his head. Apparently, whatever he'd been having wasn't sex.

"Well, then, that's another fuckin' shame, pup." Tucker frowned, a twinkle in his eyes. "Them city boys don't even know what they missing."

"I never let 'em." Patch tried not to think about how exposed he was, how trapped.

"Good." Breathing audibly, Tucker bent his knee and tied the ankle to the thigh with three or four loops. He strung the rope in a tight bowline up to the bed's brass headboard. "That's real nice." A slow tug lifted Patch's bent leg off the mattress. That leg wasn't going anywhere soon.

Patch breathed raggedly. Having only one limb loose felt alien and dangerous. His erection faltered and the sweat sprang out all over his flesh. Even with one leg bound, cool air told him how exposed his butt was. He straightened the other leg and flexed it hard.

Tucker grunted and a wry smile tightened his lips. He was sweating too.

Patch stared straight ahead, trying to steady his breath. He didn't want Tucker to know how much—

"Ain't nothing gonna happen you don't want, huh?" Tucker leaned in till their faces were *this* close. "I gotcha." He repeated the process: knee bent, ankle to thigh, roped and raised on the brass headboard.

Spread open.

Patch swallowed and squirmed against the brass at his back and the sheets beneath him. A tickle of perspiration down his ribs. His armpits felt exposed, and his belly and his butthole. His dumb dick trapped against his abdomen only made him feel powerless and panicky. Obviously he wanted it, which only made it worse.

"Look at me. Look here." Smile. "Don't fret. We just having some fun, is all."

Patch nodded, freaked and obedient. "I'm okay."

Tucker smiled at that, like he doubted it. "Okay, then." His huge hands clenched and released as if impatient to make a mess of Patch. "Good so far?"

"Promise." His pulse jerked in his throat and under the knots on his chest. It felt strange to be so close, so naked, and so powerless. Sweat slid between his back and the brass.

"Now anything you don't like, you say."

He blinked, self-conscious. "Same."

Tucker grinned and sighed, sitting back on his heels to regard his work. "There ain't nothing I don't like right now."

Calm down. Patch focused on the trail of dark fuzz leading into Tucker's fly. He tasted his own lip, wanting Tucker to stand on the bed in front of him and make him take that thing all the way to the root, choke him with the pitiless width of it. He worked his jaw open and shut.

Tucker chuckled. "That so?"

"You're distracting." He swallowed saliva.

Snort. "Pup, I'm too beat-up to go climbing around."

"Bullshit. All you gotta do is stand, old man. Put it where it goes."

"I ain't all that decrepit, smartass." Grin. "I'm patient, is all."

"Not me." Patch chuckled, embarrassed by his own relief. He needed to take a second to get his heart under control.

"And none of them city fellas ever tied you down. That's just all kindsa crazy."

Blink. "No." He'd never have let them if they'd tried, but Tucker was... something else. "Sir."

"Hmmph." Tucker smile-frowned and bent close, closer. His thumb traced Patch's lip. "Too fast to catch you." He squinted unblinking into Patch's eyes till the quiet became uncomfortable. "Now... last trick."

He's gonna kiss me. But he didn't, which weirded Patch out even more.

Instead, Tucker took hold of Patch's thickened, spongy cock. "I want to cover up your eyes."

Patch swallowed and nodded.

"Blindfold you. Help calm you down." A hand stroked his thigh. "You good with that?"

He wanted to watch, but watching also left him panicked and queasy. "I think so. I guess." His mind raced. *What next?*

Tucker held up a twisted bandana. "Let's see, then say. And if you ain't okay, you say."

He nodded again. The snug, damp press of the rope kept him squirming at the edge of struggle. Dark might help. He couldn't move and didn't want to think about it, so he focused on Tucker.

Tucker palmed his balls a second then rocked forward slowly. He pressed the blindfold against Patch's eyes and reached back to tie it behind his head.

Dark.

As Tucker's fingers worked back there, the bulge in his jeans bumped Patch's chest. The dull musk of his scent rose sharply, so familiar and strange that Patch forgot to feel afraid or frustrated. "That's it. That's all it is."

Being held in place against the headboard, trapped and blind in Tucker's bed, made him feel… what, exactly? Safe? Crazy? Horny? Happy? Hopeful? He was panting like a sprinter, and he couldn't move an inch. Well, not most of his inches. Several inches were doing plenty of moving, but he had no control over that reflex. His own breath sounded loud in his ears. His slick skin hummed under the ropes. But feeling Tucker's meat pressed against his heart paralyzed him.

You don't scare me anymore. Feeling his fantasy all horned up had loosened some terrible knot inside him.

The third thing Patch learned was that when applied with imagination, stuff that feels good can eventually make you scream.

Tucker shifted. Sound of a squirt bottle. When he shifted back, his hands had gotten greasier. "Adding some gravy to the meat."

Patch pressed back into the headboard. The goo on Tucker's hands was as warm and viscous as fresh semen. "Unff. Fuck."

"Good, huh?" His hand around Patch's pole traveled slowly from tip to root. "Best lube."

No lie. The uncanny slickness eased the friction so much that Patch had to fuck his hand harder to get the rub he needed.

Tucker slid the hand up and down in an unhurried glide. "Stays slippery for hours. All night, if y'need."

"Great."

Tucker gave a low exhale of laughter. "Yeah. You'll learn to appreciate that feature." His confident grip didn't vary or tighten.

Patch tightened his arms against the knots, then let go again. He had never been one to waste time jerking off. He copped it, popped it, and mopped up.

Tucker obviously had different ideas about where his time was best spent. He took hold of Patch's meat and tugged it with a steady, loose rhythm. The contact felt casual and impersonal, as if Tucker was testing a piece of equipment or checking livestock.

He's milking me.

Worst of all, the maddening slow tug, the lazy slip of the rough grip never sped up or varied. *Bastard.* He worked methodically, testing for reactions and teasing Patch's pleasure out of him. Tucker took his goddamned time throughout.

Blind and frustrated, Patch shook his head. "Tucker, I can't—"

"Did I ask you to, pup?" The older man cleared his throat. "Just take what I'm givin'."

"'Kay." He trembled then, unable to participate or resist. The blindfold focused his attention at the edges of his body, charging his skin and other senses.

He felt Tucker rock back on the bed, then a damp hand on his upper thigh.

"Hold your horses now. You ain't going nowhere."

Patch smiled at the boyish satisfaction in his voice.

"Mmph. Look at you." Squirming and grunting on the bed as Tucker shifted. Breath brushed his balls. Tucker was stretched out between his splayed thighs. One rough paw stroked his flank. "I swear."

The happy glow of vanity wormed through him. Praise did this to him. And he knew Tucker liked looking at him.

"Stay right here with me. You feel that? Pay attention where it's at." Gradually his hand slowed, stilled, stopped... then nothing.

"*Grwaah.* C'mon!" He licked his dry lips, wishing he could see and grateful he couldn't. "Please, Tucker."

"Please what?"

"You know." He ducked his head toward his straining flesh.

"I do know. Make it last long as we can. All we got is time. Let me get it right. Let me." Tucker squirmed closer, his breath brushing Patch's balls.

Patch arched and panted, swatting his panic down and forcing his body to relax, release, respond.

The slow stroke resumed. "Yeah. *Yeaaah*. Good boy. See? Fuck!"

The praise lit him up inside, a bright cinder he could nurse into flame if he was careful and patient. Except he'd never been either. *Just pretend.*

Tucker began a piercing punishing polish that made him go out of his skull with frustration. Nothing was supposed to feel this good. Getting away with it meant they'd get caught eventually, right?

Tucker's rough jaw grazed his thigh and the tender inside of his cheeks. He fought the burning tickle until even that seemed pointless as Tucker slowly, deliberately fried his nerve endings one touch at a time.

"*Please,* Tucker. You got no idea. Even a little more."

Tucker grunted but didn't budge. Apparently he *knew* that Patch needed him to go faster and didn't give a good goddamn. *Asshole.*

Patch swallowed and wheezed, squirming against the brass and ropes with mounting frustration. His legs tightened and released at the same horrible tempo. His hoarse breath matched it until his heart did, as well, and all his other muscles. His toes clenched and spread, his butt tensed and gave against the damp sheets, his arms pulled at the ropes and brass, his jaw trembled and clenched. His entire body ran with sweat in the cold air. He couldn't speed anything up or slow any of it down.

Still Tucker coaxed the jam out of him with brutal patience, using the endless slip of that home-brewed lube to test every inch.

Relief just out of reach.

A madness rose up in Patch, a wild, angry impatience he couldn't control or measure. At first he tugged at his wrists, arching his back away from the brass headboard. He squirmed and curled his hips off the bed, driving his spike into empty space, exposing his crack more and not caring. He tried to twist, to buck, to make contact with anything, but the rope and the brass held him immobile.

Somewhere to his right Tucker sighed. "You sure look nice fighting the air like that." A slippery hand squeezed his leg.

Patch stilled instantly, his whole being focused on that hand: the hard palm, the thick fingers, the slow build of heat the longer their skin met. Mesmerized, he whimpered and in the same moment forgot why he shouldn't show weakness.

Another hand on his other thigh, then both sliding up but stopping just shy of nudging his balls with the knuckles.

Please. Patch flinched and froze again, afraid to break the spell. If he hid his reactions, Tucker might give him enough friction by accident.

Tucker kneaded the muscle hard enough to make him flinch; the lube let his muscles slither past the hard hands with electrifying relief.

Patch yelped. Something tickled the underside of his cock. *Precum again.* A thin slick of juice snuck down the underside of the shaft toward his balls. He'd never leaked like this in his life, not with anyone, and certainly not by himself. "Jesus." Or was that the freaky lube?

"Good boy." Tucker sounded hoarse now. "That's what we get for taking our time. See?" He shifted closer and lower on the bed between Patch's legs. "Look at that. Look at that good stuff you're making." His breath brushed Patch's fevered flesh, and something in his voice made Patch pause.

He doesn't want me to see him all turned on. Even now Tucker was hiding, eight inches from his crotch and breathing hard.

Still, seductive to have all that attention to himself from someone who'd never noticed him, never given him any indication. All those fantasies, anxious spying, quarts of semen spilled in the dark over a fantasy he never should have wanted.

Tucker's breath stirred the fine hairs on his inner thigh, brushed his balls, and cooled the stripe of precum that hadn't stopped running from him.

Or he wants me too much to let me see him wanting me.

Tucker shifted on the bed, and something brushed across Patch's shins. More rope? How much more bound could he be?

A drop of sweat trickled from his hairline toward his eyebrow. Without thinking he tried to raise a hand to wipe it, and reminded himself of exactly how immobilized he was. He fell still.

Rough fingers stroked his shoulders, tugged at his nipples, and grazed his ribs just this side of tickling.

Patch froze. The impulse to bolt, to fight, to flee ballooned within him. Crazy. *What the hell have I done?*

Tucker moving again, but he couldn't be sure how. Sound from the nightstand, and a skim of skin as the big body stretched past him, reaching, then returned.

His blindness was a reddish black and hot as balls. He tested the rope against the brass. He clamped his toes tight, and the knots at his ankles gave nothing.

"Hold up, there." A hand on his belly and what felt like a kiss on the cheek. "I got plans for you. You just stay put, hear?"

Patch nodded. He could move his head, at least, but the rest of him belonged to Tucker. He panted and twitched as panic chased down his limbs, a trembling agitation that knotted his stomach. His toes flexed and his quads. He swallowed, but his mouth was dry.

His cock rose like granite between his legs. It knew what he wanted even if he didn't.

No shame in that.

"Good boy." Drawling pleasure from Tucker. "I wish you could see." A chuckle. "But I dunno, maybe not." His warm, hard palm brushed the belly of Patch's erection, once, twice.

Patch shivered.

"Look at that." Tucker's fingers closed around him and squeezed without letting go. "Jesus Christmas." He stroked it lightly, pressing his thumb into the ooze at the crown and smearing it.

At that, Patch bucked and hissed, dizzy with strain. His arms fought the rope and his heels flexed. Every part of him wanted to protect his flesh, to cover his crotch, to wriggle free and run.

Just like that, Tucker let go of him.

"Naw. I don't think so." Tucker shucked the skin all the way back, exposing the crown again and squeezing the base roughly. "We got work to do, you and me." His other hand tapped Patch's balls and scrubbed back over the hard taint.

Then Tucker started to play with him in earnest, and Patch realized just how far he'd never gone before.

"Yuhh." Patch pressed back against the headboard. His pulse hammered in his throat, and his sweaty back slid against the brass. "God almighty! Oh, that. That's the—*Yes* sir."

He couldn't catch his breath. Sprinting in place.

Tucker had begun some kind of constant grinding stroke. One hand replacing the other forever, passing over Patch's greasy hardness, right then left then right, hand over hand, so that it felt like his meat was pushing down an endless tunnel of oily calloused fingers. The slithery slurp of it only made him stiffer, raising the veins into high relief under those hands, Tucker muttering praise and kissing his flesh everywhere but his mouth.

He couldn't control the twitching now, and something broke inside his head. Control, or frustration, or whatever, simply rattled into shards to leave him flying in open space.

Tucker's sure hands wrung music out of his flesh, and he couldn't make words to express the feeling. Terrible and wonderful as he hung from the brass.

"Attaboy." Tucker sounded pleased with himself. "Aww, *yeahhh.*"

The flickering spike of heat Patch associated with ejaculation didn't crest, just smoldered… slowly roasting him from the inside. Torture that didn't hurt, but he suffered all the same. *"Tuhh*—cker."

His hips stuttered and the flickering urgency rose. His cock locked, his heels braced, and his teeth ground together in primal pleasure. "Tucker. Tuck—*Haaugh.* Please let me. Ker! Jeeez-us. I'm gonna—"

Tucker let go abruptly, and he was fucking the air again.

A roar of frustration escaped his mouth. "Fraugh-*uck,* man!"

Thwat! Tucker swatted his knob, wringing a bark of protest out of him he instantly regretted. "That so?" Tucker swatted again.

Patch scowled. "Hey!" A drip of precum splatted against his thigh. "Sorry." He panted through gritted teeth, body straining.

"Course. Just a reminder." Tucker's weight shifted and his fingertips stroked Patch's balls with a precise pressure, just this side of tickling. "Calm down now. We ain't finished." He ran one soft knuckle under the cocktip like a smutty apology.

Patch groaned and flexed his butt to increase contact, but couldn't get a purchase. The sensations confused the fuck out of him. He whimpered and clamped his mouth shut to stop the pitiful sound. Behind the blindfold, his eyes stung.

Tucker laughed at him and then he laughed with it. "Good deal. You just hold on to that nut a while longer." Tucker patted his thigh lightly. "See, I want all of it, not just the cream at the top."

Patch shuddered. "Too much. You're gonna kill—"

"No, pup. No, I ain't." Tucker petted him firmly, his voice hushed. "You gotta trust me."

"Uhh." Patch sighed and writhed. "Shh. *Shhhh.*" He blew air up, lifting hair from his face. His rod flexed once, twice, and then backed away from the cliff.

"Good. Breathe it off. No rush here. That's just your body forcing a lazy squirt. Strictly mechanics, but we got nowhere else to be. Huh?" Same tone he used to calm the horses, or the Hixville High locker room, come to think of it: Coach Biggs keeping the peace in his shorts and cleats, a towel over his tan chest. "That's it there. So strong."

Patch squirmed at the thought, feeling both lucky and doomed.

"Ain't a race. Nobody's after us." Tucker kneaded his upper thighs lightly, testing the tension there. "I wanna get the good stuff out of these big fellas." One hand cupped Patch's heavy balls. "Worth working for, the two of us. Teamwork."

He nodded, dumb with lust. To his credit, he didn't whimper.

"I'm gonna take care of you." Tucker put a hand over Patch's knocking heart and leaned closer. "Promise. So good." Tucker's own stiffness brushed his hamstring, standing his hairs on end. "I promise, pup."

"'Kay." Patch consciously relaxed his arms, his calves, his back, his ass, his hands, sagging back against the headboard again, ignoring his exposed rear and the nearness of Tucker's body. Even if he wasn't strong or patient, he could pretend. *Same thing.*

"That'sa way. Yeah."

Patch swallowed, even though his mouth was dry. His meat sure wasn't. He did his best to hold still so Tucker would keep going, determined to trick him into losing control.

"Look't you. Look at how strong, huh?" The warm, pleased rumble in his words helped Patch let go completely. "Thank you."

For what? Patch didn't point out the obvious, just sat there letting Tucker worship and pleasure every inch of his body. The soft ropes creasing his muscles. That crazy grease everywhere so Tucker's hands slid too easily.

Patch struggled and shook and shouted. "I'm gonna.... Jesus, I'm so close—Tucker, you're gonna—"

And then the slick hand was gone.

"Ugh. C'mon. Ahh. Shhhh-it."

Firm, long strokes across his chest, his legs, that woke his skin. Since when were his arms that sensitive? His whole body throbbed like violin under Tucker's relentless ministrations.

Without warning, a warm press of scratchy lips on his cheek an inch from his mouth that made his hair stand. "Oh."

"See how good you are. That's the way. Hold on now. Make it last."

Rustling again, and a spatter of lube over his dick, then Tucker trapped and wrapped it.

Patch fucked the loose tunnel of fingers in a delicious slither that curled his toes, ass open. He didn't give a damn how stupid it looked. "Unh, Tuh-hucker… I'm fixin' to go soon. That's—*Shhh*-unh. Agh!"

Tucker laughed at that. "Yeah?" His hand opened, no more tunnel. Fingers scraped and plucked at the ridge of Patch's cockhead.

One hand wrapped around his nuts and pulled, yanking them away from his body, a harsh ache that almost made him cry out. Pride kept him quiet until he couldn't stop himself. "*Haugh*! Ffft."

Tucker snorted somewhere to his left. *Asshole*. He must be enjoying this.

"Fuck, man. C'mon."

"C'mon where? 'S what I meant about patience, pup." Another stroke, up and down, then release. "If you wanna get good, you gotta practice, practice, practice." He punctuated the repeat by twisting a greasy hand around Patch's knob. Then nothing.

Patch growled and glowered. Sitting there exposed and powerless drove him out of his mind in the best and worst way.

"What's your hurry? It feels good, don't it?" Tucker stroked him again three times slowly. *A-one, a-two, a-three*. Then let go, leaving the erection to bob in space, and feather-stroked his tight sac. "This is the good part."

"Fuck you."

"Is that so?" Tucker shifted on the mattress. "Tell you what. I'm gonna count. You gotta earn it."

"Like math?" He scowled. What did that mean?

The hand gripped his joint again. "Ten, nine, eight—"

Patch tightened, struggling toward the finish.

"Seven, six, five, four—" But it was too slow, too even, too light.

He could feel the bare edge of the release, but he couldn't reach it. He gritted his teeth and strained toward it.

"Three, two. And one." Release.

Patch hissed in irritation. His cock waggled in front of him in the cool air, and his balls began to ache, a dull, hungry, heartbeat throb.

"Again. Now ask nice. Ten…." So Tucker counted him down. His hand never tightened or sped up, just the same steady slide driving him out of his skull… and then his dick bouncing and dripping in the cool air. "Again."

"C'mon. Please. Please, Tucker."

Tucker never varied. "Please what? Don't this feel good?"

Patch frowned. *Hold still. Keep still.*

"Again. Ten... nine...." Tucker put him through his paces. "See how nice that is? We can do this all night."

Patch whimpered. It felt like torture, but good too. Confused the shit out of him, but he didn't want the hands or the trance to stop. "Asshole."

"Well, sure, pup. If you say so." A hand squeezed his thigh and then a greasy finger at his rear pushed and petted the little iris of muscle between his cheeks. Patch shivered and tightened, but Tucker wasn't about to go easy on him. "How long you reckon you can last? Ten, nine, eight...."

Patch began to sweat in earnest, not from heat but from his heart rate. This felt like running a race with his dick. Tucker shifted, and Patch heard the cap of a bottle.

"Oh yeah." The finger at his hole slipped in slightly. More oil this time, which felt... great, actually. Another kiss on his cheek, because this time he felt the stubble, and it was all he could do not to turn his mouth to catch it.

Patch tensed at that but the strange pressure inside nudged him closer to climax, so fuck if he was gonna complain. If this was a game, he was determined to get his. He grunted and strained forward, trying to get a little more sensation to speed things up a hair. Anything. His damp curls fell in his face over the blindfold. "Please, sir." Begging for a reward. A tear slipped out under the blindfold.

Sure enough, Tucker bent his wrist and that blunt digit inside him felt mighty good all of a sudden; the leak from his cock became a steady flow. *Whoa!* Warmth spread though his pelvis, a coiled sizzle at the base of his spine unwrapped itself and flowed along his limbs like sunlight.

He's milking my gland. And it was scary, freaky good. For the first time, he could feel a clear certain path to his orgasm. He'd have to work his way there, but that outrageously thick finger made it possible.

"Ask for it. There we go. Now it's waking up."

Patch nodded and blew hard to move the hair off his face.

Tucker smoothed it back and patted his cheek, but the fist never stopped stroking the ten count he'd learned to loathe.

"Please don't stop. Can I? Tucker, please. *Oh-ah!*" He vibrated with frustration, yanking at his restraints. "Go. Keep going. I can't, I can't last, I *swear* I can't. Aww, man."

Tucker let go, then swatted at his pole and laughed at his involuntary flinch.

"Fuck you."

Tucker answered with his coach voice. "That is not very polite, young man." He held Patch fast with his skin, with those powerful hands. Movement on the bed as Tucker shifted closer between his legs. Breath against his inner thighs and his taint.

He can see my hole. Embarrassment seemed ridiculous, but he couldn't help himself.

Tucker tapped it. "Don't tighten up. I wanna see you wanting me." Tucker's next ten-stroke shucked off his shyness, and this time when Tucker let go, his mouth found the space between Patch's cheeks to lick his greasy aperture, pushing inside while both hands kneaded and squeezed the cap of his cock above.

"We got all the time you need, pup." Tucker kissed his leg. A scrape of stubble. "But I don't need to even touch your honker to get that seed out." Low laugh.

"C'mon," Patch begged.

"I got a way better idea." He pressed forward and dragged his scruffy jaw across the underside of Patch's exposed trench, and the abrasive tickle made him flinch and twist in the knots.

Stop fighting. Patch held his breath. He couldn't control himself. Wouldn't have if he could.

With a grunt, Tucker licked his crack, pulling the plump cheeks apart to stretch the tiny muscle between them. "Beautiful." He said the word against the raw skin and didn't stop tasting it. "Fuck. Fuck me."

Patch coughed and choked and squealed. *Help.* But he didn't want any assistance he wasn't getting already. "Awww, Tuck. Oh man." Trussed to the bed, legs back, hole bare, and a horny cowboy determined to wreck him eight ways from Sunday.

Tucker growled and chewed at his cheeks, slobbered over the hole and prodded it with his blunt fingertips.

For once in his life Patch simply stopped right there where he was and let it happen to him, all of it.

A brief, bright hurting, like fireworks.

He gave in, with tears leaking from between his lashes. And for the first time he understood what that meant: giving in. All the outward effort sloshed back inside him toward the frantic center where his fear, lust, and anger churned. *Inside.*

At some point, he simply stopped resisting, and Tucker's approval blasted through any lingering shame. Experiencing Tucker's pride and lust and confidence up close did something awful inside him, and he surrendered willingly.

A chuckle between his legs. "Whaddaya reckon? How many licks does it take?"

Patch opened his mouth wide but no sound came out. Pressure on his gland again. The lazy warmth washed over him again, holding him aloft and pinning him in place, locked in his dumb lust. Maybe his butt wasn't off limits, or if it was, not to Tucker.

Patch's feet locked and an embarrassing squeal burst from him. Tucker knew exactly where to push. Something slipped inside the little iris, Tucker's fingertip, maybe, or his tongue. "I'm gonna go. I'm gonna *go*, Tucker."

Sweat on the back of his legs because of his bent knees pressing calf to thigh.

His muscles gave. His need to speak. The tension, the terror. Even his terrible urge to run. He tossed it all into the dark hole at his core like bloody sacrifices to a hungry god.

Sure enough, Tucker was there at the edges keeping him safe, stroking his skin, mapping the boundary between safe and sane with those slick, stubborn, meaty fingers.

Patch blinked, his breathing labored, and his ribs expanded under the rope.

The rough hands soft on him again and the drawl drizzled over him like oil. "Good boy, good boy. Lasting so long." Another rough kiss on his sweaty face, this one closer to his lips.

Patch hadn't moved but suddenly he was soaring unencumbered by weight unbound by gravity. His flesh was fire. His skin was starlight. His heart was helium. He exhaled in relief. As soon as he stopped pushing out, the whole universe poured inward with a thunderclap silence.

Flying. Not the climax but the climb.

"That's the way. Right on the edge. Look how beautiful you are." Tucker stroked his legs, his chest.

Somewhere down below he could feel the involuntary tightening in his balls, but with no tension, only a rushing lift. He sagged against smooth brass. His head rolled to the side, exposing his throat. His brow and cheekbone slid against the hot metal and a drip of sweat fell from his chin to his chest. *Give in, give in.* His cock became lazy, melting iron.

Tucker licked again, lapped hard and pressed in, worshiping the sweaty crack with his face and milking the stiffness above him with infinite patience. "You don't know." A moan and Tucker drilled inside him with that tongue before taking a swipe up the trail of precum to taste the tip and suck it hard for a moment.

Patch shuddered and grunted. *Too much, too much.* But he asked for more in a guttural voice he didn't recognize.

His breath rose and fell, deep and slow, and the muggy air tasted like lightning. Never in his life had he been with someone like this. No sex had ever slammed on the brakes like this or pulled him inside out. The sizzle at his nerve endings stole his impatience.

Tucker sucked his inner thigh and his stubble scraped, but he stayed down there breathing deeply. "That's it. Take your time, all the time you need, pup. We're right here and we got all the time in the world, you and me." Seemed like he meant it. His tongue again, darting across Patch's goose bumps, mapped a rising storm.

Four fingers gripped one cheek hard enough to mark, so Tucker's thumb had to be inside him on that spot with his tongue wetting the way.

Patch couldn't even make words, and the craziness that came out was a hoarse plaintive roar that hurt his own ears. He hissed and whistled through his teeth. He begged with spit running from his stretched mouth to drip onto his chest and his muscles spasming, legs straining against the ropes. His ankles and wrists pushed against the knots. "Ha. Ugh. Please can I go? *Agh!* Tuck—"

Ruthless and gentle, Tucker never stopped milking his shaft, teasing his pleasure and pleas out of him right up into the light.

Blind like this, Patch could hear Tucker's ragged breathing and sense the tension in his sure hands. Being wanted and worshiped like this made him insane. His wet back dragged against the brass loops.

"Ten, nine, eight...." Instead of a frantic a ramble to get off, Tucker was forcing him to give in. For once he didn't fight, couldn't have if he'd tried. His need was too great and the urge too deep to resist. *Pleasepleaseplease.*

"That's it. There it is." Maybe this time Tucker would take him over the edge.

Patch began to float, or else gravity took a break that left him suspended in midair, pinned like a butterfly to the smooth brass rack with a rushing thunder in his ears and waves of delirium cooking his skin from inside. No weight, nothing holding him to the earth but Tucker's oily hand twisting around him till he was a single point of white hot light, a spike of lightning fighting the storm.

"TUHGHHKH!" The raw sound tore him open and semen boiled out of him. Heat spattered his face and hair—he could taste himself on his mouth, and the warm slide of it on his torso. He spasmed and bowed against the knots. A hushed roaring in his ears. Tucker patting and stroking his charged skin as if holding his spirit inside his broken body.

Tucker growled. "All of it. Everything."

He couldn't stop cumming, and Tucker wouldn't let up even then. It kept running and running out of him like syrup, a torrent of molten seed that turned his skull inside out. Even as the spurts slowed, those rough fingers kept pulling the fire free so it could lick his limbs.

Thank you. Jesus. Thank you, sir.

"You're welcome, pup."

Patch tensed in confusion. Had he said that out loud? Or had Tucker read his mind. Did it even matter? He licked his lips and made sure he said it. "Please. I mean, thank you. Thank you. You don't know."

Tucker pulled the blindfold loose, and then the light blinded him.

"I do know." Tucker's gray eyes on his, close enough to see the splintered silver in them. The lower half of his face was smeary with musky spit. "I know now." The big hands held Patch's face and the big smile shone on him like a lamp. "Oh man, do I know."

Patch twitched and shivered, the grogginess overwhelming and the relief impossible. Tucker squeezed his softening cock, which wrung a gasp and groan loose. He still felt the climax chasing along his spine, his whole quaking body, the kind of pleasure that made folks say stupid things.

Plucking at the knots with one hand, Tucker hummed and stroked him like a blue-ribbon horse. "You done real good."

The ropes at Patch's left wrist gave. Working methodically, Tucker unlaced that arm and then the other. He gripped and kneaded the muscles lightly, driving the blood and sense back into them. "That's it, that's right."

Patch didn't even try to help. He soaked in the languorous afterburn, some part of him sad to feel the knots vanishing.

He must've made a noise because Tucker chuckled and looked back up to wink.

"Don't you worry none. There's plenty more where that came from, I reckon." Tucker untied and stroked and freed him inch by inch, knot by knot until Patch was simply lying in bed, propped against the brass headboard, semen sliding down his chest and around his ribs.

"Y'gave yourself a helluva facial." Tucker sounded proud. "Damn well glazed yourself."

Patch panted a moment, still soaring on the crazy charge rushing through him like water sloshed in an empty tub. He exhaled in a rush. He hadn't realized he was holding his breath through the woozy aftershocks.

"That was something else. You are something else, pup."

Patch tried to nod. Even with his eyes closed, sparks flickered at the edges of his vision still and the tumbling energy wouldn't let him go. Fingers on his wet face, then in his mouth letting him taste his own sweet seed. Rather than bugging him, it unlocked some slumbering hunger he'd never acknowledged, and he ate the warmth off Tucker's thick, slick fingers and licked the webs between them.

"Good boy. Look't you now. Get all that good stuff. *Fu-huck* yeah. Hungry boy." Tucker muttered something under his breath, his eyes dilated almost solid black. "All that. Huh?" He sighed and Patch sighed in reply. "Better."

"The best." Patch grinned and flexed like a cat. "I'm too lazy to move." In truth, he didn't trust his short-circuiting muscles to obey him, and he didn't want to put any distance between them. "Agh!" He shuddered again.

"Sounds good to me, pup." Tucker crawled back up his body and shifted to sit beside him. He raised his hand and licked the thumb. "Mmmmph."

"Did you just—?"

"I sure did." *Shore.* "Fuckin' delicious. I ain't gonna waste it." He reached across to catch a drip over Patch's nipple. "Now on, you better not either or I don't know what might happen to you." A sexy threat and a promise, both.

Gradually the fizz in Patch settled and he realized how selfish he'd been. "What about you?" He glanced down at the wad in Tucker's jeans.

Tucker made a face and raised his eyebrows. "Serious?" He popped the button on his jeans and unzipped, exposing his dark pubic hair. "I busted soon as I tasted your butt. *Wham.*"

"No way." Lazy, happy pride washed over his limbs.

Tucker tugged the flaps wider, and sure enough his thick semi rolled in a gummy puddle that mashed the hair into wet sworls. "Hell, I almost popped another when you got your nut."

"That's crazy." He twisted and slid down the mattress for a closer look.

"Hands-free is my favorite." Tucker sounded proud as hell.

Sure enough, the starchy smutty smell of it filled his nostrils. "Just like that."

"I'm whatcha call oral." Tucker tasted his lower lip. "Like to get my licks in."

He grinned up at Tucker again. "Cool."

"Almost had a heart attack." Tucker sighed. "But I'da died happy." He flexed his butt, lifting his crotch toward Patch's face a moment.

They laughed low at each other.

Patch rubbed his lips. "Aw, man. You smell so damn good." He inhaled Tucker's dusty musk and the male sourness of his sweat.

"Yeah?" Tucker reached for him. "Come on up here." He tugged and Patch followed until he was next to Tucker, face pillowed against his hard chest. Tucker's ribs rose and fell under him, slow and strong.

Patch whispered, "Thanks." Coulda been for the tug or the hug, and he didn't specify.

"Sexy fucker." Tucker squeezed him against his chest tighter than rope and shook him playfully. "What'm I gonna do with you?"

"Anything you want." He murmured the words into the hard skin before he regretted them.

Tucker pulled him again, trying to raise him eye to eye, and Patch let himself be moved despite the obvious danger. "What'd you say?"

He shook his head.

Tucker did too, but he'd obviously heard. He scanned Patch's flushed face, his rope-kissed body. They stared at each other from three inches away. Their breath heated the ripe space between them. "Then I guess I gotta." His gray eyes were warm and dangerous.

"Yeah." Patch waited to be kissed, watching Tucker ask the question without saying anything.

Tucker raised a hand and cupped his sweaty head gently, burying his fingers in the damp tangle of Patch's hair.

"Tucker?" No response. *Just once.* "You can if you want."

"Lord, I wish you hadn't said that."

"Why?"

"Because." Tucker eyed him warily. "What the hell am I gonna do if I can't stop?"

Patch held himself still, counting the dull throbs in his throat. *All the time in the world.* He could pretend, right? Easy enough with Tucker's scent all over him and their lips an inch apart.

Run fast, stand still.

Tucker searched his eyes and raised the other big hand to cup his head. Patch searched his face, not breathing and not needing to.

A lazy blink and Tucker shook his head as he leaned in with wounded eyes. He brushed his hard mouth against Patch's lips, back and forth, back and forth, before his tongue slipped out and in. He groaned and pressed forward, slowly tasting his way as he pushed both hands into Patch's hair, holding him fast, and drove his tongue deep, savoring the slip and the slow drag of their seed between them. *Quick-quick, slow, slow.*

Patch froze. He stiffened and opened his mouth, opened himself, and they both gave in, gave in. The hungry kiss sent roots and blossoms chasing along his flesh and wove into the brass scroll behind him, coiled around them, burning soft as fireflies, sweeter and sharper and stronger than anything in his life. No knots necessary.

Maybe they made out more than they needed. Maybe the moon rose while they talked easy and laughed often. Maybe their grips left handprints on the headboard. Maybe Botchy padded around outside the bedroom door, nails striking the linoleum in the hall. Maybe the lube eased the friction between them. Maybe the sheets tangled around their legs. Maybe they made love again before they were still enough to stop.

"Stay with me." Tucker probably meant for the night, but for Patch the words hung in the air like sweet smoke.

Maybe he did.

CHAPTER SEVEN

MORNING ON the farm came right up out of the soil, quiet and fragile as flowers, and pushed the moon aside.

Patch woke after Tucker, around five, at the ass crack of dawn. The sky shone pale at its indigo edge.

He'd fought sleep as long as he was able, trying to memorize Tucker's breath at his nape, Tucker's fingers tracing the rope marks, Tucker's muscle wrapped around him, and Tucker's heartbeat at his back or under his cheek as they shifted against each other easy as laced fingers. He'd savored every point of contact until dreams dragged him under.

Now Tucker sat silhouetted on the windowsill smiling at him, a thick hog sticking out the fly of his boxers. "Chores all done."

"You shoulda got me up."

"I like to get it all out the way 'fore it gets hot." Tucker shrugged a shoulder and came to the side of the bed. "Shh. Go back t'sleep, pup."

He sighed into the warm pillows and stretched. "Chilly."

"No, it ain't." Tucker tugged the sheet back up over him and patted his upper thigh.

"Mmph." He stretched under Tucker's gaze. "Huh. Well, thank you."

Then Tucker lay down on top of the covers to spoon up against his back, all rust and sawdust, and he did sleep.

When he woke again the trailer was eerily silent, but there was coffee in the pot and a note on the counter said, *Fishing, T.*

Patch stretched in patient pleasure. He couldn't remember ever feeling so sated, so comfortable, so alive in his own skin without being in motion.

He didn't need coffee, or food, even. He hadn't slept that well in… ever, actually. He rolled his shoulder and went out to the porch, watching the hens doing their jerky patrol of the toilets and tubs and old tractor parts. Gradually, the morning haze stained the wide Texas horizon from black to dusty blue.

Once the sun had cleared the horizon for good, Patch made his way to the yard, not bothering with shoes. He followed the windbreak trail down the rise past the beeches marking the little homegrown cemetery.

The leaves whispered above him. For two seconds as he passed and paused, he wondered if he should have his parents buried here on the farm, until he remembered that any day now Texaco would be drilling for crude where he stood. In a few months, his little parentheses angel and all the worn gravestones would migrate with their dead owners, somewhere close to his parents, probably. In the end they'd all be buried together anyway.

He didn't know how to feel about that inevitable future. His stomach rumbled as he stepped out of the live oak onto the pond's shore.

Tucker had settled under the bald cypress with Botchy's square pale head pillowed on one leg. He had a fishing rod, but he didn't seem to be paying much attention to it. A steady breeze rippled the surface and scattered the ducks.

Patch's voice came out hoarse and soft. "G'mornin'."

"Hey." Tucker looked up. A pleased smile. "You're still nekkid, boy."

"Yup." Patch shrugged. For whatever reason, he had forgotten to put anything on. Not like anyone could see them, and truth be told, he liked feeling the air on his skin. Under the boughs, the air seemed near chilly.

"Mmgh." Tucker smiled at him. Botchy raised an ear and stood stiffly before ambling over for affection. "You look awful nice like that, mister." He shook his head and blinked.

"Yeah?" Patch planted his bare butt down on the cool grass and his back against the trunk. His skin had gone brown in the past week from all the sun. "Likewise, I'm sure." *Shore.*

Tucker wore old boxer shorts and nothing else, which was no hardship as far as Patch was concerned.

Botchy went to the water's edge and lapped noisily. *Glob-glop-glub-glop.*

Patch tried to stop his thoughts racing, but he never sat around. *Ever.* Too much to do. And the house still needed clearing out. His leg bounced.

Tucker turned. "If y'got shit to do, I don' mind."

"No." Patch tried to relax. "Too early anyways." Truth was, he wanted to stay out here, feeling like he belonged somewhere.

"You said you hadta run them toys down to Beaumont. Thought I could make us supper some kind."

Patch nodded and stroked Tucker's fuck-rumpled hair. "Oh." Tucker wanted to cook for him?

"If you like catfish. Nothing fancy."

He hadn't known these catfish were edible. Hopefully they were. "You make it, I'll eat it."

Tucker cupped Patch's crotch. "That's the damn truth." He kept his big, veined hand there, kneading without urgency.

A bird swooped over the water, and Botchy took off hell for leather, as if running fast enough would let pit bulls grow wings.

Patch laughed, trying not to fidget. Was he supposed to fish? As a kid he couldn't stand all the good-ol'-boy activities he was supposed to love, mainly because he felt like a fraud. *Not now.* Tucker made him feel like he belonged out here under the leaves waiting for the day to heat up. "So quiet."

Tucker draped an arm across their bumped knees but didn't take it further. "The best."

Cicadas ticked in the trees.

Looking at their legs together, Patch could measure the gap in their ages and experience.

Tucker's skin was rougher, weathered by work and all its tiny injuries. The thick veins in his hand sat right under the tan skin, without Patch's puppy fat. He looked hard because he'd lived hard: the crow's-feet, the broad torso, the unshaven jaw, the flecks of silver at his temples all telegraphed his place at the top of the food chain; his battle scars showed how much he could survive.

"You fishing today, pup? I brought you a pole." He nodded toward the big rock.

"If you want. I don't know."

"Best not." Tucker blinked bright gray eyes at him. "You're my bait."

Patch sniffed. "I smell like sweat and cum."

"Do I care?" Tucker kissed his shoulder. "You can rinse if you want. Pond's plenty clean."

"Cleaner'n me, at least." He rubbed his slick chest. And the marks. He could still feel that crazy grease too.

"I like it. My stuff on you." Tucker's joint raised a salute in his boxers but he didn't acknowledge it. "Nasty, huh?"

"Nossir." Patch rubbed the rope burns on his wrists, and his cock swelled in a heartbeat throb. "I like it too."

Fishing and chewing on a piece of straw, Tucker looked happier and younger than he ever had. Rested too.

Patch didn't mention any of that.

Some sneaky part of him hoped the farm would never sell, that Tucker would stay in his trailer out by the pond forever so they could fuck and laugh and kiss and talk whenever he wanted out here in the sticks.

"I almost stayed up there, just to see what you'd do if I wasn't up yet."

Tucker's shadowed gaze climbed up him from the ground to his face. "You did, huh?" He took the straw out of his mouth.

Patch saw the lust bloom and pushed back with gentle pressure, just like the dancing, completing the slippery circuit between them.

Tucker grunted and licked his lips. "I'd love that: coming home and tying you down before you woke up. Milking you for hours. Eating your tail. You never knowing when and where I'd turn up. Off-balance and horned up."

Patch made a soft sound at the back of his throat.

Tucker muttered, like a promise, "I'd take care of you so good, pup. Groom you and feed you, and tap your sap regular. You don't even know how good."

But he did know. Patch could see exactly how tempting that was, all that attention focused on him from the sexiest motherfucker in a thousand miles.

"Mmph. Wanting it something awful. Like the axe wants the turkey." Tucker nodded. "Never knowing. Keeping your head on edge too."

"I'd be one lucky boy." He swallowed.

"Show up in the middle of the night. You wouldn't even know when or how I'd get to you."

Patch nodded, stunned, and his dumb cock started to rise in slow pulsing jerks, right out there in the sunlight with Botchy nosing through the cattails across the pond.

"Look at that. Lord." Tucker chewed at his stubble as he mulled and made his mind up about something.

"What?"

Tucker made an impatient sound. "I turn into a damn gorilla around you."

"And that's bad why?"

"Do I know? I just—" Tucker rocked on his seat. "I worry about it."

"I don't." Patch flashed a swift smile and went to the pond's edge. The water felt a little cool and almost oily. "And I like calling you 'sir.'"

A cautious grin. "You do, huh?"

Patch shrugged. "Uh-huh. I like you calling me… anything."

"Yeah?"

"Well… most times." He swallowed the spit pooling in his mouth. A tendril of heat coiled around his cock and tugged it up his belly. "Sir." He swallowed again.

Tucker tipped his head and squinted. "When it's just us, I like you calling me 'sir' just fine. Gets to me something awful. You takin' orders like that. Getting all riled up while I work you."

Patch nodded and his breath came in slow drowning gulps.

Without a doubt, Tucker was kinky as all get-out. What next? A rubber bit in his teeth? A saddle. *Texas crude.*

His cock hardened completely, and he frowned at his own small-town bullshit. He wasn't some local yokel. Hadn't he outgrown his own hang-ups? They'd had fun. Why did it have to mean more?

"Maybe I will rinse, so you can mess me up again."

Tucker called out, "While you're at it, try and scare them fish over here."

Patch waded in slowly into water almost warm as his skin.

"Hey. I'm all slippery again." He rubbed his arms and legs and belly experimentally. Sure enough, last night's lube had gotten slick as spit the minute it touched water.

It took a while to wash the lube off even partially. "Man! What the hell was that gunk you used to butter me up?"

"J-Lube. They use it for foaling." Tucker grinned. "Y'mix it from powder."

"No way!"

Tucker wound his line and shifted it in the water. "Rancher's delight. I'm not careful, you gonna learn all my secrets."

Patch wrinkled his nose, wishing he could feel grossed out, but no way could he go back to Astroglide now. "Fuck." Even now his soft cock slipped through his fingers too easy to seem natural.

"If it bugs you, I got salt'll take it off. Up the barn."

"Naw." He shrugged and tugged at himself distractedly. "Not really. Just, I dunno, weird. Natural or something. Feels good."

"No lie." Tucker laughed. "Better than, in the right hands." He dropped his gaze to the water, but a smug smile played over his face.

Your hands.

"No lie," he said in the same down-home drawl without meaning to. Or maybe it was playacting part of the fantasy. He frowned at the sky.

Tucker smiled at something.

"What?"

"I like it when you sound country, when that little twang sneaks out. You still a Texas boy."

Patch *didn't* like it, but he floated on his back, soaking up the stillness until his erection lost its steam.

At one point, a flock of birds took wing suddenly, chittering and rustling in a wide loop over the pond. Botchy barked and barked, and before Patch turned to see her, she'd torn off back toward the trailer. "The hell?"

Tucker chuckled and shook his head in that direction. "Botchy's always been barn-shy." Meaning she headed for home whenever she could. Barn-shy horses headed back to their stalls soon as they spooked. "Second there's trouble, she's off, back, guarding the house. You good?"

"Better than, man." He hadn't gone this long without being chained to his cell phone in five years.

They sat out most the morning. Around ten, Tucker went up to the house and returned with a plate of fresh watermelon, cold from the fridge. He sat back down and used a pepper grinder to dust the melon.

Sitting beside him on the warm rocks, Patch scoffed, "Who eats melon with pepper instead of salt?"

"You try it and see."

Patch took a bite of the sweet, wet fruit, juice running down his chin. "Ohh." Sure enough, the pepper was delicious, actually, a kind of dusty tang that muted the sweetness. He took another bite.

"Uh-huh."

"Well, how's I to know? Ma always salted." He blinked at the gentle memory. Summers at the Honey Island pool. She'd make him a baggie of huge slices, and just enough salt to make him thirsty. He took another bite, blinking at the memory. He'd forgotten how much fun they'd had growing up.

"Tastes good, huh?" Tucker reached over and wiped juice right off his chin and then sucked the finger. "That's some mouth you got, pup."

Patch took his time and stayed on the shore long enough to finish that slice and another, enjoying Tucker's touch and lazy perusal of his body. Face and throat sticky with the sweetness, he plunged back into the pond again to rinse, then strode back dripping.

The sun had gone hot now and a couple yellow jackets drifted over the watermelon, lifting and settling in dozy loops but too sugar-drunk to sting.

Tucker picked up the plate and stood as he approached. "You gonna burn, f'we don't get you dressed." He hadn't caught any catfish.

Patch looked at him strangely. "Since when do I burn?" True enough, his skin tended toward a light tan, but he rarely turned pink even in direct noonday sun. But he followed nevertheless, taking the plate of melon rinds. Maybe Tucker wanted to get him back inside to fool around again. He certainly wouldn't object.

Nope.

Inside, when Patch went to rinse off again in the shower, Tucker knocked on the wall and said, "I'm gonna feed the animals. Run up to Lumberton." His voice sounded tight.

Had something happened? "Uh. Okay. Yeah."

"That tedder popped a cotter pin last week, and I ain't replaced it." The tedder fluffed the straw for drying. Pay or no pay, maybe Tucker felt the need to prove he was still pulling his weight as a hired hand. "I can pick up stuff for Frito pie for dinner. If you want an' all." A thump on the wall. "I don't wanna keep you all day." And just like that he was gone.

Patch heard the pickup leave before he'd even stepped out of the little shower and toweled off.

Confused, disappointed, and more than a little sullen, he went to Tucker's crowded bedroom and pulled on last night's clothing, feeling like a sucker. Just 'cause they'd messed around didn't mean shit. *Fool.* The big brass bed didn't contradict him.

As usual, he'd been in such a hurry he'd ignored the glaring signs.

He shook himself. He knew better. *Much.* How many horny dupes had Tucker fucked up with this kinda play? Keeping folks on the hook and nailed in place where he wanted them. Women and men, apparently.

Maybe Tucker had been trying to get rid of him all morning. What if he'd overstayed his welcome?

He rubbed his face. The bed's brass was cold again, chilled by the relentless air conditioner. Outside the trailer, a couple chickens huffed and squawked at each other.

Tucker had seemed nervous. *Why?*

Frito pie was just chili on chips, something served at football games and livestock shows. Delicious and terrible, like most things worth eating. Not much more than a delivery system for salt and grease.

Out back, visible through the foggy kitchen window, Botchy nosed around the yard between stall and the two rusty henhouse trailers.

Tucker wanted to make dinner for him but couldn't afford a bunch of groceries.

I'm an asshole.

To Patch, this farm only offered capital to buy a shortcut for his career. For Tucker, it had been a lifeline. He'd done his best to take care of it. And he'd been willing to give up his claim because he felt it was the honorable thing to do. He was trying to make peace between Patch and Royce after the old man wouldn't and couldn't do it himself.

Patch's ma used to say the best way to know a man was to learn his needs and deeds. *Ay-fucking-men.*

He hadn't realized how broke Tucker was. Losing a place to park this trailer would create serious problems. What savings did he have? Rodeo cowboys and assistant coaches weren't known for their robust investment portfolios.

Patch took a good look at the trailer. For the first time since he'd come back, he ignored Tucker's indelible presence and looked at the home he'd made for himself in the last place on Earth that wouldn't kick him out.

What he saw was… *time*. Years of scraping by and stretching a dime, Salvation Army furniture, and solitary nights. Jerking off for hours at a time, lonely as a scarecrow in a burnt field.

That's the thing about leaving. Some people don't.

Blanket over the old couch to cover the ragged cushions. A rug worn flat by boots and bleached by drying in the sun. Torn screens on the windows. Everything clean and tidy, but strictly functional. Canned corn and patched soles. Even the pictures on the shelves and wall were just thumbtacked into place. Like a dorm or a dressing room. Tucker treated this place like a barracks because he didn't have any other option. After all, who cared how your double-wide looked?

The only thing even close to decor was the fresh flowers on the table, and he knew that Tucker had put those out for him. *Being a gentleman.*

Patch paid more for a month in his little studio in Hell's Kitchen than Tucker spent in a year.

Best thing he could do for Tucker was offer him a leg up, a shortcut, a solid nest egg to help get him out of this dump. The Texaco deal would open so many doors for both of them.

Before he did anything crazy or heartfelt, he headed out the front door and up the drive in the hot sun back toward his parents' house, wondering how to fix what they'd broken together.

IN HIS bedroom an hour later, his phone buzzed on the nightstand. The vibration and jittering motion scared this piss out of him.

He expected Tucker, but it was Ms. Landry with excellent news about Texaco and did he want to come by the office to look through the papers? They were offering one-point-seven million, which she thought was low, but since he was in a hurry.... He should have felt relief or excitement, but mainly he felt carsick. She sounded pleased about the offer, so he pretended he was. He promised he'd swing by in the afternoon.

Patch rinsed again and changed into his "packing" clothes. He heard a truck crunch over the drive by the main barn and went to the little window to see.

Sure enough, Tucker had pulled up with a trailer of hay and was loading straw into the stalls where they'd kept a couple horses some years back. Whoever he was talking to wasn't visible at this angle.

Patch hesitated. Next to the window frame, the pine wall had bled another little sticky tear of sap. *Hot day coming.* The sunlight pounded down on the yard like a slow, scalding hammer he could feel through the panes.

Even so, he headed over to the barn. The metal building wasn't fancy, and the row of four stalls was now piled with two-string bales. Each of the stall doors split into top and bottom gates, and all four hung open. He could hear Tucker working in the third stall, whistling tunelessly.

"Tuck?"

The whistling stopped. "Yessir." Tucker poked his head out, holding a bale with both hands in work gloves.

"Who you talking to?

"Nobody. Myself." Tucker shook his head. "Mrs. Aldridge coming by for the petting zoo up the VA, so I moved this up here to save a trip to the back barn."

"Nice." Twice a year the church ladies did a petting zoo for kids in the local hospitals. Nothing fancy, just a chance for the kids to get out in the sun if they could and touch something soft and alive. "Can I help?"

"Naw. 'Bout done now." He didn't come closer, so whatever weirdness had been there hadn't dissipated. "House coming?"

"Sure. Yeah. Uh. Fine. All the big stuff's done. Papers. Just small bits now." And that would go to Goodwill over the next couple days. He'd just run it in loads on the hay trailer if need be.

"Good." He didn't make it sound good. Tucker tossed another bale onto the pile in the stall.

"I came out because Texaco's made us a firm offer. On the farm."

Tucker blinked. His mouth opened and closed in a grim line. His deep-set eyes shifted uneasily as he turned to toss the next bale.

"Serious money too." The amount seemed obscene, so he kept it to himself. No point in being insulting. Tucker could do the math.

He grabbed another bale and heaved it onto the low pile. "Good deal."

"It is a good deal. I wanna talk with you about that. I think you should take a piece so you—"

The half door swung back, too fast to duck, and slammed into Tucker's skull. He collapsed into the dust.

Without thinking Patch found himself running. He'd distracted the man while he worked, with the money and Texaco and all. *Stupid.*

"Stupid." Tucker struggled to push himself onto an elbow. "Sorry." Bloody nostril.

God.

"Don't move."

"It ain't a concussion, pup. Believe me. I's just surprised." Tucker's words came out as mushy and blank as oatmeal. He knelt a moment in the barn dust and swiped at the trickle of blood.

"Hey. Hey, man, I'm right here."

Tucker frowned and his eyes closed in pain. "Just gimme two shakes."

Patch crouched beside Tucker in the dust. "The hell I will. Blurry?"

A tight nod. "I just need one second and I'm fine. Too old for this shit."

He wondered what would've happened if Tucker had been alone out here. Who would have helped him to his feet, gotten him inside, driven him to the emergency room?

Nobody.

"Hold on, now."

"Bullshit." He knelt and looped Tucker's arm around his neck. The thick bicep flexed against his shoulder.

"Pup, you are not gonna"—Patch braced his legs and rose unsteadily. His biceps tightened and he stood—"lift me. You can't."

"Just did." He really had grown up at some point. Carrying Tucker felt surreal. Held like this, the older man seemed vulnerable, and more human. "You're not so heavy, cowboy."

"You're pretty strong." Chuckle, then Tucker winced at something. His eyes squeezed shut and a trickle of blood cut through the dust on his lip. "Pretty and strong." A joke to cover his discomfort.

"Stubborn sumbuck." Patch slowed down, working to steady his hold and struggling back toward the tack room.

"This a pretty good deal. Now on, I'm gone let you haul my lazy ass around."

Patch took him to the square bales to set him down. "I don't like that."

Snort. "Me neither."

"No. I mean I want you to get checked out."

"Pup, I don't need a doctor for a knocked head."

He wavered. Maybe Tucker didn't have insurance.

"Just need a second and I'll be fine."

Instead of arguing, Patch went to the sink and filled a mug and carried it back, not knowing what else Tucker would let him do to help.

"Texaco made you an offer."

The gruff tone stopped him where he stood. So Tucker had been listening. "Yeah. Ms. Landry said they're eager. That's something, at least. This whole town's fixing to dry up and blow away."

Tucker raised his gaze with a strained smile. "That is a true statement. Royce fought 'em off for years." A nod, and crow's-feet framed his eyes.

"Tucker, nobody else has even nibbled at this place. Least nobody serious. We're stuck."

"Well." Tucker bobbed his head, his brow creased and his mouth set. "It's just... oil folks can be rough on a town."

"She says other folks have sold to 'em, no trouble." Patch brought the water to him, more slowly now. "Besides, this close to Big Thicket, the EPA keeps their hands tied, right? They can't poison folks."

Tucker accepted the mug and took a swallow. "They got plenty pull, that's a fact." He tipped the mug to wet his hands and wiped his face with his dripping hands. The mud darkened the creases there, making him look more worn and beat than he seemed.

Patch sat down beside him to make his case as gently as he could. He had to let Tucker know he'd have a place after, that Patch would take care of him too.

"Texaco will pay. Enough to give me a shot and give you a down payment of your own and more." He wished he could make Tucker laugh, or smile, even. "Not exactly a piece of cake, but maybe a slice of pie?"

"Huh." Tucker's reaction didn't exactly rattle the rafters. Maybe his head hurt worse than he let on. His mouth worked silently and the dirty lines in his face deepened.

"I want you to have a couple bucks for… whatever. My pa would've wanted it. I do."

Tucker pressed his lips together. Either his head hurt or the Texaco did.

"I figured you'd be psyched. That's a win." He knew this was the right thing, for both of them. Velocity would open in time for next summer. He'd jump into the fast lane. Tucker could finally get out of his rut. "Win-win-win."

"Hey." Tucker shrugged and didn't look psyched in the least. "Can't lose 'em all."

For a heartbeat, he expected Tucker to pop his jeans open right there to distract him or change the subject.

Instead, he stood up and brushed the straw off. "We gotta get a move on."

"You sure?" Patch thrust his hands into his pockets.

"That tedder ain't gonna repair itself." Tucker winked. "And you're just about packed. No time to waste."

"I think that's the first time you ever told somebody to hurry up."

"Well, not the first…." Tucker chuckled.

"Me, then." He hesitated, wanting to invite Tucker into the house, but unsure if he should. Wasn't too much left to make it a house, actually.

Tucker had yet to sleep over here, which bugged the bejesus out of him. Then again, he hadn't exactly made the place inviting. Power off, no lights or furniture, boxes of bullshit. He knew he wasn't being fair to either of them.

I'm leaving in a couple days.

As he watched, Tucker ambled back to his truck and started it.

Up on the porch, Patch stared through the windows into the dark living room, the cartons heaped against the wall in orderly clumps by their eventual destination.

They always stayed up at the trailer. Why didn't Tucker want to come inside?

Maybe he didn't want any reminders of Royce, or maybe he compared the trailer to the Hastles' house in his mind. *Jesus.* Patch thought of every time he'd bragged about New York, traveling, and party bullshit.

He deserves better. Right then, Patch decided to give Tucker seed money, like a settlement. Ten grand, twenty. Nothing crazy, but enough to get himself re-situated in a good spot. It wouldn't have acreage, or a fishing hole or a hayloft for Botchy to climb... but at least he wouldn't have to move into some trailer in Clute with Bix.

The thought turned Patch's stomach.

Damn it all. Why couldn't his father have given Tucker something, anything to live on? But of course he had: the land. A life estate on a place he loved.

If Patch wasn't in a hurry, if he could just use this place for collateral, maybe Tucker could stay here and he could still make Velocity happen in New York. Happy ending for everyone.

The Texaco offer had made that impossible. Their plans required bulldozing this property along with its neighbors, probably. *Progress.*

Every option sucked. For the first time, maybe ever, Patch wished the decision wasn't his to make.

Man up, y'fucking sissy. Coach Biggs's voice and eyes scorched the inside of his head. Another Tucker, from years ago, shaming him in the locker room for seeming different, for watching the other boys bone up in the shower. Funny thing? Tonight Tucker wasn't saying it. Patch was.

They weren't the same people they'd been seven years ago. Or if they were, they knew themselves better and worse.

Patch hated the thought, but he knew it was honest.

Back when he was young, dumb, full of cum, Tucker hadn't been a *person* to him. And vice versa, obviously. While he'd been fantasizing, Tucker hadn't even seen more in him than a headstrong pain in the ass trying to get dead.

What would've happened at sixteen? If Coach Biggs had read the signals and come to him in the shower, made out with him under the spray, then wrestled him down the tile and ravished him and ruined both their lives. The fantasy had been so real, he could smell the cut grass and the pit stains, hear the steamy hiss and the clip-clop of cleats, Coach's big hand's bending him over, making him beg.

Or if Tucker had caught him in the barn and tied him to the beams above the hay and stuck fingers in him and more, what next? The sleazy ranch hand tonguing him open and making him take it like an animal, breeding him rough with his parents across the yard. Snuck into his room at night. What would he have done?

Not a damn thing. Because none of that shit was real.

He'd been horny and a kid and he hadn't known any better. He barely knew better now, but at least he realized how lucky he was that *none* of his porno scenarios had played out. He'd never have escaped the rut if it felt good. The fantasy would have fucked up the rest of his life.

How many small-town guys ended up locked in lives they resented after getting a quick dose of hick dick that kept them pinned in place, going nowhere? *Rural gay bait*… like teen pregnancy but worse because the possibility was all in your head and led nowhere safe or sane.

And Tucker wasn't like that. Kinky he might be, but nobody that'd hurt a kid. All the folks he'd fucked over in his forty-three years had gone in eyes open. Plenty of lonely to go around down here.

Patch knew firsthand.

Steeling himself against the dead air inside, he opened the door and went back inside his folks' house.

For the next few hours he ran all the boxes to Goodwill, the VA, and the dump. Books, bric-a-brac, and appliances all. He made sure to get receipts for his taxes to offset the sale price. For Velocity to start right, he needed every dime he could bring to the table.

Faster than seemed possible, he'd emptied the house down to a few boxes of family papers he planned to ship north and a few large items that called for a truck: a wardrobe, the dressers, the couch, fridge. Goodwill had said they'd send a truck over the weekend to mop up.

Now in the late afternoon, the house echoed strangely. No longer hidden by the contents, twenty years of grime and dust lay exposed. He considered cleaning but couldn't see the point. Texaco would probably tear this place down or build it out as a field office. Whatever the trouble they bought with the place, it wasn't his.

Before he checked the closets and corners, he opened all the windows in the hopes a stray breeze would stir the stale air. *Nope.* He'd done the job creditably. The house was well and truly bare.

He didn't know quite what to do with himself. Nothing had gone as he'd intended. The lazy, horny side of him wanted to drive up to Tucker's and mess around. The sensible side could see what a trap that was.

According to his original plan, after the funeral tomorrow he'd head home on the next available flight, and Tucker would be heading, well, nowhere fast. Only, that seemed impossible now.

No matter how good the sex was, or how much fun they had screwing around doing nothing smart, he knew where he needed to go and why. Tucker and he had no business spending a whole lot more time together. His feelings were complicated enough as it was.

Big tough cowboy, broken and hurting. Even in the abstract, Tucker's vulnerability pierced him. It would have been so easy to give in.

Even Frito pie was too much to risk. He made up his mind to drive into Port Arthur for Tex-Mex just to get as far gone as he could manage but then sat there dithering and second-guessing for near on an hour. *No good reason but one.*

And sure enough, Tucker's truck turned into the drive and right up to the porch easy as you please, exactly as he hadn't wanted. He raised his hand, and Patch raised one in answer, angry at the sweet spike of pleasure that went through him as he went down to say hey.

Fool.

Tucker hopped down and immediately skinned out of his muddy T-shirt. "Long-ass day, pup." He rubbed his damp chest and smelled his pit, grimacing at Patch.

He'd never admit it out loud, but even like this he dug Tucker's light musty odor, a blend of Ivory soap and honest sweat over his sawed-wood scent. Patch looked away. You knew you were broke to a guy when his sweat didn't bug you.

Tucker sat down on the porch steps and pulled off his boots. He stood and slapped the dust and straw off his legs. "That tedder's fixed, at least. And I rode the back fence just to check."

"You didn't have to do that."

Tucker gave him a funny squint. "Well, s'got to get done. 'Specially if you're selling."

Patch knew he was right but wanted to ignore the tightness in his gut at the prospect, as if this could work still, for both of them.

Tucker walked to the corner of the porch and turned on the hose. He bent and rinsed off his head and torso, the water gleaming on his lush muscle as Patch watched, hypnotized.

He could imagine a whole fake scenario of him on the farm: *Old MacDonald had a kink.* Tucker eating his tail by the pond. Patch groping him on the tractor. Tucker riding him bareback in the hayloft. Sitting on the porch swing to drink and stroke till it was time for rope and rutting in one of their beds.

Stop it. He almost shook himself. The longer he lingered in Hixville, the bigger the lie. He was running out of excuses to stay.

Better that he store up memories, knowing that time would pass and he'd vanish back to New York and Velocity after the funeral and the closing.

Tucker scraped the water off himself. Somehow only the waistband of his jeans had soaked up the spray. The top button of Tucker's jeans hung open, and the little strip of hair led down from his navel behind the zipper, hot as fuck. Patch scowled at himself. *Not just a hot fuck.*

"What'sa matter?"

Patch shook his head. "Nothing. Looking."

"That's bad?"

"Looking at you like a piece of meat is. You're not just handsome, Tucker. More than, I mean. I don't think you realize."

Tucker beamed and his damn dimples packed a wallop. "You think *I'm* handsome?"

"Fuck off. You know I do."

"Me too. Think you are, I mean. Not meat."

"Thanks," Patch murmured.

Awkward silence.

Tucker plucked at the rail. "People ever come atcha? Looking like you did?" Water dripped off his hand, his hair.

"No." Had they? Patch didn't remember anyone bothering him like that, at least not in a way that he couldn't handle. "You mean like trolls? Creeps."

He sounded serious. "You ever let someone touch you, you didn't want touching you?"

Patch blinked. He knew what Tucker was saying. "No." He'd gotten close a couple times, when he first landed broke in NYC, but nothing more than dates picking up dinners he never could have afforded. He knew guys who had hustled, but he'd never.

"Good." Tucker pursed his lips at the window.

Patch studied his tight expression. "What about you? Looking like you did." Murky waters and he dipped a toe.

"It weren't good." He held the beer hard. "It weren't easy. Getting blowed by ol' men."

"Tuck." Feathery sadness drifted over him and choked off his air. Had Pa suspected this shit, known his friend well enough to worry? How had Tucker survived at all?

"Not when I was little, but older. Y'know." Tucker shrugged and his gaze faded. "Twenty bucks means bed and food. But it ain't nothing you wanna do." He pursed his lips and ducked his head. "Least not me. Not then."

"Sorry." Sex was sex, but fucking scumbags so you didn't starve wasn't sex at all. "I mean, I get it, but I wish your family had—"

"Yeah." Tucker scowled. "Sad song."

Was that why Tucker had been so ugly to him in high school? Protecting him and warning him both, like a wary shepherd in wolf's clothing? Doing what his parents hadn't and Patch's wouldn't. Some kind of sick sense about scaring him straight.

Tucker looked up, eyes bright. "That's why I hated my eyes. My dick." He scuffed at the ground. "Every ugly motherfucker I never met wanting something didn't feel like mine to give."

"I get that."

"Most times folks seeing what they put on me they-selves. Ketchup on eggs." He shrugged. "Can't taste nothing else. Eventually you play the part they give you."

"You don't have to."

"There's worse things. I figger I got lucky." The porch swing rocked back and forth on a breeze. "I ain't a cripple or a halfwit. Plenty strong. Have fun. And I guess I weren't hard to look at."

"Uh, no."

"Pretty good life I got. Suits me."

Patch nodded. "That's what matters." *Bullshit.* "You ever wonder—?"

"Me?" A line between his brows.

"—what you coulda done if you'd gotten out?"

"Naw. Why? They's folks worse off." Tucker made it sound like moving into a comfortable coffin.

"I guess."

"They's plenty space between where I started and where I ended up, pup." Tucker nodded. "My folks? Hungry all the time. No school to speak of. Jobs anyone coulda got." He grinned at the yard again. "Now I got a double-wide, plenty rope, and a smartass city boy honking my horn hands-free all over Hardin County. No rivers gonna get wept over me."

Patch almost squeezed Tucker's leg but changed his mind halfway there so he dropped his hand on the swing.

"Good deal." Tucker winked. "Patch, I ain't upset or nothing. About that time. You asked, is all. Ancient history and I'm here. Fair and square."

Patch tried to make light of it. Tucker deserved better, but that wasn't his row to hoe. "Yeah. You're not fair or square, ya big galoot."

"I could be dead in some desert or dying of some disease in a ward. Folks I needed stepped up to make sure that didn't happen."

Patch smiled at that. "I get it." *The way you made sure, with me.* "I really do get it." When he'd first landed in Houston or New York, that's exactly what he had done. Found people who weren't monsters, who laughed at his jokes and treated him right. Like most gay folks lucky enough to grow up in one piece.

"You build y'own family."

"Exactly." Patch had never felt closer to another person in his life. It couldn't last, could it?

Says who?

Tucker's big smile drove the shadows off. "You want a beer? I got a six-pack inna barn." Without pausing, he clomped down the steps to the dirt and looked back up. The sunset carved his face in stern stone. "I'm gonna grab us another." He winked.

Patch nodded, not really hearing. *What if we didn't stop?*

Like a spark on straw, the notion smoldered in his mind.

Without Tucker tied to the farm anymore, he could come and party with Patch now and then. Why not? They were consenting adults. A long-distance thing didn't have to be, like, some dumb romance.

Sure, he'd head back to New York, but nobody was dying. Velocity would go and they could go on. Hell, he traveled two weeks out of the month. They'd be friends and fuck buddies.

The idea caught fire. Part of him liked the idea of showing up at Circuit parties with a hot cowboy daddy on his arm in the middle of all the pimps and posers. He could imagine the reactions, envy and lust. Having Tucker squire him once or twice a year would keep his stalkers at bay and give them time to hang out together. Everyone who accused him of being standoffish would have to back down. Hell, Tucker's rough pigginess would up his reputation.

Plus, Tucker would groove on the attention. *Probably.* Guard dog and sex toy. They'd eat him up.

After years of being the hottest thing in Hardin County, Tucker would finally be able to spread his wings. Travel. Trick.

Just roll over and play Dad.

A whole bunch of hot guys would be thrilled to get bossed around by a real live cowboy.

He frowned at himself. *That ain't fair.*

Tucker didn't have to be anyone's daddy to keep 'em interested.

In fact, whatever daddy fantasy he entertained had fuck all to do with Royce and everything to do with *manhood.* What he felt wasn't envy or weakness or shame.

Fuck Freud.

The thought of his actual pa's naked body or sex life made him queasy... hostile, even. *No.* By all accounts, Tucker was a rotten father, but he sure as nightfall made a perfect daddy.

Maybe all Patch's farmboy exes had been flimsy imitations of the guy-ness, the male-ness, the *dad*-ness of Tucker. Maybe the porno fantasies just gave him an excuse to dismantle that impossible manliness up close. Like busting a watch to see the pieces, but not knowing how to make it run, after.

Once the suspicion took hold, he couldn't shake it.

Maybe fantasizing about some daddy was never about literal fathers, and more about fatherhood as a notion: honor, protection, integrity, discipline, grit. What screwed-up small-town boy hadn't felt the gravitational pull of steady strength that punished and rewarded? The crude power of making and taking, faults and all? Maleness on the hoof that didn't ask permission.

Maybe *daddy* just meant someone strong enough to stand firm and love without limits... a man who couldn't care less and always cared more. Patch shook his head, scowling at his own dangerous logic, but he couldn't look at Tucker the same once it took root.

All of his triggers and kinks laid bare. *Quick-quick, slow, slow.*

"Head's-up, pup." Tucker's warm call made him turn, and sure enough a bottle arced toward him.

To his improbable delight, he caught the beer and snorted in pleasure at his own coordination.

"You musta played football." Tucker's eyes twinkled. "Good catch."

"Good coach." He raised the beer in a toast.

"It may come as a shock…." Tucker flicked the cap off his own bottle into the flowerbed as he climbed the steps. "But I am highly susceptible to flattery, pup."

"Not shocked." Patch twisted off his own cap and took a swig.

Almost like they'd planned it, they found themselves on the porch nursing their beers as if riding the prow of a trawler in companionable silence.

Patch sat on his mama's creaky bench swing that faced out over the fields.

After a moment, Tucker joined him, knocking their bottles together with a clink. "You think it'll hold both us." He settled himself close against Patch, and the swing held them easily. "Lookit." Tucker pointed up at something he couldn't see. "Even the stars fall for you."

"Ugh! *Tucker*." But he laughed and shoved his big cowboy, jogging the swing a moment, but he took the compliment while he could. Next week he'd be home in New York.

Sitting there, Patch couldn't think of anything else that needed saying, and Tucker seemed to feel the same. The swing shifted gently under them and every once in a while, he caught Tucker glancing at him.

The empty house seemed to loom behind them and the fireflies were out. Glowing pinpricks dotted the night around the house, bobbing like tipsy stars.

Patch took a sip and tipped his beer toward the tiny drifting lights. "I always wanted to catch 'em. Fireflies."

"Me too." Tucker nodded and sighed, peeling the label off his bottle. "Kids do."

They swung a few gentle inches, back and forth, in a breeze sweet with fresh-mowed grass. Patch smiled, even though no one could see.

"What?" Tucker turned, as if he'd felt the smile happen.

"Drove me nuts when I was young. Younger. All the stuff you can't have."

"Well." Tucker winked and rocked some more. "You know the absolute best way to catch lightning bugs?" He made it sound dirty.

Patch turned his head. "Mmh?"

"Live close and invite 'em over." Tucker ran the back of his hand along Patch's forearm. "They'll catch themselves just fine without a jar. Live longer too."

Patch screwed up his mouth and scoffed. "Pssshh. Yeah."

"Can't make things live where they don't wanna."

Patch blinked. What'd that mean? He squeezed Tucker's hand and turned to see his expression.

A kind of brightness lit Tucker's eyes, a lambent brandy glow behind the cracks in the stern gray. Patch could just about see the boy he'd been before life beat the stuffing out of him.

"Pup, you thinking again?"

"Nossir."

Tucker shifted back on the swing. "Good deal."

Without asking permission or testing first, Patch lowered his head to Tucker's shoulder. Tucker grunted and hitched closer, chin notched against his head where it fit.

One of them sighed, and the other did the same while the swing swung softly and tiny drunken stars drifted around them on the warm breeze, exactly where they wanted to be.

FUNERALS SUCKED.

Patch wore the loose black suit he'd picked up at the charity shop in Kountze, and he spent the whole day heading for the door no matter where he was, at home, the viewing, the church, the burial.

Mostly Patch ran a slow-motion sprint between ugly emotional scenes with people who didn't know or care about him.

Well, mostly.

To keep himself in one place, he kept pretending he was tied to the brass bed in Tucker's dark trailer... like a game, a trial, a test. Struggling against imaginary knots gave him something to do so he wouldn't go nuts.

Mercifully, Pastor Snell kept things short and sour: two hymns, no anecdotes. The Keister sisters did a merciful job with the organ (loud) and flowers (lilies) and only squabbled a little, and after the fact. Vicky drove over from Kountze with her three kids and gangly Fred in tow, bless her. She even stopped to hug him and say a few plausible things, which he appreciated, then let him alone, which he appreciated even more.

In theory, a funeral was a group-hug good-bye so a community could leave their regret six feet below their soles.

He kept wishing he could have somehow snuck Botchy into church beside him. She could have kept him company without asking him things he couldn't answer and making promises she didn't mean. Truth be told, she probably would've felt what was happening more than most of these other hypocrites.

In practice, a funeral ended up being a wedding in black, except you married the dirt.

Tucker drove him from the church and to the cemetery but hung back throughout, a relief and disappointment, both.

Janet and Dave flanked him at the grave, while Tucker stood behind him like a wounded sentry. Even they couldn't stave off the waves of sympathy threatening to suffocate him. After years of overuse, he found he'd started to run out of fake smiles.

No rain today. The blinding sunlight over the graveside turned the two holes into a hungry equal sign.

Anywhere but here sounded good. Supposedly, funerals made folks horny, but mainly he felt exhausted, shaky, and hysterical. By the time the coffins were fed into the parallel plots, Patch had decided he wanted to be cremated and would have given his whole right arm to be in bed with someone grouchy, handsome, and hard-handed. Not horniness—self-preservation. Only the thought of Tucker's stubble on his skin kept him from snapping and splitting right there in front of all those well-wishers wishing him well in front of witnesses.

He hadn't wanted any reception, but Ms. Landry swanned in and organized something at the low sheet-metal hall by the church: finger sandwiches and limp handshakes. He stood stiff inside the foyer drowning in condolences while his parents' parish sniffed and grazed on soggy hors d'oeuvres.

A panic rose in him occasionally, a frantic laugh and rush that wanted loose and gone. Adrenaline scoured his insides like a jangling alarm, and any second he needed to bolt, *quick-quick*. Patch only kept himself nailed in place by closing his eyes and imagining his hands rubbing the scars on Botchy's coat or simply feeling the sweet slip of that brass bed under his back while Tucker spoke slow, slow truth to his skin.

Imaginary knots. *Hold your horses.*

"Slow, slow," he whispered under his breath whenever his hands shook. *Slow, slow.*

Janet kept most of the well-wishers off him beyond the clucks and clasps, swooping in to steer them away to the table of Wonder Bread and mayonnaise. And Tucker stood guard, hovering a few yards away like a stern storm, handsome in his baggy suit. He didn't flirt or joke with anyone who said *hi*. And after the first ten minutes, he didn't look at anyone but Patch.

Exactly fifty-nine minutes into the reception, there was a hard hand at his elbow. "Time to go, pup." Tucker nodded at him, moving him toward the door firmly. "You don't even need to say nothing to none of 'em." He shook his head at Janet as she approached, looking worried. "Let's go home. I gotcha."

Patch nodded and closed his eyes, letting his caretaker take care of him. With that hand on his arm, he wouldn't stumble. He walked blind and steady through the murmuring room and only knew the outside by the sun on his face.

"You with me still," Tucker told him, not asking, low and concerned at his ear. Then he asked, "Pup?"

Patch nodded, dumb and docile. He could sleep standing right here. Opening his eyes, he found himself beside Tucker's truck. The imaginary knots had fallen into imaginary rope around his feet.

"We gonna go now. Okay by you?"

Another nod. Something was broken inside, or was that a preexisting condition? *Objects in mirror are closer than they appear.*

Tucker opened the door and sort of boosted him into the seat before jogging around to the driver side and climbing in. "They shouldn't have done that. Sandwiches an' all. They mean well, but Chris'sakes."

Patch closed his eyes again, and the truck started and pulled out, looping around to head back toward Hixville. He exhaled all the way, forcing the air out so he wouldn't bring it home with him.

Tucker put one hand on his leg and stroked it roughly.

"I shoulda got my hair cut like Ma liked." Patch scratched the curly mess on his head.

"Naw, pup." Tucker sounded confused.

His eyes drifted shut again. "All off, crew cut."

"I wouldn'ta let you. You look… perfect."

"Thank you, Tucker." Then he turned to look at Tucker's rugged profile, the hand on the wheel, the bleached farms rolling past them outside, the road home. "Thanks."

Tucker pursed his lips and nodded, looking sheepish, but he left the other hand on Patch's leg where it belonged. "You gonna take a break tomorrow. Anything you want. You say, we'll do it."

Patch opened his mouth but couldn't think of anything normal to say. The idea of going back to New York felt like driving ninety miles an hour into a brick wall. "And you too?"

"I reckon I might, if you said so."

"I say so." Exhale. "Sir."

Tucker smiled at the road. "Good deal."

Little by little, lulled by the speed and the quiet, Patch dozed off.

Back at the trailer, Tucker fed him chili and made him stretch out on the couch to nap. "You don't need nothing but sleep."

He was right.

Patch woke up starving and bleary around ten that night and ate another bowl of Tucker's chuck chili without fully waking up. He refilled Botchy's water on the porch and bumped right into a brawny naked cowboy.

Tucker held open one arm, and Patch leaned against him without comment, staring over the fields. They leaned together a moment in the warm stillness, the gentle pressure like dancing without moving.

Patch sighed, spent and content. "What do you reckon?"

Tucker shook his head slowly. "I got nothing."

"Well. Not quite nothing."

"Near enough, pup." Tucker stroked his ribs steadily, as if calming a colt. "No idea. Just a feeling, I got."

Patch frowned at the night. In a couple days, he was s'posed to fly home, and he could hardly walk. He should have bought the ticket already. He should have done a lot of things. How was he going to go back to New York and forget the past week? "Sorry."

"No, I mean thoughts. Too fast, too much."

And then Tucker wouldn't say more, just watched the night in uneasy silence.

Patch lifted the muscular hand from his side and laced their fingers. "Tucker, you know I'll do—"

"Naw. This my trouble an' all. It's just— It's like…." He wiped his face. "Heaven don't want me and hell's afraid I'll take over."

He grinned. "You, me, both."

Tucker straightened and regarded him carefully, reading something in his face. Whatever he saw, his brow wrinkled and he herded Patch toward the screen door. "C'mon, pup. Bed."

Patch let himself be turned and stumbled inside, down the narrow hallway to Tucker's room, crawling in and pulling Tucker's arm over him, not even caring what it meant.

He didn't dream at all and when he woke in the big brass bed, Tucker was still spooned up against him, breathing deeply. He squirmed in dozy pleasure.

Tucker squirmed in slow reply. "Mmmh. Good," he said, or maybe "God."

Patch rocked his face down into the pillow and lay hopelessly horizontal, matching Tucker's slow, deep inhale-exhale until his eyes drifted closed.

Around 8:00 a.m. he heard something small and high-pitched. Probably Botchy whining outside, or mice, or his imagination.

Tucker's arms were a steady weight over and under his ribs. What would they do today? Everything seemed possible and appealing, as if a suffocating weight had lifted while he slept. He remembered yesterday, parts of it, at least, and even then he could breathe easy.

Tucker never slept in, but he'd obviously decided to take the day off after the funeral, which was kind and smart, both. The down comforter smelled like sawdust. Maybe this was where Tucker got the smell, or vice versa.

Stop it. He'd started to wake up and his head had cranked into gear. Again the squeaking or cheeping. He turned a bit in Tucker's arms.

Tucker's eyes were closed.

He tried to pinpoint the sound. "You hear them squeaks?"

"Mmmh." Tucker squeezed him lightly.

Now he was wide-awake. "'S that the dog?"

"Chicks," Tucker muttered.

Patch squinted at the craggy face. "What girl squeals like that?"

"Chickens." Tucker opened his eyes a slit. "Bathroom. Sleep." He chewed his lip and closed them again, shamelessly dozing off and tempting him to do the same.

Patch couldn't let it rest. He slipped out of the bed, ignoring the grumbling sexiness he left behind in the bed, and went to the closest bathroom. No chickens there, and the creaking seemed further away.

Rubbing his face, Patch followed his ears to the other end of the trailer to the spare bedroom and the other—

"Chicks." He laughed in the doorway of the unused back bathroom.

The whole bathtub was filled with a layer of straw and pale yellow and white and brown balls of fluff cheeping indignantly at the draft of air. A couple slept in wobbly heaps together. A tiny space heater kept the room uncomfortably warm, probably for them, and one high window lit it dimly. The close space made the peeps seem louder than they were.

He squatted and reached out to touch. "So soft! Hey."

The fluffy army did not like this big monster leaning over them one bit. Most moved back from his hand, but a few brave or stupid babies stayed near enough to peck at his fingers. They felt like little silky clouds brushing past. "Look at you guys."

"Sorry 'bout them." Tucker stood in the doorway, handsome as hell in his boxers and rumpled hair. "I was hoping you'd sleep in, get some rest."

Patch shook his head and gestured at the tub of meeping fluffballs as if he'd discovered a new continent. "Chicks."

Tucker rolled his eyes. "I tol' you."

"Well, you didn't say clear, so how could I know? They're hilarious." Obviously they thought voices meant food because they were agitated now. "They hungry?"

"When ain't they?"

His folks had hated chickens and refused to keep birds all his life, even for fresh eggs. "I didn't realize you were raising chickens too."

"Just business. Last year I done so good selling eggs on the side, I figgered they's an investment. Folks come by from all over. Fresh eggs is good money. Three bucks a dozen. Five-six dozen a day. And Janet takes my extras up the Feed & Seed."

Patch nodded, ashamed. *That's* how broke Tucker was: seventy or eighty bucks a week made a difference. He felt like a grade-A asshole.

Leaning against the doorway, Tucker considered him with soft affection. "Them little bastards like you plenty, huh. You got the touch."

Patch beamed back. "Can I feed 'em?"

"Sure." *Shore*. He tapped a bucket by the door with his foot. "They get this high-protein grind mixed with other stuff. Gimme two secs. 'F you want, you can refill their water."

Tucker disappeared, and Patch grabbed the two flat dishes crisscrossed with rubber bands. What purpose the bands served he had no idea, but he emptied both in the sink and refilled them. After returning it to the tub, he stroked one brave brown chick with his knuckle till it conked out.

Tucker called from the kitchen, "That's my chores you doin', so I figger I'll have to reward you somehow. Special an' all."

Patch laughed and called back, "Looks like you will."

Tucker returned with two bowls, mashing something with a spoon.

Patch pointed at the napping chick. "He passed out. He okay?"

"Yeah, they always zipping around, so they wear out fast and wake up the same." He passed the bowls. "Not even you can keep up."

Patch put the food down and suddenly his left hand was an object of gleeful adoration at both ends of the tub. The chicks pressed forward and pecked at the gritty contents, meeping their approval.

"They dig around. Instinct, I guess. So I mix the grind with crumbled yolk, shred lettuce, boiled rice. Gives 'em something to look for."

"Nice." For no very good reason, Patch felt better than he had all week, sitting on this bathroom floor looking at a tubful of baby birds. Cleaner, somehow, and steadier. "What's with the rubber bands?"

"So they don't drown." Tucker shook his head with a rueful grin. "Them little guys so crazy they fall over in the water and choke because they don't know better. They always zooming around, so you gotta look out for 'em."

"Makes sense to me." Patch tried to count the chicks, but they kept bobbing and bouncing off each other too quickly. Three collided near the water and knocked each other down in a heap like fluffy drunks. He gave a wheeze of sympathetic laughter. He stroked another curious visitor pecking the straw near him.

Tucker shook his head slowly, as if baffled. "I didn't know you favored animals so much."

"Do I?"

"Well, them there you do." He nodded at the tub. "And Botchy. Nugget. Lightning bugs. You a farmboy an' all." He offered a hand to pull him up.

"Well, I am." Patch took the hand and stood, brushing his palms on his legs. "They're terrific." *You're terrific*, he wanted to say but didn't know how it would sound, after everything.

"You okay?" Tucker brushed Patch's hair out of his eyes so they could see each other clearly. "Yesterday an' all."

Patch nodded. "I think so." He glanced back at the chicks. "I was wiped out, I think. I don't remember making it home. Or lots of things, I guess."

"Well, you ain't working today for nothing. You try and I'll whup you."

"Oh you think so?"

"Amen and church after." A flash of white teeth in the stubbled face. "Pup, are you doubting my word?"

"Nossir."

Tucker winked and ambled off down the hall. Without turning, he said, "Don't make me get out them ropes."

Patch smiled at the tub of fluff. Something had shifted between them, and he couldn't say what.

He took another look at the bobbing chicks and then headed out in search of some breakfast. As he reached the kitchen, his phone buzzed and skittered on the counter where Tucker must have plugged it in last night.

Midsip, Tucker nodded at the vibrations over his coffee. "Been buzzing a bunch, that thing."

He picked it up and discovered a text from Priscilla, a Latina DJ he'd met in Mykonos last winter.

SCOTTY SAYS YR DOWN SOUTH started a chain of texts she'd sent in the wee hours, offering him two key gigs spinning at Southern Decadence. By the tenth or eleventh text she apologized and essentially begged, *NEED A LAST MIN. COVER, PRONTO.*

New Orleans always drew a big crowd and so close. *Crazy opportunity*. He could make the drive in three hours if he lead-footed it. Nine hundred guaranteed for Friday and over double that if the tea dance was a go. The clock on Tucker's wall said seven, so maybe he hadn't missed out. He texted back in the affirmative. *Hey girl! In East TX, I'm down if NOLA gig still open.*

Tucker filled his coffee cup carefully, and creamed and sugared it again. "What happened?"

Another buzz. "Last-minute job." He clapped his hands and bobbed his head as he scooped up the phone again. "Near here."

Tucker made a "no shit" face and took another sip.

On his phone Priscilla closed the deal with hearts and kisses. *SOLD, MIJO! WILL CONFIRM WITH PROMOTER.*

"Good news an' all?"

"Real good. Big gig." He had a definite set at the Bourbon Pub Friday night prime time. And a solid lead on a private tea dance Saturday afternoon if he got on it today. "Maybe a bonus too, if I kill it."

Tucker said, "See? Shit grows roses."

"Please and thank you."

The big cowboy grinned as if he'd predicted the offer. "Is this music or model stuff?"

"DJing a huge party on the Circuit." Soon as he said it, he realized Tucker couldn't imagine what that meant or how much fun they'd have together exploring New Orleans. And just like that, Patch wanted to show him. He turned the smile on Tucker, full blast, and braced his hands. "Come with me."

Tucker choked on the sip he was taking, then put the coffee down on the counter between 'em. "To a party? This that disco rodeo thing?"

He nodded. "New Orleans."

"I ain't never been."

"C'mon. That's impossible." Patch regretted the words as soon as they made it out.

Tucker didn't take offense, though. "Why would I? No work for me out there. And I never been much for travel, huh?" He shrugged.

"Food. Fun. I promise you'll love it. Gig's on Friday and Saturday— we'd be back fast."

"That don't matter, pup." His grin grew. "You mean it?"

Clear a few grand. Show Tucker the sights. Eat, drink, and get hairy. Get away from this place for a couple days, just the two of them. *Oxygen with a side of beef.* "That's why I asked."

"Then I guess so. Yep." He drained his mug with a smug smile. "Two days, Janet and Dave'll watch the animals if we ask. They done it before."

Patch laughed in triumph. "I promise. All you gotta do is kick back and enjoy."

"That's my kinda weekend." He laughed back, and the happy sound bouncing in the trailer's snug kitchen made Patch feel like he'd won the lottery. "Good deal."

"Thanks, Tucker. Thank you." Taking this trip seemed right, important, necessary. *Secret sojourn.* When else would they have a chance to spend this kind of time together?

He shot the tea dance promoter an e-mail with links to his site, confident his underwear shots and mixes would seal the deal. Sure enough, within ten minutes, he got a reply with the subject line "LIFESAVER!" and the Saturday tea dance set was his as well, along with another grand and extra travel money.

Outside a sleepy rooster crowed, and crowed again, working up his nerve on the job.

Tucker grabbed the pot to pour himself another cup of coffee. He filled the mug halfway, then topped it up with heavy cream and spoons of sugar: one-two-three-four. The black swill turned pale beige. He stirred it lazily, his spoon *tinking* against the bottom. He lifted an eyebrow and his crow's-feet deepened. "Whatzat?"

Baffled by the entire process, Patch paused and asked, "Why you drink it so sweet?" He glanced at the mug on the counter.

Tucker didn't answer at first, just took a swallow and traced the mug's handle with a broad fingertip for a moment, frowning. "When I's a kid, my folks wasn't good about food. Keeping it in the house an'—" He grinned, but his eyes didn't. "Meals an' all. We lived on other folks' ranches mostly. Mama cleaned and my daddy worked stock when he could stand up sober. Most mornings I'd walk over to the office in the barn, and they'd be all this coffee inna pot. Nasty, black stuff. Strong enough to run a mouse across it. Thick and burnt."

Patch knew what barn coffee smelled like, especially on a big outfit. Most hands used it primarily to keep their gloves warm in cold weather.

"Them guys'd just reheat it and reheat it all year long. Never washed the durn pot." He grimaced. "But it was hot and free, and I was hungry."

Patch nodded and made sure he didn't blink, not once. *Jesus.* He tried to watch Tucker's stony face as gently as he could.

"So I'd pour me a half mug of grown-up coffee like I was one-a the hands, fill up the other half with milk and sugar. Guys musta knowed why, but they never said nothing." Tucker looked up then, eyes glittering.

"Two, three cups, I'd be set for the day. Who needs eggs?" He took a swallow from his mug.

Out back that rooster crowed again, a good clean one that split the air and poked the sun.

Patch frowned, eyes dry. "Some families don't deserve kids."

"Sure. Some kids don't have a family to start with." His gaze so clear, hands so strong.

For a moment Patch saw the little boy Tucker had been: farmer tan, boots plugged with cardboard, ragged hand-me-downs from someone else's clothesline. His shitty parents leaving him to rot in the dust like a groundfall pear.

"What?" Tucker was eying him uncomfortably. The low drawl, the dimpled whiskered chin, and the work-hard muscle almost didn't matter. *Bait.* "Pretty dumb, huh."

Cowboy, coach, daddy, dom, bastard, buddy: all the easy, sleazy fantasies pulled back to show the kid Tucker could have been, the person he was, the man he wanted to be.

I love you, Tucker Biggs.

Patch squeezed his hands into weak fists and didn't even fight the feeling. The unshakable certainty looped over his head and heart and hope and tugged against his ribs like rope until he couldn't move, didn't want to.

What else could he do?

Unable to say the words, or take another breath on his own, he rose up and forward until their chests scrubbed together, laying his brow and cheek into the hollow of Tucker's throat.

Tucker kissed the top of his head. "Mmph. Smell pretty good, pup." His breath was hot in Patch's curly hair. "You figgered what we gone do today?"

Patch muttered apologies against his Adam's apple.

"Yessir. Somethin' good." Tucker raised his rough hands and brought their faces together. Sandpaper on Patch's jawline. That smile, that wink, that rumble. "Who needs sugar?"

Patch kissed the sweet, scratchy lips and left their mouths together to whisper, "Not you."

CHAPTER EIGHT

FRIDAY, THEY woke before first light because Tucker's clock only had one setting, and left too early to see clear or sit straight.

Patch needed to check in and test his equipment with the sound team, and this way they'd reach New Orleans by seven, well before the party kicked off at noon. He offered to drive in shifts, but Tucker side-eyed him and took the wheel.

"Pup, I been driving to rodeos cross-country since the Dead Sea was still sick." He started the engine. "Not even speeding, we'll be there for sunrise breakfast."

"Perfect. Beignets at Du Monde."

"Do what?"

Patch lifted his eyebrows and put his boot up on the dash. "You'll see."

Silence as Tucker's tires ate the road taking them out of Hixville, past the pine woods of the Big Thicket, east to Louisiana on a highway empty all the way to the horizon.

True to his word, Tucker stayed five miles over the speed limit even this early in the day. Patch let him pick the music (bluegrass) and traffic stayed sparse heading east up I-10.

About five in the morning, Tucker pulled off at Buc-ees, a huge truck stop outside Lake Charles, for a piss and a Coke. "Gotta get ridda all that coffee. You comin?"

He did, but just because he wanted to stretch his legs. For his part, Patch ignored bleary truckers eying them and stayed out of the echoing bathroom. He could hear showers running in there, and out in the sticks, the wrong kinda look could get you beat. He felt safer with Tucker standing over his shoulder, but they didn't need any ugly episodes this weekend.

The whole purpose of this trip was to smooth things over for him: leaving the farm, Patch going back to NYC, Tucker finding some job and a place.

Patch widened his eyes and blew his hair out of his face. "Well, that was freaky as fuck."

Tucker squinted at him over the hood and climbed inside, reaching across to unlock the door. "Buc-ees was?"

"All those truckers circling for dick. You didn't notice? Them scoping each other, cruising us."

"Not— No. I guess not." Tucker reversed out and circled back to the highway. "Well, no. I didn't. I ain't a gay, Patch. What I get up to in bed's got fuck all to do with how I live or what I listen to."

"Well, no." Patch knew he shouldn't push but couldn't help himself. "Until someone tells you no."

"Whatzat mean?" Tucker's face was stiff with obvious confusion. If ever he'd thought about this stuff, it hadn't been much.

"That there's a whole world around you. Everything doesn't end at the fence line just because it's easier that way. Folks get beat. Kids get taken away. Hell, down in Sour Lake there's preachers who'd burn us both alive just for holding hands, let alone what we did last night and we're fixing to do later more'n once."

Tucker made a grumpy sound. "Well, that's stupid. That don't have to be."

"No, it doesn't, but only 'cause some *gays* made a fuss."

"Who wants a fuss? Not me." Tucker changed lanes without checking his mirrors.

Patch shook his head, impotent, impatient. This was every fight he'd ever had with his parents, his pa especially. And this was the same. "No different than those kids with the flag't got you so honked off. Stars and bars. It matters."

"It's nobody's business."

"Agreed. Which is why it's important to make sure it stays nobody's business."

Tucker didn't say anything, folded in on himself like a bagged lunch. "Not for me. Sorry, pup. I ain't that way." Whether he meant gay or brave or grateful, he didn't indicate, but he dropped the subject like a rattlesnake.

Awkward. Patch didn't push the issue and let the radio fill the silence.

In another hour they hit the outskirts of Baton Rouge and not much later Metairie, before taking the looping ramp down into the Quarter.

"So, uhhh... I never asked." Tucker held his spread hand outside the window to catch the breeze. He gave Patch a crooked, fuzzy smile. "These guys come all this way for a party? That's gotta be some party."

"The Circuit's…." Patch shook his head and looked at the pickup's ceiling. How could he explain an army of juiced-up muscle models paying a couple grand to hump each other to cutting-edge dance music for a few days straight? He opted for the rose-colored glasses version. "Sort of a sexy nightclub carnival on steroids. It's like a… I dunno, a string of migrating parties that last up to seventy-two hours at a time." *Please let that sound fun to him.*

"That's a lotta party. All guys, all gay?"

"Well, yeah. Whole other level. Olympic-level fun with lightning rods and no limits and surprise pop stars. The hottest guys you ever seen all flying in, cutting loose, hooking up. Sex on stage. Legit celebrities. High octane everything. You'll love it." He hoped.

Tucker blinked at the road. "Mmh." He seemed dubious.

"You can't imagine. Loud, crazy, sweaty shenanigans with the sexiest guys in the most beautiful places on earth."

"And you know all them gay guys?" Tucker squinted over at Patch, wary.

So that was it. "Not like— Well, no. But I got plenty of friends on the Circuit. DJing for these promoters builds your name and pays serious bank."

"Good deal for you."

"Yup." Patch had never navigated this kind of shit because he'd never been with anyone who didn't understand the Circuit. "So you're okay with folks looking."

"Who's gone be looking?"

"At me, Tucker." Patch crossed his arms over the seat belt. "Folks'll look. That's part of the DJ thing. I'm part of the show."

Tucker stopped, scowled hard enough a line appeared between his brows. "Huh."

"'S why I take care of myself."

A sly smile as Tucker glanced over. "Why you been doing push-ups and sit-ups and squats too, I bet."

Busted. "Not just me, I mean. Some Circuit guys lift strictly for these weekends. Train hard at the gym just so they can get their beef out. But I attract attention."

"Amen." Tucker shrugged. "I ain't bothered. What's-a point? Men's men. We check the goods, I figger. Gays same as us."

"Well, yeah." Patch didn't push anything there. Tucker seemed to have a pretty loose idea of this fooling-around-with-dudes deal. "They're gonna look at you too."

"Well, hell, that's anybody. Guys are guys. Am I gone look back? Sure. Everybody's gotta go to the fair and pet the pig." Tucker huffed, eyebrows up.

"Hey!"

"That's not what I said." Tucker grinned. "Well, it is, but it ain't what I meant." He shook his head calmly. "Who wouldn't wanna look at you?"

Patch soaked up the praise.

"They won't bother you none, 'cause they do I'm gonna have words for 'em. But I don't own you," Tucker said.

He stopped smiling. "No." The shortest lie he'd ever told.

At the Bourbon Pub, he left Tucker napping in the truck and checked the feeds and levels. *No sweat.* According to the sound tech, Thursday's parties had gone smoothly, and they expected a hundred and fifty thousand folks in the city by tonight. A good weekend ahead.

They parked the truck at a garage near their hotel and dumped the bags. Tucker couldn't get over their view, looking down at a little courtyard with "a real fountain."

His boyish wonder shook Patch like a happy can of hot soda. After, they walked deeper into the Quarter, slowly making their way along Decatur to Jackson Square. People swept and hosed the sidewalks, and the streets were still empty enough to not worry about cars.

"Right up there." Patch pointed at the open-air cafe, sparsely populated this time of morning and this time of year. Summer in New Orleans the hotels were cheap as dirt, which was how Southern Decadence had kicked off and grown so fast. Good food, warm locals, and friendly bars.

They sat and Tucker made him order, looking out toward the river. "No walls. This ain't what I thought you'd want at all." He frowned and shrugged.

"Good. I like surprising you."

"That is a true statement." Tucker blinked at him. "I think I'm hungry, pup. What all'd you order now?"

"Coffee. Beignets." He tapped the menu on the napkin dispenser. "Au lait just means with milk. And sweet already. Way you like. I'm telling you."

In no time, the waiter came back with two big bowls of coffee and a plate of beignets under a thick drift of powdered sugar.

Tucker added his spoons of sugar and took a careful sip. "Mmgh. That tastes like… chocolate? Man, that's good." Another, deeper sip.

"'S the chicory." Patch nudged the beignet plate, feeling pretty confident of the reaction. "And for my next trick, give one of them a try. Hands is fine."

Looking nervous, Tucker wiped his fingers and took hold of one, not even shaking the loose sugar. He took a wide bite and froze. His eyes melted and he grunted in pleasure, speaking with his mouth full and no apologies. "Jesus H. Crickets."

"Try it with the coffee."

Tucker was a goner.

From there, three beignets became a dozen, with a gallon of cafe au lait alongside. And the only reason it stopped was because Tucker called it quits. "I'm fixin' to bust my pants. And you gotta be bored watching me eat."

"No sir. Much as you dig it? I could watch you eat stuff, groaning and licking, all damn day."

Tucker looked up then, sucking the powdered sugar off his fingers with slow relish. "That so?"

Patch stared at his cowboy, blood thudding in his ears like anything.

With a lazy grin, Tucker licked sugar from one side of the bristly whiskers. "I love it sweet and hot, you know that."

"Fuck, Tucker." He gripped his crotch. "Now I got a damn boner. No fucking underwear. Jesus, what you do to me."

"Yeah?" Tucker wiped his mouth. "I told you to put them shorts on."

"Well, I didn't. And now I'm bent wrong and it's too hard to flip."

Tucker took another swallow of coffee, in no kinda hurry. "And?"

"And I'm gonna have to go to the john to get rid of this before I can walk past them families. Bust and go before I get arrested." He nodded at the gabbling patrons dotting the cafe even at this hour.

"No, you won't." Tucker scowled and took his wrist, gripping it firmly. "That's mine, there."

He nodded, startled.

"Are you funnin' me or you really need a nut that bad?" He sucked the pad of his thumb and winked. Maybe he'd pull Patch off in the truck while driving, so he sprayed the dash. Or at a rest stop. Or in the hotel. Maybe all of the above and gold star for playing.

Free-range lust.

Patch realized Tucker would do it, drag him into a public john in a twenty-four-hour cafe and milk his nut with folks outside a thin door and in the street besides. Do it? Hell, he'd enjoy it more, *savor* the slow suffering. "Nossir. I'm good right here with you. I'd better wait."

"You got a problem, you bring it to me. Y'hear? Don't you waste it. Not while you're here."

Here, French Quarter? Here, road trip? Here, visiting Hixville? He had no idea. "Yessir."

Tucker squinted and blinked, maybe teasing or maybe not. He ate another beignet, taking his sweet Texas time.

Now that the day had gotten underway, the streets began to bubble around them, and Patch took Tucker on a wandering tour. He'd played plenty of parties here and knew enough to be entertaining. They stopped to eat a couple times, and wandered into galleries they couldn't afford, but more than anything they took their time, together.

Somewhere in the past week, Patch had learned how to wait once in a while. When it counted.

On the way back to their little hotel that afternoon, Tucker eyed his reflection in a dark store window. "I need a shave." In fact, he hadn't shaved since the funeral, so the stubble had started to cross the line into beard, mostly dark with less silver than up top.

"If you want. I like it both ways." Without thinking, Patch reached across and scratched at it. The streets were mostly empty, but Tucker didn't seem to mind a bit.

He smiled. "Well... I'll clean up once we get settled. I don't wanna look like a damn hick."

"Speak for yourself." Then he realized this was Tucker's first trip out of state. He probably wanted to dress up. "It's New Orleans. We can dress however." A plan began to simmer in Patch's mind. He waved at the garish window displays on both sides of Toulouse. "I mean, like flip-flops and a towel if you wanna. Honest."

Tucker sounded skeptical. "I ain't gone embarrass you, pup. You work for these goobers. If I ain't got the right shirt, we can go buy something."

"Naw," Patch drawled. Why did he feel so goddamned Texan whenever he left Texas? He caught Tucker smiling, knew why, and fought the urge to play the hayseed. "In the Quarter? You could show up in overalls or a dress or body-glitter-balls-naked, and no one would blink. Well, not *blink*. They might kidnap you and chain you to a bed. The flesh is weak."

Tucker didn't take the bait. "You fix me however you want." So he was nervous, then.

"You don't need fixing."

"I'm serious." He scrunched his lips over his teeth. "You put me together how you want. 'Kay?"

"Deal. Same."

Tucker did turn then. "Me dress you? No way."

"Fair's fair. It's a chill gig, and I'm in the booth anyways. You get me up however you want, and I'll go along." He squeezed Tucker's knotty thigh. "But I get to do the same. I want to show you off to all them rich perverts."

"Jesus wept." Tucker sighed, but he looked calmer and walked back to the hotel without any other comments. They stopped to pick up a couple six-packs for the fridge: Tucker grabbed the Bud, Patch countered with Guinness, and they left with both.

Upstairs in their hotel room they stripped down and split a cold Guinness in a glass before rinsing off and getting off so Patch could calm down. Tucker held his wrists high and jerked him off fast in the shower and then knelt down to suck him clean while he busted a hot mess on Patch's calves.

Watching his big cowboy servicing him hungrily did Patch's jitters a world of good. Afterward, when he stood to rinse again and kissed Patch under the shower spray, he tasted like cock and beer.

Obviously this weekend, anything might happen and probably would.

After they'd dried off, they dropped their bags on the bed between them. Patch held out a hand to shake. "Anything's fair game."

Tucker took it, bemused. "I figger I'm in a heap of trouble now." He cracked open another Guinness and refilled the glass. "This stout stuff's good. Rich." He licked foam off his stache.

First Patch dug through the contents of Tucker's knapsack. He had packed for a rodeo: pearl-button shirts and ironed jeans, a couple faded T-shirts.

Made sense. Rodeos were the only chance Tucker'd ever had to get fancy for strangers.

The only thing Patch grabbed out of the pile was socks, the ridged black boots (alligator), and a black rodeo belt (ostrich) with a wide prize buckle (*BULLDOGGING*). He picked up briefs, weighed them, and then, eyes on Tucker, tossed the folded underwear back on the bed like an undersized catfish.

Tucker sighed, "Oh Lord." But he sounded pleased. "Do I get pants, at least?" He opened the bathroom door.

"What you think you're doing?"

"I needta shave at least, 'fore you parade my ass up Bourbon."

He swatted Tucker. "The hell you will."

"What? Patch, what?" Tucker grimaced. "Okay, now you look evil."

He held up clippers and clicked them on. "Can I do something to your mustache?"

Tucker shrugged. "Your go."

Three minutes later he wiped them both down with a damp towel and let Tucker see himself.

"Lord." He'd trimmed the thick bristle into a proper old-school porno handlebar that framed Tucker's hard mouth and cleft chin. He looked like a cocky outlaw in a spaghetti western.

"Looks sharp." Tucker grinned and winked at him in the mirror.

"Just like that." He ran a hand over the raspy jaw and flicked the cleft chin. "You don't even know. You can't."

"You should see how you're looking at me 'bout now."

Patch blushed, the pink crawling up his chest and neck to his temples. "I'm gonna go to hell."

Tucker stepped up behind him and tucked his chin into Patch's collarbone. "Save me a seat, huh?" He turned and kissed Patch's hair.

"Now duds." Patch pushed him back out toward the bed.

Tucker smiled indulgently and let him play porno dress up, pulling on his boot socks while he stood there. He took another deep swig of stout that drained the glass, then raised it. "Courage."

Patch upended his own bag on the bedspread and rummaged. A whisper-thin undershirt. A pair of oversized black Diesels, baggy for him but tight on Tucker.

Stuffing himself into the jeans, Tucker scowled. "Hold on, pup. I'm freeballing? And where's my shirt?"

Patch handed him the white tank. "It's for effect. If you get sweaty you can tuck it or ditch it."

"Effect. Huh." Tucker bunched the tank and tugged it onto himself.

Truth was, the sheer cotton made him look more naked than naked because of the way it hugged his pecs and abdomen. Plus Tucker sliding bare chested against him in a sweaty back room sounded ideal. The trick would be keeping everyone else off him.

Tucker tucked the tank, adjusted his junk, and zipped, then sat to tug on the boots.

Patch enjoyed the view, mightily. *Why am I not taking pictures of this?* "Sunglasses too." He handed over a pair of mirrored shades circa 1977, and on they went.

Tucker straightened and growled at the big mirror. "Fuck."

Fuck.

"Hello, Trouble."

The low-rise jeans hauled Tucker's cock into a rounded wad to the left of his zipper under a buckle the size of a burger. Standing in those hornback boots, veins wrapped up his arms, his square chest, retro handlebar, and the silver aviators shading his smoky eyes, Tucker looked illegal.

Tucker shifted his weight. "Am I okay?"

"Uhh." Patch closed his mouth. "You're—" He pressed his hand to Tucker's back. "Yes."

"You say so." Tucker frowned, as if he wasn't seeing the same thing. "Your turn."

"My turn." Patch loved dressing to go out but he had no idea what Tucker had in mind for him, or even what he'd want to see.

"Whatever I want?"

"Freaky as you feel like." Patch had no idea what Tucker would pull out of his duffel of party clothes. Tux? Boy Scout uniform? Chaps and a pigtail butt plug?

Instead Tucker reached into his own pile and pulled out a plain white Hanes T-shirt and a pair of Wranglers that would be loose on him. He caught Patch's confused stare. "What?"

"Not a thing." What was he up to? Now Patch really was digging this goofy game.

"They'll fit fine. You'll have to wear your own boots." Tucker licked his whiskers, squinting at something. "And you don't get underwear neither." He pursed his lips.

Patch had no problem with that option. "Anything else?"

"I like your hair curly. Y'know? All loose and wild."

"My agent calls it freshly fucked."

Tucker raised an eyebrow. "Oh yeah? I like that."

"But we're on a schedule, so don't get any ideas," said Patch.

"Well, fresh-fucked, then. Yeah. So I can put my hands in it."

"Dealer's choice." Patch fingercombed a dab of product through his hair, then dried it roughly with a towel. It would curl in the damp air by the time they arrived.

Tucker bobbed his head. "Mmh. That's the deal."

Next he pulled on the socks and jeans, straightening to button them shut. They hung low and loose, his hips sharp above them, his inguinal crease exposed right down almost to his bush.

"Now hang on one sec." Tucker squinted at him a moment. "Naw. Naw. Keep going. I want the white too. 'Cause I get to take it off."

Grinning to himself, Patch slid the plain shirt over his head, and Tucker smoothed it down, regarding him in the mirror.

Wholesome. Was this how Tucker imagined him, all strong and sturdy? The T-shirt hung loose, the jeans bunched at his ankles. Hardly club wear and not kinky at all. He looked like a hip young dad headed to a sports bar.

Patch gazed at Tucker in the mirror. "I figured you'd go for payback. A jock or chaps or something."

"You don't need none of that." Tucker blinked, eyes soft. "Looking like you do. I don't need nothing else to see how beautiful you are."

Patch closed his yap and nodded, a cold lump in his throat. No way was he serious.

Then Patch looked back and the mirror proved him wrong: they looked like a matched set, Tucker hot and polished and Patch scrubbed clean. *Daddy, boy.*

Tucker scowled and muttered. "'Sides, I don't want folks seeing that much-a you on my say-so."

"Yessir."

"Hell, if you didn't have work, I'd rather stay right here and take all that off you for a couple hours."

Patch swallowed. This hadn't gone at all as he'd planned. He turned back to face his cowboy. "Really?" He felt like Tucker was trying to tell him something, show him something he couldn't see.

Tucker whistled between his teeth and stepped close. "I swear. You give me urges, pup."

"Oh yeah?" He wasn't too proud to fish for a compliment. "What kind of urges?

"Strong ones." Tucker shook his head.

His cheeks and chest heated at the expression on Tucker's face.

"Exactly." He cupped Patch's backside through the denim. A light squeeze, and his fingers pressed into the crack. "Made for eatin'. You feel that?"

He did. Tucker's thumb pressed at the little opening under the denim in a way that paralyzed him, that made him want to agree to anything, everything. Patch inhaled sharply, legs shaking, but didn't answer. Their eyes met in the mirror, saying something scary, something sweet.

Outside, a crowd laughed and hooted down in the street at something they couldn't see. Their room was on the second floor over a tiny flagstone courtyard, with stairs leading right down and an alley that opened onto Chartres so they could still hear the slap and tickle of the weekend crowd.

Patch nodded and scanned the room one last time. Feeling nervous seemed stupid with his résumé, but he always did. "Cowboy up."

Tucker opened the door and picked up the laptop case waiting there. "All you need's in this war bag? Nothing in your pockets or whatever?"

"Just ID and a fifty in my shoe for emergencies." Patch pulled the door closed and headed for the stairs and down. "Full moon tonight, so… it might get manic."

Down here the night air was mild and the crowd louder.

Tucker laughed behind him, coming down into the empty courtyard. "You do like I do."

"Howzat?"

"Rodeo ready. Empty pockets and dress for battle."

Patch puzzled over that one. "I guess. Music's on the laptop, key's at the desk." He nodded toward the lobby. "We'll drink free."

"Exactly. Never ride in a rodeo with money in your pocket." Tucker took off the sunglasses and eyed him solemnly.

Patch laughed. "Why the hell not?"

"Empty pocket gives money somewhere to go."

"We're not at a rodeo."

"Same deal." Tucker frowned, mule stubborn. "We ain't so different, you-me. Not like you say."

Patch grinned down at the flagstones. "Says you." He took the laptop and headed for the arched alley and Chartres beyond.

"I can carry something." Tucker scooted up beside him into the little archway. "Hold up. One sec."

Patch shifted the laptop strap. "I got it." Maybe Tucker was nervous too? Of course he was. "We got plenty of time. I'm not on till eleven."

Tucker stared at him a minute, smoothed the white T-shirt, then squeezed his shoulder.

"Better?"

"Mmmmh. Full moon, pup." Tucker's eyes glittered in the half-lit alley, and he put the mirrored aviators back on, showing Patch his own dark reflection. "We're gonna wake snakes."

Patch grinned and they walked right out into Southern Decadence, side by side.

NIGHT HAD gotten loose in the Quarter, so the boys were out and the streets were boisterous. Watching Tucker get a load of the insanity gave him the strangest charge, like watching a kid open Christmas in his PJs... a big scary kid with hormones and a handlebar.

At the corner of Bienville, Tucker took a handful of his hair and tugged, right at the edge of rough. "I'm kinda hungry, pup."

"Oh."

"You weren't gonna eat, huh?"

"Later. I mean breakfast. I usually grab something at the end of the night."

"That ain't healthy. And my navel's 'bout to hit my backbone, we don't put some protein in there."

Which is how they came to be wandering up Dauphine in search of a muffuletta.

"A moofa-what?" Tucker looked skeptical.

"Big sandwich, Italian. Trust me. Salami and peppers, olives and cheese, and you'll love it, so calm down, cowboy."

He did. They split one and Tucker ended up eating three quarters of it. "Best damn thing I ever ate." He cupped Patch's ass in the doorway. "Well, second best."

Eating anything on the way to a set made Patch feel stuffed and greasy, but it definitely calmed him down. "Food coma. I feel like I just smoked a blunt."

Tucker hooked a thick bicep around his neck and kissed the side of his head. "Boy, y'gonna get me another one of them on the way back. I got an appetite."

"Yes, sir."

"Good pup." A kiss and a sigh on the side of Patch's head. "We're gonna need all your energy."

"What about *your* energy?"

"That you don't need to worry 'bout."

Dauphine was busy but at 10:00 p.m. Bourbon Street was in full hurricane.

Friday night of Southern Decadence at the Bourbon Pub & Parade meant a huge-ass crowd and dudes getting their dicks out. Even before sundown, Bourbon was thick with Circuit boys… muscles jacked, clothes off, and beads swinging already. Many had been up since last night and had no intention of sleeping before Monday on the flight home.

Again Patch let Tucker take his time as they went. The man'd never been anywhere, and they had plenty of time before his set. Seeing Tucker's boyish pleasure did something odd to him, turned him patient and protective in turn.

All the way into the Quarter, they made some damn impression, for sure, especially as they headed northwest toward the gayer section. Southern Decadence had a rep for attracting lookers and hookers, so these guys should've had their fill of eye candy, but folks started snapping photos, with and without permission.

The model in him was keenly aware of the picture they created on Bourbon Street, sauntering together in easy concert. Even before sundown, the crowd between the Bourbon and Oz was bound to be rowdy and grabby, but they pulled back as Tucker and Patch came up Bourbon. One photographer trailed them until Tucker turned and glared to make him scamper off.

Patch had done underwear runways and knew how to get a reaction, but Tucker was something else without even realizing.

Maybe it was the loose-jointed cowboy muscle ambling down the middle of Bourbon. Maybe it was the stern jaw and dom daddy duds. Maybe it was the wad of meat under his buckle, the cocky smile of ownership, and the gentle hand on Patch's back.

As he passed, folks stopped drinking, swiveled to stare, and in one case, gawked and walked right into a street sign while friends teased the poor guy. More pictures too, on phones and a couple actual cameras. Patch should've expected that, and it certainly weren't a bad thing for his cred. As they entered the club, the guys made a path for them as if their arrival had been choreographed.

And that, boys and girls, is what a damn entrance looks like.

Tucker didn't seem to notice the reactions and couldn't have known there was anything odd about the space they made standing next to each other. Patch introduced him to the promoter, the bartender, and a few of the staff, just to keep the drinks free and Tucker safe. To a man, they fell all over Patch's big "assistant." Double beef for half price.

Tucker came as far as the stairs to the booth and then nodded back at the bar. "You thirsty?"

"'S okay. They bring me water. Gotta keep clear."

Tucker smiled then, making a strange picture with his stache and sunglasses. "You gonna do great, pup. You need me, I'm right here." His nod made it a promise, and Patch watched him walk away through his admirers. At least they got right out of his way.

Up in the booth, Patch poked his head in and then dropped his bag on an empty chair.

"'S up, slick?" A skinny black guy saluted him and thumped his back with huge hands. "Them all been brewing for Patch." A wide white grin with crooked lower teeth and a hearty handshake. "Amadeu." He wore a soccer jersey (Sao Paolo) and his accent (Portuguese?) gave his words a slurry, soft rustle. "Crush thos' bitches f'me. Make 'em pay."

Patch spread his hands. "I'll do what a boy can."

Amadeu turned back in the doorway to ask, "Drank?"

"Water's fine. Bottle." He blinked thanks and didn't apologize for his paranoia about spills.

A short beefy staffer with a tribal collar tattoo came back with three cold bottles of Fiji, just passing them through the doorway and vanishing. Even in the era of digital music, folks could be superstitious about the booth.

His phone buzzed, and he discovered a chain of texts from Scotty from an hour ago: *Good luck tonight, boo. SDecadence, right?* Then about five minutes later. *XXX. With you in spirit. Proud AF.*

Scotty was unjealous about pimping anybody's successes, rare in some DJs. Southern Decadence was a popular gig, and Scotty knew what this could mean for Velocity besides: big crowds chanting your name made a difference when you talked to the bank.

Patch thanked him with a *TY. Wild down here.*

Scotty came back with *You are the G.O.A.T. Roll down like thunder....*

Below, Patch spotted Tucker by the lights flashing off his sunglasses, not dancing but leaning against a column while jocks circled him like starved gators. As if he could feel Patch's gaze, Tucker raised his face just then and gave him a wry nod.

Amadeu's last track began to fade, and Patch cued up some craziness to announce himself: low drums, and a sample of Beyoncé breathing. Sure enough, the crowd shouted in recognition and reached up to him, so as a reward he dropped in that new *Hamilton* remix, just two men rapping in hushed voices over bass and synth.

"Here we go." And there they went, right where he wanted.

He bent *Hamilton* into Disclosure just to mess with their heads, then a tickle of Madonna at the margins, which gradually took it all down. *Boss.*

His laptop fed music into the mixer while he read the crowd and shifted options on his deck. This part of DJing nobody could teach: knowing how to coax emotion out of a sweaty horde, how to keep them clip-clopping along a cliff of exhaustion without going over, the way Tucker loved to edge his dick. *Anticipation.* And in just the same way they needed to strain and ache and leak before he gave them any release.

His phone buzzed on the deck. *You blowing up twitter.* Scotty sending him good vibes. *Make them eat it and Imma tweet it long as I can.*

Patch could have ignored it just then, but he didn't. For whatever dumb reason, he needed to tell somebody what was happening. Somebody safe. So he tapped out *I think I met someone. #TrueStory.* Why had he said it that way? He'd known Tucker for years, but then again, maybe not.

!!!!!!! came back. *Da fuck? Deets!*

#LongStory too. No time. Spinning. And then he added *I think he taught me how to dance.*

Scotty sent him *Happy AF to hear that. <3* back.

Just then Patch did dance, heart racing the beat, leaning out to give the crowd a show because he'd shared a piece of the truth with his friend and his body wouldn't contain how great he felt. The crowd hollered and waved up at him gratefully.

Next track, sips of water, and the next. *Fast.* Time whipping by the way he loved because long as he spun for that first hour, the whole world was keeping up with him, straining to pass him or lap him, even.

He felt like a fiery angel hovering above hell, wings scraping the mirror ball. Untouchable.

A hand gripped the back of his neck, rough and familiar.

"Hey." Tucker smelled like Wild Turkey and rust.

"How'd you get up—?"

"Pup, ain't nobody keeps me outta where I want to be." His big cowboy swayed slightly. Sweaty now and bare chested, he looked even better in the club clothes. A lipstick print on his throat. A curved scrape of silver body paint under his left nipple. His teeth blazed white under the dark handlebar. His fingers petted the spray of hair that dragged Patch's eyes below his belt buckle. "Maybe 'cause I look nice."

Patch swallowed thickly. "Nossir. You look pretty mean."

Porno cowboy coach daddy. Just Tucker.

"Still an' all, everybody's been real friendly."

Patch could imagine. The crowd probably thought Tucker was a porn star dressed for trade or a big city dom trolling for twinks on Bourbon Street.

"*You* look nice." A grin and then Tucker grabbed the back of his neck, one hand tangled in Patch's hair, and planted a wet crooked kiss on him, pushing that smoky tongue inside while the bass line throbbed into the bridge for the next track. "Died an' gone to heaven, I did."

Patch blinked as he pulled back and smiled. "Amen."

"I lost your shirt, I think." Tucker shook his head ruefully.

Patch shrugged, still speechless. Seeing him like this was worth anything.

"Or here it is." Tucker plucked the wet tank tucked into his back pocket and squeezed till it dripped over his wide knuckles. "Even that street's crazy. Hell, outside I ran into a couple fellas I know."

"How'd they like your clothes?"

"They liked 'em fine. I like mine on you better, pup. You look so nice, and I get to make the mess. Right?"

"Yessir. You sure do." *Shore.*

Below he could see the crowd straining at the bit, so Patch bent over his laptop and chose a beater to lift them easy and light. Nicki Minaj, a capella, then full-funk fuckery.

Tucker stroked his back casually, affectionately.

Why couldn't he have this every day? Why couldn't Tucker stand beside him in Milan and Hong Kong and Rio and Palm Springs? He checked his watch. "Another thirty-five, I think. You good?"

"Mmh." Tucker crossed his arms and squeezed himself. "Patch, I wanna thank you for dragging me along to watch you work an' all. You didn't haveta, and I—"

"No. Thank you for driving me and coming, both." Patch nodded. "Better than flying, anyways." *Except Tucker's never been on a plane.* Just like that, Patch felt warm, powerful, responsible for Tucker's well-being. His own man. *Who's your daddy?*

"I never done nothing so fun. Great party. Dancing like that. All them lights. New Orleans. And I loved that Muffa-latte doodad." His Boy Scout smile turned the sleazy costume into a complicated lie. "So, thanks."

Patch nodded. The protective tenderness pierced him. "You hungry again?"

"Starving." Tucker pushed his wad of half-hard cock against Patch's buttcheek. "You got no idea."

"Deal. Wait till we get some étouffée in you. My treat."

"Whatever you say, boy. I'm all yours… with interest."

Patch smiled at the tipsy, earnest announcement and refused to read anything into it. He checked his laptops and bumped up the double David Guetta track he wanted as his capper. One day he'd make his own music too, one day the world would keep up. He'd run the race and set the pace. He had so much to do and no time, no time, no time.

Tucker watched him cue and set the next transition in silence. "I'd sure like a dance."

Patch screwed up his face. "I don't—"

"Now hold on. You stomped with me just fine on the porch."

"That's—"

Tucker gestured down at the happy crowd. "And you got all them nice folks worked up. Ain't nobody gonna hassle you none, and if they try, they gotta go through me. And good *luck*." He patted his gleaming, glittered chest, then smeared the sweat up to the lipstick smear on his throat. "Just, I'd like one dance tonight." A shy nod. "With you."

Before he could second-guess himself, Patch nodded. "My set's up in thirty minutes. The house DJ's back at one."

"That's just fine. I get one song with you. Down there." Tucker pointed at him. "You tell him to make it a good one."

The next half hour crawled. Patch never danced, and rarely descended into the throng at any party he worked. Mystique mattered, and staying in motion kept party promoters chasing him. He nodded, excited in spite of himself. *One dance.* Tucker Biggs all to himself right out in public in a city that took plenty of prisoners and told no tales.

Amadeu popped back into the booth, his head and then the rest of his narrow body, the soccer jersey wet now and smelling of beer. "Nice set, bruh." Fist bump.

Patch cleared the deck and untangled his laptop's cables.

"You're not gonna split?"

"Nah. Long day, but I'm all pumped now."

"Good man. Never hurts to have a model in the mix down there. Stirrin' the soup."

"Hardly." Patch looked down at his nondescript clothes.

"*Xodó*, hell, they only know me from a couple CockyBoys clips. I seen your Andrew Christian ad, you twerking in your smalls." He watched Patch packing up, his shaky hands. "You okay?"

"I owe somebody a dance, and I never dance."

"Some *body* or somebody." Amadeu leaned back, regarding him.

"He's… I dunno."

"Big buff stache daddy in gator boots?"

Patch laughed. "You saw?"

"Your cowboy? Man, all them kids did. They's like fleas on a fucking dog." He flashed his eyes appreciatively. "Know him?"

"Long time." Patch nodded. "And he asked for a dance."

"Leave your shit up here till you're ready." Amadeu set the case on a folding chair. "Any requests?"

"Yeah." Patch held his breath and his gaze a moment before he answered, "Make it a great one."

"Tha's a promise."

He trotted down the narrow stairs in search of Tucker. Standing in the crowd seemed surreal after the bird's-eye booth view.

Above him, Amadeu had begun to thread a snaky backbeat into the subsonics that jarred the floor. *Nice.* Strings under a moaning contralto he didn't recognize.

The rural club queens and rhinestone rednecks pretending not to stare at Patch probably just saw a pretty farm boy dressed for the sticks.

No way they knew he'd been spinning up there. No glitz, no armor, no posturing, no assembly required.

This is our first date.

He'd never been on much of a date that didn't come after a club hookup. He'd never let someone dress him or take charge in public or watch him work.

Come to think of it, he'd never once been on a date where he didn't have to pretend anything.

Tucker couldn't have planned this. Hell, they'd only decided to come a couple days ago. Even the clothes had happened because he wanted to ease Tucker's nerves. Apparently, the concern went both ways. Magical accidents and last-minute miracles.

Patch paused at the bar and surveyed the floor, staring between bobbing heads and the strippers' shaved calves. Catching his eye, a trio of gym bunnies waved hopefully at him from the floor, but he just smiled, ambled back toward the front.

"Wanna dance?" A bass drawl, low and rough as gravel.

Jesus Christ.

Tucker stood against a column nursing a whiskey and Coke. If he noticed the groomed barflies buzzing around him, he showed no sign. The aviator glasses reflected Patch's face back at him in confetti colors. He offered his glass and licked his lips.

Patch accepted the drink and drained it down to the melting cubes and left the empty against the rail.

Tucker chuckled and leaned forward. "C'mon, boy. 'Fore I bust inside your nice pants." He stroked his bulge through the borrowed jeans.

"Sure." Amadeu's backbeat took hold of the floor, a dubstep tympani pulse that coiled out of the walls and up to the lights, slicing the air into bright ribbons. "Good stuff."

"Mmh. Works for me."

Patch tried to place the melody. A woman belted out something about coming home to an empty bed. "Some voice."

"That's—" Tucker stopped and looked up at the booth. The singer's voice made an arcing, smoky plea. "Goddamn. He's playing Reba McEntire for us."

"A good one?" Patch turned and gave the booth a thumbs-up and mouthed the words: "Amadeu! Thanks!" The DJ pointed and nodded by way of a reply.

When he turned back, Tucker gave a big predatory smile and then backed him into the center of the floor surrounded by the bouncing bodies. He stepped into the circle of Patch's arms and pressed their torsos together.

Patch blinked and gasped. "You're crazy."

"You're beautiful." A raw whisper against his face. Not a declaration for the crowd, just him.

Patch didn't know how to answer or where to put himself.

"Dance with me." An arm around his back, and then they did, *quick-quick-slow-slowing* in one spot, two-stepping without traveling much of anywhere. Pressed into each other, their wet muscle slid together inside the music and the crowd. Tucker bobbed and weaved in a tight square, keeping their bodies close and humming into Patch's sweaty curls. "Mmph."

"Oh." Patch put his face against the hard chest and relaxed, letting Tucker lead because it felt so good to follow.

"I gotcha." Tucker's wet chest slid under his cheek. "I gotcha there." The room, the bodies fell away, leaving them coiled around each other describing lazy circles. "Like smoke." He laughed under his breath. "I never knew how to dance before."

"Me neither." *Quick-quick, slow, slow.*

"You taught me."

Combs of light raked the crowd from the double derbies overhead. Reba's homesick crooning wove through a pounding drumline that shook the room like Bollywood thunder. Tucker sang along under his breath, so close that Patch felt like he knew the words too.

I never danced with anybody before.

When Patch opened his eyes again he realized that half the dance floor had pulled back to watch Tucker lead him in dreamy loops that bloomed outward. *Quick-quick, slow, slow.* Only now they traveled under the lights and smoke in a trance, making room where none was.

Tucker's breath in his hair, gruff baritone making the remix into a lullaby. His hand was tucked into the top of Patch's jeans, fingers tracing the base of his spine.

Patch let go, pushing with Tucker instead of pushing back as Reba's voice fell over them like petals.

Tucker chuckled. "There ya go. Good boy. All we got is time."

Patch swallowed and grunted in the affirmative. Under him, his feet knew where to go. As long as their hands held that loop and Tucker kept crooning quietly that close, he could go anywhere, anytime.

"God... damn," said some local boy close by, and Patch knew exactly what he meant. *He's mine and I'm his.*

Second by second, they spun in slow rocking circles, and the happy, hunky crowd slid aside to watch them move together like one flesh.

The DJ in him could feel the verse's windup, the end ahead, not wanting it to stop and wondering how long one song could last.

All too soon, Reba's contralto scorched the air one last time, fading away under the electro beat as silver light floated around them like champagne cinders.

Just Tucker.

"Patrick." Tucker's hand slid around his waist and fished down the sweaty slope of his back into the top of his jeans till the fingers pressed at his crease.

Patch's pulse jerked under his jaw so hard it made his ears hurt. *He's gonna kiss me in front of all them folks. He wants to put his mark on me right here in public.*

Between them, Tucker's soaked undershirt dragged over their hot skin till he pulled it up to let their muscle slide easy. The music swirled on and the crowd reclaimed the floor to Alicia Keys, pressing close and patting them appreciatively.

Patch shifted his weight, and Tucker's arms tightened.

"Hold your horses. Where do you think you're going, huh?" Apparently, Tucker wasn't done dancing with him.

"I'm not. I promise." Patch muttered the words into the wet chest. He tasted salt.

Tucker whispered into his hair, "There's nothing else in the world. Nowhere to be. Just you."

Amadeu's Bollywood drums pounded back into life around them in the flickering dark. The air felt humid and heavy on his shoulders as their hips ground together in a daze, as their cocks knocked over each other. They weren't leaving and that seemed just fine by him.

"I wish I could put you in my big ol' bed right now." Rough, unhurried hands smoothed Patch's face, asking something. "Grease. Rope."

"Please." Patch nodded, dizzy with the slowness. His bone ached and sparked in his jeans.

"Any second now I'm fixing to take you back, tie you down, and take you apart, pup." And with that, Tucker bent down and brushed his bristles against Patch's lips till they opened and then he was inside, impatient and hungry, and Patch stopped fighting, stopped racing, stopped right where he needed to be and let Tucker pull his sanity apart on the dance floor in blinding handfuls without moving a muscle.

Patch grunted and his heart *ka-thudded* under his sternum. Tucker could collar him, tattoo him, brand him if he wanted. The mark didn't matter because it was already there.

I love you. But he wouldn't say it, didn't say it.

Moaning, Tucker sucked at his tongue gently and swallowed their blended spit without relenting. He fumbled between them, lifting the borrowed undershirt to tug open the buttons at Patch's fly impatiently and then his own, grasping their leaky cocks together in the thudding dark. His looser, juicier skin slid between them with electric pressure. "What you do t'me."

The crowd jostled around them, oblivious or envious.

"Can I? You'll make me—" Patch spoke quietly and without protest. "I'll come too fast."

"Good boy." The rough farmer hands tug-tug-tugging below Patch's hem with hypnotic patience, pulling him under, giving him permission. "I told you I was starved." Tucker bent his head and drooled whiskey spit onto their erections. "You gone feed me quick?"

Patch nodded. The gossamer slide pinned him in place; he couldn't move if he'd wanted, and he didn't want.

Tucker's slick calluses scraped and milked his stiffness, tugging the pleasure loose, set it racing through him under the hazy, swooping lights.

He shivered and shook, moaning against Tucker's throat too loud to pretend. His hips stuttered and his knotty resistance fell away like loops of burning rope. *Anything, sir.* Mesmerized by the languor, he ground into the slick tunnel between Tucker's rough palm and his own flexing belly. "Can I go?"

"Every fucking drop, I wannit all. In my hand. Y'hear?" Tucker shivered and leaned in to suck his lobe. "Forever and ever amen."

"Yessir." With the whispered words, he fell forward and his cock locked into a pitiless spike and the first squirt reached his chest. Cresting pleasure tightened his hips, and then he sagged, spilling his scalding juice over Tucker's hard fingers and zipper for too long to stand steady.

"I gotcha, pup. I gotcha right here." Tucker milked him firmly and held him up and close. "Gimme all your seed."

Patch whimpered and fought to stay standing in the drumming dark pressed against the only man he'd ever wanted. *Please, please*. He gasped as the wet ribbons lashed Tucker's knuckles, as Tucker smeared heat between them with his torso.

"'At's it. 'At's it, man. Cream it." Tucker kneaded their hard-ons together with a slippery coaxing industry. He cupped their meat and scraped the seed onto his fingers. "Gimme it all."

Surely the men around them could smell his semen, could see Tucker scooping it up even under the glinting lights, but standing up took too much effort for Patch to worry about witnesses. Tucker's coarse hands scrubbed his knob clean.

A growl. "You give me all your stuff. I need it. Y'don't know." Without blinking or hesitating, he brought his sticky fingers up and sucked his thick thumb clean with a groan and a grin. "I'm about starvin'." He sucked the juice off his hand like they were alone, like it wasn't anyone's business but theirs.

Shaky and dazed still, Patch reached down to put himself away, although the buttons were beyond him.

"Thanks." Each finger, Tucker ate the slickness off with fierce relish. "Tasty sauce." He winked and licked his palm, smearing his handlebar, then kissing Patch to share the brine.

His. He had nowhere to be but here and permission to stay.

There must have been music, colored lights, bodies pressed, but mostly everything left was Tucker, filling his view and arms like a horizon.

If anyone had seen, Patch didn't care. If he never worked in this club again, he had no regrets. If their picture ended up on Buzzfeed, he wanted copies for Christmas cards. If he never touched Tucker Biggs again, he'd never forget the scorched eyes on him as Tucker ate his load while everyone watched and wished.

Finally, Tucker sighed and pulled him close, rubbing his back in lazy, dozy circles. "Home?"

He meant the hotel, but a yearning certainty drifted over Patch. The idea of missing home had always seemed impossible. He'd joked that homesickness was what drove kids to ditch their families. Home made you so sick you had to split.

"Yes, sir." And for the first time in his life Patch was truly homesick without having a home to be sick for.

CHAPTER NINE

THE DOOR closing quietly woke Patch, sore and sated with the cool sheets tangled around his legs.

Tucker had returned with a paper bag. "Didn't mean to wake you. I couldn't sleep no more."

He nodded. Ten o'clock was midday for someone on a farm clock. Outside the streets were still quiet; in New Orleans that could mean anytime before noon.

"I got you coffee and some kinda egg thing." Tucker chewed and grinned, obviously proud of his foraging expedition.

Patch yawned and scraped the hair back so he could see clearly. "Thanks."

"Or you can have one-a my sweet rolls. I found this bakery run by a nice gal four-five streets over, don't even have a sign. I just followed my nose and whaddayaknow?"

"Surprised you didn't go score another muffuletta too."

Tucker stopped chewing, eyes wide. "I didn't even think. I coulda, huh? Or them beignet things. Lord, the food's good here." He patted his flat belly again.

"The hell do you put it all? Work it off."

Tucker's eyebrows flicked higher and he tugged his belt. "You keep feeding me like this and I'm gonna have to buy me some new pants." He stepped closer, leaving about eight inches between them. Definitely eight inches. His damp cockhead bumped into Patch's bicep.

Grinning, Patch twisted to rest his cheek against the hard wall of Tucker's abdomen. "I'll get you all the damn pants you want."

As he reached for the hard cock, Tucker stepped back, teasing him, then plunked down in the chair, thighs wide as he ate. "What's the plan, my man?"

"I play this afternoon, but we got all morning then all night after." He handed Tucker the card.

"Am I invited to this thing?"

"Jeez. Of course!" He should've said. "It's just dancing. Of course you are."

"At two in the afternoon." Tucker looked skeptical as he tore off another hunk of sweet roll.

"That's why they call it a tea dance." He propped himself up. "I'm gonna be working, but they'd love you. And I thought—" Truth was, he knew plenty of men who lived out in the boonies who lived for the Circuit. Tucker might even find a couple kindred spirits, come out of his shell, make some friends. *Secret agenda.*

Saturday was the biggest event, and Patch had agreed to spin at a private tea dance out by the levee. Some online porn producer with money to blow, which Patch didn't share with Tucker. The weekend had already forced him into plenty of freaky firsts.

The host was Russian but based out of Brooklyn: Alek something. *Hot Cocks, Hot Hunks?* Something like that. Southern Decadence made these porn companies a ton of money, and they spent a ton to make it so.

"Well, I'll come watch you do your deal, I guess." Tucker chewed his new whiskers and wiped his face with a napkin.

"You wanna take a shower."

"Yessir." Tucker looked up with a grin. "I'm feeling pretty dirty again." He unbuckled his jeans. "Filthier than you, I bet."

Sure enough, their shower took about an hour and a half. By the time they dried off, Patch felt cleaner than he had in his entire life and Tucker's cat-cream grin looked to be a permanent fixture.

They took Patch's laptop with them and did the tourist wander all the way over to the Marigny Street address he'd been given.

"This a garden?" Tucker eyed the glass roof.

"Parties book a big local space and just bling the hell out of it." But sure enough inside the massive doors, it was a greenhouse about seventy-five yards deep and thirty across. The glass had been covered with dark tarps; condensation beaded and ran on the inside from the thumping bodies and low A/C. "First time I seen a setup like this."

"HotHead.com, huh?" Tucker nodded at a banner featuring a swarthy cop with his belt unbuckled to his black pubes. "Yeah."

"Sponsor. Porn site." Patch shrugged. "I mean, they're not gonna be shooting in here." Not that he knew of. Shit, he should've gotten more details. Tea dances tended to be pretty casual, so Patch had opted for tight slacks and a fitted dress shirt unbuttoned to the navel with some artful smears of body glitter on the exposed cuts of his muscle. "Guys in uniform is their thing, so no."

"Okay."

"I just play music, Tuck." Well, with his shirt off and flirting with the crowd, but Tucker didn't care about that shit. "Pay's great, folks dance, all good."

Tucker looked at the porn company banner again then back. "And you gotta work all twelve hours?"

"No-no!" Patch laughed. "No way! Two hours max. I'm a guest spot is all, but I'll make bank." He couldn't even tell Tucker how much he'd make because the numbers would freak him out. "I'm only booked for this afternoon."

"Good deal."

He bumped Tucker's shoulder. "Then I'm all yours. We can dance or eat or, I dunno, go crabbing in our jockeys if you want." Grin. "You pick."

"Oh." Tucker's shoulders relaxed. "Oh good. I'm just having a good time with you."

"Same, mister."

Inside the greenhouse, the party was already cranking at an easy clip, and the whole room smelled like cut leaves and chemical fog. A working florist warehouse, then, with a low platform against one wall serving as the DJ's booth. The guests seemed young, dumb, and tweaked, mostly. The party was working some kind of jungle theme, emerald gels and a lot of animal-print Lycra on the guests. He wasn't really dressed, but he'd take off his shirt and paint some and be fine. As weekends went, Southern Decadence was pretty low-key, but with an invite-only porn crowd, things might get *crunk*.

Tucker looked anxious or serious or something. "You're sure these clothes is okay." He plucked at the black T and eyed his chaps and Wranglers skeptically.

"Cross my heart, cowboy. I don't want them porn dudes scouting you."

"Yeah, right."

Down on the floor a couple familiar faces pointed up at him, and he pointed back. *Thumbs-up, mofo.* He saw them checking Tucker out and decided he'd made the right call. In two hours he'd take Tucker for oysters and beer and help him unwind.

Patch checked with the promoter, set up his laptop, and still Tucker didn't crack a smile. "You okay?" He started to sweat and just peeled out of his shirt. "Get comfortable if you want. Dance if you want. Or hang here with me."

"I'm— Yeah. I'm good." Tucker nodded at the polished jocks grinding below them. A young crowd. "Loud."

"Yeah." Maybe this part had been a dumb idea. Last night had been a dance night in a local bar with a scatter of tourists and fruit flies, but this was a Circuit scene, no question: amped, cramped, and damp. Circuit parties could overwhelm even experienced partiers and Tucker had never been outside Texas.

Patch shook off his apprehension, trying to find his groove. Up here no one could get near them, at least. He hovered above the swirling mob, a shaman stirring a jeweled cauldron with nothing but rhythm.

He spotted a couple porn pros on boxes teasing the punters, but no cocks-out, rocks-out clusters. This wasn't Hustlaball. Just smiling faces and hard flesh grinding under the Fresnels. Even the hustlers were here to unwind and put on a couple pounds eating real butter.

He glanced at his watch about forty minutes in. He smeared the next track into position and queued a baseline he'd pulled out of an old Jamiroquai B-side. He took a swig of water, already sweating heavy in the greenhouse humidity.

"Patch?" Tucker stood close by, squinting at him. "I think I'm gonna step out and get some air."

"Sure!" Patch flashed a happy grin. "No sweat. You got your wristband?"

Tucker fingered his wrist. "Yeah, but I think I need a breather. 'S nothing wrong. You got 'em going good." He looked down, sheepish. "It's a lot. This's a lot for me. Them guys."

Patch stood and put a reassuring hand on his chest. "I know. Sorry. I just—I totally understand, man." He didn't want to strain the connection they'd found or force Tucker to stick around if he was freaked. "You wanna go back to the hotel?"

"Naw. Might grab a beer. Y'know. Sit a spell." Tucker sounded embarrassed. "Air. Sounds dumb to say, but I just want some space 'round me. That okay? You good?"

"Tucker, I really do get it. This is a madhouse, huh? I just wanted you to see. Sorry. You go on." He glanced at the laptop's clock. "One hour and twenty-six minutes, I am all yours."

"Yeah?" They shared a dirty smile.

"Yessir. Anything you wanna do. With me. For me. To me." Wink. "Dealer's choice."

"Well." Tucker raised his eyebrows. "You'd best rest up, then. I got two or three things in mind."

"I bet." He checked the crowd (jacked), the track (six minutes), and the promoters on their platform (high). "I'll text you soon as I'm out."

Tucker whispered, "'Kay." He swayed close like he was about to kiss Patch, but then he didn't.

Awkward pause. And then a longer beat when neither of them broke the awkward pause and realized it.

"Okay, then." Tucker smiled again and saluted before ducking out, leaving Patch with a funny anxiety he couldn't nail down.

Patch muttered to himself, "I shoulda said." But what, exactly, he had no idea.

TWO HOURS and nine minutes later, Patch stepped out into the afternoon glare on Dauphine Street with a roll of hundreds in his pocket and his phone in his hand. Emerging into daylight from a party always felt like climbing out of the Looking Glass, Technicolor fading into black and white.

HEY he texted to Tucker's phone. He cracked his neck and leaned back against an iron gate, ignoring the mob jostling at the curb. He opened and shut his jaw wide a couple times to stop his ears ringing.

A couple seconds later, Tucker replied, *We bought you a beer* along with a picture of a bar sign at Bourbon and St. Ann's. *OZ.*

Well, shit. Oz was a touristy disco in the French Quarter known for its beefy Cajun strippers who'd dip their dicks in your drink if the tips came thick enough. That corner was a hub for Southern Decadence, so the crowd would be looney tunes. So much for Tucker needing space.

He considered the text again: "We bought you a beer." *Who's we?* Dauphine looked black and white and gray all over. A petty, selfish jealousy took hold. Of course Tucker had collected a couple skeezy bar buddies in the past hour, and now he'd have to go make nice to plan their escape.

Patch crossed the street, frowning. After playing his set, he didn't feel like being pawed by strangers. Tourists and strippers sounded like a bummer, but he'd already dragged Tucker somewhere uncomfortable, so he could hardly complain.

"Suck it up, buttercup," he chided himself as he trudged into the Quarter, aiming his feet toward the noise.

Now the day was fading, and the boys were out in force. He kept his eyes down and headed south for Bourbon, wanting Tucker and that beer. He texted his cowboy again and picked up the pace.

Closer he got to the gay stretch, the louder and brighter everything got. A drag queen on a cast iron balcony blowing bubbles over the street. Five spray-tanned bodybuilders in a clump wearing nothing but combat boots and red bandanas tying their dicks to their legs in heavy lumps… asses out, technically dressed, but only by letter of the law. Bourbon got busier and louder, until he reached the corner of St. Ann between the Bourbon Club and Oz.

No Tucker.

How the hell were they gonna find each other in this madhouse? The dull roar was deafening, and the more he scanned the crowd, the more guys thought he was cruising them. *Tricky.* He stepped up onto the curb for a better vantage point but saw no sign of Tucker's handsome face.

Someone grabbed him from behind, wrapping beefy arms around him and lifting him off the concrete by the waist, but it was not Tucker and he was not in the mood.

"Where you fixin' to go, good-lookin'?" Voice familiar, innuendo guttural. A soft beard on his neck and cheek and the breath forty-proof and bottom-shelf.

A couple of tourists hooted and pointed from the bar and surrounding balconies.

Patch stiffened, twisted, and then his boots were back on the ground, the big stranger's body still laminated to his hindquarters, a firm lump notched against him.

"Don't fuss, boy."

He shoved free. "I'm not your—"

Bix.

"Fuck. They's more meat on a taco." Bix laughed, skunk-drunk and unsteady on his big legs, a loop of chain swaying at his hip, battered jeans, biker boots, and his black leather vest over his gold-fuzzy chest and belly. "We been over t'the Phoenix for beer bust." The local leather bar. "Pitchers, they servin', and I had me three." He held up two, then three fingers with a satisfied grin. His beard was wet.

"Who's we?" Patch tried to stop frowning and eyed the sozzled crowd. He didn't mention Tucker because if they hadn't found each other, he had no intention of making that happen.

"Muscle Bear contest. *Grrrr*." Bix opened one side of the vest, revealing bruised ribs and one stiff nipple as if that explained everything. A passing twink tugged his tit, but Bix didn't take his eyes off Patch. "Dishonorable mention." He wiped his damp, loose mouth again, breathing booze.

"Yeah. Good." Patch stepped up on the curb, putting an extra yard between them and scanning the intersection for Tucker's stern profile.

"Arm wrestling I lost. No head for it." Bix pursed his lips skeptically. "*Pfft*. Tucker coulda. He says so hisself. That big fucker can pop the heads off rattlesnakes with his bare hands." He squeezed his eyes shut and rubbed them with a multistamped hand.

Patch said, "Bar hopping, then."

Bix nodded and eyed the crowd. "Boy. You 'lone."

A coldness right through his limbs, like ice water clinking in his veins. Patch didn't answer. He pretended not to hear.

Bix moseyed close again and put his hands on Patch's shoulders. "You are one pretty fella." He stank of cheap gin and his lips were wet. He stuck his tongue out all the way, licking the air. "Mmph. Woof."

Tucker was nowhere to be seen in any direction.

"You come on wit' me, boy. I'll fix you good." Bix raised his chin. "Play some. We got unfinished business, you-me."

"I'm working. Music. I'm a DJ." Patch pointed inside as if that were proof. Had Tucker said something, promised something, even inadvertently? "I got a job to do, Bix."

"Shame, that." He raised his big hand again, but he didn't touch. "We need a drink. Imma fetch you a drink, boy. Wet that whistle. Calm you down."

Patch scanned the crowd and checked his phone again. *Nothing*. Ignoring the sharks circling him, he whispered, "C'mon, Tucker. Get me out of here."

Bix must've imagined an opening. "We can hang two secs. Get friendlier." He gripped his basket like a convict with blue balls.

Patch scowled, angry at himself for feeling horny. Southern Decadence, after all. Why couldn't they hook up with Bix, or anyone else for that matter? He'd had plenty of iffy three-ways that meant nothing and punched his buzzer. What did he care? No big deal.

No. Big deal.

Because he didn't want to share Tucker with anyone, let alone some horny roughneck who knew his worst urges too well already. Bix wanted to horn in because he knew he could, because Tucker would let him, because Patch was just a tourist, after all.

A hand pushed down the back of Patch's pants, a finger tracing his crack, crooked for his opening.

"Hey." Patch jerked back, twisted away, and shoved hard with one arm. "Hey! Fuck off."

Bix's stupid drawl and sloppy grin. "I was just funning with ya, boy. Kicks with Bix."

The crowd skittered back, sensing danger in his raw anger. Patch shook his hand like it burned.

"There's no call to crawl my hump." Hands up and off. Bix wiped his wet beard and licked the offending digits. Was he seriously trying to start something? "S'all good, boy." He winked.

"Says who?" He lowered his arms, glaring at the clown. "And don't call me that."

"All right, all right." Bix swayed, drunk. He drew a sharp breath and shook his head. "Everybody's friendly."

Patch stepped back again. He hated himself for his animal arousal and the sleazy paralysis that froze him there. He hated himself for thinking of the two roughnecks making him do things. He hated missing Tucker and not being able to find anyone but this drunk greasebag.

"You say when." Nod. "We both friendly with Tucker, and I'd sure like to help you out."

"Fuck off, genius. I'm busy."

"What's got you wrapped around the axle?" He wiped his loose mouth drunkenly. "This Decadence, ain't it?"

"Not for me. I got a job to do, Bix. Solo."

Bix gave a woozy nod and clapped his bare shoulder with one rough paw. "Sure thing. You come on when you're ripe to slam the ham." He clumped back down the stairs in search of trouble. A stud, no doubt, and exactly the kind of bossy daddy pig Patch used to fantasize about.

Before I knew it for fake.

His needy impatience frustrated him, but he'd never been one to hunt around for anyone. *Tucker, where the hell are you?*

"There y'are," Tucker said from somewhere nearby.

Patch turned, looking, looking for him in the sea of sweaty bodies. The sharp relief embarrassed him.

"Pup!" Tucker waved at someone behind him. Several strands of cheap Mardi Gras beads swung from his neck. "All done?"

Patch nodded, annoyed, and annoyed that he was annoyed. Bix had gotten under his skin. "Got some beads, I see."

Tucker nodded. "They asked me to show my pecker but I held out for a firmer offer." Tucker put a hand on his waist, not embracing him, but marking territory. "Wan' a drink? Anything?"

Patch shook his head. He wanted to be somewhere else. "Sorry I'm late. I got an offer for New Year's in Vienna. Austria." Might as well be Mars. He should've kept his mouth shut. Everything he said sounded wrong here.

"Bix is here somewhere."

Patch stiffened. "I seen him."

"He done some contest." He chuckled. "Stuck something up his tail, he says. Curly plug something. I dunno. Crazy sumbuck." More tipsy laughter.

Patch watched him, unable to laugh along. He ignored the rush of nerves and regret that surged through him. He hated wanting to go back and fix things, change things, make things different.

Tucker and Bix. They had years of history, sex, jokes, and more between them. What all did Bix do that Patch wouldn't or couldn't?

A rush of loathing and jealousy so strong it turned his stomach. Frankly, Bix taking off was probably a blessing, He'd happily slice the canny bastard lengthwise and sew him up with barbed wire.

"You okay, pup?"

"No." Patch glared at Tucker, weighing the risk before he lobbed the grenade over the wall. "Bix been trying to fuck me for ten minutes."

Tucker gave a wheezy laugh that didn't reach his eyes. "Howzat?"

"Here. While I was looking for you. Right under your nose. Just now."

"Then you'd best check my feet for horseshoes, 'cause I don't see him trying anything." Tucker crossed his big arms, looking absurdly reasonable bare chested in chaps and crocodile boots while costumed drunks eyed them from a safe distance.

"He said some things. About you."

Tucker acted like it was all a joke. "Now, pup, he's just having fun. All them fellas havin' fun and flirting. Nobody's hurt."

"Made some kinda dickhead three-way play."

"Course he did. He's achin' for the bacon, and you're hot as hell." Tucker squinted.

More of the guys around them had paused to watch the embarrassing scene unfold in public.

He could feel his voice and eyes sharpening. "Tucker, he seemed to think we had an understanding. You and me."

"Well, then, he's wrong, right? Patch, I been messin' around with Wayne Bixby near four years, you think I don't know when his tail's waggin'? Course he's sniffing after you. Till you say otherwise, that's between y'all." Tucker didn't sound jealous, or annoyed, even.

"That's not— I'm trying to explain. I meant you." Frown. What *did* he mean? "Your boyfriend."

"Patch, he ain't my *boyfriend*. He's my… nothing. Bix crashes at my house a few nights a year when he's passing through."

Patch nodded. Bix hadn't actually done anything, but the crazy impatience flickered inside him.

"Well, an' he's gone now. See?" Tucker crossed his arms and stepped away from the mob at Oz's front door. "You played the hell outta that party. Done real good. Great day. We's here."

Patch nodded, fidgeting.

"Now all a sudden, you're madder than a mosquito in a mannequin factory. The hell is that?" He shifted again to put them in shadow. At least the crowd couldn't watch them as easily. "Is that it, pup? You figger he knows me better than you do?"

"I don't…. No." Sigh. "The way he said it. I thought you'd given him the go. He practically said as much." He scanned the crowd for the asshole in question, like proof would help. "Bix just now."

"Look, I'm just here killing time for you: half hour ago Bix come up roostered as all get-out, cain't hardly stand, some stripper's load in his chest hair, and said a bunch of nothing. And I said the same back." Tucker shrugged a shoulder. "I told him to go find his own bed." He grinned, not upset at all. "We got our own."

"We do? What've we got?" *Hold your horses, hold your horses.* "A rented room, I guess. Twenty feet of rope and a tub of grease back in Hixville." He started to back away, not caring if he fell.

"Now hold on." Tucker didn't smile. "Bix may be a humbugger, but he's straight with me. He says sorry when he should, an' asks for the things he wants, an' fucks off when he oughtta."

"Not me. He wants *you*, Tucker."

That stopped Tucker. "Oh pup. Now that's…."

"You don't see." Patch choked on the hard kernel of jealousy. "He's doing everything he can to screw us up, stake a claim. He wants you."

"I'm not for *sale*. And they ain't a scheming bone in his body because Bix don't want nothing he don't have already. He's too screwed-up to screw anyone else."

Patch thought of the big hand cupping his backside, the two fingers, imagined that hand on Tucker and wanted to kill someone. "He'd take you in a heartbeat."

"Nobody can *take* me. I'm a man." Tucker pushed his chin out. "I got a mind of my own, believe it or not. The life I got I made, just like everybody ever."

"We don't have a chance. No chance in hell." Patch shook the hands off and backed up till he hit the wall. *Too fast. Too fast.*

"Now wait up." Tucker held up his hands as if Patch were a skittish colt. "You ain't making sense. You ain't being fair."

Patch knew that better than anyone. He was bad as Bix. He'd brought Tucker out here to show him off like a bull at auction. He wanted all these hicks to slobber over the thick stud cowboy wearing his brand.

Just pretend. And he had. Like his pa said, *Nothing's fair and it never was.* This whole trip to delay the inevitable moment when he fucked off back to New York and left Tucker to rot like everyone else in his life. Like burning a barnful of hay. *Both our lives.*

And though neither moved, a cavernous space opened between them.

Patch blinked. "I didn't think this through."

Tucker said, "A good time. That's what you said. Ain't we having a good time? Hell, come Monday or so, you fly off to where the fuck ever and leave my bony ass anyways. What do you care if I get my stick wet after you gone?" He didn't look psyched at the prospect.

"You're right. You're right." He'd never flipped out or fought over anyone like this. Because he cared enough? Because he didn't care? Dealer's choice.

Patch shook his head slowly, seeing everything with vicious clarity. They'd fooled each other, just like they'd fooled the people in their separate lives. Two guys with smiles that packed a wallop playing to the cheap seats.

Patch laughed, a short ugly bark. "Right." A movement drew his eye, and there stood Bix on the curb, swaying with a nervous frown between his bushy blond brows while a couple hundred Circuit boys drifted between them like feathers from a split pillow.

"Don't you wanna?" Tucker looked so lost on Bourbon under the neon and night sky.

Run. His whole body burned with the urge. Now he just wanted to be gone. *Quick-quick.* To get away before everyone started telling a bunch of truth designed to pin him down. "Places to do. People to be."

"Aww, Patch. Don't. Let's go, huh? You and me. I'm starving anyways." Tucker was using the coach voice now, reasonable and sturdy, which only made him feel more frantic. "If we can't make some kinda decision, we gonna stand here till the sky goes red on doomsday. C'mon, son."

"In a month we won't even remember why this was a good idea." Patch hugged himself. *Just pretend.* "I'll be a dirty story you tell all your tug buds."

"Look, pup... I don't know what's what. I want t'be here with you while I can." He shrugged, his arms hanging loose. "I just figure everybody oughtta be happy. Even me. Our lives are too short to be miserable."

"I—" *Guess?* He didn't know how to finish the sentence. *Give up? Give in?* "Want to go somewhere, anywhere else." Scanning the pavement, Patch began to stride away from Oz.

Tucker kept pace, trying to slow him down, until finally he tugged at Patch's elbow, forcing him to turn in the gutter in front of an abandoned bar with chains on the doors and soaped windows. "Hey. Hey, pup! You still with me?"

Patch blinked stupidly. He'd forgotten this feeling: wanting someone who didn't want him back the same way. *I'm fifteen under the bleachers.*

"You're not listening to me, even. Already gone." Tucker crossed his thick arms and cocked his head. "After all this, past couple weeks and tonight and all, you're not even here with me. I'm just some old redneck you sorta remember."

"That easy for—"

"None of this is easy. Patch, I didn't even know you till two weeks ago."

"Bullshit. You watched me grow up."

"You was a kid! Royce's pissy kid who raised hell from go. Rushing around raising a ruckus. Everything I knew was you being some asshole teenager who kept getting hisself into trouble over bullshit. Wild as a corn-crib rat. Guys beating the hell out of you while you go back for more of the same."

"Some stupid queer."

"That's not what I said." He looked angry now.

"Tucker, they fucking terrorized me."

"Well, now, see…." Tucker paused, his face set and his eyes hooded. "You scared us plenty."

"You should talk."

"And you should listen, Patch."

"*You* terrorized me." Patch took his hands out of his pockets but found he had nowhere to put them.

"To keep you *safe*. Pickin' fights with anyone who stood still long enough. Screwing around with boys as could hurt you. Or men willing to I dunno *what*. That's fucking stupid. You knew better."

"I was…." Patch hadn't thought about their side of it. *Dumb. Stubborn. Horny.* "Mad."

"You was a *kid*. Teachers and coaches all trying to keep you safe. Town looking to keep you safe. Your daddy fighting to keep you safe best he could. Like hugging a rosebush. If we did it wrong, least you're still alive."

"Fucking hypocrites."

"Maybe so. Well, tough break, son. You kept getting caught doing shit weren't safe, weren't legal, even. That's a fact. I'm not even gonna get into everybody's Jesus or whatever."

"They tried to snuff me out."

"So you run off and found your life where you could. Good deal. You're twenty."

"Two."

"And I'm twice that. I made a life down here that I liked fine. I figgered this was what happy looked like. I had it good, I figgered."

Patch shook his head.

"Then you show up in a hurry." Blink. "Run me down. Drag me along. Make me happy. All I done is hold on while I could. I knew you was goin'-goin'-gone soon as you could. You tol' me."

"Strangers."

"Then, yeah." Tucker blinked and held his arms wide. "But I know you now."

"You've known me my whole life."

"Bullshit." Tucker shifted his weight awkwardly. "I seen ya. I talked to ya when I came by the house. I busted on ya at the school. But I didn't—"

"Well, I knew *you*. All my life you swoopin' in and making me feel like a failure, a fuckup, a *fag*. Got to where I could beat myself up better than you could." Patch wiped his nose with his shaking hand and hoped that was only sweat on his face. "Even after I'd run, you were giving me hell in my head. I knew you plenty." He sneered. "Talk shit, get hit."

"Patch, you didn't know me. You knew stuff *about* me."

"How can you say that?"

Up on his curb by Oz, Bix laughed loud with a circle of leathered-up muscle bears, no longer even paying attention. His belt was open, his zipper down to his bush, and he was rubbing his belly absently.

"All that crap was in our heads. It ain't real. None of it." Tucker's face fell, as if he'd remembered something simple and sad. "None of it." He rocked onto his heels and took a couple steps back, looking up at the Bourbon Street lights as if seeing them for the first time.

Patch said, "I'm not a boy anymore."

"No." The light died in his eyes. "But I ain't a boy neither. Not young or hopeful or nothing." Tucker scowled. "Hell, I was out of the Army when you weren't no more than a tussle in the backseat of a car."

"And you'd know all about tussles. Huh?" Patch's eyes went dead; he could feel the green turn cold and poisonous. "Sneaking around to bang other people's wives and worse. What you can get wherever you can steal it, right?"

"That's enough, pup." Tucker swallowed and closed his mouth in a tight line. "They ain't no education in the second kick of a mule."

Patch shut his mouth. He wondered what he'd said and if he'd meant it.

Tucker seemed dead certain. "I got it the first time."

"You could have anything, Tucker."

"No, Patch." He closed his mouth and exhaled, a smile and a sigh that made him look like the goddamned Marlboro Man. "Nobody can have that."

"More, then. So much more than...." Than what? Tractors? Sunsets? Botchy? A cold beer on a hot day? Fireflies? Patch realized how insulting he sounded, but couldn't figure out how to compare their lives equitably. "You expect less than you oughtta."

"That may be so. People don't never want the same things, though." Without moving, Tucker moved away from him. "Sad song."

Patch hesitated. "I should know." Tears danced at the edges of his lashes. "I thought you and me...." *Would what?* What future did they have? Why was he mad if Tucker had used him back or if he hadn't? Where did they have a chance to end up together? "I guess none of this matters."

"Hold on now. What don't matter? You're gonna go home to all that New York concrete. And I'm going to Kountze or Honey Island, or wherever I can find hookups for my trailer. We're both going somewhere, and it ain't together. You said so, pup." His eyes were dirty nickels. "You kept telling me and telling me."

Did I?

Patch wanted to contradict him, say something, make some crazy promise. A thousand things impossible to name.

The queasy silence stretched and wobbled between them. Their brief hot window of shared time was closing while they stood there stone cold sober on Bourbon.

The rowdy crowd swept past them, not caring, not even pausing to see them in the middle of Southern Decadence. A river of easy mischief and no answers.

"Exactly. And that's that. You go on back to your buddies, and I'm gonna hang with mine." Tucker looked stoic.

Patch straightened. "Fuck you." So he'd just been a piece of hot meat after all. The second things got serious, Tucker turned tail. *Like always.* "What do I care anyways?"

"Boy." Tucker's voice was disappointed and soft. "Don't be that way."

"What way?" This was their trip. He felt betrayed but couldn't find a reaction that didn't feel humiliating. "You're leaving."

"Yeah, uh, at least… I don't think you're staying. You got places to be I don't belong, pup."

Anger and relentless disappointment rushed through him. "Just like that."

"Like what?"

"Like Bix knows the truth. Like you don't. Like I'm one more horny shitkicker sneaking home with a hickey once you're done. Like none of it means anything and you don't give a good goddamn."

"That's as may be." Tucker shrugged and looked absently at the dark sky. "God'll forgive me. It's his job."

"You know what I'm saying. You say you don't. You don't want to, even, but you stand there stuck, Tucker Biggs, waving while the world walks away." Patch shoved him off. "And I know it because I seen you… balls to bones."

Tucker spread his hands and held them up as if Patch were aiming a shotgun at his ribs. "Son, you got all this stuff in your head ain't real."

Patch glared at him, at the caustic truth he didn't need dragged out in the middle of Bourbon with Bix standing up the block ignoring a mess he hadn't actually made.

"We got a problem. You got work. And I got a ride. Simple as that." Tucker shook his head.

Simple.

Patch frowned. "Go rodeo with the clown."

Tucker's mustache shifted over his teeth, as if the truth might spill any second. "I don't know what you want, pup."

That makes two of us.

"No." Before he could fool himself into believing the fantasy again, Patch covered his eyes and walked blind up Bourbon through a crowd of happy, hunky, hungry sailors looking to drown.

CHAPTER TEN

PATCH ONLY stopped at the hotel for his bag and then spent a grim night at a Travelodge by the bus station. He paid in crisp cash from the tea dance envelope, like a dirty cop paying a bribe. He rinsed off the glitter but didn't sleep worth a damn. Sunday went worse. He tried to eat, tried to move, but never managed.

About eleven Monday morning, he caught a local bus to Beaumont and, after sleeping in a chair that night, made a transfer to Lumberton, which meant he didn't make it back into Hardin County until Tuesday afternoon.

He climbed out at the Shop-n-Go feeling like fifty pounds of shit in a five-pound bag. Thankfully his phone had two bars here, so he could call the funeral parlor and beg poor, stunned Vicky to pick him up.

An emergency, he said. Fast as she could, was her reply.

While he waited, he tried to sleep or eat, but couldn't make his eyes shut or his tight stomach ease up. He sent Scotty a text to let him now he was coming back to reclaim the Beige gig and a confirmation that the Velocity money was incoming. He typed three messages to Tucker he tried and failed to send, before he gave up and went to stand by the road in his Diesel jeans like a refugee from an expensive warzone.

Vicky pulled up a couple hours later, looking fidgety and terrified as she popped open the passenger door. "Lord, Patch. You look pretty rough." Her throaty contralto and earnest expression made the observation sound like lyrics from a Patsy Cline ballad. "Anything I need to know?"

"Long, terrible story. I got—" What could he say that sounded sane? "Stuck."

To her credit, Vicky just nodded and drove all twenty-one miles to the farm without peppering him with questions. Easy listening radio filled the dead air, which suited him fine. The clouds hung low and thick as dirty wool, swollen with some sullen storm refusing to break.

At the house, he thanked Vicky and made her take forty bucks for the gas she'd wasted before startling her with a grateful hug. She gave him another squeeze before she took off again, looking back at him with a worried look on her face.

No shit, sister.

After unlocking the door, he tossed his bag inside and went right back out to the bright rental car. The curdled clouds looked lower, duller, greener as he drove into Hixville.

The Feed & Seed was locked with a Be Back sign on the door, so Patch made his way up the drive to the Rodmans' rambly clapboard house out back. A grumpy rooster eyed him from a mailbox on a post. Dave waved from the roof, a hammer in his hand.

"There he is." Janet's booming voice from the store's backside, where they stashed the dumpster between the sheds. "What's up, big city?"

"Whatcha doing?"

"Thinking." Inside the big hay shed, Janet stood in a temporary pen of four foot wire, feeding chickens. She looked down at the birds. "They're helping." A handful of grain. "Me think, I mean."

"Who—?" He walked closer and spotted a familiar horse trailer stacked with laying boxes. "Those are Tucker's chickens." He'd never seen them penned up. Normally they just roamed the cluttered yard around Tucker's place.

"I'm just watching 'em till he gets back from wherever."

A cold kernel of fear lodged in his stomach. "Where's that?"

"Do I know?" She raised her eyebrows, skeptical as anything. "Silsbee or Batson. Someplace else. He went off, like he does when he's got no choice." She tossed a loose handful of grain from the bucket at her hip. "I expect he had no choice." Ostensibly she said it to the chickens, but he knew better.

He walked to the enclosure. "Everybody's got choices, Janet."

"Ha!" She snorted and her face flushed. "That boy grew up stuck. Every place he shows up, the whole fucking county like a hangman barbershop tying the noose while they sing another round of 'For he's a jolly good failure.'"

He knew that for truth. He'd done it too, his whole life, while he fantasized and followed the poor guy around. *Loose cannon. Hair trigger. Train wreck.*

That last thought made him flinch.

"Even your daddy, rest him. You think Tucker wanted everything ever happened?" Janet toed the chickens out of her way to the gate. "He drifted. Like you, like anyone."

"I got to go, Janet. I mean, I knew it and you did too. But now I got no choice."

"What about Tucker?" She didn't or wouldn't look at him.

"What about?"

She raised her chin at something behind him. "He left me a present."

For the first time, he turned and saw the towering mountain of bales piled right up to the beams overhead. In the dimness, he'd mistaken it for a wall. "Jeez."

"Last night about ten, he brung it. Scared Dave halfway to Christmas." She crossed her arms over her bosom. "I come out here in my robe, and he's unloading his trailer into the shed. Six trips and driving slow because he was over the legal load. Then the hens. Nugget up the barn." She nodded that way. "It's a goddamn soup-sandwich, is what."

He shook his head. "But why?"

"'Cleaning up,' he says. You're selling." She sniffed. "You selling?"

Just like that, the decision got made. Ha hadn't known what happened next until he said the words out loud to her.

"Yup. Buying my club. Velocity." He rocked on his feet, straddling an imaginary line. He hadn't said the words out loud because once he did, the decision would be made and no turning back. "Soon as I sign the papers with the lawyer. I think she made a pretty good deal." Then why did he feel like puking?

"Older, richer, and wiser, that's you, kiddo." She considered the overfull shed and plucked a piece of straw off her blouse. "Lotta fuckin' hay."

"Jiggs, he said." He scowled at the strand in her hand. "He put in some new Bermuda grows like anything."

"That's the beauty there." She spun the straw in her fingers. "It's best fresh and it'll grow till you cut it." She gave him a hard look then.

Patch shook his head, not wanting to hear whatever she was not saying. "Give the money to him. Whatever these bales sell for." The least he could do for Tucker, who'd done the work anyway.

"Fair 'nuff." Janet looked unconvinced.

He couldn't tell if she was congratulating him on his savvy or scolding him for his cowardice. *Maybe both.* "And I'm gonna sign over a cut of the Texaco money. In place of the life estate my pa left him."

"Hmmf." She didn't clarify.

"You think that's right, don't you?"

"Hope so." She favored the hens with more feed. "Whatever you do gets done for good. Otherwise you better hold your fuckin' water. Think fast. Choose slow. Your move, kiddo."

"I made it already." Patch didn't say anything about the goat rope in New Orleans, or the long stinking bus ride back, or getting Vicky to take him out to the farm on a Tuesday midday. Nobody knew all that but him, and the scab hadn't even set enough to scratch.

She searched his face a moment. "Well, I say that's fine. You know 'xactly what you want, then."

"I hope I do." He crossed his arms so he wouldn't fidget.

"So you go on back to the city. Dance around and make some fast money. Pretty boys and easy answers. What do you care anyhow?"

Patch agreed. "I don't."

"Then don't. And if you did, you burned that bridge before you crossed it, kiddo." A sudden gust whipped her thick ponytail sideways. "And we got chickens to feed."

Patch wondered where all chicks were, or Botchy, but he was afraid to ask for fear she'd know, and worse, tell him. "I know this is the right thing. For—" *Him.* He blinked, embarrassed. "Everybody."

"Then you gotta find a way to get out of the doubt, huh?" She poked his chest. "Head off someplace that's no place like home and forget."

He frowned. "Forget?"

"That happens easy enough. What's home, anyway? It feels big when you're a kid, but home shrinks. Weren't all that much time, y'know. Sixteen years of dreaming and bullshit and memories you cain't remember."

He already had. The past couple of weeks he'd dismantled so many mistakes and misunderstandings. Stupid fantasies about cowboys and coaches he'd kept fresh while he dated slick idiots in a hurry.

All we got is time. Tucker's soft growl in his head, rough hands on his body. *Quick-quick, slow, slow.*

The wet wind picked up around them, rustling the hungry chickens, and Patch leaned out to look up. Something nasty brewing, no question. The sky had congealed and dropped closer like ominous mashed potatoes.

"Know something?" She blinked and swallowed. "You look like you been ate by a coyote and shit off a cliff."

"Naw. I'm not so bad off." It even sounded like a lie, soon as he said it.

"How you figure?" Janet's brow clouded as if she'd caught him smoking a cigarette in the boys' bathroom, as if she wanted to whup him. "I never see'd you look so rotten, kiddo."

"Not really. The Texaco deal's going through. Everybody gets taken care of. Tucker gets his folding money. I got my club coming up any second. They get their rigs in to pump whatever's under that ground."

"I guess so." She shrugged and smoothed a few loose strands of hair back toward the thick ponytail. "Hard on him, though. They's no retirement on a farm. You work till death kicks your legs out."

He nodded, silent and sour.

"Lookit Dave...." Janet sniffed. "That dumb bastard can't count to twenty-one unless he's naked. Best man I ever married."

"Only man, you mean."

"I guess I do." She patted his arm with her freckled hand.

"The right person."

She watched him then, as if she knew. Maybe she did. "Sometimes your knight in shining armor turns out to be a shitkicker in faded jeans."

Hot tears then, and he let them go, humiliated and all.

Janet didn't seem to mind. "Siddown already. You're fixin' to fall over."

He sat on a bale, his back against the shed's wall. His hands shook.

"Patch, we only fall in love to find out just exactly how much we can tolerate."

Patch nodded, dazed. "He weren't anything but wonderful since I been home, and I let him. All this time, an' I let him because I was gonna fix things somehow. Clear a path, y'know? So it'd work out, everything with...."

"Y'all." She didn't blink and the question rested there between them. The chickens drifted around her ankles.

He didn't move at first. "Have you ever done the right thing for the wrong reason and the right person?" He shook his head. "That came out wrong."

She wiped her hands on the towel slung over her shoulder and toed past the squawking birds, considering him with a patient gaze. She unlatched the gate carefully before she asked without asking. "You didn't say who 'he' was, kiddo."

Nod. Swallow. "Tucker. I mean Tucker." Saying the name aloud to her while he was so raw felt like slow knives across his soft parts.

For one stinging second, he worried he'd done the wrong thing, coming clean. His urge to run rose up, and he braced to bolt. But no.

She emerged from the pen and hugged him. She smelled like pears. "C'mon out in the light."

She pushed him out toward the battered bench behind the store where she snuck cigarettes when she was squabbling with Dave.

Patch sat again, crossing his arms over his hollow chest. He squinted up at her. "You didn't know."

"How in hell would I know? I don't know what Dave's doing half the time, and he's ten yards away every damn day. It's none of my business." She smiled and hugged herself, pleased as pie. "Heh. You and Tucker. Well, I'll be a clam salad."

"He's old enough to—"

"To know what's what." She jabbed his chest with a finger. "And you're old enough to get the hell over yourself, so hush. You're both old enough to do right by each other, and that's fuckin' plenty. *Pfft*. Old enough!" She held him.

"I'm so messed-up, Janet. Broke. And it's me who done it. Maybe some bad stuff happened, but I held it so long I can't feel right. Love right."

"I can see that."

"There's nothing left inside me. No hope, trust, or love. Like I ran out at some point." He wiped his nose.

"Naw, Patch. You can't never run out of love. It sweats out of us." She rocked him and stroked his head, shushing and humming.

"I did something terrible. To him. I thought it was the right thing, but I did something he can't ever forgive." He squeezed his eyes shut, hot with shame. "He made me happy."

"Oh kiddo. Love don't exist to make folks happy." Janet sat back and smoothed his messy hair. "It's there to tear us up and make us over. To teach us how much we can survive 'fore we keel over. It's like sunshine. Makes things grow and burns your ass both."

He choke-laughed on his tears. "No shit."

"Lord, you two know how to make some mess," she brayed. "Thank Christ for that."

"Why?"

"Both y'all so lonely, horny, messed-up." She snorted and chortled in satisfaction.

Patch frowned at the dirt. "I didn't think it'd be that way. Think that he'd want me. Think we'd give a damn. Nothing, really. I guess I didn't think."

"Folks more flexible than you think." She dropped her gaze but didn't share.

"I been pretty scared. You know how it is out here. He didn't hide it, but we didn't exactly put up a billboard."

"Well, some of my pink places wish you'd told me, but all same I'm glad you didn't. I mean, I'd love to see them sex tapes y'all made, but—"

"Gross!"

"Sue me. I'm human. And you boys sure do—"

He laughed. She'd made him laugh, so at least he was breathing. *Baby steps, baby steps.* He'd come out about Tucker to someone who mattered when it was too late to make a difference.

"But I think maybe some things don't need sharing." Her lips made a little tight line and she squinted at the sky. "Real life." The not-fantasy, she meant.

"No, ma'am."

"But I'm sure happy you told me. Happy for both y'all."

His face broke and whatever control he'd had over his sadness went with it.

"What? What, kiddo?" Her arms circled him. "I'm not gone tell nobody."

He bit his lip, clamped his mouth shut.

She eyed his wet face. "He done something."

"No. I did."

"Big whoop, kiddo. Must've been what you wanted or you wouldn't have."

He shook his head. "No."

Janet blinked but didn't give him any grease.

"I just—I rushed around and ran him down. Ugly." He shook his head but couldn't find his voice till he cleared his throat.

Janet gave a clipped nod. "You a full-grown man with two ears and a head stuck in between 'em. Whatever you did, you done."

"Something pretty awful."

"Well... awful. That's just folks. Some bitch and go. Some stay the same. Some folks will complain if you hang them with a new rope."
Rope.
"Yeah." He exhaled with effort. "I think I forgot how young I was. Back then." Shrug. "Now, even."
"That's what young is. How could you remember?"
For once in his life everything was moving faster than he could handle. For once, he needed a breather, with the pedal to the metal and the brakes shot. He squeezed his hand to stop it shaking. *Fool.*
"I miss—" He stared at the chickens, at the straw. He wondered if Botchy was with her daddy, if he'd ever see her again, slobbering on top of some hay mountain. "Everything."
Maybe Tucker could forgive him being young and stupid. He had before. Even if nothing else happened, even if he'd blown their shot, maybe he could make things right and apologize before he flew back to New York.
"You sure things bad as you say? Tucker's pretty steady in a saddle. All might blow over."
"Maybe once. But not anymore. He brought them hens. Horse." He nodded toward Tucker's animals.
"You think?" She sat back. "Well, men are dumb 'bout some things."
"He's done. I'm dumb and good riddance." He blinked and wiped the water from his lashes. "Maybe I learned my lesson."
"Least that's something." She didn't look too happy about it, though. "Aww, Patch. If I could, I'd give you the world, and fence it in too." She patted him.
He let her, just trying to breathe and nothing else while the sky churned above them. Any second it'd pour. "Maybe I go back up to New York, but stop running around so much. Maybe slow down some. Maybe I know better next time."
"That's as may be." Janet smoothed the loose strands back again, squinting up at the scudding sky. "Who knows? Not me."
"About time I act like a man." *Just pretend.* His father's advice in his head didn't make him cringe. "I ain't spun glass." He could pretend until it became the truth.
"Kiddo, you get to pick. That's all it is, being an adult. You pick." She spread her freckled hands, the battered gold band glinting. "You can be a mirror or you can be a window."

Patch frowned. "Howzat?"

"Sometimes you want to show folks what they are, bounce it all back, but sometimes you can show 'em something that's past you."

And then he knew exactly what she meant. Tucker had been that, done that. Patch had watched both. All his life, actually. "Past."

"That one's harder for most people. Staying clear without getting broke. Getting themselves outta the way so folks can see past and through to the other side of something." She patted his leg.

He turned to meet her gaze. "You think so?"

"People look, but they can't see always. You gotta help 'em."

"Thanks, Ms. Rodman." Patch smiled then and gave her a grateful hug. He wasn't hopeful, but at least he knew what needed to happen, even if he wasn't sure he could do it. "You're a wise old broad."

"Tell Dave." She grinned at that and slapped at him playfully. "Look at me still teachin' shit standing by a chicken coop with a storm brewing."

She stood and watched him walk back to his car, waving at him as he pulled away.

As Patch made the turn onto the highway, he saw her slowly heading back to the straw shed, studying the gravel at her feet.

The drive home took him right into the ugly storm brewing.

Before any bad storm, the Big Thicket hung heavy with color, the leaves and needles swollen with a soupy green that showed at no other time and only lasted till the lightning. For those few hours, the trunks oozed chilly sweat, and sensible animals found someplace to hole up.

This one looked to be a doozy.

Somehow he felt certain Tucker would be waiting at the trailer, in the house, by the pond, or up the barn pitching hay. He planned to hand over the tea dance envelope. Aside from the personal shit, fifteen hundred in cash was the least he could give Tucker for all the work he'd done out here, plus the hay money. They'd talk, at least, and even if he'd messed that up he could apologize and do right by the only person who deserved better.

Patch drove back to the farm ready to say sorry, to tell truth, to stand still and take his damn medicine so the two of them could figure out what a way forward might look like, even if it was apart.

He nosed into Tucker's drive, and a sorrier sight he'd never seen.

The fixtures in the yard were gone, and the windows of Tucker's trailer dead. Out back, one of the henhouse trailers sat silent and rusted through on its cracked axle. Of the other, nothing remained but a rectangle of the stunted weeds that had grown underneath.

Tucker hadn't gone off for a couple days—he'd up and left. *No mistake.*

Patch climbed out of the Impala, ignoring the damp wind. Up the steps, the little porch was bare too, and swept besides. All the planters gone. No hens roamed the yard depositing ninja eggs willy-nilly, because they'd gone to the Feed & Seed.

He tried to ignore the cold tension hollow in his gut, certain he'd walk into some horrible surprise he couldn't handle. Then he knew.

Please no.

At his touch, the chipped door swung open, unlocked and unloved.

Inside, Tucker's trailer had been emptied of every single stick of furniture and clutter, in a hurry by the look of it.

Patch's footsteps creaked in the small space, echoing oddly. Without the contents, the entire double-wide had shrunk somehow, as if disgorging all of Tucker's belongings had left it shriveled and crooked as a punctured tire.

"Bastard cleaned right out." He should feel happy.

Out back, Nugget's still stall sat wide open beside the abandoned henhouse trailer propped on blocks. Botchy's bowl and chewed tennis balls had vanished too. The back bathroom empty of straw and chicks both. The cabinets and fridge empty and wiped down. No food, no plates, not even a roll of paper towels.

Everything.

He'd never seen a bleaker sight in his life.

He walked straight back to Tucker's bedroom and froze in the doorway, hands shaking on the doorknob.

Tucker's big brass bed still filled the bare room, the ornate frame he'd dragged all over creation for most of his life. The only thing left in the whole trailer was that old frame hunched at one end like a monstrous gold skeleton guarding his bedroom... no sheets, no mattress, just the gleaming coils of metal.

Of all things, why would he leave this?

Maybe he'd run out of time. Maybe he planned to come back for it. Maybe he hadn't had room in the U-Haul and just stored it here till he got settled.

Dumb bastard, meaning him or Tucker or whoever else fit the bill. The edges of his eyes did some preweep prickling until he wiped them hard enough to sting.

What in hell had Tucker done? Patch frowned. He'd moved, was what. Just as he'd said he would, just as Patch had told him to. He'd taken care of all the loose ends the way he'd promised and left Patch without a mess to clean up. *Well, mostly.*

Patch braced his hands on the foot of the bed frame that sat waiting for him in the dim like a long, handwritten letter in a foreign language, golden cursive. *Jesus.* This was the only part of Tucker's past he'd managed to keep, and he'd abandoned it.

He gave it to you, asshole.

Queasy terror coiled around him, pumping him full of too much adrenaline with nowhere to go. Patch wiped his mouth and got the hell out of the trailer.

The hell have I done?

He drove slowly back to the main house, trying to pinpoint exactly where things had gone so wrong so quick, so easy.

Finally he made a decision, of sorts. He'd drive over to Ms. Landry's to sign the Texaco paperwork to authorize the survey and sample. A formality at this point. They'd wanted the land for years. No reason to wait, and the clock was ticking on Velocity anyway. Even if things had gone a little wobbly, his original plan was still a good one.

He washed and dressed in the dark house, steeling himself against the storm.

For a million reasons, the drive to the lawyer's didn't go the way it should have. The roads, the blackening sky, his discombobulation conspired to knock him off course. Somehow he passed the same unhelpful Texaco station twice. He kept getting turned around as the wind and rain picked up, as if deliberately misleading him. Eventually he made it, but by a weird route he couldn't have found again if he tried.

By the time he was back in Hixville, he'd used half a tank of gas trying to take a twenty-minute drive, and the knotted, woolen sky had drifted close enough to touch.

Back inside the house, Patch lay stiff on the blue carpet of his childhood room listening to the storm boil. Not a hurricane, but definitely a big county-wide mess come morning. Lightning lit his parents' empty house, revealing the bare rooms in sporadic flashes of blinding white that left him blind and jittery. About eleven, the first pebbles hit the window and soon after, what sounded like rocks on the roof.

Sure enough, when he peeked outside it was hailing like hell. Chips and knots of ice pelted the drive and rattled on the shingles. Because of the humidity, hailstorms could get nasty out here in hurricane season; he'd seen it punch through a windshield and beat a car's paint down to the primer.

Braving the wet cold, he sprinted for the rental, holding his dad's old slicker over his head. Hailstones hit him hard enough to hurt. Most were the size of nickels, but he spotted a few clumps of ice big as his fist as he dodged puddles and downed branches. The wet trees drooped and the lawn was pocked with mud.

Jumping into the Impala, he steered it into the sagging barn just so it didn't get hammered. Last thing he needed was a bodywork bill when he turned the damn rental in.

Crossing the yard again, he circled the house and closed all the shutters best he could, covering the exposed panes, at least. He'd helped his pa put these up in seventh grade as a Mother's Day surprise, and the hinges were stiff with disuse.

Back indoors, he stripped out of his soaked clothes, dried with a towel, and braced for a bad night. The wind and hail echoed strangely in the empty rooms.

Twenty bucks said the power would go out, which made no difference as he'd been without it this whole time, but that meant cell towers too. Folks would be cut off till morning all over Hixville. Reason number five million why he'd moved to the city, right? As storms went, this one wouldn't set any records, but out here in the sticks, nature liked to remind people exactly who owned what every now and again.

After a couple hours, he fell asleep alone on the floor, listening to the angry hail knocking on the roof like gigantic knuckles, not knowing how to answer and hoping Tucker was safe, somewhere out where he didn't belong.

CHAPTER ELEVEN

EVENTUALLY THE storm blew itself to smithereens, leaving the farm bruised and silent.

Patch woke up exhausted, tight-nerved as if keyed to a subsonic whistle that kept him on edge, inaudible but incessant. His whole body wanted to bolt for any exit available, to flee so fast the flesh melted from his bones.

Outside, the muggy, woozy air still hadn't warmed or moved enough to feel clean. A few stubborn chunks of hail still salted the puddles of stripped dirt in the yard. His mama's azaleas and roses were pulped. The livid sky had been scoured to the bone.

Without any cover, the fields were worse. The new grass was flattened, Tucker's last discing pounded into green mush. No matter. Texaco wouldn't be baling any of this hay anyway.

Thank God he'd parked the car in the barn.

If he wanted to, he could be on the road to Houston by noon and back in New York by sundown. And after all, didn't he want that?

He finished stacking boxes against the wall for shipping. And crammed his crap into the duffel, wondering if he'd be better off just burning these clothes. He could afford to. After all, this wasn't the end; it was the start of everything he'd always wanted.

At the last, he went to say good-bye to the cemetery, and the pond. He'd never see 'em again.

Hail had stripped the leaves and broken branches. The uneven ground was soaked, and in some shadowed places the biggest chunks of ice lay melting like misshapen golf balls. The kudzu-draped trees must've sheltered the graves from the smaller pellets. He wondered if the folks buried here appreciated the trees' sacrifice, and paused.

In all his years using this place as a hideaway, he'd never really thought about the actual human remains underfoot. As a kid, he'd treated the markers as little more than grubby scenery.

Sixteen pitted gravestones, the names and dates almost scoured smooth by a hundred years of rain. Nine of them were plain sandstone squares sticking up like loose teeth. They'd been here so long that a beech stand had grown up around them, even the tiny angel statue, folded wings curved forward like protective parentheses over some forgotten kid. This morning, the bowed wings sheltered a lone hailstone the size of his fist.

He didn't even know their names, this family buried out here. His mama had tried once to find out when she went through her scrapbooking phase, but no public records existed.

The Slope family had farmed this land since before Texas had joined the United States, but beyond title to the acreage, the town records were lost, and the family history. Couldn't have been easy, surviving the hot summers and hurricanes to scratch a living out of the dirt back before there were any real cities to escape to, when Texas was still a country.

Not like drilling for crude would disturb these bones. Then again, he wasn't a geologist.

Patch stared at his parentheses angel and wondered about the child under it. These people had families too, folks who loved them enough to put them in the ground nearby and remember them.

Irritated, he yanked a weed from the angel's base that had survived the fat hailstone. What kind of dolt would try to live here in the sticks to make a life? They must've been dim, desperate, or unhinged. The nameless child bothered him, a pebble in his boot.

Sure enough, the surviving Slope descendants had abandoned their past and gone out into the world: Austin, Chicago, and maybe even New York. Maybe some queer son of theirs had joined the circus, launched a business, fucked off to find a life.

Home sick.

He tugged another weed loose.

They'd be moved, probably, the bones. It didn't matter. Who'd notice besides him? Eight or nine farmers too stubborn to find a better place to live. They all deserved to be left behind, except for the kid.

Tucker's words haunted him. *Some people don't have a family to start with.*

The angel's face, weathered flat and featureless, stared back at him. Something sad about your bones being shuffled around like a car in a city parking lot.

A crow squawked overhead.

"I hate this place." But that was a lie too. He loved this green, quiet bubble. Some things out here he did miss, he did love. Some part of him would always live here.

Goddamn Tucker for reminding him about the good parts he'd forgotten. For making a simple life out here with nothing but his charm, his dick, and his dog.

Another weed and another pulled. The soil beneath was cool and reddish with clay.

Patch wondered what the kid had been like. How old he was when he died. How much that angel had cost. How far it had traveled. How much his folks had sacrificed to put it out here under the beech trees for the rain to rub smooth. At least in New York, a million miles a minute, someone was always watching.

I never should have come back here.

He'd have been better off just staying away and wiping his hands, making up a childhood that worked better.

He frowned at the idea of lying that much, trying to erase his family. He whispered, "Stop."

Good-bye, good-bye.

A tear fell, and another. *Stupid.* He didn't even know the dead kid under the angel, and here he sat blubbering about him.

Well, mostly. And his parents too probably. And Tucker.

Patch wiped his wet face with the back of his hand, ashamed of his sadness and his doubt. He picked up the angel's big slick hailstone, letting it melt in his palm and not caring if it hurt.

"I love you." Tucker's voice came as a low rumble behind him, and the raw words tore an ugly hole in his chest.

Patch turned as if underwater, silence roaring in his ears and his skin tingling with gooseflesh.

Tucker stood at the edge of the grove, straw work hat in his hand and Botchy sitting at his leg. They both looked serious. "You knew that, I figure, but I wouldn't say it."

"What are you doing here?" His throat was gluey and tender.

"Saying it."

"Tucker." Patch squeezed his eyes shut against tears and blinked.

"I didn't— You didn't give me a chance to explain." Tucker's mouth looked broken. "I said I love you, Patrick. I never said that to nobody in my whole crappy life."

He looked back at the little angel, weighing the hailstone like an icy heart.

Botchy came to Patch slowly, her stumpy tail going, eyes like hot solder, but her champagne face steady and sweet. *How do dogs know when we're upset?* She licked his hand and the hail, and leaned against him, scars and all, smelling of straw.

"Look at me, pup. Please."

Patch didn't.

"I tried to tell you in New Orleans. At the bar. In bed. In the damn truck, driving there. Every second." Tucker came no closer, just held his hat and breathed with effort. He swallowed. "But I got messed up. The dancing. Dunno. My bed. Bix's bullshit. Everything got crazy an' all."

Patch thrust his chin in the direction of the empty trailer, eyes dead. "You cleaned out fast enough."

"You didn't want me here, pup. You said as much, and I listened. I hadn't ought to have been here to start with. Living off your folks. But I'm not brave like you."

"Yeah. Running away. Real fuckin' brave." He laughed. "I ran away from home, but I didn't run *to* anywhere. That's blind, not brave."

"I could never go to a city, stand up and start over. I'm a slow learner. Stubborn and lazy."

"You're not."

Tucker frowned.

"You were right when it mattered." Patch gave a lopsided shrug. "Figured everything faster than me. Told truth when I couldn't. Saw through all my shit. Saved me. Back then. Now." Another stupid tear sliced down his cheek and he didn't wipe it. He rubbed Botchy's sturdy, scarred back—*where her wings were*—and she licked his salty face again.

"That ain't so." Tucker squatted. His hands shook. "I'm a mess, pup. I loved you too much to let you love me back, 'cause I don't want to wreck you like I wrecked every other thing ever put in my hands."

"That's not true."

"Patch." A short sigh. "You know better."

Patch rolled the slippery hailstone in his cold fingers. *Do I?*

Tucker pointed at his dog as she wandered back toward the pond. "You know she run off last night? Middle of a damn storm and that mutt hares off, hell for leather into the dark. Sky about broke open and she's gone I don't know where. I ain't slept yet 'cause I been looking and looking."

Patch nodded at her. "Damn dog's smarter than any of us."

"That is a true statement. She came right back. Here, I mean. Ten miles or something. Scared the piss outta me. I drive out, she was up the barn, nosing around, wondering where her haystack went."

"How'd you know she'd come here?"

"I didn't." Tucker squatted down. "I came looking for you. Only she got here first. My best bitch." He chuckled then, and rubbed his palms together.

"I'm glad." He swallowed, not sure where Tucker was headed.

"Patch." Tucker blinked rapidly. "I got this feeling now. Like I never had." He looked up then, his hands open. "If I just let you go off, if I just decide to do nothing, I'll be stuck the rest of my days with my whole life gone to sticks and splinters, jerking off while I wait on nothing."

"You took the words...." Patch coughed and wiped his eyes. "That's me, same. Same fucking thing. Like a hurricane with no houses to hit."

"So no." Tucker took his empty hand then, carefully. "I'm not gonna do *nothing*, now. Not ever again. There's one thing you done, it's got me out the dirt and looking out, out there." He turned to look past the little pond where Botchy stood up to her hocks in the shallows looking back, water dripping from her muzzle.

Patch grinned to himself. "I'm not ashamed of that."

"And I ain't grousing. Look, pup." Tucker stared at the small angel, as though his tongue had just discovered a hole in one of his molars. "You're young. Smart. Handsome. Lord knows. Easy on the eyes, hard on the heart."

Patch shook his head. "None of that mat—"

Tucker said, "I don't mean how you seem or say, I mean what you do, who you are, Patch. Live wire. Run around making lightning bugs into *lightning*. That's—" He paused.

"Like a jackass."

"No. When you showed up and things happened, I thought we were playing. Just a game, a gimme. Nobody loses 'cause it don't matter," Tucker said.

Shrug. "I get that. Sure." He'd thought the same thing. He'd snuck over and spied in the dark and sneered at all of it, everyone, but most of all Tucker.

"Until it mattered. Except the way you come back, I figgered you didn't want nobody close. You wanted to hate me, so things was simpler. Both ways." Tucker pointed between them. "Like you was somewhere else the whole time. We was both safe 'cause no one was home."

Patch squinted back before answering as best he could. "Maybe when we started, or maybe back when I was in school. Maybe back when I was trying to get fucked to death and you couldn't stop me trying or tell my folks." Shrug. "But now? Huh-uh."

"Only I been that way my whole life. Rode hard and put away wet and 'Fuck you, Biggs.' I didn't—" Tucker smoothed his handlebar. "I wanna say this right: I stayed where I was so no one new could get at me."

Patch nodded.

"No matter how close they got. Whoever it was, I could hit 'em, quit 'em, hump 'em, dump 'em, but they couldn't hurt me none." Tucker looked up. "And you the same. You just the same."

"Messed-up."

"Or messed-up enough to not be scared of being with someone messed-up." Tucker wiped his mouth and sighed. "Like, anybody who could put up with me had to be messed-up too."

Patch snorted. "Messed-up enough to survive. Yeah."

"So, I guess I stay. You go. Last couple weeks just a crazy memory to pull out sometime. Messed up the best way, I guess."

Patch considered the little parentheses angel for a quiet moment. Wind stroked the branches overhead and the kudzu beside the pond.

"Pup, am I right?"

He shrugged, shamed all the same. "My whole life I've been running in place. Racing around so the right people think my life's going somewhere."

Tucker pressed his lips together in an odd grimace. "My wife used to say 'never confuse motion with action.' Ex-wife. You know."

"Luanne. I do." Patch remembered full well. He had been too jealous of her to be nice, and glad when she split to El Paso. "She had my number, then. Seems like all I did was mix up motion and action."

"But Patch, I done the same." Tucker pressed his lips together before he continued. "I confused standing still with doing nothing. Sitting on my tail out here, I done plenty of harm to plenty of folks. All them women gone. All them kids grown up in other men's houses 'cause I figgered my bad luck was contagious. I shoulda tried sooner. Work, sex, nothing. I let my whole life go by. I chose that. I done that, better and worse. An' that's wrong too."

"Barn-shy." He'd run for home.

Tucker dipped his head. "Yeah. An' worse. Didn't I come running back home just now trying to catch lightning in a jar? Ain't I here?"

"Don't be sorry for that." Patch squeezed the big slick piece of hail, rolling it like soap in his fingers. "I shouldn't have said all that shit in New Orleans. I was wrong."

"We was both wrong. But we were right together, and you knew it and I knew it. Folks fight and that's fine."

"I didn't want to fight."

"No. But you wanted me to love you back, and I did, and worse. I *needed* you terrible, and we couldn't go nowhere together after that weekend. Not ever again. Last chance, standing middle of the street with a million other lonely dumbasses."

"Sorry."

"Me too. Sorrier'n you know." Tucker gripped his hat and looked down at it in his hands. "I couldn't move and then all I did was chase around for fear I'd miss a step when it counted." He rubbed his big hands together. "Two-step and struck by lightning bugs."

They smiled tentatively at each other. "You and me both."

"How'd you get home?" Tucker took a step closer, set his hat on a tombstone.

"Bus. Vicky." Another handful of plucked weeds. "Janet 'bout roasted me for what I did."

"Tell me. I cleaned out the trailer. Drove half my shit to the dump 'cause I didn't care and it didn't seem to matter. Dropped off them birds with Janet and Dave, but I wouldn't tell her nothing. Then night." Tucker sighed. "Hail like hell, right? I'm sleeping in my truck parked in a ranch lot outside Honey Island I used to bunk at five, ten years ago." He frowned and bowed his head. "My whole life scattered. Clothes in garbage bags. Furniture in the pastor's garage. Chickens and Nugget up the Feed & Seed. Scattered to hell and don't I know the feeling."

Botchy chose that moment to mosey back up to them, sniffing at the mud and broken weeds. She sat beside her daddy and put her head on his knee.

He stroked her silver-pink ears absently. "Storm cracking and spitting. Pickup's under a horse shed, but I can hear the hail. Dog's whining and shaking in the truck bed, so's I get out to bring her in the cab. Right? Untie her, and boom, she tears off, on a mission." A dry wheeze of unsmiling laughter. "I 'bout died. Chased after. Can't find her, can't find her. I drive all night, looking and praying."

"She's fine, though. Fine now." Patch nodded.

"I dunno. Everything. I drove around blind in that storm. All my shit scattered, scattered. Ice pinging the cab like the sky's broke up there. All busted to hell and falling in chunks around my truck. I swear." Tucker looked up, his mouth a sad rictus till he closed it. "Nowhere. Driving, driving. I had no idea, until I did."

He patted Botchy's ribs roughly and rubbed them. She twisted her head, tongue lolling and grinned at him proudly.

"So finally, finally I come back out here looking for my durn dog. Nowhere to go. Last place I wan' to be 'cause I know you're gone off somewhere with someone smarter'n me, better'n me and I'm already dead inside." Head shake. "She's up the barn, looking for something. Nothing. And I come down here." Frown. "Find you standing here with hope in your heart and a piece of broken sky in your hand, like you knew to wait." Tucker put a hand on the back of his neck.

Patch leaned forward.

"For me." Tucker stared at him, unblinking. "You waited for me."

Patch smiled then and bowed his head. "I guess I did. I never waited for anything in my damn life 'cept you."

"Except me." He brushed Patch's hair back and cupped the back. "And for that I am grateful like you will never know in this world, pup. I don't s'pose I could explain if I tried."

Patch gazed into those big gray eyes and saw... what?

Everything. Fireflies, Rope, sweet coffee, Botchy's scars, creaking floors, that big brass bed waiting for him too like golden cursive.

"I know, Tucker. I really do." He tipped their foreheads together, sighed, and his shoulders settled for the first time in two days. He dropped the big hailstone in the grass to melt and held Tucker's ribs through the faded cotton.

"'Kay." His whisper was nearly inaudible. He cleared his throat. "So. Well. That's that. Huh? You got a plane an' all." Tucker's rugged face gave nothing away. "Sad song."

He whispered. "No, sir."

"No, what?"

"Why is 'that that'? Says who?" Patch sniffed in impatience. "I didn't say that, Tucker. You did. I swear you're the smartest dumbass I ever met."

"Well, I just mean—"

Now Patch found his full voice and said it again. "No, Tuck. Running around doesn't mean you get anywhere. *Fuck* fast. No way I'm gonna spend rest my life twisted 'round to look backwards wondering what-if when I already know good and goddamn well."

Tucker didn't reply.

"I want to be with you." Patch took a breath. "You, Tucker Dray Biggs... and your boots and your bluegrass and your daily egg hunt and your coffee and all your duct-tape, halfway bullshit genius." A grin. "Because it's not bullshit, none of it. I love you and it can work if you hush up and let it."

Tucker nodded, lips shut, eyes shiny.

"I mean, you do what you want. We both get a say if we want that, the two of us. But if you're asking, that's what I say." He kissed Tucker's face and eyes, tasting the mineral sting of tears on his tongue after. "We'll figure it out."

"I guess we will." Tucker cleared his throat. "Cain't lose 'em all, right?"

"Nossir." Then Patch kissed him, a slow certain press of their lips under the trees and the wind with the little angel at their knees. "We can't lose."

A grunt, and then Tucker kissed him back but good, pushing thick fingers into his hair and pulling his face close, not letting him go, tasting the inside of his mouth and groaning like a thirsty man, face tipped up in summer rain.

Patch didn't fight it, just gave back the same gentle pressure he had when they'd danced... in the drive, in New Orleans. He leaned into the soft, stooping give-take they made against each other, tipping his head to get closer as Tucker ran a calloused hand under his shirt and up his back. Their cocks knocked together, *slow-slow*, and the friction between them quickened the air, heated their skin.

Tucker pulled back and at first Patch followed, not wanting him to stop. "Hey now. Hang on."

He chuckled at his own hunger.

Tucker stroked his shoulders with steady, calming pressure. "Lord, I missed you, pup. Two days an' you'd think it were a year in prison."

"We're going to take our time and figure this out." Patch rocked back. "Measure twice, cut once."

Tucker exhaled. "I'm selfish enough to agree, but I worry you're gonna get frustrated with me plenty."

"Likewise, I bet. And if I can't be patient, then I'll just pretend, huh?"

"That I'd like to see."

"If we take our time, it's our time to take, right? Besides, if there's one thing you taught me, being frustrated ain't all bad, huh? Rope, grease." He chuckled then, a low teasing sound. "A little friendly restraint never hurt nobody."

"I guess not." A wet globber as Botchy licked and licked the big hailstone. Tucker snorted. "Damn dog."

"Best bitch." He rubbed her ghosty, gleaming coat.

"That is a true statement." Tucker studied his face for a moment. "You gone be able to stand living somewhere quiet with me?"

"More than stand it, now that I understand it." Patch hoped Tucker understood what he wanted to say. "I guess there's no place like home. And there never was."

"I don't think that's it, exactly."

He shook his head. "No, Tuck, I mean… I was running too fast to see around me too clearly. I forgot how young I was." A dry laugh came out of Patch unbidden. "Am."

"Pup." Tucker smiled back at him, patient and proud. "There's no place like home because home ain't a place." He pressed his big hand to Patch's heart. "Not somewhere we go."

Patch leaned into it, like dancing. "You sure make it sound easy."

"It is easy." Tucker blinked. "After. If y'smart, you hang on like you're bulldogging. Rope it and wrestle it to the ground so it don't go nowhere."

He butted Tucker's forehead with his. "It ain't going nowhere."

"Good deal. What'm I gonna do?"

"Tucker. You can open a damn petting zoo. Sell eggs. Barbecue stand. Just ride around on Nugget and be in my bed at night. We got time to decide."

"Yeah?"

"Plenty of."

Tucker looked out through the trees at the storm-battered farm. "Then I figger we'll just move, pup."

"You think?"

"Yeah I think. It don't much matter. Not necessarily a bad deal. Not farming, though. 'Cause hay's good, but ain't many people around regular. We'll just find a piece of land up the road a piece. Dunno. Barbecue ain't a bad idea. Maybe some place people wanna come hang out. Like a juke joint. You could play music some. Dancing, maybe." Tucker blinked and winked. "I can supervise and eat all the profits. You can go on that Circuit when you got to."

"Barbecue." He smiled at the idea. They had the insurance anyway. "I think that's a fine idea, Tuck."

"Like a... redneck destination. You seen Slick Dick's—they's folks drive hours for somewhere to go. Space for parties and such." Brandy glow lit the stern gray of his eyes again, the boyish troublemaker under the bruised man. "Birthday, rodeo, wedding an' all. Someplace ours."

"Yeah?" He knew Tucker would be good at playing host. He could make anybody feel welcome and safe. He would have been a great dad, in some other life, with some other family behind him, doing right by him. "Mechanical bull."

"Hell, I could just put horns on Botchy and she'd pitch in." He rubbed her ribs roughly, and she wiggled and circled them.

"But you think we need to move."

Tucker looked confused.

Patch rubbed his unshaven face. "More I think on it, I think we're better here. I don't want to sell this place."

Tucker turned back to him, squinting. "You signed them papers, though."

"I did not." Patch scowled at the memory and shook his head.

"Serious?"

"Twice I drove there and back to that office with the papers in my hand in that crappy car. Ms. Landry thinks I'm a loony, or more of one than she did already. But I just couldn't do it. I tried and tried and I knew it was wrong. So I stalled." He exhaled and looked at his parentheses angel. "Run fast, stand still, right?"

"So it ain't sold." Tucker straightened. "None of it."

"Nope. Velocity doesn't have to happen either if we don't want. I gotta go back to New York to wrap up, but we'll just take our time and decide whatever we want. Together. I had this stupid idea I needed, I dunno, that club and all so I could stay in the fast lane. But I think this is something we decide, you and me, like you say."

Tucker looked poleaxed, eyes glistening. "We will? I did?"

"Unless you know of someone else who needs a vote…. Maybe the damn dog." Botchy's ears perked up, and she loped back in their direction, ready to climb a mountain.

"C'mere, pup." Tucker opened his arms, and Patch stepped into them so that slow lazy rushing pleasure soaked through him, rooting him where he belonged. "I gotcha. I gotcha."

Patch nodded and grunted. A little winnowing breeze shifted the grass in the graves and Botchy's blocky head bumped their pressed legs.

"I swear." Tucker kissed his hair and inhaled. "Some times." A sigh that turned into a happy mumble.

"Sometimes what?"

Head shake and a squeeze. "Sometimes everything."

CHAPTER TWELVE

NEW YORK hadn't noticed his absence and welcomed him back like an angry cake visited by a crumb.

About a week after the storm, Patch went back long enough to pack up his life, and after eleven days in Manhattan, he couldn't remember why he had ever fought to make a home here.

Now the jittery, caffeinated rush and fumble of the city felt less like a rhythm and more like an illness. For the first time, walking through the crowds made him a salmon struggling upstream. Why fight for what you don't want?

He no longer felt like a resident, but a tourist. Worse, his business partner and his friends, all the people he relied on, had replaced him swiftly, perfectly willing to fill the gap created by his trip to Hixville with some other hot bohunk who hated home.

Not me.

As a DJ, he could do his job from anywhere. Velocity didn't need him to happen. Scotty had settled quite comfortably into Patch's gig at Beige. And if he wasn't trying to climb the nightlife heap, what good was a hipster club that needed him to sprint like hell to stay in one place?

His little walk-up apartment in Hell's Kitchen and all the sexy, silly city-isms he'd come to love had soured somehow. All he wanted now waited for him in a stolen double-wide in East Texas, stretched out on a brass bed wearing crocodile boots and an easy grin.

Patch didn't waste one second. The apartment was so small that boxing it only took two days, shipping it two hours. In just over a week he'd slipped most the nets that held him in New York. He figured on a couple of weeks to untangle himself and ship his crap back home. He'd take his leave and haul ass back to Tucker ASAP.

Nope. The modeling agency barely blinked, but breaking his lease and his bills turned out to be more complicated than expected, so he decided to sublet. The delay preyed on him. He talked to Tucker on the phone a few times a day, which helped, but it felt weird not seeing him, not touching him when they spoke.

To his surprise, he caught himself getting nostalgic for dirt roads and county fairs but knew it for what it was. He didn't miss Hixville; he missed feeling like he was in the right place with the right man.

Scotty and the rest of his friends kept stalling, kept him running in place: an after-hours birthday, a last-minute go-see, an impromptu farewell dinner, one more toast and roast. *A couple more days, a couple more days,* until ten days had passed with him stuck fast.

Then one day at the end of that second weird week, ambling through a crosswalk on Broadway and Twenty-Third, he paused and what felt like half of New York began honking at him in unison. *Cacophony.* Stopped him dead in his cowboy boots. Some surly woman in a custom Porsche shouted, "Hurry the fuck up, jagoff. Sheesh!"

Without thinking Patch smiled at her, because he was from Texas and not in a hurry at all, and drawled, "Hold your horses, ma'am." Hearing himself saying it woke him right up. *Bam.* Right in front of all them honking cabs.

Next thing he knew he was buying a full-fare plane ticket on his phone and making Scotty promise to meet the movers. He told himself to calm down and thought of his pa's advice with understanding: *Just pretend.* He'd never be patient, but he could pretend… which got close enough to count.

And on the night of day eleven, he threw his duffel bag into a yellow cab and got his ass to the airport (Newark) and a one-way to Baton Rouge (exit row), and he was too happy to gripe about getting stuck with the middle seat. He didn't even call to tell Tucker, hoping to surprise him a couple days early. For once he didn't think Tucker would mind him rushing.

He reached Louisiana after one in the morning and the farm long after four. Skipping the house, he headed right to Tucker's trailer but found it dark and empty as he'd left it.

Well, hell.

Downside of surprising someone: usually they don't know their steps. *Quick-quick, slow, slow.*

Disappointed and anxious, Patch dragged his ass back to his parents' house, wishing for once he'd planned this better. Where had Tucker gone? Was this a mistake? A cold sliver of doubt wormed its way between his ribs.

Fools rush in.

In no hurry now and sullen at his own screwy impulse, Patch slung the duffel over his shoulder and scuffed up the driveway toward the barn. He was halfway to the porch when he spotted the old truck, and, tucked into the base of the kitchen pear tree, a perfect white egg glowing in the moonlight like a giant pearl.

He laughed then and rescued the warm egg in one careful hand. Doubt turned to hot hope and his feet carried him to the porch in a carbonated rush. *He's here*. Waiting.

On the swing, Botchy raised her head and whuffed quietly. Her tongue lolled as he rubbed her head roughly in greeting.

"Hey, girl. Hey there. Look at you. Lord, but it's good to be home." She bumped his leg with her square head and then rolled onto her back so he could tickle her powder-pink belly. "Yeah? Good girl. Where's your daddy at, huh? Where's daddy?" He left her guarding the little house in earnest, watching for the moonset.

Inside, the hall was neat and dark, the den empty and freshly painted. All the boxes had been stacked along the living room wall and a cool breeze drifted through the screens. He left the egg to rock in the key dish by the door.

"Tucker?" he murmured into the cool blue spaces of the house.

But the rooms were dark. He glanced at his watch: almost five o'clock. Practically daybreak for decent folks out here.

Grinning, he sat in the mudroom to tug off his boots and socks. The dark kitchen was equally bare, but the fridge hid a twelve-pack of Bud and a half-empty gallon of milk. He paused to rinse the dog smell off his hands and dried them with a faded tea towel. He smiled and doubled back through the dark rooms. *Come out, come out wherever you are.*

In a quiet voice Patch asked the silence, "You here, Tucker?" He crept down the hall toward the bedrooms without turning on the lights. The floors were clean, the walls were bare, and the house welcomed him with easy silence. *Home.*

His room, nothing. The sewing room, nothing. But an amber glow beckoned him from his parents' room, the door ajar. The grin on his face broadened into something steadier, calmer. He pushed the door open, and the last knots of his tension unraveled and fell to the floor, into dust, into sweet relief.

Patch sighed. *There.*

Tucker's big brass bed now filled the master bedroom, with the man himself stretched out on ironed sheets dozing in nothing but a pair of unbuttoned jeans. One thick arm cradled his face and his toes twitched in his sleep.

What's the opposite of homesick? Whatever it was, he was.

Holding his breath, Patch snuck to Tucker's side to gaze down at his dozing cowboy.

Hey, bud.

Tucker probably hadn't shaved since he'd left for New York. There were fresh scratches on his sun-browned forearms and the creamy bicep bunched under his cheek. His face looked contented, almost innocent in sleep, even with his gray-flecked hair and his craggy features. His pale ribs rose and fell in gentle rhythm, powerful and peaceful.

The raw sawdust and iron smell of him permeated the room, probably because he must've been sleeping here. *Since I left.* Were these walls painted too? With primer, it looked like. And when had he moved the bed?

Patch realized it didn't matter. It belonged in here as much as Tucker did. If anything, he wished he'd been here to help Tucker put it where it needed to be with less hassle.

"I missed you, mister," Patch whispered to his sleeping cowboy. "Like you wouldn't believe." He dropped his watch and wallet on the nightstand and skinned out of his damp shirt. "So much."

Tucker dozed on, oblivious and trusting.

Patch closed the door slowly and stepped quietly to the bed. "Tucker?" A sneaky, snaky idea put a grin on his face.

Tucker looked so relaxed, his lips curled and slightly open as if he was about to tell a dirty story.

Feeling wicked and willful, Patch decided to roll the dice for once just like Tucker had asked. Before he had time to doubt himself or ask for permission, he opened the nightstand and grabbed the coil of rope he knew he'd find there. With quick fingers he made a double loop and a hitch.

Tucker had it coming.

Doing his best to keep quiet, Patch slid the loop over Tucker's right wrist but didn't pull it taut. He flicked the rope behind the headboard and made another hitch and loop to match for the broad left wrist. *So strong.* Even at rest, the muscle bunched and gave under the skin like filthy poetry.

Wheezing in suppressed laughter, he put one knee and then the other on the bed, straddling Tucker before he had time to wake fully.

"What the—? Hey, buddy." Big contented smile as Tucker stretched awake under him. "Mmmh. Tha's nice. I must be dreaming, huh?"

"Could be."

"Good dream. I think I fell asleep." He scrunched his groggy face at the ropes.

"You sure did." *Shore.* Patch imitated his accent and tugged at the rope till Tucker's wrists rose off the mattress like a marionette's.

"The hell you done, pup?" But he didn't resist, just favored the idea with a lazy smile and the fat rammer under Patch's seat. "I seem to be in some kind of trouble."

Patch sat back on the ridge of rigid flesh. "Mmmph. That so?"

"Seems someone's taken advantage of my trusting nature."

They grinned at each other.

Patch tugged the rope the rest of the way, lifting Tucker's arms to meet the brass. "And here I thought you'd want to welcome me home."

"I was gonna. But now...." Tucker cocked his head and tasted his lower lip slowly. "I ain't gone be much help, looks like."

"Excuses, excuses." Patch bent forward to kiss the corner of his mouth and whispered against his smile. "Lazy sumbuck." Reaching behind Tucker, he secured the ends to the headboard over them.

"Unnph. See?" Tucker flexed his hips under them both. "I like it when you talk right."

"You do, huh?"

He hunched again, grinding against Patch's ass. "A lot."

Patch flexed his hips in answer. "Well, I like what you did to the room. The bed."

"Good deal."

He tested the rope again, checking the knots. "We need a sturdy bed."

"Yes, sir." Tucker sighed and squirmed under him. "I hope you ain't done with me."

"No chance." Just like that, everything the same and different and perfect. "Yeah?" But he wasn't really asking. Nervous and horny as hell, he secured Tucker's hard arms to the headboard from wrist to shoulder.

Rising up to hitch the knots and lace those arms to the brass loops put his crotch about two inches from Tucker's face.

Tucker closed the distance hungrily to nuzzle at the zipper.

One of them groaned, though Patch couldn't say who. His nuts ached and within a few minutes he had secured Tucker's arms and torso to the headboard in broad loops that trapped and displayed the heavy muscle.

"What's got into you, I wonder?" Tucker didn't sound too distressed.

"I wonder." He tested the rope, tracing the wrap and probing the knots to make sure nothing pinched and stroking the lush flesh.

Below him, Tucker looked flushed and frustrated, his mouth wet with spit. "I got worried—" He stopped and closed his mouth. "Bullshit. I been thinking 'bout you."

"Yeah?" Patch sat back again, his cock jammed against denim. They were both sweating a little now and breathing deeply against each other. "Good. I like how you think."

For the first time, Tucker pulled against his restraints. His chest and biceps bunched and his hands squeezed into fists as he tested the slack. "Sneaky bastard. How am I even gonna touch you like I need?"

"Hold your horses." Patch stroked the hard abdomen all the way down to the fuzzy trail leading into his pants. Tucker jumped and flinched. "Are you... *ticklish*, cowboy?"

"Whoa!" Sure enough, the big body bucked under him as Tucker tried to get away without going anywhere. "Wait up! Hold on now."

"I think you are. I did not know that particular detail."

Tucker swallowed and panted. "Neither did I. Fucker."

"See now? That just ain't polite. And I—" Patch braced his hands on Tucker's chest and slid them up into his armpits. "—am gonna have to teach you a lesson."

"Hold up, Patch." Tucker's hips rose off the bed as he tried to dismount his tormentor. "That ain't fair."

"No?"

"C'mon now. Now... I ain't done nothing. Just laying here all alone, all nice and polite, waiting for you to come back to me."

Lifting up, Patch dug his fingers in again. "Poor fella." He used Tucker's twisting and bowing to tug the jeans off him, revealing the lean line of his naked muscle.

Tucker struggled and arched, wheezing with tense laughter. "Now... now.... That ain't right. *Fucker!*" His hips rose again, pushing up off the mattress, and he dug in with his heels to no avail. "Agh! Wait. Okay. Okay? Please, *Patrick*!" He yelped.

Patch stopped to straddle him again and settled his hips back on top of Tucker's. *Weird*. The power made him feel woozy, sluggish with banked pleasure. *Good deal.*

"Please."

"What did you call me?" He squinted at Tucker.

"Your name. Patrick is your name, ain't it?" Tucker's hard breathing lifted and lowered him. His voice dropped. "Sir?"

Patrick nodded. Why did that make him feel so strange?

Little by little the tension drained out of Tucker's rigid body, but his eyes glittered hard and hungry. "That okay?"

"Better than." He exhaled and smiled. *Equals*. He leaned forward, pressing his lips to Tucker's, then dipping in with his tongue. Tucker groaned into his mouth and tipped his hips again to ride him from below. Patch pushed deeper, savoring the salty tobacco sweetness of his mouth, his mouth, his mouth.

"Oh my God." Tucker dropped his head back against the brass and rolled it side to side. "Crazy."

"What's the matter?" Patch kissed the pulse under his jawline and tongued the skin, then slid down his warm body to crouch between his legs.

"I want to touch you."

"Well, ain't that just too bad?" Patch wrapped his hand around the slick pole straining above Tucker's lap. "Because I want to touch you instead."

Tucker swallowed.

Patch stroked the stiffness slowly, running his thumb over the wet plum at the top. "You're fucking juicy." He bent to suck the sauce off.

Tucker nodded and pressed his lips together. "I'm so old I leak." His eyes twinkled.

Patch sank his mouth over it, taking it deep as he could manage at this angle, then letting his tongue drag on the upstroke and kissing the crown with loose lips.

"*Jee*-sus." Tucker bit his lip, looking hypnotized. His cock flexed hard for a moment, and he closed his eyes. "Pup."

"All that sweet sap." Patch smeared precum over the knob and back down the shaft so he could squeeze it tight. He tasted the head again. "Feels like you're carrying a heavy load, huh? Let me see. You got something for me, cowboy?"

Tucker's gray eyes were bright, the whiskey splinters wet and soft as he growled and grunted under Patch's fingers. "Yessir. I saved it."

"For ten days?"

"Eleven days." Tucker shook his head.

Patch whistled. "Pretty fucking foolish." He milked the full curved length all the way to the crown, forcing a gleaming bead free. He swiped it away with his tongue.

"Please, pup." Tucker shuddered. Another drizzle of precum slid out under Patch's thumb. "Patch. You're killing me."

"Hold... your... horses." Patch kept up the steady stroke, squeezing hard enough to hurt and licking up the leaks. "Oh, you can dish it out, but you can't take it? You gonna ask nice?"

Tucker did not complain. "I can't. I can't. Please." The plaintive ache in his voice did something funny to Patch's stomach. "It's too much. *Please*, man."

They both stared down at Patch's hand milking his bone patiently, hypnotized by the slow duet, bone and groan. Patch leaned forward to suck the tip again. The musky heat of it got his mouth wetter than it should've been, but the taste made him crazy, and he could feel when Tucker got close by the sudden rigidity under his mouth.

"Hang on. Hold on now." He sat back. "I wanna see."

"No." Tucker panted and shook a moment. His nipples were stiff and his abs stood out in hard relief. Finally, he braced his heels on the bed and his shoulders settled again against the brass and knots. "I dunno how long I can."

Patch's own cock sparked and ground inside his jeans. The aching shivery pressure wrapped his midsection, threaded back into his bones. He knew he could go like this, just like this, with very little effort. The slow aching climb tightened everything at his center, pushing him up the crest involuntarily, inexorably. He tipped his hip to show Tucker the bulge lifting his button fly. "Look what you do to me."

Tucker looked and licked his mustache. "Ungh."

Patch nodded. "I know, right? You're gonna get my nut without laying a finger on me. I can't even control it." Tucker's stiffness flexed in his hand. "You like that."

Tucker nodded.

"You like making me do it."

Another nod and his eyes glittered with permission. "A lot."

"Me too." Patch stroked it slow and hard, stretching the loose skin up over the knob, a trace of veins mapping Tucker's impatience. "You making me." Pulling it forward, peeling it back. "Me making you."

Tucker swallowed, hypnotized by his crown swelling to a slick brick-brown above Patch's fist.

He scrubbed the cockhead with his palm and tickled the tender gather where the knob dimpled. "Why is that, huh?"

"Patch," Tucker begged.

"Them nuts feel pretty full, pardner." He tapped them.

Tucker winced and shivered. His balls shifted in their fuzzy sac, and the firm mound under them flexed, once-twice, making his meat bounce above.

Patch kept milking the impossible girth till he stiffened, then tightened his fist again just this side of hurting. The tip swelled dark and shiny.

"Uh, yeah. If you don't—You're gonna make me go. I'm gonna go!"

He released Tucker to bob and jerk in the air like a ruddy spike.

Tucker scowled. "Fuck!"

"Language, cowboy."

"Prick. 'At's language too."

Patch raised his hips to kick out of his own jeans, not rushing and happy to watch Tucker wait.

"Lord."

Crawling back onto the mattress, he put his face right back down in the middle of things so he could see the veins stand and the head bulge, fascinated by the spectacle of Tucker's surrender. Yet somehow he no longer felt paralyzed; he felt *calm*.

Quick-quick, slow, slow.

Tucker's legs quaked and flexed on either side of him. Using every trick Tucker had taught him, he started at the base and mapped the shaft a millimeter at a time, the firm veins, the plump ridge, the sloppy skin, learning where Tucker flinched, yelped, and whimpered. Obviously, he needed some practice but he did his best.

And then because he couldn't stop himself he lowered his face and sucked Tucker's nutsack. Tucker's legs flexed on either side of him as he nuzzled lower, pushing at the fuzzy trench beneath.

Tucker hissed. "Hungh-puhh. *Lord.*"

Patch gave him a good long lick, pushing closer and swabbing his tiny hole hard with steady, slick pressure.

Tucker went boneless above him, his thighs falling open and his arms sagging in the rope. His fat branch jabbed the air above and his breath came in ragged gasps.

Little by little, the snug muscle surrendered to Patch's mouth, but he didn't relent. He spread the cheeks and dug in, suckling and kneading down here, which elicited drastic, spastic reactions. Lifting up, he kissed the juice off Tucker's knob.

"Huh-*unnnngh.*" Tucker grunted as his lean hips rose off the bed involuntarily. "Put a finger in. Gimme one."

Patch paused. Had he heard right? He remembered Tucker poking himself that night in the trailer. How long ago?

"Please. In my butt." Tucker grunted and hitched his pelvis again. "Gimme it. Put it in me, pup. C'mon."

Patch's cock was leaky marble as he obeyed. A lick and then he sank his index finger in one go. Tucker bucked above him. He twisted, searching. "Yeah?"

"Ho!" Tucker grunted and ground down on his hand. "*Hsss-yeah.* Fuck, man. Auuggghh. *Hah.* That's the spot."

Patch could see that. He licked the sparse fuzz in the trench again and slid his finger out as Tucker's hole flexed at his knuckle.

Tucker whimpered above him, arms pinned and bent legs twitching. "Naw. C'mon. Gimme a couple where it counts. They's grease in the stand."

There was, a clear squeeze bottle filled with his magical viscous farm goo. *J-Lube.* "This stuff's crazy." He squeezed a little ropy puddle into his palm, then closed his fingers over the grease, wringing and rubbing them through it one-handed. He grinned and licked his teeth with filthy appetite. "It's gonna get everywhere."

"Mmh. That'sa idea." Tucker's broad cock darkened to a dull rose, wrapped in raised veins and already slick with ooze and saliva.

Patch wrapped his slimy hand around Tucker's shaft and tugged up it once to slick the hot skin.

Tucker's eyes widened. He gritted his teeth and hissed. "Please."

"Hold your horses." He reached under to Tucker's ass. "I gotcha. I'm right there already." Dropping down, he got in another two licks and then pushed two lubed fingers inside. "Huh?" He tried to feel for the place, blind and eager. Having so much control over the flexing flesh made him crazy.

"Almost. Wait a—Jesus, Patch. Oh my fucking... *there*!" Tucker panted and bellowed like a bull. He rocked in the ropes, his hips punching the air in urgent staccato. "Yuh. Yeah." His chest heaved rapidly.

Patch worked to stay at that slick, sweet pad while Tucker's muscles pulled at him, asking for what they both wanted. He didn't dare touch himself. His own boner had grown too stiff to shift. It obviously liked the idea, and if he wasn't careful—

"Ugh. Ugh, fuck. Al-*most*." Tucker pulled at the ropes, his muscles shaken by whatever internal battle he was fighting. "Down a little. Yeah that! *Ohmi*-JesusCrickets.... Patch...." His butt clamped down again and his ruddy meat reared.

He sagged back against the headboard, and Patch followed, pushing his hard thighs back and open, pressing forward with his face and fingers, licking the soft skin where his digits sank inside before pushing in after.

Tucker's thighs shook as he went nuts above and his legs shook on either side of Patch's spit-smeared face. "Yeah, man. Lick it open." He growled and grunted and sighed, relaxing against the ropes and pulling Patch closer. "Ssst-*ha*." He chuckled and flexed his hole on Patch's tongue. "'At's it. *Hssss-ungh*." A low grunt. "Agh, yessir. Yes sir."

I wanna fuck him. Patch blinked sweat out of his eyes. He'd never wanted that. *Before.* All he had to do was rise to his knees and line things up, and he could sink inside.

"Unh. *Huh*." Panting, frantic, Tucker began to shake and mutter. "Do it."

What does he mean?

"C'mon, pup. Put it inside. Give it to me quick 'fore I nut." Tucker hitched his butt and glared hungrily at him. "Please." His labored breath came low and fast, then he growled, "Sir."

Patch nodded, knowing he might squirt before he could get where he needed to go. Already he was clip-clopping on the edge. He kneewalked back and let Tucker rest those lean legs over his shoulders. "Tuck, y'sure?" *Shore.*

Tucker nodded, eyes hungry and scared and hopeful. "All of it, one go. Quick, pup. I'm fixin' to—" He bit his lip.

"Yeah." Patch lined his bare knob up with the slick squeezing ring of muscle. "Wait for—"

"*Fuh.* Oh my—Yeah, man. Right—" His powerful hamstrings clamped around Patch's ribs, then his waist, tugging him closer. His ankles crossed behind Patch's back, urging him deeper-harder-rougher. "*There!* Yessir. God-yes-sir. That's *it.* Hunh-ugh!"

Patch fell forward into heaven, and the slow, delirious slide did impossible things to them both, locking them together. *One Mississippi, two Mississippi.* He flexed his cock hard, clamping inside and straining against his own climax, fighting like hell not to pop so quick. "Kkk-whuh. Oh, Tucker."

Tucker bucked and hissed under him. His slippery sheath gripped every hard inch of Patch with a tender, relentless pressure that edged him more perfectly than his massive hands. *Help.* Trapped between their slick torsos, Tucker's cock thumped and slid easy in grease and sweat.

"Don't you move or I'll—" Patch held his breath and let it out slowly. "Ohh." He panted, choked, squeezed handfuls of the bedclothes in his fists. "Don't."

Immobile, they rode the crest together in slippery tandem, staring at each other in frozen surprise. "You're making me."

"Jeeez-us. Hang on, man. I mean it." Patch held himself back using every trick he'd learned in Tucker's ropes, holding still and focusing on the sharp edge of sensation, but Tucker was milking him hands-free at the intersection of their bodies. "Y'hear? Whoa... don't you move a muscle."

Tucker licked his throat, his cheek, then deep into his mouth with careful insistence. His body quaked in the ropes, his rod throbbed against Patch's breathing torso. His growl became a guttural scream as his head twisted against the headboard and he arched helplessly. His legs locked around Patch's slick hips. "Fuck *mmm—*"

Hot goo struck his chest as Tucker broke open beneath him.

His own climax balanced on a greasy razor's edge, buoyed by the lazy, straining pressure of his need and his seed. Patch held his breath, not moving while Tucker howled into his hair.

Tucker's hole went crazy on Patch's shaft, milking it root to tip, over and over and over with relentless, gentle urgency... a slick wanting he couldn't, he didn't fight. The ring of muscle squeezed at his root, not letting him go, so that he had no choice but to push that bit deeper and crush Tucker beneath him.

Patch pressed Tucker back into the knots and brass while the big cowboy muttered thankful moans and mashed his cum between them. He shook, shuddered, then fell irrevocably and splintered into slippery shards inside him, and they fell back to Earth together.

Tucker hummed and skimmed his whiskers against Patch's lips lightly, then gave him a sweet peck. "Howdy," he whispered.

"Pardner." Patch pushed his hips forward so his softening cock shifted.

"*Fu*-uck." Tucker's eyes closed dreamily. His butthole tightened and relaxed around Patch's length. A shiver chased up his torso and he exhaled happily. "Yes, *sir*."

"Jeez."

"I needed that something awful." Tucker sighed. Another shudder. "Phew. You don't know."

"I guess so. I guess I did too."

Tucker closed his mouth and studied Patch's eyes. "You stuck me pretty good, pup."

"I'm a mess." Patch kissed him carefully, not wanting to break the trance. "Your arms gotta be sore. Huh?" He sat back on his heels. "You look pretty smug."

Actually, Tucker looked *spoiled*. His thick arms were laced against the brass headboard, his dark hair damp, and the pearly smear of seed on his torso and his cheek. One loose knee fell to the bed and the other bent casually.

"Handsome an' all," he drawled to get a smile out of Tucker.

Tucker regarded him with a dozy, lazy grace and tasted his lower lip. "You 'bout turned me inside out." With Patch off him, his cock rolled to the side drowsily and down over his loose sac.

Now he wanted Tucker wrapped around him, and that meant ditching those ropes. "I wanna turn you loose."

Tucker blinked and sighed. His eyes drifted shut as Patch set him free. "You say so. I could sleep like this right here."

Patch straddled him. "Fuck, Tucker."

Tucker's blissed-out grin told the whole story.

"You're still flying." He lifted forward, reached up, and his wet dick brushed Tucker's chest. "Ain'tcha?"

"Mmffh." Tucker smiled easy, watching him loose the slipknots.

Patch untied his left arm to his wrist, catching it before it fell. He kissed the salty hand and lowered it to Tucker's sticky torso.

"Mmh. Hi." Tucker cupped his own dick. "Welcome home, pup."

He freed the right wrist from the nylon loops just as easily. He kissed that hand too and lowered it carefully to Tucker's lap.

Tucker gazed up at him, powerless and potent. He nodded. "You take all the time you need. You fixed me up good." A deep sigh.

Patch unwrapped Tucker's torso, rubbing the muscle roughly. "If... *that's* gonna happen every time I come home, I'm fixing to travel pretty regular."

"Sure." *Shore.* "Anywhere you wanna go, I'm game. Have boner, will travel."

Patch kneaded his arms and shoulders and eased him down into the pillows.

"C'mere." Tucker didn't even rub the marks on his wrists, just curled onto his side and pulled Patch in front of him, spooning him from behind. Semen slipped between them. "Y'feel good."

"Y'kidding?" Patch lifted their laced fingers to his lips and nodded. He felt steady. *Sturdy.* "No hands and you milked me anyways."

"No lie."

A protective rush made him pause, like he was still in charge in a good way. "Hey." He twisted and then rolled in Tucker's arms so he could face him square. Their semisoft cocks knocked together. "Butt okay?"

"Better than." Tucker made a silly face. "Humming pretty good an' all. *Mmmgh.* I ain't never gone like that. *Whew.*"

"I mean it." Patch reached down Tucker's back and squeezed the meaty cheeks apologetically.

"So do I. Hell, you stuck me too good. Jeez. That took the *buckle*, pup. Don't you worry." Tucker seemed unfazed and uninterested in making a big deal out of getting roped and railed. "You saw me bust."

Patch nodded. "I never...."

"Put your crank in someone's tail?"

Head shake.

"Well, that's fine." He kissed Patch's cheekbone, his eye, his mouth. "I like that just fine. Being first." He purred and pulled Patch closer, mashing their wet cocks together. "We got all kindsa time to figure us out. *Mmh.* Nice."

Patch grunted in assent and squeezed him. If Tucker liked it that much, he definitely wanted a chance to return the favor.

Tucker fitted his face against Patch's throat, and his wet exhales heated the skin. He lipped Patch's neck where it met his shoulder. "Salt. You hungry?"

Patch lifted up and laughed. "Seriously?"

"I dunno. You flew around wherever. I didn't know you was coming, but I got fajitas in the fridge." Tucker frowned. "I'm... I wanna take care of you too."

"Likewise, I'm sure." He pressed a hand to Tucker's sweaty pecs. He rubbed the light creased stain of rope marks across Tucker's shoulders and biceps and forearms. He knew from experience how they tingled and floated, after.

"Howzat City?" Tucker even said it with a capital *C*.

"Fine." He shrugged. "Naw. It was... *fast*. Ain't home."

"No?"

Head shake and a hitch closer. "I missed you, mister."

"Good." Tucker smiled at that. "Same. Something fierce. I didn't sleep right for twelve days, and you know I love to sleep."

"Amen."

Tucker sat up against the headboard and glanced around the dim room. "I put primer on them walls so you could pick."

"The color?"

"I figgered you know and I don't." A contented shrug.

"'Kay." Patch inhaled and let it out, trying to think of what they needed to wake up to every morning. "Well, it looks like we got work to do."

"I been thinking about that. Hay and all. And fixing the barn. Maybe start looking for a place fit for barbecue, if you still wanna. Juke joint."

Patch stretched and exhaled. "That too. DJing too. I'm gonna need an assistant, a couple times a month. Weekends, mostly, but it means getting on a plane." He hoped Tucker got what he was getting at, the crazy future he'd dreamed up for them.

"Them parties." Tucker squinted at the word like it might rattle and strike.

"Yeah. Well, no. You'd go with me. But they're—"

"In New York."

Patch frowned. "Everywhere. With me."

"Then that's where I'm gonna be." Tucker sounded adamant.

"Weekends, mostly. I mean." He knew it might seem scary. He suspected Tucker would balk. Patch petted him as if he was a barn-shy horse. "'S okay, Tuck."

Tucker just looked back, grim-faced and pie-eyed with unspoken questions.

"We'd be here, I guess, until we book a party, and then we go wherever. If you wanted. So I can spin. All over. Together."

"Serious?"

"I wanna be here. With you. I don't see how I could be anywhere else." Patch crossed his arms.

Tucker's shoulders relaxed. "I didn't know."

"What's the matter?"

Tucker pressed his bruised eyelids and wiped them. "I been trying to work up the nerve for New York. I didn't think you could do it, and I figgered I could. You got all your life up there, and I'm just—"

"Nope." Patch kissed him, tasted the salt with his tongue, and kissed him again. "You're mine, Tucker Biggs. Every stubborn inch."

"No. I figure you're mine. I got seniority and experience and the fucking gray hairs you gave me, so I say you're mine and no two ways."

"Like I said."

Tucker eyed him. "Leaving the old coot to stew and fret."

"Old?" Patch shoved his chest. "Now you're old? When you were poking half the county you weren't old. Or when you were dancing till 3:00 a.m. in New Orleans torturing all them boys, you weren't old."

Tucker nodded and crossed his arms, settling back against the brass headboard. "Mature. That's me. Lived one way all my life till some kid shows up and tries to tie me down."

Patch rolled his eyes. "Next thing, you're going to growl out a chorus of 'Don't Fence Me In.'"

"Fuck off." Tucker laughed, though. "I ain't that bad. You get more jealous than I do."

"Fucking right. Before I let you out of my sight in some Circuit party, I'm fixing to brand you. Right—" Patch pressed his fingers into Tucker's left buttcheek. "About there."

Tucker raised an eyebrow. "Slippery when wet."

"Naw." Patch stroked the skin and stole a kiss. "Big Hassle Farms." Would he go for it or was he too proud? "Y'think?"

"Say, now...." Tucker's eyes lit and wavered. He raised his eyebrows and bobbed his head. "I *like* that."

"It's the damn truth." Patch tried to stay still, no sudden movements. "Or not. Y'know. We can decide together."

"Big Hassle." Tucker squeezed his ribs, sighed, and kissed the hollow of this throat. "I like that just fine." His hands slid down to Patch's backside and pulled his full length closer. "And getting hassled hard, I *love*." *Luhhhhv.* "Feels like you 'bout ready to hassle me again, pup."

No surprise, Patch's cock plumped between them in that big hand.

"Then I might have to hassle you right back." Up close, the soft brandy glow lit the flecks in Tucker's gray eyes. He nuzzled Patch's throat, rasping across it with his prickly chin till he flinched. "More'n once, even."

"That sounds like a pretty good plan, sir." Patch bit his shoulder until Tucker turned to chuckle.

Outside, the grumpy rooster gave a warmup squawk.

"Sun's nearly up." Tucker stood and squinted out the window.

Sure enough, faint lemon tickled the horizon.

"Well.... Up's a stretch." Propped up against the damp pillows, Patch grinned. "Not what I'd call up just yet. We got a couple hours yet. Come on back to bed."

"That's what you get for traveling so late at night. Waking decent folks up... sneaking in so late it's early." Tucker turned off the lamp, and now the bedroom was lit only by the predawn glow and the numbers on the clock. "Don't forget: we both of us got chores."

"Good deal. I'm ready." Now he really was sleepy. All the panic and push had leaked out of him somewhere along the way. "You tell me what needs doing."

Quick-quick, slow, slow.

"Well...." Tucker grabbed the base of his cock and shook it. "I'm all slicked up still. Your stuff all over me, besides. Shame to waste."

He chuckle-sighed. "I told you I was fixing to make a damn mess."

"You did. I ain't complainin'. I'll take care of it."

Patch raised his drowsy eyebrows. "Mmh?"

"Caretaker." Tucker blinked and brushed a hand over his chest, his smile easy.

"Mmnh. C'mere." Patch shifted to make a space in the big brass bed. "I guess that makes me your hired hand, huh?"

"Guess so. You sure?" *Shore.* Tucker sauntered back to him with a slow grin. "Hard worker too, what I hear. Quick on your feet. Flexible too." He wiped his lips.

"Well, sir, I'd say I am interested in whatever position's open."

"That so, pup. Well…." His voice rumbled in the dim room. Tucker crawled into bed like he meant to stay there a spell and then gathered Patch in his arms to growl in his ear, "You took your damn time."

Patch twisted to kiss him. "I got here fast as I could."

DAMON SUEDE grew up out-'n'-proud deep in the anus of right-wing America, and escaped as soon as it was legal. Having lived all over, he's earned his crust as a model, a messenger, a promoter, a programmer, a sculptor, a singer, a stripper, a bookkeeper, a bartender, a techie, a teacher, a director... but writing has ever been his bread and butter. He has been happily partnered for over fifteen years with the most loving, handsome, shrewd, hilarious, noble man to walk this planet.

Damon is a proud member of the Romance Writers of America and currently serves on its national Board of Directors. Though new to romance fiction, Damon has been writing for print, stage, and screen for over two decades, which is both more and less glamorous than you might imagine. He's won some awards, but counts his blessings more often: his amazing friends, his demented family, his beautiful husband, his loyal fans, and his silly, stern, seductive Muse who keeps whispering in his ear, year after year.

Damon would love to hear from you...

Website: www.DamonSuede.com
Twitter: @DamonSuede
Facebook: www.facebook.com/damon.suede.author
Goodreads: www.goodreads.com/damonsuede

BAD IDEA

DAMON SUEDE

Bad Idea: Some mistakes are worth making.

Reclusive comic book artist Trip Spector spends his life doodling supersquare, straitlaced superheroes, hiding from his fans, and crushing on his unattainable boss until he meets the dork of his dreams. Silas Goolsby is a rowdy FX makeup creator with a loveless love life and a secret streak of geek who yearns for unlikely rescues and a truly creative partnership.

Against their better judgment, they fall victim to chemistry, and what starts as infatuation quickly grows tender and terrifying. With Silas's help, Trip gambles his heart and his art on a rotten plan: sketching out Scratch, a "very graphic novel" that will either make his name or wreck his career. But even a smash can't save their world if Trip retreats into his mild-mannered rut, leaving Silas to grapple with betrayal and emotions he can't escape.

What will it take for this dynamic duo to discover that heroes never play it safe?

www.dreamspinnerpress.com

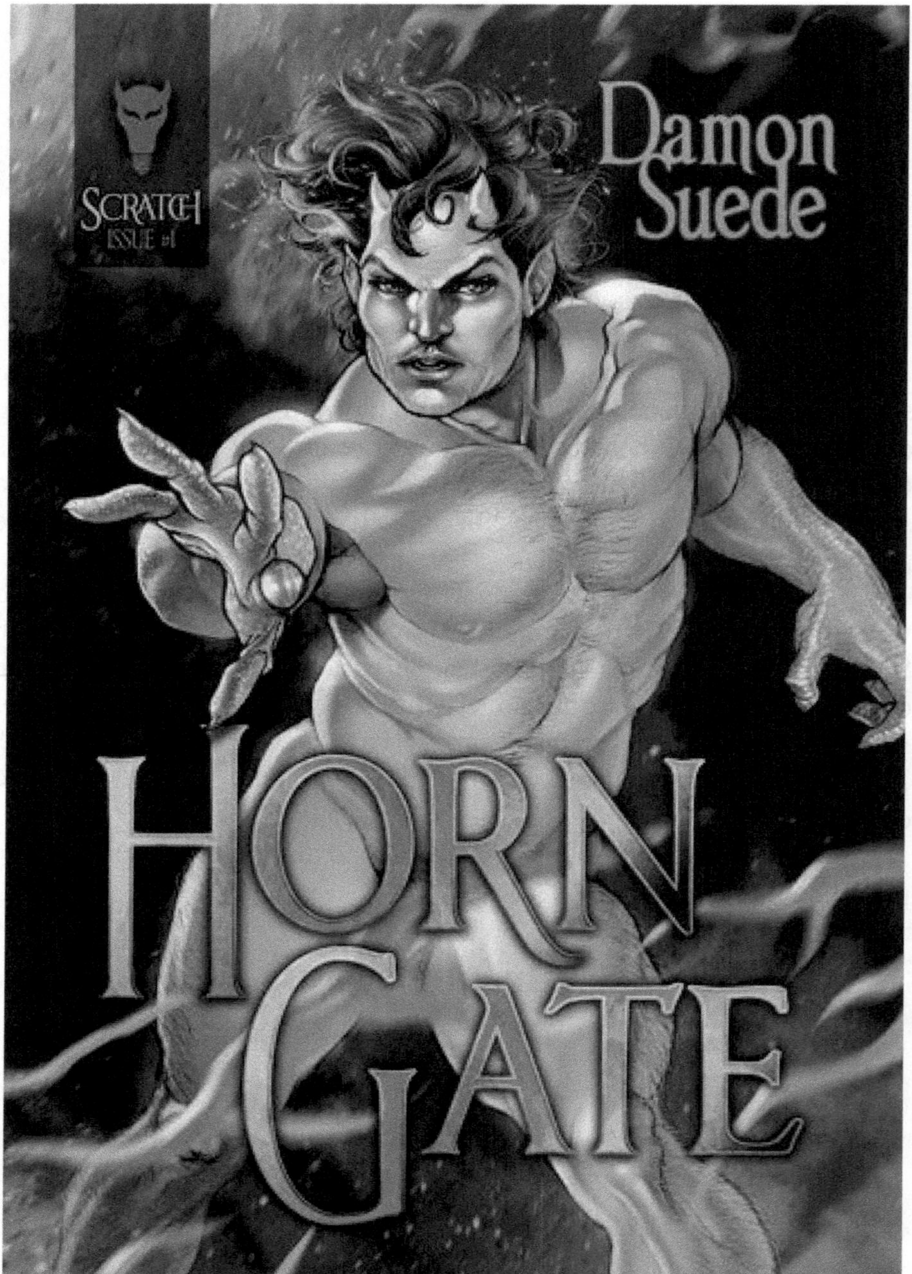
SCRATCH
ISSUE #1
Damon
Suede
HORN
GATE

HORN GATE: Open at your own risk.

Librarian Isaac Stein spends his lumpy, lonely days restoring forgotten books, until the night he steals an invitation to a scandalous club steeped in sin. Descending into its bowels, he accidentally discovers Scratch, a wounded demon who feeds on lust.

Consorting with a mortal is a bad idea, but Scratch can't resist the man who knows how to open the portal that will free him and his kind. After centuries of possessing mortals, he finds himself longing to surrender.

To be together, Isaac and Scratch must flirt with damnation and escape an inhuman trafficking ring—and they have to open their hearts or they will never unlock the Horn Gate.

www.dreamspinnerpress.com

DAMON SUEDE

HOT
HEAD

Where there's smoke, there's fire...

Since 9/11, Brooklyn firefighter Griff Muir has wrestled with impossible feelings for his best friend and partner at Ladder 181, Dante Anastagio. Unfortunately, Dante is strictly a ladies' man, and the FDNY isn't exactly gay-friendly. For ten years, Griff has hidden his heart in a half-life of public heroics and private anguish.

Griff's caution and Dante's cockiness make them an unbeatable team. To protect his buddy, there's nothing Griff wouldn't do... until a nearly bankrupt Dante proposes the worst possible solution: HotHead. com, a gay porn website where uniformed hunks get down and dirty. And Dante wants them to appear there—*together*. Griff may have to guard his heart and live out his darkest fantasies on camera. Can he rescue the man he loves without wrecking their careers, their families, or their friendship?

www.dreamspinnerpress.com

CPSIA information can be obtained
at www.ICGtesting.com
Printed in the USA
FSHW020459300819
61574FS